SURROUND ME

MARGUERITE MARTIN GRAY

The journey continues...

Marguerite Gray
'21

Second Print: 2018

Celebrate Lit Publishing

www.celebratelitpublishing.com

ISBN: 978-0-9995370-3-9

❀ Created with Vellum

To my husband and best friend Wayne.
Thank you for sharing in this amazing journey called life. You have taught me to be humble, gentle, patient, and forgiving. Because of your love, you continue to make allowances for my faults (Ephesians 4:2).
Thank you for adding editor and publicist to your list of talents.
I love you.

CHAPTER 1

 *ordeaux, France*
June 1773

His hands tightly gripped the railing, turning his knuckles a startling white compared to his wind-chapped and tanned skin. The pressure in his grasp mimicked the turmoil in his head. Louis Lestarjette's gaze lifted to a sea of deep-blue waves. Charles Town and any semblance of land had disappeared weeks ago. Why the upheaval now when he had already had weeks to prepare for his journey and his family reunion? Could a prodigal son truly go back home? How would he be received? The same questions rolled over and over in his head.

If he had made a mistake, he would never forgive himself. All the what- ifs jumbled in his mind, tumbling into compartments he thought he'd closed in order to keep away doubts and insecurities. Where was the peace he had claimed? The voyage was a necessity for business, for the colony of South Carolina, and for his family. He had determined even after the first five weeks on the ocean that his love for Elizabeth Elliott would only increase with time.

He hoped the strained relationship with his brother didn't make the stay more difficult. They'd had a year to heal from their parting words. Louis had to believe they would work better without having had their previous day-to-day confrontations. At least in their working relationship, the distance between France and South Carolina had seemed to do the trick, alleviating brotherly competition.

Each evening, right when the sun was setting to the west and sending threads of yellow and orange across the vast Atlantic, Louis dreamed of Elizabeth with her blue-gray eyes and curly light-brown hair. He reached for the hope she had dispersed in his once troublesome, wayward life. Would she be waiting when he returned? Why the doubts now? Many watery miles away from his heart's desire, he longed for his fiancée, wanting to release the secret they kept from her family.

His ship, the *Rose*, rocked at the dock in Bordeaux. It didn't take him long to find and embrace his mother and older brother. "*Maman*, André. You haven't changed at all in the past year."

In his brief contact with André's eyes, Louis detected a question. Was he concerned that perhaps Louis had not changed at all?

Speaking in French separated him from his other home, drawing him closer to his roots. "Where's Jean? Did you leave him in charge of everything at home?" His younger brother by three years ran the small estate and helped André with the business.

His mother reached to touch Louis' cheek. "Of course. You'll see him soon enough."

Even though he reveled in the presence of his family, he didn't want them to guess his heart was thousands of miles away in a foreign land. Part of him wanted to keep his secrets for a while longer. Anyway, he had a job to do and a purpose to achieve. His personal story could wait.

He knew his petite mother had had a hard time letting go of him a year ago. She hadn't surmised the real reason for Louis' leaving. Perhaps André had spilled the news to her later. They had worked out their need for individual space and ventures without involving her.

As he watched his mother, her resemblance to her sister Jeannette in South Carolina made Louis homesick for Charles Town. How could home be in two places? How could he miss his life there so much, while here with his mother?

His heart knew the answer. *Elizabeth. One day at a time. Enjoy these moments. How often will I be able to return to France?*

André stepped closer and interjected. "The trunks will be delivered to the inn, so we can take the carriage there now, and we'll stay the night. Follow me." He took charge. Always. At least across the ocean Louis had made a stab at independence and success. Although his separation from his brother had resulted in a part ownership of a ship, along with buying, trading, and transporting merchandise between France and the New World, Louis still maintained a share of his family business.

They left his ship resting in the port at Bordeaux in Captain Robert Cochran's capable hands. Louis appreciated the quick friendship he had established with this thirty-year-old man whose strength in stature contrasted with his gentle smile and laughing eyes. It helped that Robert's wife Anne was Elizabeth's sister. Louis wanted what Robert had—a wife, family, and contentment.

The ship would be loaded with additional cargo. The bottom of the crates would be filled with those "questionable" items such as guns, ammunition, and various other weapons. Topped with common goods like wine, oil, canvas, spices, glassware, and material would make them passable to the average eye. Neither Louis nor André were comfortable with the contraband goods, but Louis was now a full-fledged member of the Sons of Liberty and the independence movement in the colonies. He couldn't imagine this journey to France outside of his connection with the Patriots. Gone were the thoughts of becoming a wealthy merchant going about his own business. His business had taken a turn and went hand-in-hand with supporting the cause.

As they began walking, André turned to a topic they both knew held top priority. Louis appreciated his brother's openness and inclusion of Louis in the process. At least Louis hoped he was genuine. "We have more contracts with the colonists up and down the coast, including New York and Boston," André said. "Business has increased and so have the profits. I couldn't put it all in a letter, so the books will be interesting to you."

Louis nodded and added, "I have ledgers to share and some ideas, too." Perhaps after a year, André would now trust Louis enough to heed some of his New World wisdom.

A delicious meal awaited them at the inn in the middle of the bustling town. Real food—French fare like pheasant and vegetables with olive oil and spices. Actually, anything not resembling ship food was a treat. Louis breathed in the aroma, imagining it distributing nourishment even before the first bite.

André handed the biscuits to Louis. "I suppose you know the new Tea Act passed on May tenth."

"No." Louis held the hot biscuit in his hand. So much for savoring the rich flavors. Politics with the first bite. "I suspected as much, though. It seems all my actions on this journey align with the inevitable changes the new act will bring—like boycotts and embargoes. I'll be ready when I return to Charles Town."

Mother interrupted by waving her napkin in surrender. "Are you two going to talk business every minute?"

Louis placed his hand over hers, feeling guilty for his lack of attention to her. "Of course not, *Maman*. Business isn't my only reason for coming back," Louis assured her. "So, how are you?"

Ten years ago, her monologue would've detailed the latest soirées, marriages, fashions, and estates, but now she concentrated on her church and her family.

"Life isn't as easy anymore. Now I can see the plight of

someone else as more important than mine. After all, I have a nice home, money, and family. Does anyone need more than that?" Her contented smile answered it all.

No, a person didn't need title, estates, power, or prestige. They had enjoyed all that in the past, but not now. All had been given up for faith and contentment. Louis sat back and admired her.

"*Maman*, you would love living with Tante Jeannette. She has such a good, solid life without all the trimmings and concerns of the wealthy. You would also love the church she attends. Although it is Church of England, not Huguenot, she's free to worship as she pleases."

His mother stopped and faced Louis, placing her hand on his cheek. "Louis, you've changed. What is it about you that's so different? Will you tell me now?"

He returned her gaze and offered her a huge grin. "We have time. Believe me, I have so many stories to share. I promise you'll hear them all."

After dinner, his family reclined in the comfortable parlor and let their mother bombard Louis with the kind of questions a mother would ask: health, rest, friends. Business and the more practical details—the ones André would be interested in would have to wait.

He gained control of his wandering thoughts as he felt the prickles of his mother trying to get in amongst them with her stare. Her blue eyes wouldn't let him escape. "You are harboring a few secrets, Louis. Although you're not bursting to tell them, I'm on the edge of my seat to hear. *S'il te plait, dis-moi.*"

"You are inquisitive, Maman. Are you really that interested?" He knew his letters weren't detailed enough, for he never burdened her with any conflicts, and he hadn't mentioned Elizabeth.

"Of course. Don't keep your poor old mother in suspense."

His head rolled back in laughter. "Well, you are neither poor nor old," Louis volleyed. "Where do you want me to begin? What information do you need?" There was no way to hide much from her, not after he hadn't seen her in months. So, he sat back, laced his fingers behind his head and waited.

"Let's start with how you fit in socially." Her eyebrow seemed to form a question mark. "If I remember correctly, you were at the point of avoiding all social events when you left here a year ago." She had loved to emphasize to all of her sons that they would never find wives without social commitments.

Pulling in a deep breath, he let it out quickly, knowing how important this was to her. "I was invited to more soirées and galas than I accepted. I don't know if I could have attended all of them even if I had wanted to. Without the coaxing of Tante Jeannette, I would never have set foot in any parlor or ballroom. Uncle Henry helped by reminding me of the numerous business associates who would be in attendance." He laughed, knowing their intentions dripped from hearts of abundant love. "They are a perfect couple when it comes to manipulation."

From a settee next to his mother, André shuffled his boots reminding Louis of his presence. "I have no doubt you were the best-dressed," André ventured. This from a man sporting the latest Parisian attire. Louis felt a bit provincial with his colonial-style three-cornered hat and jacket *sans* ornamentation. It would have to do for now.

Louis chuckled. "That wasn't hard to do considering the colonists are always a year or more behind London and Paris. When I return, I'll only take back the essential new clothes and leave the fancy stuff for you, *cher frère.*"

His mother cleared her throat and did her own shuffling, rear-ranging her skirt. "So, you attended a few balls. Ate a lot of interesting food. *Et quoi?*" His mother wasn't giving up very easily.

He knew what question gnawed at his mother, but Louis aimed to make her wait.

Instead, he sat forward and offered his other important information. He had no qualms about sharing what she had wanted for him for years. "Let's see. On a more serious note, after years of your praying, *Maman*, I have finally found a personal relationship with God." Her eyes opened wide, and her hands clapped as in a pose of prayer. "I know. Don't be too shocked. I had too many questions and problems to continue alone. I've finally grasped what you have had for years." He paused to let his mother wipe her tears. He couldn't let her tears stop him just yet. "After months of questions and talking to the Huguenot minister and then the Church of England minister, I couldn't deny the need for someone to take over my complicated, purposeless life. I understand now what you tried to tell me all along." He reached for his mother and embraced her. A prodigal son's embrace.

His mother blinked through her remaining tears. "Is there more, Louis? Not that I can take much more."

Louis stood and paced. "Well, yes, there is." He reached inside his jacket and retrieved his treasure—or the image of his treasure. "The next most important decision I made was about this beautiful woman, the love of my life. I have asked Miss Elizabeth Elliott to be my wife."

He handed the locket, holding Elizabeth's tiny likeness, to his mother. The artist had captured the hint of mischievousness peering through her lashes. His mother grasped it as it rested in his hand.

She jumped to her feet. "Louis, are you truly in love? After all you experienced, you've found someone?" After kissing his cheeks, she returned her gaze to Elizabeth.

Air whistled through his teeth in relief as his mother's approval relieved pent up nerves. "She is beautiful, inside and out. She's nineteen years old with curly light-brown hair and blue-gray eyes. She has to be the sweetest, smartest, most talented girl in the colonies. In the world. And the most amazing thing is that she loves me." He pointed to his heart. *Me.*

Clasping the locket in her hand, she returned it to Louis,

holding his hand in both of hers. "Well, I can see that you love her. Congratulations! If only I could meet her."

Louis led a separate life an ocean away, but he wanted to allow his mother to dream. "I do hope one day that you can meet her. At the present time, it seems impossible. I gave her the ring that you gave to me before I left. So, she has a part of you and my family with her at this moment."

She patted his hand. "Thank you, Louis. She couldn't be dearer to me than if she were my own daughter. Now, while you are home, you must have your portrait set in a locket for her. My gift to her."

"I'll do that for you, Maman." Louis kissed his mother's cheeks, embracing her acceptance of his beloved.

André cleared his throat and rose to his feet. "I say, that's enough for one evening. It appears both of you could go on all night. My advice is to leave something for tomorrow." He extended his hand to Louis. "Congratulations."

"And to you too, André. I almost forgot that you are recently engaged." Louis was embarrassed that he'd been so wrapped up in his own story that he had forgotten about his brother's news.

André's broad grin expressed his genuine contentment. "Yes, and you will be present to attend the occasion and stand up for me in the ceremony the second week of July." If only Louis could be as transparent about his love while in Charles Town. André didn't have to hide any of his feelings behind false expressions.

Louis bowed his head, then met his brother's eyes. "Gladly. An honor." *One I thought I would never have, considering our past words.* Forgiveness had found its intended mark.

Their mother stepped between them and looped her arms through theirs. "Off to bed for all of us. There is a month that we can spend reminiscing and planning." She kissed them both and sent them to bed as if they were children again.

For the next six weeks, Louis resided with his family at a country estate outside of Angoulême about two days travel from Bordeaux. Louis remembered spending time there as a child with a friend of the family. His mother and brother had rented it for the summer, since it was close to André's fiancée. As time allowed, André and Louis delved into the business side of their lives.

A large table in a drawing room posed as an office in their temporary home. Maps and ledgers occupied much of the space, leaving a small area on each side of the table for Louis and André to take notes, lay out their papers, and formulate written plans. After glancing around the room this morning, Louis noticed the sunlight streaming through the sheer curtains, the heavy drapes pulled out of the rays' path with sashes. The shadows danced across the floor and furniture bringing life to the place. Crossing his arms, he stared at the patterns and wondered what Elizabeth was planning for his house, their future home in Charles Town. Would she choose sheer window covering to let in the light? Would the furniture beg to be enjoyed by a lively family? How he would love to be with her now. The footsteps in the foyer reminded him that wish would not be granted for a few months.

Turning, Louis faced his brother, changing his thoughts to business. There was not room for Elizabeth and homesickness on the full table.

André took the top ledger and sat down, placing his elbows on the table. "You're down early."

Louis smiled. "I think I'm still used to the up-before-dawn life on the ship." Louis took his seat and glanced at his papers, a list of priorities staring at him. "I'll have to meet with your contacts soon," Louis said. "Are these men willing to supply the Sons of Liberty, or the Partisans, as they are now called in the colonies, with needed items?"

André drummed his fingers on the table before leaning back in his chair. "You'll be happy to hear that a strong group of Frenchmen have their minds tuned in to the concerns of America.

Longtime enemies of the supporters of Britain—or Loyalists, as you call them—watch with wonder at the progress abroad," André explained.

Although not encouraged or condemned by the French government, men actively conversed with the Partisans. Louis knew that names like Benjamin Franklin, Silas Deane, and Thomas Jefferson were frequently mentioned in the political arena and in the business world. His friends in Charles Town like Christopher Gadsden used the names often at rallies. Letters circulated connecting the prominent names with French contacts. Louis understood that finances and goods depended on many political decisions, yet André assured him Frenchmen were eager to join forces with the Sons of Liberty when the time came. Was that time now? Was this path toward war set with no turning back? Those were things Louis hoped to find out while he was here.

After meeting the suppliers, Louis realized his purpose and his role in the future. He was willing to coordinate shipments of arms and ammunition if the need arose. The word "smuggling" never surfaced, but in a way, he was lending his aid to the Partisans to defeat the Loyalists with the help of the French. His small role would be just one more step to the larger goal. He had committed in Charles Town. Now, he was committed in France. How he could feel at peace with his decision had everything to do with his peace with God, not with Partisans or Frenchmen.

One afternoon around their office table, André set aside his ledger and laced his fingers in front of him. "Louis, I want to ask you a question."

For his brother to place his work to the side, it had to be important. So, Louis did the same with his charts. "All right. What do you want to know?"

"Are you planning to become a citizen of South Carolina to the point of fighting a war if needed?" Concern was written all over André's face as he squinted his eyes then opened them wide.

10

How could his brother understand the transformation the New World and the people had wrought on his life, not forgetting his new spiritual change? "Yes, I have made that commitment, although I still pray King George will make it right."

"You are willing to give your life and your wealth on foreign soil for this cause?"

André just put into his question what Louis had taken almost a year to work through. Louis had decided the course of his life. He could not stay in France, safe from turmoil. He had to go home to Charles Town—to a world on the verge of eruption. Any logical man would choose to stay in France far from the conflict. But what about a man in love?

Turning to André, Louis spoke with a new passion. "I see no other direction for my life, even if it means death. God has given me a purpose, a woman to love, a home, and a desire to protect my new way of life. I will not turn back. I embrace it fully, consequences and all."

Eyebrows arched, André's look probably meant Louis had once again bewildered him. It wasn't as if this declaration was much different from taking off for the New World. "And you realize with the new Tea Act in place, Britain is not backing down," André added.

Louis nodded. "I know. I can only imagine what the major ports are doing. Charles Town will have to make decisions about British cargo. That is one reason I will need to get back as soon as possible."

"Don't leave too soon. At least not before a few social events and especially my wedding." Was André seeking confirmation that Louis wouldn't run away again?

This time he wouldn't run, for he was returning to his home, his love. "Don't worry. I won't leave without saying goodbye like I did last time."

One of the social gatherings was a large dinner party in André and Madeline's honor given in late June. Finding his brother free from the well-wishers, Louis draped his arm over his shoulders and added his encouragement. "Madeline is perfect for you. She's level-headed and doesn't seem to cater to every high society matron. How does she manage to be the center of a party but does not bow to every whim of society?"

Raising his glass in Madeline's direction, his brother didn't take his eyes off her. "She uses her intelligence to make her own decisions about life. It works for me. Her love and support are worth the occasional whispers."

Louis' mind traversed the ocean, visualizing Elizabeth at a party like this. "She and Elizabeth would become fast friends. Recently, Elizabeth has taken an independent stand about her decreased loyalty to Britain, labeling her a rebel in her parents' social class. She's not the only young colonist to do so, though. Her views are becoming widespread. I think she could find her place among your friends. I have a feeling she could convince quite a few to turn to the Partisan view." Louis laughed, totally believing she could.

In between business and social events, Louis found time to pose for his portrait to place in a locket and to add small pieces of furniture, paintings, and collectibles to his ship's hold to grace his new house. He remembered his talk about making the house Elizabeth's own—to buy what she wanted in order to make it a truly special, homey place. Since Aunt Jeannette had access to his accounts and was free to spend what it took, he wondered what had been done to the house on Church Street.

Every day Louis anticipated letters from Charles Town. Today, he wasn't disappointed. A bunch of correspondence graced the foyer table, many with Elizabeth's feminine penmanship. Cloistered in his room, Louis checked the dates and started with the earliest. He knew the stack would stay on his night stand, bringing him closer to her and his departure.

3 June

Dearest Louis, the days don't go by as quickly as I'd like with you so far away. Jeannette and I spend lots of time together, working on the house. I want to get as much done as possible before I leave for Boston. Six weeks with my grandmother will make the time fly, I hope. As of yet, my parents do not suspect a thing about us. That is another good reason for me to leave: to get away from their watchful eyes...

Father continues to try to find a young man for me ever since I disappointed him over William. So, it's time to flee before Mother joins him in the quest...

I miss you and hope your time with your family is all you hope for. Come home soon. Lovingly, Elizabeth

He, too, was faithful to write, sharing the details of his life, some encoded or minus the specific details that would expose his contacts or merchandise plans. Unfortunately, he couldn't send his letters directly to her. Louis sent them via his aunt, a woman they could both trust with their secret. It pained Louis that it had to be this way, but he couldn't leave her to the consequences of their love and future plans if he were not there to protect her. If her father and brother had knowledge of their impending marriage, Elizabeth would have been under constant scrutiny, always questioned and discouraged, maybe even whisked away to Boston. No, while he was away, the best thing for now was to nourish their love secretly. Time would reveal it, and together they would face the consequences.

A letter from Christopher Gadsden, his business partner, filled in some of Louis' questions about life in Charles Town in his absence.

The Tea Act was not received by the colonists as positive news. The Sons of Liberty in New York, Philadelphia, Boston, and Charles Town as well as every place in between, are making plans to refuse to cooperate. What that means is not clear...just know that plans are underfoot. Be on alert.

Samuel Evans's letter was short, minus the details of Christopher's. Louis' friend, a man who spent his days in legal research and preparation of cases, used very few words when responding to Louis. He shared briefly about the "deadness" of the town. The people of Charles Town tended to escape to the country to avoid the storms, heat, and mosquitoes during the summer.

Aunt Jeannette's letters added information about the store and who was buying what. "We need additional dinnerware, candlesticks, and lots of material for the fall and winter season. The French merchandise is a popular commodity."

While the letters made him long for home, the wedding here linked him to the present. By the first week of July, Madeline became a welcome member of the family. "She seems to make you very happy, André," Louis stated a week later.

"Complete is a good word. It makes me wonder why I waited so long."

"For the same reason I have. You waited for the right woman. What if you had married Francine or Sara or even Justine? You now know no one would be the perfect one except Madeline," Louis said. "And I would have been stuck with Janine and never have met Elizabeth. So, I see this as God's plan. He has protected us both from poor choices."

Louis' twenty-seventh birthday came on July fourteenth. Of course, his family remembered. His mother produced a wrapped package on the morning of his birthday. "Here's a gift; at least I think it's a gift," she said as she turned the item over in her hands. "It's from Elizabeth. I've saved it for today."

He received the letter and a small ornate box filled with pieces of paper from Elizabeth. Each strip contained a Bible verse. He would cherish these, knowing that she had taken the time to search for the right Scriptures to share with him. "These verses continue to comfort me," she wrote. "Hurry home. *Avec mon amour*, Elizabeth."

"What a unique gift," his mother exclaimed. "A year ago, you wouldn't have found any comfort in this gift. I'm glad we now share the same faith. I must remember to express my appreciation for her influence in your change."

Important to Elizabeth, the verses would be important to him. Like the first one he read: Psalm 103:11, "For as the heaven is high above the earth, so great is his mercy toward them that fear him."

"So great is his love that surrounds us," she had written in her letter. "It helps me keep my thoughts focused on God with all the uncertainty facing Charles Town."

Another verse, this one from Psalm 102, brought comfort for the time confronting them: "Hide not thy face from me in the day when I am in trouble."

Trouble definitely loomed in their world. France was not any calmer than the New World. His homeland was consumed with the drive to fight. Trouble at home and abroad. But one constant abided: God held his followers close, surrounding them with his love.

By the end of July, Louis' work in France was completed, the ship filled with cargo, gifts stashed away, plans confirmed, good-byes said, and tears shed. André and Jean accompanied him to the *Rose* in Bordeaux. But his mother decided to stay at the estate in order to avoid the emotions she knew would overcome her at Louis' departure. As he had embraced her, Louis realized this could be his last time to see her, to hold her. He had chosen his life in Charles Town with a renewed commitment.

Although a part of his heart would stay with his family in France, his true purpose and love awaited him in South Carolina in the arms of Elizabeth and in the pursuit of freedom.

CHAPTER 2

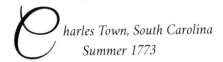

harles Town, South Carolina
Summer 1773

The summer loomed in front of Elizabeth—long, but very full. Louis had departed for France in May, leaving her alone with her thoughts and a ring—full of hope and promise. Who would imagine her being involved in a secret engagement?

At first, all the plans and logistics of the new girls' boarding school consumed her. "I'm still surprised that my opinion matters at all," Elizabeth confided to her father one afternoon. After all, she was only nineteen years old.

He stared at her from across his desk. "You have a knack for discerning personalities and characters. Mrs. Reynolds and I need your honest assessment of the girls." He once again convinced her that her word had merit.

She raised her brows and straightened her shoulders. If he really felt that way, it wouldn't hurt to add ideas and concerns where she could. "If that's the case, then I really think the group of students needs to be diverse. Not conformed to a single mold."

She waited, concerned he would set this request aside; perhaps her desire was too much, too early. But why not set the standards now?

"And I suppose that means from different classes both economically and socially," he concluded. This wasn't the first time Elizabeth came to the aid of ones less fortunate. The girls from different parts of society had the same intellectual potential. Didn't they deserve the same chance?

She held her hands tightly in front of her. Her tendency to punctuate her words with her hands and arms seemed inappropriate during the crucial decision-making time. "Yes. Why should only the wealthy upper echelon be admitted? They need to see it as an opportunity for all of society, not just a few. Anyway, the upper crust is sent away to England or has its own tutors already."

He left his side of the great desk and met her face to face. Raising her chin with his fingers, he said, "I promise to listen and be a little more open-minded. Remember, you have to convince Mrs. Reynolds and the rest of the board too."

She scheduled numerous interviews with applicants, followed by tedious reviews and letters of acceptance or rejection. Only thirty girls could be accommodated this first year. As she worked, a broad spectrum of students emerged from the stack of lifeless papers. Lower, middle, and upper classes were represented, as well as participants from common laborers, landowners, lawyers, and merchants. Seeing the final product pleased Elizabeth while it brought a few disconcerted looks from Mrs. Reynolds and her cronies.

Mrs. Reynolds drummed her fingers over the applications. "Are we sure this is the best group of girls?"

The woman's dark eyes squinted as she connected with each person in the room. But Elizabeth didn't flinch. Many prayers had surrounded the selection. Should she speak? Would her words give any sway?

Mrs. Collins, the wife of a local banker and mother of Elizabeth's best friend Sarah, spoke, taking pressure off Elizabeth for the moment. "I thought we agreed that the diverse group of girls would benefit the community and the school." Elizabeth noted that other board members nodded in agreement.

Mr. Elliott cleared his throat and laid his palms flat on the table. "We should be proud of these thirty girls. I know that after lots of prayer and our discussions, these boarders will be a nice start to the school."

Her father had the ability to bring the board back to the importance of the cause, not bending to personal agendas. She yearned for his approval and acceptance of her differences in other areas too—namely, Louis and the Partisan cause. If only he would listen as intently when the time came to gain his blessing.

Her work with the boarding school finished in late May, leaving three months for Elizabeth to fill before Louis returned. Determined not to mope around, she promised to fill her hours with pleasant activities. Since her parents didn't know about her arrangement with Louis, she needed to remain upbeat and involved, avoiding forlorn thoughts of missing him.

Elizabeth visited Jeannette, Louis' aunt, often. She was one of a few who knew about and condoned her secret affiliation with Louis. The two women had been friends long before Louis came to Charles Town. What would she have done without her friend's support?

"You are sure your parents don't know?" Jeannette Wilson asked.

Elizabeth brought her hand to her mouth. "Oh, no. I have been very careful. Since the letters from Louis will come to you, I won't have to worry about correspondence reaching Mother. I don't think Mother will ever guess about an engagement. She's so conscious of pleasing Father that she awaits his commands and never even asks about my social life unless he pushes her to question me. Father is different, though. He's constantly throwing men in my path." Elizabeth laughed.

"How do you get out of those awkward situations when he pressures you?"

Elizabeth disliked having secrets from her parents, but she saw no way to confront the truth until Louis came back. She was stronger with him beside her. "I just tell him I'm not interested. He accepts that most of the time." She bit her lip, reviewing the close calls. "Anyway, I leave for Boston soon to stay with my grandmother for six weeks, away from their scrutiny. I hate hiding this from them. I know I'm to obey my parents, so I struggle with this secret."

There was nothing Jeannette could say to change the fact that the secret must remain a secret. More harm would come by telling it at this point.

"Did you bring me your address in Boston, so I can forward Louis' letters when they arrive?"

Elizabeth pulled a folded piece of paper from her pocket "Yes, here it is. Grandmamma will never suspect if it is in an envelope from you. Thanks for your help, Jeannette."

"I'm glad to aid you and Louis," the older woman replied. Her smile turned contemplative. "You do realize this can't be a secret forever. You must tell your parents."

"I know. Don't worry. When Louis returns, we'll know when the time is right. For now, it is our dream, our secret life." Was there another way?

Jeannette patted Elizabeth's hand. "Let's think about your reunion now. We still need to finish the last touches to the house before you leave. Let's have the drapes delivered and assembled next week. Only a few pieces of furniture are yet to be completed. I can be on hand to have them set in place," Jeannette said.

Another secret—furnishing Louis' house, the one he had purchased around the corner from his aunt on Church Street.

Their house, although Elizabeth had a tough time calling it her home. She cherished the time spent making it special. Would they truly have a life within its walls? Soon?

Elizabeth clapped her hands and rose on her toes, as if a child given a threat. "With those items, we'll have furnished the front parlor, the music room, and the upstairs master bedroom. It should be livable for Louis. We've made a large dent in the list."

❀

In June, Elizabeth joined the throng of people seeking refuge elsewhere to escape from the heat and stillness of Charles Town. The ship's destination: Boston and her grandmother.

As she approached the large city bursting from its seams, pleasant memories of her childhood—roaming the streets with her mother, sister, and grandmother—bombarded her. Elizabeth, named after her grandmother, was spirited and adventurous like her faithful namesake. Grandmamma was happiest when busy with social engagements and never tired of flitting from event to event. Although not much for endless entertainment, Elizabeth adored her grandmother and her inspiring view of existence.

"Life is to be enjoyed. Put on a happy face and go live it," her grandmother said. However she did have her boundaries. "But stay within the rules of etiquette."

Always do the proper thing. Grandmother hadn't always been wealthy, so she appreciated what she had obtained. As she was very willing to share her means, Elizabeth and her sister had received numerous gifts from her through the years. But what Elizabeth loved more than anything was the time her grandmother gave to her. She cherished the hours spent in her company, watching her proper ways in all areas of society.

Even though fifty years older than Elizabeth and gray-haired, her grandmother wore the latest styles in the fashionable yellows, purples, and greens. The only time Elizabeth had ever seen her in dull, dark colors was when her grandfather died when she was a child.

Elizabeth sipped tea one morning over breakfast, her favorite part of the day with her grandmother. So often they tackled topics that didn't necessarily have easy answers. "Do you know all of the servants' names in every home you visit, Grandmamma?"

"Most of them, yes."

Well, Elizabeth expected as much if her recent observation proved true. "And every clerk in every store is greeted personally by you. How do you do it? I have a hard-enough time in my own house and the few stops I frequent often. You have a real talent." Her grandmother's rare character trait captivated Elizabeth.

"I don't know about talent." Grandmamma set her cup in the saucer. "I think everyone should be greeted personally, if at all possible. I just tune my ear to that one detail. God wants us to treat all of his children with love and respect."

Elbows on the table, Elizabeth rested her chin in her open hands. "I'll have to work on remembering better. I'm so bad with names unless I see someone over and over." Elizabeth knew her excuse was feeble. If a seventy-year-old woman could remember and recall details such as names, so could she. The part she liked best was her inclusion of her staff and servants. Elizabeth's mother was not quite so friendly and respectful in that area.

After receiving letters from Louis recently, Elizabeth was dying to share her news with her grandmother. *How can I? What if Grandmamma told Father?* Elizabeth sighed. Such a secret had to be guarded—her future with Louis depended on it. Secrets surrounded Elizabeth. The letters were just another example. When would it end? In one of his letters, after stating his "purposeless" existence without her, Louis focused on his family and the wedding of his brother. She cherished the three detailed pages.

Mother spends every moment on the upcoming wedding of my

brother and makes sure I sample every French food and experience every
possible event. She thinks I'll forget my French heritage, I guess.

She is very happy about us. More than anything she wants to meet
you and welcome you into the family. She knows deep down that's not
possible—at least not yet. I won't crush her dreams for the future. One
never knows...

Amour, Louis.

She could tell that devotion to his mother and brothers ranked high. What would it be like to meet his family? Would that ever be a possibility? With the way the unrest in the colonies grew, Elizabeth doubted there would be a voyage across the ocean for pleasure any time soon. She remembered slipping the letter into the back of her desk drawer with the others after sealing it with a kiss.

"What news did you receive recently from home?" Grandmamma asked.

Elizabeth stared at her, no words forming. *Again. Do I cover the secrets again?*

Grandmamma tilted her head and spoke softly. "Did you have any bad news?"

Elizabeth's chin shot up as she latched onto her grandmother's gaze. Did her words give her away? Probably not. But her reactions to letters she opened or couples strolling arm in arm or stories of engagements quite possibly did. The added bounce to her step depicted joy and cheerfulness, probably inspiring others to assume she exuded contentment.

On some occasions, however, Elizabeth's brief lapses into melancholy produced questions of concern. These lapses were short-lived—a few little doubts about Louis' return, his safety, or his commitment to her—but her demeanor was noted.

"No...no bad news. But I can't keep silent anymore." She needed to share her confidence, her secret with this woman whom she loved and trusted. "Please don't spill a word of what I am about to tell you to anyone," Elizabeth pleaded.

"I promise. Whom would I tell? The cat or dog?" her grand-mother quipped, causing Elizabeth to relax her clinched fists.

A deep breath in and then slowly released. Now. "I have to tell you. I'm about to burst. I know you have promised to keep this private. You'll see why in a moment. If Father finds out before I'm ready, I'm afraid of what he'll do."

Even with that dreaded thought, Elizabeth was able to smile. Her grandmother grabbed Elizabeth's hand across the table and squeezed it, spurring Elizabeth on to confession.

After bowing her head, possibly in prayer, her grandmother whispered, "Tell me, child."

A brief pause gave her courage. "I'm just going to blurt it out." Elizabeth squeezed her eyes closed before opening them wide with enthusiasm. "I'm in love. That's it. I'm in love with a wonderful man." She felt such a relief to say the words. The mere words produced a reality that tingled to her fingers and toes.

Her grandmother's smile resembled Elizabeth's. "Now that wasn't so bad. I'm sure your father expects that to happen."

"No, you don't understand." Courage pushed her on. "I'm in love with a Frenchman, a highly educated successful merchant and ship owner," Elizabeth said with pride.

Her grandmother smiled again. "And that is not hard to digest either. What is the problem, Elizabeth? So far I am overjoyed for you."

Now the clincher. "And he is a sympathizer of the Sons of Liberty. You could say a strong supporter, even a member. Do you see my predicament? Father would forbid it."

Her wise grandmother nodded. "Now, I understand. The daughter of a stout Loyalist attached to a staunch Partisan. I think there is more you are not sharing."

Elizabeth gazed at her sympathetic grandmother, one who was loyal to a few things—her God and her family—but not yet to a political view.

"Grandmamma, have you not experienced and seen what is

happening to the colonies? Surely you remember the Boston Massacre, the boycotts, the rallies, the harsh words. You lived right in the middle of them. I don't know about you, but I can't be quiet for much longer. I'm afraid our lives will be changed forever if things continue the way they are." She tried to see events from her grandmother's perspective. Boston was such a center of patriotic leanings. Would her grandmother be caught in the middle if it boiled over?

Elizabeth rose and walked to the window, pulling aside the sheer curtains to view the activity on the street in the distance. Turning back, she ran her fingers along the mantle before bracing herself on the back of the chair facing her grandmother. "Long before Louis came into my life, I joined the Daughters of Liberty in Charles Town. I am as far from Father politically as I can be. And now Louis has committed his life to the cause. Father knows I don't agree with the Loyalists, but if he knew I had signed on to oppose them, he would be devastated. He already figured out Louis' commitment and fired him from teaching at the college. All the negatives are lined up against us. But I can't seem to stop myself from going in deeper and deeper." The passion spilled over with her words, giving them a life of their own, the power to convince and prove her case.

Grandmamma pushed herself up to standing and joined her, placing her firm hands on Elizabeth's shoulders. "You are no longer a child. I see that now. God has given you a purpose beyond the obvious one of worshipping Him. You, and possibly your Louis, have made strong, heartfelt decisions. I only pray that you are strong enough to endure the battle. Because if what you say is true, you will need each other and God's strength. I'm not as ignorant or unconcerned as you might think. I feel the turmoil. But it will be mostly your generation that will make the change," As Grandmamma finished, tears filled her eyes. Her grandmother loved her so much. Elizabeth knew that the beloved older lady spoke the truth.

Strength and courage, hand in hand. They would need those commodities to endure whatever lay ahead of them. With God all things were possible. And with Louis by her side, the burden shared, Elizabeth felt lighter and more confident.

❀

Home again in August, Elizabeth welcomed the school preparations for her thirty fresh, eager girls, a new beginning and adventure for them. The challenge gave her a purpose, filling her days with needed activity.

Sarah also returned to Charles Town from her country stay. The added color to her cheeks and shine to her hair made Elizabeth's friend appear healthier, happier, and even prettier.

Elizabeth greeted her friend in the front parlor with laughter and hugs. "Are you sure you don't prefer the country life, Sarah?"

Something was different about Sarah. What exactly? Elizabeth couldn't quite put her finger on it.

"Not necessarily. I do know that I'm going to follow your example and get outside more. I'm making a vow in front of you to step outside of my shallow world at home and do something with my life." A different young woman indeed.

"Well, good for you. Have you thought any more about helping at the boarding school?"

Sarah bowed her head and stared at her folded hands. "Yes, I have, although the prospect of being in charge of girls of any age scares me. If you will help guide me, I'll try."

"Great. It will be fun working together. I will tell Mistress Reynolds that news and have her put you on the same schedule that I have on Tuesday, Wednesday, and Thursday. I'll be working from ten in the morning until three in the afternoon," Elizabeth explained. "I don't think the girls will let you down. Anyway, you don't have to teach them. Just be an extra set of hands and legs. They will love you."

Sarah shrugged her shoulders. Elizabeth sensed the trust her friend had in her—enough to try. Their personalities were opposite, but from their first encounter three years ago, they had been fast and steady friends. Best friends. Of the same age and same class, they bonded quickly and permanently. One shy and introverted; one talkative and outgoing. One pessimistic and afraid; one optimistic and secure. One paranoid; one hopeful. Elizabeth thought her friend was so very special in her sweetness, her loving gestures, her willingness to help others, her kind words, her promptness. The list went on. They did complement each other. Somehow, their faults were not so obvious when with each other.

"So, have you heard from Louis?" Sarah asked.

"Oh, yes. Quite a few letters. He should be on his ship right now headed home." Home to her. Home to the changes made to his—their—house. She chose to believe her love drew him closer and kept his love steadfast. Elizabeth shook. "And have you heard from Samuel?" Elizabeth returned.

A forced smile didn't reach her eyes. "No. Not a word from him. I guess our few outings together were just to pass the time. He found out right away that he didn't like me. I really didn't expect to hear from him," Sarah shared.

Elizabeth hadn't expected her friend's answer. Samuel was a good friend of Louis', and the four of them had attended a few events together in the spring. Nothing more, though—no promises, no plan for the future. Elizabeth tried to be positive for her friend. "Well, maybe it is because you have been gone for so long."

"Don't make excuses, Elizabeth. I haven't. He's a nice man, but we're not right for each other."

"I know there will be someone else soon."

"Or maybe not. I'll stay busy as I am determined to get out of my house more. You'll see. The old, boring, inactive Sarah will metamorphose into a social lady." Sarah giggled, letting Elizabeth see a light, carefree side of her friend. Sarah appeared to be butterfly, no longer a moth.

"Don't change too much, Sarah. I won't recognize you." Elizabeth laughed. "Speaking of change, I'm ready for the heat and mosquitoes to disappear. Fall is my favorite time of year. Especially this year because…" She stopped.

Because Louis was coming home. They would announce their engagement, and they could plan their wedding. But she couldn't tell Sarah yet. And what if it didn't happen that way at all?

Sarah crossed her arms and prodded. "Because why?"

The seconds seemed like minutes. Why wasn't she ready with an answer? "Oh, just because of the new things happening with the school. That's it."

Did I convince her?

It appeared her friend would let the subject drop, for now. In time all would be revealed, exposed to the world—exposed to her parents. Elizabeth shook the unpleasant thoughts from her mind. The end result would be worth the drama to come.

"Let's go to the boarding house right now and check on the progress in the classrooms." A change of scenery would allow Elizabeth to transmit her energy and thoughts to a neutral ground.

A few days later Elizabeth journeyed to her sister Anne's house. She knew Anne liked her company since it added a bit of variety from constant care of the children. Her two sons, ages six and eight, kept her sister busy and confined at times.

"Hello, Aunt Elizabeth." Two eager boys attached themselves to her skirt and pulled her into the drawing room.

"How did you know I was coming?" Elizabeth tussled their hair.

Robert, the oldest, laughed. "We saw you through the window." She was surprised he didn't add "silly" to his answer.

Elizabeth loved the atmosphere of the happy home. "Where's your mother?" Her little hosts took her by the hands to Anne's side.

Elizabeth saw the books piled on the table and the blocks on the floor. "Did I interrupt anything?"

"Not at all. The boys are trying to build the tallest tower yet. One that will let them see their father pull into the port." Like Elizabeth, her sister anticipated the arrival of Louis' ship, where her husband Robert Cochran served as captain of the vessel.

"You miss him, don't you?" She'd seen that faraway look in her sister's eyes before, usually right before Robert was expected home.

Anne motioned with her hands at the boys' architecture. "Yes. But the boys keep me occupied and focused on them."

Because of many similar interests, the girls remained close friends and shared many of the secrets that Elizabeth could not voice to their parents. Both were Partisan sympathizers closely tied with the Daughters of Liberty. This fact remained a secret to their father, although Mother had figured it out last winter. She disagreed with her daughters' affiliation only because her husband was a fierce Loyalist.

Elizabeth helped the children add the wooden townspeople to the buildings. "At home I have no one who understands my longing for Louis. If it weren't for you and Jeannette, I would feel so very alone."

"Well, Louis did entrust us to take care of you, and I think we have done a good job, don't you?"

"Of course. You have helped immensely." A true friend and confidant had made the days more bearable. "Have you heard anything, Anne, about when they will return?"

"Robert's latest letter said the departure date was August first just like Louis predicted. So, assuming that happened, it should be the first or second week of September."

Grabbing a block that fell from a tower, Elizabeth tossed it back and forth in her hands. "I don't know if I can wait that long. How do you do this waiting so often?"

"I won't say I've gotten used to it, but I do know how to cope." Anne picked up a few stray blocks and placed them in a chest out of the way. "I knew I was marrying a ship captain and the consequences of that lifestyle. It does make the homecoming in the fall and winter seasons a time of blessing, growth, and love. When he's home, he really is here day to day, one hundred percent."

"You will let me know right away when you hear news of the ship's arrival. I want to be there waiting for Louis. From his letters I think Louis is as anxious as I am."

Anne secured Elizabeth's hand in hers. "I believe you have nothing to fear. Even Robert said Louis talks about you constantly."

Nothing to fear. The true test would not be the time they had apart, but the time ahead of them when obstacles loomed as impregnable walls. Her thoughts always stopped there at the walls. She couldn't seem to wrap her mind around the possible scenarios. She would face that when the time came, with Louis and with God. Surely with that strong threefold cord, they could overcome anything.

CHAPTER 3

eptember 1773

Tuesday morning, Anne entered Elizabeth's classroom at the boarding school. Ten pairs of curious eyes peered at the sisters as they huddled in the doorway.

Anne clasped Elizabeth's hands in hers and bounced up and down. "The ship has been seen off the coast. They're almost home, Elizabeth. Only a few more hours. Can you get free?" Anne questioned as she stood back, allowing Elizabeth to breathe.

Elizabeth had stood by the sea wall every day for the past two weeks, anticipating the sighting of the *Rose* and Louis. *Is his love as strong as three months ago?* His letters encouraged her with his words of devotion and plans for the future. But once he saw her, would his dreams still be the same as hers?

Shaking the shadows away, Elizabeth closed her eyes tightly for a second, seeing only Louis' face full of love. "Nothing will stop me. I'll have Sarah cover my classes this afternoon." She had dreamed of this moment for so long. Louis. Home again. What would that mean? She could hardly expect endless hours at his side when her father stood ready to question his every move.

Anne left to have lunch with her children and alert the servants that Captain Cochran was coming home today. Elizabeth found Sarah, with an armload of books, helping the literature teacher. "Sarah, do you think you could watch my two classes this afternoon for me? I have an urgent...ah, an important meeting that came up all of a sudden," she whispered, knowing her friend wouldn't mind.

"I can guess what it is." Sarah smiled. Although Elizabeth hadn't shared any details, Sarah had tried to pry information out of her all summer. All she could possibly know was that Elizabeth was anxious about Louis' arrival. So far, she had held her secret. But not for long, now.

She should just blurt it out like she'd wanted to for months. Like she had with her grandmother. That had gone well. She did trust Sarah as her dearest friend, but a part of Elizabeth needed this kept quiet, the part full of fear and doubt. Was it fear on her part of something going wrong? Fear that others would find out? Fear of her love? Or just a selfish desire to keep Louis to herself for now?

"I'll tell you, but please keep it quiet. I don't want the whole school asking questions." After her friend had deposited her books, Elizabeth guided Sarah to the back of the room. "Anne said the ship has been spotted and is headed in now. Louis is coming home. Finally coming home." She squeezed Sarah's upper arm, needing the contact. Perhaps Elizabeth needed to be pinched to make it feel real.

"I want to know all the details," Sarah said. "Promise me no more secrets." Her brown eyes pleaded with Elizabeth for the truth.

"I promise. But right now, I need to see Louis."

Elizabeth left before she said too much. It really didn't matter if Sarah knew now. Soon, all of Charles Town would know of their engagement and their love. No more secrets in the near future.

Before heading to the wharf, Elizabeth raced to Wilson's Mercantile. Her gait was between a skip and a jump, her arms swinging by her side. Her reticule, wrapped around her wrist, jostled with the beat of her feet.

Perhaps Jeannette didn't need to hear the news with words, as Elizabeth's bouncing into the store said it all. "He's back isn't he? Louis is home." Her friend's hands pressed against her lips, covering her excitement.

Elizabeth stretched her hands out, clutching Jeannette's fingers. "Almost. I'm on my way now. How do I look?" She ran her hands down the front and sides of her skirt, checking the folds of blue striped fabric for flaws and wrinkles. "Should I change?"

Jeannette tried to hold her still by bracing her hands on Elizabeth's shoulders. "You look beautiful. Excitement is glowing on your cheeks. Louis doesn't need anything but you just like this."

"Really?" Elizabeth bit her lower lip lightly and raised her eyebrow in question. "All right. Then give me a hug for good luck."

"Why do you need luck? You know how he feels. That has not changed, unless it has gotten stronger," Jeannette encouraged. "His eyes will light up when he sees you pacing the pier."

"Well, give me a hug because I'm about to explode."

The two women embraced, calming Elizabeth's nerves and replacing them with encouragement. Placing Elizabeth's face between her hands, Jeannette commanded her attention. "Go. Give him my love. We'll have a big celebration tonight. You, my dear, are invited. We will have all his favorite dishes. I'll put the cook on it right now. Go. Go."

It didn't take much persuasion to push Elizabeth out of the door. Before going to the pier, Elizabeth strolled briskly to the seawall facing the water. Yes, there. She could see it, although just a shadow on the vast expanse of blue. Others using spyglasses had seen the ship and identified it as the *Rose*. She waved and threw the ship a kiss, not caring that Louis couldn't see her.

Mesmerized for at least half an hour, Elizabeth soaked in the sun, the breeze, and the sounds of the water lapping against the wall. Peace. She was actually still. She didn't try to think beyond the next few hours. She had debated her situation all summer, racked her brain for solutions, wished away her problems, all to no avail. But for right now, the future did not matter. Only the present. With the slow advance of the ship, the details became clearer and sharper every minute.

Elizabeth remembered when Louis had first set foot in Charles Town one year ago. Now he was doing it for a second time after his three-month journey. Elizabeth waited. And then she saw him. At least to her eyes, she saw him standing at the bow of the huge ship, holding onto a heavy rope and looking her way. She wanted it to be him. That was where she would have been—standing or pacing, ready to jump in to make the distance shorter. She followed her instinct and waved to him with big circular motions over her head.

The blur of an image moving with the same motion confirmed that the person had seen her. It had to be Louis. Were his thoughts the same as hers? Hopefully, he didn't doubt her love and commitment.

She unfastened her ring from the inside of her bodice. She studied it, a gold band with rubies and diamonds, cherishing the memory of Louis' placing it on her finger in May. She took off her left glove and returned the ring to its proper place on her finger, a symbol of his love for her. Soon, that would be its permanent place.

Holding her hat in place, Elizabeth ran along the wall, passing numerous piers before she turned onto the familiar one, where she had last said her goodbyes to Louis. This time her hope and love would be sailing into port instead of away.

Elizabeth saw Christopher exit his office with Samuel close behind him. Excitement poured out with her questions and comments, skipping the polite greetings. "Did you see the *Rose*? How much longer? Do you know anything about Louis and Robert? Are they well?" Her hand pulled on Samuel's jacket sleeve.

"And good afternoon to you, Elizabeth," Christopher said, as he broke into her string of questions. His grin matched his companion's. Both men laughed behind their smiles.

Placing her hands on her hips, Elizabeth pursed her lips in a pout. "You're laughing at me."

Christopher mimicked her stance minus the pout. "Well, you are a pleasant sight. Like a child waiting for Christmas. I think we were both wishing we had someone waiting for us like you." He elbowed Samuel in the ribs. "I'm sure Louis will practically jump off the ship before she's docked when he sees you."

She straightened her hat, gloves, and skirt. "In other words, I need to calm down and act my age," she suggested.

Samuel peered around Christopher's shoulders. "No need, Elizabeth. Louis does not expect a porcelain doll greeting him. We are just glad to see your enthusiasm."

Walking a few feet farther on the pier, Christopher gestured toward the vast ocean. "To answer your questions, yes, we saw the *Rose* through the glass. She will arrive in about half an hour. And last word I had from a smaller vessel two hours ago was that both men and the crew are just fine. Anything else?"

Elizabeth knew Christopher had reason to be as anxious as Elizabeth since his cargo and ship were involved.

A few minutes later Anne arrived with all the dignity of an older woman, something Elizabeth wished she had herself. Even if Anne's feet weren't lifting off the ground, Elizabeth guessed her sister's heart pounded and her mind centered on the arrival of her husband.

"I see, gentlemen, that you have not managed to keep my sister still in one place," Anne remarked.

Elizabeth couldn't help the bounce or the pacing. "I don't think I'll ever get used to it like you. How do you manage, Anne? Robert is gone so often." Elizabeth's brows furrowed as she tried to imagine a husband on the sea six months out of the year.

The sisters linked arms and strolled to a bench placed on the pier about halfway down. "I concentrate on the time he has at home when we enjoy his presence every day, all day," Anne said. Elizabeth appreciated her sister's attempt to distract her, until increasing waves lapped onto the pier and the sound of crashing water interrupted conversations. Then the huge body of the ship appeared and headed straight to the pier, steered to perfection. Men readied to secure the ship.

A silent prayer of thanksgiving for Louis' return pierced her heart. Nothing else mattered to her. Louis, with his windblown hair, weathered face, and wrinkled clothes was the perfect vision. He was home.

Louis was the first man off the ship after the vessel was secure. Elizabeth bounced on her toes, her dress flowing around her and her wind-tousled hair framing her face. Within minutes, they were in each other's arms, spinning and floating, trying to balance as they slowed down. He kissed her hair, her cheeks, and briefly her lips. Such public display was uncustomary, but who was to see —the crew, the Cochrans, Christopher, Samuel? She giggled. So what if all of Charles Town saw Louis publicly showing the world that he loved her?

But it did matter a bit. She remembered her grandmother— "careful with etiquette." As Elizabeth found her footing, she took a step back in order to see Louis' face, to touch his cheek. "Welcome home, my love."

"Oh, Elizabeth, how I have wanted to be home with you. You were always with me in my thoughts, my heart, and my prayers. In fact, this locket never left my body." He pulled out the gold chain with a locket attached from his inner pocket. Her miniature portrait was in it, a gift she had given him before he left. "Always close to my heart."

Robert and Anne enjoyed their own reunion as passionately as a couple could on the pier. The rest of those present were greeted in turn. Louis seemed genuinely glad to see Christopher and Samuel. Elizabeth knew hours would be spent detailing the last few months, exchanging news from France and South Carolina.

She didn't release Louis' arm as they walked past Christopher's office. The unloading and distributing of the cargo would wait until tomorrow. Personal luggage would be delivered that afternoon. So Louis was free to roam the city with Elizabeth. Without plans or discussion, they found themselves in the city park overlooking the vast waters. "Do you mind if we walk or stand for a while? I need to get my land legs back. It usually takes me several hours to adjust."

"Not at all. I don't think I could sit still now anyway. I just want to look at you," Elizabeth confessed as she gazed at him.

He hadn't changed in any noticeable way. The creases around his eyes appeared to be from lack of sleep rather than from stress or discomfort. Overall, by his healthy stance and lack of pallor, he appeared to have weathered the arduous voyage as a true sailor. The blue of his eyes matched the afternoon sky—clear and light, as if they could see into her soul.

Does he know, truly know, how I feel? How can I show him?

He winked at her, catching her daydreaming. "I believe you did miss me, Elizabeth. Maybe as much as I missed you."

She had no reason to dream and wish. Louis stood right in front of her. "Do you want the honest truth? I was miserable at first. I thought there was no way to survive the summer. Then, with the wisdom of your aunt and Anne, I threw myself into projects. In order to avoid pining and whining, I accomplished more than I thought possible." She faced him as much as she could without tripping. "One recipient of my energy was your house. I think you will be pleased."

He lifted her chin, forcing her eyes to focus on his. "You mean 'our house'—don't you? You were to turn it into a home for both of us."

"I know." She tilted her head, knowing all he said was in fact true, although hard to believe. "And as I worked and planned, I did so want it to be mine. But I don't feel I can claim it until we make our engagement public. I can't talk about our house to just anyone. I'm sorry, I just couldn't."

"Don't apologize. I understand entirely. And I did ask you to keep our secret. That is the only way you could be protected during my absence. Now I'm home. If you can trust me a little longer, I'll obtain your father's consent, and you'll have a proper engagement and wedding. I promise." He wiped a tear from her cheek. "What did I do to deserve your love and trust?"

"Louis, what if—"

He silenced her with a finger to her lips. "Not now. Remember how we knew God was holding us close this past year? That He had a plan and a purpose? Well, I still believe that more each day. Somehow His love is surrounding us. Elizabeth, I can't explain it, but I know that you and I will be together. The big obstacle is your father, I know. Pray that he will grant us the permission we desire. But if he doesn't, *mon amour*, I'll not be deterred for long. I promise you will be mine."

The strength and certainty in his words caused her to touch him again, convincing herself of the reality. God's promise. Yes, she remembered. "I don't know what to say. Already I feel stronger just with you here. My doubts seem so silly when put up against God's love."

A few moments of silence allowed their thoughts to focus and even fuse together. They would face the hurdles together in the days to come.

Lacing her arm through his, Elizabeth pulled him forward.

"Now, Louis, another item. You are to be escorted to the Wilsons' by none other than me. I promised your aunt and uncle I would not keep you to myself too long. Are you ready?" *Am I ready to share what I have waited all summer to see, to hold...and to kiss? Yes, with those thoughts, it is better for me to share Louis!*

He rubbed her fingers, pressing his heat into her body. He bent his head closer to her ear, rustling her hair with his breathe. "If I must. I certainly can't stay with you for hours alone. What scandal that would bring. But one day I will have you all to myself."

"Louis." Elizabeth rubbed her free hand across her forehead, feigning a shock she didn't feel. Yes, one day. The bounce returned to her step as they slowly strolled to the house on Tradd Street.

Once Louis was welcomed home by his aunt and uncle, Elizabeth left after promising to return for dinner at seven. She regretfully released Louis' arm, but joy spurred her homeward, knowing in only a few hours she would be back by his side.

Now, a difficult task. Even when faced with a dilemma, Elizabeth could not erase the telltale signs of her extreme joy at having Louis home; she couldn't hide her constant smile and motion. It was as if Louis' arrival transformed her inside and out.

Is it normal to be this excited?

She informed her mother she had accepted an invitation to dine at the Wilsons'. That would not be strange to her parents, for every few weeks Jeannette extended her hospitality to Elizabeth. No, the surprise was probably Elizabeth's adding the information about Louis.

"So, Mr. Lestarjette is back from France. I really never expected us to hear from him again," Mother commented as she sat straight backed and regal in her parlor. Elizabeth could tell her mother's defenses were up. Not only did she see concern, but signs of fear.

Elizabeth clucked her tongue. "Mother, you knew he would return. I told you he had every intention of working with Mr.

Gadsden and the Wilsons. He even bought a house. Then why are you surprised?"

"But plans change. His family might have had an influence on him. They might have encouraged him to stay in France." All hope was gone from her mother's voice as she swallowed this information.

All this time, Elizabeth knew the negative feelings existed, yet now they were tangible, evident on her mother's face. "Do you dislike him so much, Mother?" Elizabeth asked, hoping her mother would be honest. Usually, her mother was not prejudiced or mean at heart.

"Of course, I like him. All the times I have seen him, he has been very polite, displaying impeccable manners. His charming French ways are a delight. But your father says he's up to no good. That he's only out for profit and to deceive the British." Her mother leaned closer and whispered, "And maybe he is a spy."

Elizabeth's jaw opened her mouth to an "O." A spy? Louis? "Mother, now you are gossiping. You let him into your house every Sunday for a year. Do you really believe he would harm me or you or Father? Just because his views are different from Father's doesn't mean he is a spy. Anyway, you know where I stand politically—the opposite side of Father. So, am I a spy?" She fidgeted with her gloves, remembering just in time that her ring graced her finger. She had to return it to her bodice as soon as possible.

"Of course not, Elizabeth. Maybe you're right. Just be careful. Enjoy your dinner with him. Don't make it a habit though. Your father won't approve."

Elizabeth kissed her mother on the cheek. She prayed a silent prayer that her mother would one day take a stand for her own beliefs and not always be a puppet of her father's.

During the remaining hours of the afternoon, Elizabeth soothed her racing thoughts with music. She attacked the keyboard with fervor. Slowly, her feelings calmed, and a peace returned as she switched from a lively Haydn piece to Mozart's Kyrie in D. Her soul wrapped around the chords of the sacred work, and her pensive meandering settled on God's plan for Louis and herself.

Although the two of them continued to be surrounded by unsettling events, unpleasant people, and even an uncertain future, she could focus on her faith. It engulfed her even in her solitude. She was not alone. God promised to always be with her through his son, Jesus. His love surrounded her. And because Louis believed and trusted in Jesus, his love for her as a woman added to her ability to prevail.

His luggage safely deposited in his room, Louis joined Aunt Jeannette and Uncle Henry in the Wilson's Mercantile next door. He wanted to reacquaint himself with his life and people here. As he perused the shelves, he remembered he had arrived back in town just in time for the change of season. Stocking of fall items had begun.

"Hello, son." Uncle Henry wrapped him in a bear hug. "Welcome back to the mercantile. I was so used to your help that I had to hire a young man to help me in your absence." Henry nodded his head toward the storeroom door. "I thought I might keep him on. He works hard, and his family needs the money. What do you think?"

Louis nodded his approval, knowing that Henry wouldn't hire anyone he didn't trust. "That would help us both out. Well, do you want to introduce me?" Louis suggested, taking the initiative toward the young man.

They entered the storeroom. The pungent fish odor from a recently opened barrel of pickled sardines hung in the air. Bags of flour and corn lined the walls. The young man bent over a crate of bottles of oil and wine and proceeded to put a few on the shelf.

Henry cleared his throat. "Tom Engle, this is my nephew, Louis Lestarjette."

Tom extended his hand. "Pleased to meet you, sir."

Louis liked the look of the boy, about sixteen years old, medium height, well mannered, and strong. "Likewise. Thank you for helping my uncle. I'll let you get back to work."

His uncle filled him in on the general ins and outs of the summer business. He implied that the clientele had shifted and actually increased since Parliament's bill in May.

"I guess you could say that our customers tend to see things the way we do. It's as if we put a sign on the door: 'Partisans welcome.' The political lines are more defined now. Rarely do we see a Loyalist darken our doors. But on the other hand, business has increased. People we hadn't seen before now do their business here. I can't wait to hear your knowledge on the situation over-seas." Henry and Louis completed their tour of the store. "I will give as many details as possible, Uncle. For now, put me to work after I give Aunt Jeannette a little attention."

He found her alone at the front window, adjusting a sash on a dress. Sneaking up, he surprised her with a big hug from the side.

"Oh, Louis, you scared me. You know I'm not used to that. Why even your uncle gives me warning." She turned to face him, spreading her arms as if to encompass the entire store. "Well, what do you think of the shop? As you see, we continued to implement your suggestions. And all the goods you ordered are quickly purchased. I can't wait to see the shipment you brought with you."

He laughed. His aunt had a habit of not pausing for anyone to answer her questions. He loved to hear her ramble. But since she seemed to have finished at present, he said, "I think you have done a marvelous job. The new items will be delivered tomorrow, which will keep you occupied for a while."

After catching up a bit more, she then convinced him to rest for an hour or so and to begin work the next day. He obeyed, but only after his uncle had coaxed him as well, knowing cool lemon water in the sunroom was just what he needed.

By seven o'clock the sideboards in the dining room were filled with steaming dishes. The aroma in the house hinted of fresh baked bread and peppered sausage, making it hard for Louis to concentrate on his reading. He turned from his perusal of a book on European garden designs at the sound of light footsteps. A portrait of indescribable beauty dressed in her light-blue skirt and bodice trimmed with pink ribbons, Elizabeth entered the parlor with no introduction. He stood, admiring her hair hanging in ringlets around her rosy cheeks and her bright eyes beaming at him. Finally, he shook himself in order to lift the spell mesmerizing him. In two steps Louis was in front of her, taking her hand and kissing it.

"How did you enter without a fuss, so quietly?" he whispered now that he had found his voice.

"Your aunt anticipated my arrival and let me in," she explained. She ran her fingers down the lapel of his flawless jacket, though plainer than usual. "Are your clothes new?"

He nodded, taking her hand as it traveled over his heart. "I decided to buy some practical items." He looked down at his beige dinner jacket and brown trousers. "No ruffles and lace tonight." Louis paused and stared, becoming lost in her blue-gray eyes peering at him through her dark lashes. "Why are we talking about me when you look so beautiful? Let's sit in here and wait for Jeannette and Henry. By the way, what did you do with her?"

As they walked across the plush wool carpet decorated with a scattering of flowers, leaves, and palmettos on a blue background, Elizabeth giggled. "Jeannette said she had to help Henry with his cravat. Can you believe that?"

She fingered Louis' cravat, then lightly touched his chin and cheek with her soft fingers. He captured her hand, although he favored her fingers on his face. She stepped back, taking his hand with her.

Elizabeth looked toward the dining room, breaking their contact. "By the smells from the dining room, it appears your aunt has concocted a feast. I know they didn't eat like this while you were gone. I think you are good for them, Louis. A reason for them to celebrate and open their home. And I'm glad to be included."

He guided her to the sofa, facing a beautiful vase of yellow roses. "I have so much to tell you," he began, as he touched the ring on her finger—the one he had placed there months ago. "I'm glad you feel comfortable wearing this here. I have thought of little else. Everything I did in France got me closer to coming home to you. Do you believe that?"

She sighed. "Yes, I know it now. I'll admit I had a few doubts. I thought, what if you found a beautiful French woman, someone who could give you an easier life without the drama attached to me. Oh, Louis, I thought—" She paused, lowering her head to glance at his hand still holding hers, "I thought when you were away, you might realize the difficulties of this life were not worth it. I--"

Louis stopped her with a shake of his head as he squeezed her hand. "I assure you I never for one moment wanted to change my mind. It is you I love. You I want to marry and take care of, even with the conflicts around us. I accept the challenges of this life. This time last year, I would have run from them, and I could have done just that. But I didn't. Now I have a purpose, a reason to commit. So, I'm glad that you see I am here to be with you. I promise we'll work it out."

He reached in his pocket and pulled out a small leather box. Opening her hand, he turned her palm upward and placed it in the center.

"What is this, Louis?" Elizabeth's fingers hovered over the box. Slowly, she lifted the lid. "Oh, it is wonderful. Perfect. A treasure." She brought the gold locket with Louis' likeness inside close to her heart.

"It matches the one you had given me. I hope if I'm ever not with you the image can bring you comfort."

"Yes, although, you are always in my heart, closer than any portrait." She took off the gold chain from around her neck, the one that she had secured her ring on all summer and placed the locket there.

Taking the necklace from her hand, Louis got down on one knee and as Elizabeth lifted her hair he secured the clasp behind her neck. Rising, he kissed her forehead. "Perfect."

Jeannette chose that moment to make her entrance. "I hope I'm not disturbing you, but dinner is ready, and I want Louis to finally have a nice meal after so many weeks in a less than inviting situation."

A servant uncovered the dishes and released more of the tantalizing aromas: mushroom-and-onion soup, ham, sausage, asparagus, yams with molasses, cabbage, and yeast biscuits with fresh butter. Louis filled his plate from rim to rim.

"I've never seen this pattern on your plates, Jeannette. Is it new?" Elizabeth asked. Louis noticed her plate was not nearly as full as his. He couldn't even see the pattern.

"No. I've had it for a few years," Jeannette said. "I fell in love with the flowers and butterflies."

Smiling at the images, Elizabeth set her plate in front of her. "It reminds me of my garden in the spring and summer."

"Are you wondering what your china will look like? That is something you two will have to decide," Jeannette said, setting her plate on the table. "Now let's eat."

Louis laughed, and Henry changed the subject from china to business, which they discussed at length. "Are you ready to work tomorrow, Louis? I have a feeling it will take weeks to properly display and sort the cargo you brought."

"Yes, I am. Weeks on the ship made me want the everyday activity of the store. I'm sure I'll be there early," Louis promised.

As an afterthought he added, "How much have you told Tom Engle?"

"Not anything that would hurt us or bring up questions. He keeps to the front floor and back storeroom. He knows nothing about the other places," his uncle explained. "I try to keep an eye on him since his father recently passed away. Mr. Engle was a member of the Sons of Liberty. I don't know the boy's stand. I do know he needs the work to support his mother and sister. For now, I'm not going to give him anything to lead the Loyalists here, just in case."

Louis didn't usually question loyalties, but his uncle's storeroom could spark a lot of questions. One word to the wrong person and all of his uncle's work would be exposed. "I'll keep an eye on him too." With that, he turned his attention to his aunt. "The meal was superb."

Her features softened as she blushed and grinned. "We'll have dessert in the parlor in a few minutes. Tonight, we're not letting you men disappear to the library. Louis, you must stay with us and enlighten us on your voyage. Come, let's get a little more comfortable," Jeannette suggested.

They all moved to the adjoining room and arranged themselves on the sofas under the glittering glow of the chandelier. Louis didn't debate for a moment that his place was right next to Elizabeth.

Before long, the lemon custard and tray of tea were situated on the table between the couches. Jeannette served the hot amber liquid in her butterfly cups. Between sips of tea and bites of the creamy sweet, Louis related bits and pieces of his time in France. He answered their questions, enjoying the memories of his family.

"You would have been pleased with the wedding, Aunt Jeannette. It was stylish without being extravagant. André and Madeline are a happy couple, from what I could tell. And Maman was content to finally have another female in the family. She has been outnumbered all these years. I wish you all could have been there."

He related other details to satisfy their curiosity, but the time finally came when Elizabeth needed to get home. As Louis and Elizabeth waited for the arrival of her carriage, they spoke in whispers of love and the future, of pure faith and dreams to come, not of the realities of the present. Dreams and realities were different at this time. Dreams included a pleasant public engagement, a perfect wedding shared with friends and family, a peaceful day-to-day life in their new home, a brood of children, and a pure love for each other.

Reality lurked around the corner, threatening to make an appearance. It forced them to talk of disapproving parents, of a dangerous daily existence with the threat of war, and a dismal time to start a family.

Louis led her to the carriage. "I plan to talk to your father soon. We will then be able to plan all these things we only whisper about now. Don't lose that hope that made you not give up on me."

Elizabeth arranged her skirt around her on the seat. "I know. My hope is too deeply rooted in God to lose it."

"That's the part I'm working on every day—the deep roots. I've wasted so much time doing things my way. But slowly my doubts and fears are being replaced by purpose and strength. We'll hold on together, surrounded by God's love and our love for each other." He kissed her cheeks and planted a promising kiss on her ring finger. Then he signaled the driver to move on, taking Elizabeth to her home.

I promise, Lord, to seek your will in all of this, especially where it concerns Elizabeth. His prayer disappeared in the still dark sky.

CHAPTER 4

*T*he next day, Louis joined Christopher on the docks. Dispersal of the goods in an organized manner was top priority. "Here are the orders I have from several French merchants whenever we're able to fill them. Basic goods as before. Some were impressed with the local pottery and the items made from hardwood. Besides that, it's mostly rice and cotton they want."

"And the other contacts?" Christopher asked, never taking his eyes off the cargo leaving the ship.

"A few of the men were very open and receptive. I'm surprised at the sentiment in France." Louis had taken part in many heated discussions. Would the New World go to war with France's enemy? "Daily, their dislike of the British grows as their love for the colonists increases. Frenchmen are waiting for a fight. I avoided any talk of revolution, hoping it won't come to that. There's no need to excite an excitable people."

He heard footsteps on the dock and turned as James Laurens, a local landowner and planter, joined them.

"Welcome back, Mr. Lestarjette." The distinguished man offered Louis his hand as they renewed their acquaintance.

"Thank you, sir. Since this is to be home now, I was anxious to return." Louis trusted the gentleman. He was a staunch leader in the Sons of Liberty.

"I'm interested to hear how your fellow countrymen view our situation," Mr. Laurens said.

Were all of his acquaintances this curious about Frenchmen? "With great interest. Ready, maybe too ready, to enter the fight. As you know, nothing incites the blood of the French as a fight against the British," Louis replied.

Mr. Laurens continued the probe. "And the king? Where does he stand?"

Louis had heard talk on the streets of men ready to join forces against the British crown. There just was no need yet. It wasn't France's problem, although they were itching to join the fight. "As typical of the king, he has no comments. His ministers handle all the details of foreign affairs. There are rumors of factions raising money, arms, and men to help in case of battle. It's a wait-and-see game now." Even though his countrymen wanted war, Louis prayed it could be avoided. "Well, gentlemen, I must see that my crates are delivered to the store. I look forward to talking again soon." Louis turned to depart.

Before Louis had taken two steps, Christopher called to him. "Louis, there's a meeting next Thursday night at Mr. Manigault's house. It's very important, an update on the Tea Act. I hope you'll be there."

"Of course. I need to get back in touch with the cause after my absence. Maybe I can help more now." He waved as he left.

The prospect of meeting with the Sons of Liberty brought mixed emotions. Sharing the energy of intelligent, civic-minded men stirred excitement, but not everything was peaceful.

Louis took a deep breath as he set down a crate. "Last one."

"It's about time." Henry wiped the sweat off his forehead. "It took us all afternoon to get these into the storeroom."

Louis shrugged. "I expected it to." He glanced over his shoulder. Nobody was in hearing distance. "As before, there are faux bottoms. I made sure the weapons and ammunition fit securely and discreetly inside."

"I appreciate your dedication, Louis. I know it's asking a lot of you." Henry tested the lock on the storeroom door. "All secure."

Wiping his neck with his handkerchief, Louis verbalized his disturbing realization. "If I wasn't quite sure before my last voyage, I am now. I have no other option but to support the cause." More and more he realized all the controversial stored goods would have to be used in the future.

Henry clapped his gloved hands together, releasing a cloud of dust. "Well, let's get to work. I've pried open the boxes. If we can remove the top layer, I'll let you store the other supplies quickly."

"I'll gladly manage that." Louis put his work gloves on quickly. "How many times have you done this?"

Henry laughed. "What? Unloading crates or stashing contraband?"

"The contraband." Louis grinned, lifting the lid and placing it against the wall.

Facing another box, Henry lifted out a few bottles of olive oil. "About a dozen. I've stopped counting."

And still neither Parliament nor Partisans were backing down. God would have to be the One to turn the tide. Louis knew he couldn't do it as one person.

Over the next hour or so, Louis carried items up and down the steps multiple times to the hidden basement. After housing the goods in their proper places, Louis did a quick check of the inventory. The supply was significant. Ceiling to floor on one wall of muskets and pistols. A few kegs of powder. Five crates with swords and bayonets. Was it enough to fight the British? The citizens were not trained to fight against an organized militia, men of war, although some had seen action in the French and Indian War. He hadn't heard of any strategy or plan to get these weapons into the hands of Partisans.

He closed the storage door, making sure the entrance on the floor was covered by boxes once again. Uncle Henry had made a dent in the crates; the shelves were filling up with a good supply for the fall and winter.

Stretching his back, Uncle Henry observed the items on the shelves. "I see once again you managed to procure the finest material, china, spices, and oils for our customers." His hands held two large candlesticks. "What about these, Louis? They are mighty fine for a regular client."

Taking them from his uncle, he balanced one in each hand. "These are mine. A wedding gift for Elizabeth. I'm glad to see they arrived without a scratch or dent. The finest craftsman of silver in Paris made them. What do you think?"

"Perfect, son. She will love them. I assume they are to be a surprise," Henry noted. "Young and in love, that is a good place to be. Right now, you have all the hope in the world and in your future. Wait 'til you've been married twenty years."

Louis laughed about thinking that far in the future. Today was far enough for him. "I have to get married first, then work on the next twenty years." He placed the valuable items safely on a shelf. "I'll come back for these later this evening and keep them in my room. For now, I'll go check on Tom."

Out on the main floor, Tom filled bags of flour, while Jeannette adjusted a bolt of blue satin material. Louis noticed multiple bags at Tom's feet, sugar and seed. "I suppose these go to the wagon outside, Tom? I'll help you load them."

Without looking up, Tom said, "Thank you, Mr. Lestarjette."

Louis followed the lad with his hands full. "I'm sorry to hear of the loss of your father. How are your mother and sister, Tom?"

After placing his burden in the wagon, Tom looked at Louis.

"They have both secured temporary jobs as house servants but are looking for more permanent situations."

"If I hear of anything, I'll let you know." Louis knew how the loss of a father changed a family. At least he had been a lot older and more financially secure when his father passed away.

The bell on the front door of the mercantile tinkled, announcing her entrance. On impulse, Elizabeth searched for Louis and saw him immediately. Was he waiting for her? She hadn't told him she was coming by this afternoon. After all, she'd seen him just last night.

Since she was in the presence of others, she restrained her desire to rush into his arms. Composure—an essential quality.

It seemed her hands didn't remember what to do when talking to someone. She wanted to touch his face, hug him tightly, and twirl him around. Instead, she clasped her hands together in front of her, willing them to be still. "I was hoping you'd be here, Louis. How was your day?"

He reached for her hand; obviously he tried to control his desire. But he only stole a kiss on her hand. "Busy. It has disappeared quickly, it appears. And yours? Did the girls behave today?"

"Of course, I had complete control." She giggled, knowing he knew the truth. Could thirty girls be *completely* good? "Are you free Friday night? Anne is having a dinner for the family at her house to celebrate Robert's homecoming. Please come." She didn't need to plead, but she knew Louis might hesitate when she added, "My parents will be there as well as George."

He didn't hesitant. "Well, I can't say 'no.' Anywhere you are, I want to be. What time?"

"Dinner is at seven, but you can come earlier to keep me calm around my brother. He's been helping my uncle in his firm in Boston, and hopefully, it has mellowed him somewhat."

Her need for Louis' presence wasn't an idle statement. She had a way of confronting and challenging George and his brash statements. It had ended with both of them storming out of each other's presence on numerous occasions. Gone were the happy days of sister-and-brother playfulness and carefree ways. Those had been replaced with siblings standing on opposite sides of a bridge, waiting for the other to compromise. It was getting crowded since neither would budge.

Louis' words focused meandering thoughts. "I almost forgot. Would you come by the store after class tomorrow? I want to view our house with you. I haven't seen any of the changes or additions that you and Aunt Jeannette have made."

The ribbons on her bonnet rustled as she nodded. She clapped her hands together. "Yes, I will. I just hope you're happy, Louis. Now we can fill the rest of the house together. Well, almost together. We still have to be secret until you talk to Father."

"Soon enough. Let's see how Friday turns out with him. Who knows? Maybe he's had a change of heart. We can always pray that he has." Bringing her hand to his lips, he sent her on her way. She didn't purchase a thing. She had come solely to see him.

Elizabeth thought about Louis' house—their house—all the next day. Anxious to finish her classes, she glided through her theory and history lessons, not letting the girls know she was preoccupied. But when she failed to answer Sarah's question, she was caught.

"Elizabeth, did you hear me?" Sarah repeated. "I asked if you need any more notebooks for next week."

Elizabeth snapped out of her reverie, physically jerking her head toward the voice. "I'm sorry, Sarah. To answer your question, no, I don't. The girls still have plenty of paper left in their journals."

Lowering her burden to the table, Sarah touched Elizabeth's arm. "May I ask you a personal question?" Sarah paused. Elizabeth opened her mouth to stop the chance of any more lies escaping, then closed it. Her friend had the right to question her. "I'm going to anyway. How is Louis? Is everything like you thought it would be?"

Honesty. I'm ready. But is Sarah? Is my family? The town? Elizabeth grabbed Sarah's hands and spun her around. "Yes, it is. We were able to pick up where we left off. Sarah, I'm more in love with him than ever."

"I'm so happy for you, honestly. What do your parents think? Are you getting married?" Sarah asked.

Elizabeth looked around making sure they were alone in the classroom. "Slow down. As far as I know, my parents still don't like the idea of Louis and me. But I need to tell you something, if you can keep a secret."

"I can. You know I can. Please tell me." Her friend had been faithful to her confidences for over two years. No reason to think she would break a confidence now.

Now. Could the truth flow as easily as the lies? "Well, Louis and I are engaged. We have been all summer." Done.

"Why didn't you tell me?" Sarah frowned, but only for a second.

Her excuses of fear and uncertainty could appear flimsy, but it was the truth. "I couldn't. What if Louis didn't come back? We would have talked about it every day. I needed to be sure."

A tiny tear slid down her friend's cheek, and Elizabeth could tell her friend was happy. "I knew you would share in my joy. It's just so difficult with my parents. But now that he's back, I know we can find a way to make it work."

After a few more whispered details and a last hug of excitement over the news, Elizabeth left Sarah at the school and raced to the mercantile, hoping she hadn't kept everyone waiting. At least she knew Louis wouldn't leave her stranded there.

Louis and Jeannette had turned the store over to Henry for an hour or so.

"You're here," Jeannette greeted. "We're just about ready. Louis will be back in a minute. Aren't you excited? Do you think he will like the work we've done?"

Elizabeth and Jeannette had spent hours shopping, dreaming, and laughing. "I do hope so, though I'm a little nervous. If he doesn't like it, at least we had fun doing it."

Louis came through the door as he adjusted his jacket and hat. "Ready?"

"Just waiting for you," Elizabeth said.

He tucked Elizabeth's arm in his and then laced Aunt Jeannette's with his free arm. They strolled along the sidewalk and rounded the corner onto Church Street.

The house, nestled comfortably between two structures of similar size, didn't appear vacant. "Home, or soon-to-be home," Louis commented, as he stepped back to study the three-story, brick structure with large windows and green shutters. A few steps with an ornate iron rail guarded the solid door.

Louis took the key from his coat pocket and opened the door. Once inside, Elizabeth turned around to catch Louis' expression as he walked into the parlor with hands on hips, admiring the transformation. Elizabeth held her hands to her mouth, fingers steepled. Would he like it the way she did? At least he was smiling; even the wrinkles around his eyes joined his grin. Yes, he liked it. He had to after all of their preparation. But did he love it enough to call it home?

The once bare room now had a plush, pure wool rug loomed in Turkish weave with a bold, branching flowering tree. The other colors accenting the rug were honey, brown, red, and yellow. The drapes, two sofas, and two high-backed chairs brought out the colors throughout the room, adding shadows and light in corners, mingling the rich hues. She hoped the room begged Louis to rest in the warmth. In her daydreams, she envisioned the two of them cuddled on the sofa in front of the fire, speaking of everything or of nothing at all.

After circling the room, Louis halted in front of them. Elizabeth and Jeannette had not moved an inch from their position at the door. "This is truly a home now. Somehow, you two have worked your magic." He kissed Jeannette on the cheeks and without hesitation did the same to Elizabeth. An unexpected blush graced her cheeks as her hand automatically covered where his kiss still lingered. She breathed freely, letting out the pent-up air from her lungs.

Gratefully, Louis took the lead, for Elizabeth didn't know what to do next. "Now, let's go to the music room. I hope you were able to begin making it your special place, Elizabeth."

Her silent nod wouldn't suffice for long. Her words sounded foreign and shy. "I added a few items—a music cabinet and a small table and chairs for guests as well as a desk. I have a few things I want to bring from home when the time is right. A bookcase from my grandmother and a small chair I had as a child." Elizabeth beamed as she ran her hand over the closed face of the pianoforte. Louis had surprised her with it last May—a gift and a promise that he would return. How many senseless hours had she spent wondering what she'd do with the house if he didn't return?

As they continued through the house, Jeannette commented, "We didn't do anything to the dining room. So, I hope you have some ideas, Louis. Also, we left the library for you to furnish."

Elizabeth advanced to the staircase, very glad that Jeannette was by her side. "We began the work on the master bedroom. The bed you ordered arrived in June, along with the armoires and storage chests. We picked out the material for the bed cover, the rug, and the drapes. I do hope you like it, Louis." Elizabeth was a bit nervous; after all, this was a room they would share.

She ran ahead and poked her head into the bedroom before

the others entered. The room was bright and airy. She fluffed the pillows and ran her fingers over the bedcover. Soft and inviting.

"What do you think of the colors? We tried to tone down the dark grain of the mahogany with the green and off-white hues." Elizabeth grasped a newly polished bed post and waited on Louis' response. She wanted to jump and shout all of her suppressed excitement, but she needed his honest assessment first.

"It's perfect." He touched the shaving stand and wash basin. "I can move in right away with ease."

Elizabeth tried to see the room as Louis would for the first time. The beige-colored bed cover was of a double-woven cotton matelassé, very soft and luxurious, crisscrossed with birds, fountains, animals, and flowers. Pillows in the same pattern accented the bed in white, green, and off-white. The canopy over the bed, made of light-green gauze, flowed effortlessly over the top and around the posts. The ecru drapes with green valances and sashes complemented the room.

His eyes and smile showed his approval. As he gazed at her, Elizabeth felt like she was the only one around. Without words, they shared a special moment, holding promises of things to come when they were finally married. She broke the spell, knowing that she needed to think of other things. They weren't married, not even officially engaged, and Jeannette was standing right there.

She grabbed Jeannette's hand for security and said, "Let's show him the guest rooms, although we've only applied drapes and rugs, no furniture. The same is true for the drawing room."

He followed them to the additional rooms. "You ladies have done more than enough. In time the rooms will be filled with whatever you want, Elizabeth. For now, I just need to be able to move in and begin to make it home."

Opening his arms wide, Louis welcomed them into his embrace.

Back downstairs after the tour, Louis asked, "Aunt Jeannette, do you know anything about Tom Engle's mother and sister? Do you think they would be good house help? I know they need the work."

She fluffed some pillows on the sofa and looked up. "I'll ask around. I think they're both doing odd jobs at the Singleton's now. They might be perfect for you starting out. Tom could help in his spare time."

Turning to Elizabeth, he caught her smiling and probably already making plans. "Tell me what you think, Elizabeth. We do have plenty of room to house them. It might be the answer to a lot of our needs all around," Louis concluded.

She found it hard to believe that she would be in charge of this house and the running of the household, including an additional family. Her confidence buoyed with Louis' enthusiasm. "Let me know what I can do to help," Elizabeth said.

"Believe me—you'll have the final say. I want your approval of any help that we have here. After all, you will be the one in charge of the household and the kitchen. But if the Engles work out, we'll be helping a hurting family adjust to a new life."

Elizabeth pulled on Louis' sleeve, wanting his attention. Did he approve of the house? Was it all too simple or too elaborate?

Whether he saw the questions in her eyes or not, he covered her hand and gave her the assurance she sought without having to ask out loud. "Success. The house is beautiful. Exactly what I expected from you."

She let out a deep breath—one she hadn't realized she held. Success in one area gave her confidence in the other challenges still before her—mainly her father.

CHAPTER 5

*F*riday was Elizabeth's day off from school. Instead of resting or reading or doing something for herself, she volunteered to help Anne prepare for dinner that night. She could always tend to the boys to keep them out of the way of the comings and goings of the house servants if she were not needed in the preparation.

Anne was expecting her and had already chosen a chore. She gladly turned over the flower arranging to Elizabeth. "I have no knack for this. Here are the vases and a variety of blossoms—roses, hyacinths, gladiolas, and zinnias. Do you think they will be all right?"

"Of course." Elizabeth peered at some of her favorites and brought a rose to her nose. Perfect.

Anne wrung her hands and placed her hand to her brow as if forgetting something. Elizabeth rarely saw her sister in such a distressed mood.

"Is something wrong? It's only family tonight, right?" Plus Louis, but his presence wouldn't bother Anne.

Anne wadded some dead leaves in her hand, crushing them with extra force. Thankfully, they were already trash worthy.

"Mother informed me George is bringing a guest with him. That was fine—until she told me who it might be. Can you guess?"

Shielding the fresh flowers from Anne's idle rampage, Elizabeth couldn't guess. "I have no idea who would upset you so. Just tell me."

"Miss Victoria Seymour. Do you know her?"

Elizabeth cringed, feeling spider-like sensations creeping up her arms. "Yes, I do."

Unpleasant memories came back from their introduction at the Middleton home last March. Miss Seymour had recently moved from Philadelphia, and she had made it plain she thought Charles Town and its occupants were not up to her standards. On top of that, she and her family were staunch Loyalists. That sentiment explained her attraction to George. Yet Elizabeth didn't understand why Anne fell apart at the prospect of Victoria dining with them.

"Well, I met her once," Anne said, "at a party this summer while you were in Boston. Every word out of her mouth was a criticism of a person or a place, or a promotion of herself and Philadelphia. Why, out of all the young ladies in town, did he have to choose her?"

Elizabeth's inner core echoed those feelings. There was an uneasy vibe when Miss Seymour was around. Elizabeth searched for something to ease her sister's stress. But, as she felt the same way, it was a perplexing task. "Maybe she'll be so occupied with George and ready to impress our parents that she'll show a different side tonight." Elizabeth tried to picture a demure, quiet, polite Victoria and laughed. Her show of humor released a few giggles from Anne.

After arranging the flowers and placing them on three different tables, Elizabeth went upstairs to look in on the boys, who were busy at work with their tutor. She viewed them from the hallway, not wanting to disrupt their concentration. Being a teacher, she knew how the slightest disturbance could ruin a lesson.

She returned to find her sister in the kitchen, helping with the meal preparation. Although the cook was more than capable of producing a grand dinner, Elizabeth knew Anne enjoyed baking and occasionally trying out her cooking skills. She already had her hands floured and was kneading the bread dough.

Elizabeth reached for an apron hanging on a peg on the pantry door. "What do I need to do to help?"

"Why don't you start on the lemon sponge cake?" Anne pointed to a sheet of paper on the table. "I use the recipe Grandmother gave me years ago. Have you made it before?"

Elizabeth licked her lips in anticipation of the result. "Yes, that is Mother's favorite."

Elizabeth found the bowl and the ingredients and began her work. Conversation never ceased between the sisters. Gone were the signs of stress that Elizabeth encountered earlier. They were bearing each other's burdens. In a way, they would both rather be observers than participants tonight. Still, they were determined to make the event pleasant for all.

Between the cook, the house servant, Anne, and Elizabeth, the feast was prepared in plenty of time, leaving a few hours for the sisters to dress for dinner. Elizabeth used the guest room to change. Her dress had been brought over and hung up for her. She used the time alone to collect her thoughts.

She had already gone through the worst-case scenarios of the evening but now dwelled on the best possible outcomes: Her father and George would be polite and respectful to Louis, not insisting on talking about politics and government. Miss Seymour would show virtues becoming of a guest in Anne's house by not insulting the choice of food. Also, she could add that the boys would behave, since they were invited to dine with the adults tonight. The best part of all centered around Louis' presence and his hopeful acceptance in the family.

Dressing carefully, she delighted in her choice for tonight. The bodice was solid-peach muslin, with a skirt the same color with thin brown satin stripes running down the length. Her hands pressed the brown sash close to her waist and wove small peach-colored satin ribbons into her hair. Glancing once again in the mirror, she knew that the colors gave her features a warm glow. Adjusting her ringlets around her face, Elizabeth descended the stairs in time for the first of the guests.

Her parents were always prompt, if not early, especially to Anne's house in order to see their grandsons. Robert and John raced to their grandparents before Elizabeth could reach them. She was in no hurry to speak to her parents; after all, she lived with them. But there was something about a special occasion with family that caused her to want to greet them with added affection, as if they had been parted for a long while.

As her parents joined Anne and Robert in the parlor, Louis arrived. She turned around and almost ended up in his arms. He wisely held her away, steadying her and keeping the distance between them.

"I like your warm welcome." Louis laughed for only her to hear.

"Well, I am glad you are here. Let's go in the parlor."

Her smile displayed her true joy. Why shouldn't she rejoice in his presence? Yet she kept a reasonable distance, able to admire him in his custom-fitted trousers and brown jacket, a shade darker than his trousers. Everything from his shoes to his cravat matched perfectly. She didn't mean to stare, but as he shook hands with Robert and her father, acknowledging Anne and her mother, Elizabeth's gaze lingered. To her, this was as much Louis' homecoming dinner as Robert's.

Friendly, light conversation volleyed back and forth.

Mr. Elliott, after several minutes spent depositing kisses on his grandsons' cheeks and placing his coat on the hall coat rack, approached Louis. "I'm glad about your safe return. I'm sure your aunt and uncle have missed you. I didn't know if you would decide to remain in France or not." He arched his eyebrow.

Elizabeth wondered if her father suspected Louis' other motives for his return. As Anne served water with lemon, Elizabeth held her breath a second more but quickly released her anxiety as her father appeared to be cordial.

Louis seemed to have his answers under control. He dipped his head, clasped his hands behind his back, and rose and fell on his toes and heels. "Well, Mr. Elliott, France doesn't have a hold on me anymore, even with my family living there. I decided before I left that Charles Town would be my new home." His grin proffered to Elizabeth the security she needed: he came home for her. She assured herself that his words, though guised, would confirm his commitment and love.

"I see. Your aunt and uncle are probably enthused about your decision." Elizabeth surmised what her father was doing. He wanted to place Louis in a box at the mercantile, away from the rest of the town—no connection to Robert or Christopher or her. She was glad Louis let the remark drop.

Enough noise was made in the foyer to distract everyone. George and Miss Seymour had arrived. The boys ran to their uncle and practically wrestled him down from each side. The shrieks of surprise and perhaps terror were from Miss Seymour as she moved far away from the mayhem. Anne was full of apologies as she tried to round up the boys. Robert and Louis laughed quietly at the commotion, until Anne caught Robert's eye and pleaded with him to help her.

Robert crouched down to the boys' eye level. "Now, boys, I want you to act more civilized at least for one night. Uncle George has a special guest who is not used to two little wild boys." Robert's deep, authoritative voice worked magic as the boys retreated into a corner of the parlor to begin a game of marbles.

George didn't appear to be bothered by the children. As he watched them wander a few steps away, he turned and politely ushered his guest forward. "I believe Miss Seymour has met everyone here at some point in time except Robert. This is Miss Victoria Seymour."

Robert took her hand and acknowledged her with a slight nod. "I'm pleased to finally meet you. I've heard a lot about you from my wife. Welcome to our home."

Elizabeth set about making Victoria feel at home and a part of the celebration. After all she was an invited guest as much as Louis. Of one thing she was certain, she would never have the woman completely alone, since she remained attached to George's arm throughout the evening.

Struggling with her words, Elizabeth ventured, "What have you found to occupy your time in Charles Town, Miss Seymour?" If Victoria's opinions from the past surfaced, the answer would be far from positive. *I should have asked a different question.*

The woman glanced quickly at George standing next to her. "Please call me Victoria. We'll most likely spend more time together in the future." Elizabeth noticed that, somehow, Victoria held herself rigid without a flinch or a wiggle, no expression to let anyone know her true feelings. "To answer your question, I spent the summer in Philadelphia with my mother. Other cities have so much more to offer. Anyway, my days were spent with parties, shopping, and excursions. I hear the formal fall season is a bit more full and active here than what I experienced last spring. Is that true?"

"Oh, it's full enough for me. Too many invitations for my pleasure. I hope you do find it to your liking." Even as she spoke, Elizabeth knew that was almost impossible. The big-city lady hadn't changed her opinion since the Middleton party.

She shushed her inner commentary. What if her words spilled out? Why couldn't Elizabeth accept Victoria as she was? Why take all her words personally?

"Elizabeth, I need to talk to you." Louis interrupted at the most opportune time.

Ever so thankful, Elizabeth unceremoniously jumped up, giving Louis a mouthed *"Merci."*

Louis' chuckle joined Elizabeth's laughter as he pulled her away. "I saw you needed rescuing. Don't let her upset you."

She stopped and looked around, leaning in closer to Louis. "I won't. But just so you know, she hasn't changed. Anti-Charles Town and probably still anti-French and anti-Partisan, even though the subject of politics hasn't surfaced." She shrugged, hoping the negative Victoria conversation would end. "Now tell me, how's Father?"

"Cordial. I've listened to Robert fill him in about our voyage. I added a few words but mostly affirmed what was stated. Tell me about your father's relationship with Robert. It seems so stable and full of respect on both sides."

They found a vacant sofa—Louis occupied the middle with Elizabeth hugging the arm, careful not to touch Louis' knees. "Remember, ten years ago, there were no Loyalists and Partisans. No offensive acts had been passed, no boycotts. Robert was an aspiring captain who loved Anne. Their relationship of father and son has had years to develop. So far, Father doesn't seem to know about, or at least doesn't acknowledge, Robert's involvement with the Sons of Liberty. To Father, Robert has provided a good home for Anne and the boys."

Could ten years change her world so much? It had, for she had been a child, with a childlike idolization of Anne, Robert, and her father, leaving out the government and war.

"I don't see how it will be possible to convince your father of my worth. But I will strive for a lifetime to gain his respect and acceptance," Louis promised.

"God can certainly do anything. Don't give up on that." Her hands clutched the abundant material of her skirt, forcing them from reaching out to him. "Anyway, you have a lot to offer me, and Father will see that in time." Why was it so important for Louis to fit in her father's perfect mold for a son-in-law?

"In time." Louis glanced across the room at her father. "Until then, I'm a Frenchman and a Partisan in his eyes. I want him to see a man who is capable of caring and providing for you, a man who has a sound business, a home, and above all, a man who fears God."

"That's the man I love," she concluded.

Robert announced the dinner hour. Elizabeth tucked her arm in Louis' and gathered with the others around the table. They stood behind their chairs as Father spoke. "We have joined together tonight to celebrate Robert's safe return. It is always a special occasion to have the family complete again. You are greatly missed, Robert, when you're gone. Tonight, we also are thankful to have Miss Seymour here and for George's return from Boston. And we must not forget Louis' safe return from France as well."

With heads bowed, her father said a short prayer over those present and the meal.

"We chose to serve ourselves tonight. So, ladies first." Robert coaxed Elizabeth's mother toward the sideboard.

Dishes of white chicken fricassee, beef-and-rice pie, stewed mushrooms, potatoes with caramel sauce, and peas covered the surface. Fresh rolls were on the table, as well as a hot bowl of vegetable soup at each place.

Elizabeth eased up to Anne, thankful for their easygoing relationship. "I know I'm not supposed to feel this way, especially since it's a celebration, but she puts such tension in the air."

"Calm yourself." Practical and sympathetic, Anne spouted truth. "It's one meal, right? Our attitude toward her could help keep George open to the family. Let's give this a concerted effort of geniality."

Elizabeth inhaled and counted to five. "I'll try, but no promise."

Everyone seemed satisfied with the assortment of food. The boys, occupied right away with their full plates, contributed only the sound of clinking forks against plates. Elizabeth slowed her consumption, wanting to savor the meal and time together. The others at the table tended to relax too.

Anne, as hostess, guided the servants to replenish the glasses and the roll baskets. Elizabeth noted Robert had no need to fill the host's role as conversationalist, for Father managed to keep the flow going.

"George, tell us about your work with the law firm," her father urged.

George lowered his fork and raised an eyebrow. "I think the group here would rather speak of something more interesting. Perhaps you want to know what the rebellious citizens of Boston are doing or what the British government imposes as a punishment for the Sons of Liberty?"

Elizabeth shuddered as George cut his eyes toward Louis.

Her father cleared his throat. "Later, George. That's a discussion for after dinner."

Over the next few minutes, Elizabeth's pride in her father rose a few points. Each time George tried to intimidate anyone, not just Louis or Robert, by commenting on some political theme or act of Parliament, her father would guide them to a less sensitive topic for the dinner table. Elizabeth wished she could have access —at least as an observer—to the heated conversations she knew would come after the meal, when the men would cover the forbidden topics. It would be even better to be an invisible being when the inevitable debate started. It might help her understand her father and brother.

She shook herself clear of the negative. For now, she was content at the table, sitting next to Louis and across from Robert and John, the youngest Cochrans. If only they all had nothing more than the cares of children: to love and be loved.

Louis leaned close to her and whispered, "Robert is a lucky man with two healthy sons, a beautiful wife, and a happy home. Perhaps 'blessed' would be a more appropriate word."

Was he envisioning his own life in that way—a table

surrounded by their children and her? Her heart skipped a beat, concentrating on Louis envying Robert's domestic life. She wanted that too.

Anne sent the boys upstairs with the housemaid and their share of the lemon cake for dessert. Then she invited the ladies to join her in the parlor. Elizabeth paused to watch Louis follow Robert, George, and her father into the library. She took her seat next to Mother on the settee. Dessert and tea sat on the table in front of the sofas.

"How do I choose, Anne?" Victoria perched on the edge of an overstuffed chair. "The lemon sponge cake and bread pudding are both so rich and sugary. I think I will forgo the dessert for now."

"Well, I think I'll have a small piece of each." Elizabeth filled her plate with more than she would normally take. Why did Victoria have to make a few sweets into a display of contention? She chastised herself for letting Victoria's actions rile her.

"Tea anyone?" Anne poured four cups and passed them around.

Mother balanced her cup and saucer while giving her full attention to the guest. "Victoria, I'm interested in the charity work you might have participated in this summer." Mother gave her full attention to their guest.

After clearing her throat, Victoria spouted facts as if read from a paper. "I participate with so many. My favorite is for the philharmonic society. I helped organize the reception for the opening performance of the summer."

Important, Elizabeth had no doubt, but her mother would be more concerned about the poor and the sick. Some bothersome part of Elizabeth decided to prod the woman for more information. "What about any hospital work? Or a meal program for the poor?"

Victoria fanned her hand beside her face, pushing the idea aside. "Oh, I couldn't do that personally. Mother taught me to avoid the sick and the dirty. So many others help them. I prefer the promotion of the arts."

Elizabeth stared into the amber liquid and willed her mouth shut.

The four women exhausted other subjects. Each included a long monologue from Victoria. Elizabeth noted she had a strong opinion about everything from child rearing to church services. Did Victoria even attend church? Definitely not at St. Philip's.

Even with all the talk, Elizabeth didn't feel like Victoria allowed them any access to anything other than superficial ramblings. George had to see extreme worth in some attribute deep in Victoria's being, one unseen to Elizabeth. Yet she couldn't shake the uneasy feelings the woman and George left with her. She was glad tonight hadn't shone any light on her relationship with Louis. Would Victoria have verbal opinions about their future when it was announced? Most certainly.

The men consumed their sweets between congenial comments about the weather and societal activities. The heavy scent of leather and old books settled around them. Robert claimed the chair by the window. Louis chose one adjacent to him.

Mr. Elliott occupied a high-back cushioned chair situated close to the dessert table. "I'm always glad when the social scene begins again. The summer can be such a bore with so many gone. Did you find it still the same in Boston, George?"

George fidgeted with the latch on the clock on the mantle "It wasn't too bad to me, at least. I stayed very busy with work. I was more interested in the rallies and political debates prominent in Boston Commons. It seemed there was one every day."

What isn't he saying? Is it possibly George is hiding more than I am?

Mr. Elliott jerked his head toward his son. "Really? Are things heating up?" The topic avoided at dinner was officially brought to life. The only difference existed in Mr. Elliott's allowing it and possibly encouraging it with his remark. Louis sat back, ready for words to volley between the two. He didn't trust himself to speak and stay neutral.

George now looked at Louis and Robert. "It's calmed down a bit, but I wouldn't put it past those rebels to start something out of pure spitefulness." What kind of reaction did he expect?

Robert had few words tonight, remaining quiet in general, slow to join a discussion. Likewise, Louis had decided to guard his speech, although not quite deciding on silence.

Mr. Elliott made no effort to stop George. The man was used to being in authority, and now he gave his approval to his son. Did George feel he had to mimic his father's words and beliefs? It appeared so, since they gave their matching opinions on everything.

Most of George's monologue took place on his feet as he paced the free space in front of the mantel. "Well, since I spent the summer in Boston, I was wondering how other areas were reacting to the new Tea Act." He paused. Was he seeking heated comments to spur him on? If he was, Louis didn't take him up on it.

George stopped his pacing and shoved his hands in his pockets. "The law office emphasized anyone associated with them must support the act. Of course, I agreed. But that wasn't the case all over the city. Ever since the so-called Boston Massacre, the citizens have been concerned about this heavy British rule. The militia has been stationed on Castle Island because of that event." George hesitated again. He continued to leave opportunity for others to comment.

Louis, interested in the views of others, wanted to hear more. "So, what was being said or done? Business as usual?"

George fixed his gaze on Louis. "Hardly. Some locals have boycotted British tea and have turned to drinking coffee instead. Almost daily there's a rally in the town square across from the courthouse for either action against Parliament and the Tea Act or against the rebelling colonists. I wasn't allowed to participate, as a policy of the office. But I let my voice be heard at the tavern among friends."

That sounded like George. He wasn't one to keep his words bottled inside, at least not the few times Louis had been with him.

"So, what will come of the rallies, if anything?" Mr. Elliott asked.

"As long as they're peaceful, nothing. When I left, the protesters and supporters didn't have groups any larger than twenty-five people at a time. What was said in private was different. At the tavern I frequented, a group sang a song of the militia from Castle Island about the Liberty Tree and King Hancock and warning to beware. It has a catchy tune, although I'll not sing it for you." George laughed and stared at his drink.

Since it appeared no one wanted to respond to George's bait, Louis succumbed. "That sounds threatening, if you're on the government's side." He glanced at Robert who concentrated on his tea. He wouldn't get help there. Louis wasn't surprised at his lack of response. In fact, Louis didn't know how to enter or exit the conversation.

Mr. Elliott solved the dilemma. "Being a Frenchman, Louis, not a local citizen, what do you think about the Tea Act? More generally, what do France and King Louis think?"

That question was wide open. What did he want—a personal view or a general view? The distinction Mr. Elliott made between citizen and Frenchman rattled Louis. He was put in his place once again as an outsider. An outsider who more than anything wanted to ask for Mr. Elliott's permission to marry his daughter. Would any answer be appropriate in the presence of Loyalists?

"The king has no comment. He leaves that to his ministers and asks them not to start a fight. The French people are a little different. They are eagerly waiting to see what will happen."

"And you?" Mr. Elliott prompted.

Louis chin rose as his eyes contacted Mr. Elliott's. "I have yet to see the effect of the act on this town. I'm interested to see how Boston, New York, and Philadelphia respond, as they are large port cities. I think Charles Town will follow."

Hands on hips, George asked, "Are you straddling the fence, Louis?" His stance shadowed over Louis, giving George the over-lying façade of power and confidence.

But Louis wouldn't bend under his opponent's oppressive stare. "It appears so on this issue for the time being. But I will tell you this, George: I am a strong supporter of local views involving what's best for everyone, not just those profiting from higher powers. The next few months will tell. At that point, many will have to take a stand."

Was that noncommittal enough? Would it buy him time? Time to convince Mr. Elliott to give his daughter to him in marriage? He didn't want to lie; his commitment to the cause of the Sons of Liberty was firm and true. But as of yet, he didn't honestly know what the group had decided about the repercussions of the Tea Act.

Robert chuckled, "That's wise on Louis' part. I'm in the same position. I'm going to wait and see. Maybe it will all blow over with a peaceful solution." Robert ended the conversation. "Now what about joining the ladies?" He opened the library doors and led the men to the parlor.

George grabbed Louis' sleeve before leaving the study. "I don't believe for a second that you have any intention of leaving your Partisan cronies. Father might buy your stall, but not me."

Louis pulled his arm back and shrugged his shoulders, bringing his jacket back in place. "It is not for me to placate you or your kind. Just wait and see like the rest of us. I'm confident I will choose the right course."

How could he erase the unpleasantness of his encounter, bombarded with government threats? In the next room, filled with soulful melodies of love and peace, Louis gravitated to Elizabeth, who played the piano and didn't miss a note as the men joined the ladies. With sweet melodies in the background, how could controversial conversation resurface? Louis chose a chair close to Elizabeth and admired her graceful pose and her fingers gliding expertly over the keys.

The evening ended on that pleasant note. The hours had ticked away. Louis had no time alone after dinner with Elizabeth, for he was ushered out with the others at eleven o'clock.

"Thank you for including me." He bowed to his hosts. Then he turned and touched Elizabeth's extended fingers. "*À dimanche*. Do you think you could go on a stroll with me Sunday afternoon?"

She left her hand resting in his. "I'll put you on my schedule. About four o'clock?"

"*Parfait.*"

Louis reached the open door and glanced around the foyer. Overall, even with Victoria's critical comments and George's prodding, the evening was successful. Louis suspected the Cochrans would close the door and relax within their peaceful home, leaving the conflict outside. Louis wanted to do the same. Yet so much loomed on his personal horizon.

CHAPTER 6

*L*ouis stood in front of Samuel's desk, facing his friend once again with the same proposal. "Samuel, it's not as if you've never been to church before. Join me. Our row has more room. You know Reverend Smith from the Sons of Liberty."

And once again Samuel's head shook from side to side. "Not this week. It's not for me."

Louis wanted his friend to attend, but part of him understood. He remembered having the same feelings all of his life—until last spring. The only reason he'd ever gone to church was because of family. His personal relationship with Christ had only just recently begun to grow, so he wouldn't push. But Louis knew avoiding church—and more important, God—was not the best way to live. A life without Christ as Savior was only an existence. He would keep on trying to show Samuel the way.

Louis advanced to the Wilsons' usual pew. Rows away, the light from the stained-glass windows highlighted Elizabeth's white bonnet, tied with a blue string under her chin. She stared at him. Returning her gaze, he smiled and nodded as if they were the only two in the room.

As was a habit now, Louis focused on the service, beginning

with the first hymn, "Praise the Lord Who Reigns Above." He knew Elizabeth loved the lyrics. He imagined her playing it in their home. The words became a prayer as he sang. He embraced the hope that came to mind. Politics aside, his imminent talk with Mr. Elliott loomed as a storm. Hope at that same moment surfaced to surround his problems and cover them. And hope brought him back to the point of worship.

Reverend Smith read the words from Philippians 2:12-13: "'Work out your own salvation with fear and trembling. For it is God which worketh in you both to will and to do of his good pleasure.' Paul urges each of us to look at salvation as a process full of opportunities to do what God wants. Daily you will be faced with a possible crisis as an individual or as a corporate body. How will you view the situation? He states that you must work all things out with 'fear and trembling.' Should you live in fear of the demands and uncertainties of life? By no means. God supplies each of us with the promise that He will work each situation out for good. Think of your life and see if that is true. Good comes from every situation, even the worst, if we can rise above our circumstances and view situations from God's perspective."

Louis' impending conversation with Mr. Elliott was only one of his critical situations. If he gave Louis no hope of a life with Elizabeth, how would God work it out for the good? Louis knew he only had one choice: to accept God's way. He prayed for safe passage to the other side of this dilemma. His decision to marry Elizabeth was not in question; that was one thing he felt was God-directed. But the road to the actual event was full of possible hazards and detours.

On the front steps of the church, Louis rushed to catch Elizabeth before she left. "The usual time today?" He gently touched her elbow.

"Yes." The sun illuminated her eyes and highlighted her hair. "I'll be waiting, most likely outside."

He watched as she briskly walked to regain her parents' presence. Somehow, he had to make Elizabeth his forever. It would surely be much easier if Mr. Elliott gave his blessing.

At four o'clock, the butler at the Elliotts' ushered Louis through the house to the back garden. Louis found Elizabeth pruning the blooming mums. Orange, yellow, and red blossoms fell at her feet. "Elizabeth, you never miss an opportunity to work in your garden." He watched as her cat, Cleo, wound her way around her skirt. Elizabeth's cheeks were flushed.

"Yes. There's always something to do." She stopped her chore, swooped up the cat and her gloves. "Isn't today beautiful? I'm ready to walk if you are." She stuck her head in the back door and told her mother goodbye. Then she grabbed his hand and guided him through the white gate, depositing Cleo on the inside of the fence on the way out. He chuckled at her quick exit plan.

Arm in arm they walked and enjoyed the cloudless, blue sky and slight breeze from the ocean. They strolled by the market, although it was closed on Sunday. Louis spied a single daisy beside an empty container. He picked it up and presented it to Elizabeth.

"For you." He touched her nose with the flower. "It seems this flower needs an owner."

"Thank you." She twirled it by the stem in her fingers.

Silence surrounded them as they continued walking to the seawall. He could tell by her bent head and concentration on the flower that Elizabeth wanted to speak. Why the delay?

He stopped and faced her. "What are you thinking?" Her eyes widened with the spark of energy he had witnessed so often. Knowing her, she couldn't contain her thoughts for much longer.

Her hands fluttered lightly by her sides. With the added flower as a wand, she seemed to be conducting an orchestra. "Louis, I have to know when you are going to speak to Father. I'm very nervous. But after this morning's sermon I want to be calm and confident that it will all work out for the good. Am I being selfish when the good I want is for us to be married?"

"No, you are not selfish." He took her empty hand to calm her. "I feel the same. I had already decided to talk to your father tomorrow. Like you, I am trying to be confident. There's no reason to put this off anymore. We can only begin to deal with his answer when I ask. All we can do is depend on God for the outcome."

"I know, but what if—" Elizabeth didn't conceal her doubt.

He interrupted. "Don't dwell on that now. We'll face the 'what if' later. For now, I have you alone— with fifty other people roaming the park." Louis concentrated on their solitude amidst a crowd. Laughter and joy replaced the doubt and worry as they watched children play and couples bend into their own secrets under parasols. When Louis was with Elizabeth, it was hard to concentrate on the negative—war, conflicts, insults, the enemy. In her presence, all he wanted to focus on was peace, love, and hope where war and enemies did not exist.

Mid-morning Monday, Louis entered the familiar college where he had taught last spring. He couldn't put off his mission any longer. He headed to the director's office on the first floor. Two short knocks. The door opened, and the secretary led him to the waiting area outside of Mr. Elliott's office. He felt like a little boy about to be disciplined.

Get control of yourself. You are a grown man, not a child.

He composed himself just as Mr. Elliott swung the door open. "This is a surprise. How may I help you?" Mr. Elliott smiled and ushered Louis inside.

"I need to talk to you about something very important, sir," Louis stated as he faced the man who had the power to grant his request or deny it, to give him the world, or crush every dream. Clutching his hat extra close to his side, Louis followed the man into the office.

"Have a seat over there." Mr. Elliott pointed to an area set aside from his desk that contained two chairs, a table, and a lamp forming a half circle. Louis sat while Mr. Elliott lowered himself to his chair behind his desk.

Now or never. Louis drew in a deep breath. "Mr. Elliott, as you know, Elizabeth and I have known each other for over a year. We have spent a lot of time together getting better acquainted." He twirled his hat around and stopped. He set it on the table beside him. "Our fondness for each other has become deeper and more serious." Louis zoomed in on Mr. Elliott's eyes, hoping he had his attention. "Sir, I love your daughter and would like for her to become my wife."

Louis never lost eye contact. He watched Mr. Elliott sit up straighter in his chair, eyes opening wider and lips twitching. Had Louis' words penetrated the depths of Mr. Elliott's level of acceptance?

Rising to his feet, Mr. Elliott turned his back to Louis and walked to the window. Louis rose as well and stood by his chair, hoping to use his full stature to withstand any words he encountered.

When Mr. Elliott faced him again, he controlled his words and voice. There was no surprise evident in his voice, and he didn't stumble over his words. His was almost a rehearsed speech.

"I will be honest and tell you I expected this was the case." Mr. Elliott lowered his chin and seemed to examine the upholstery on the chair, running his hand back and forth over the high back. "Elizabeth's mother and I warned her not to become involved with you on any level other than as an acquaintance." Louis stared at Mr. Elliott, following him with his head. The man returned to his desk and faced Louis. "We really didn't expect you to return. I see that we were mistaken on both accounts. Elizabeth didn't take our advice, and you returned."

Louis wasn't surprised with the facts so far, although he couldn't yet release his pent-up breath. "Sir, I understand your concern and the suddenness of our news. We do want your approval of our life together." He sighed and exhaled. His legs wobbled but remained stable.

"My first instinct would be to say no, for many reasons. I don't know your family. There's no stability in your life. You haven't been here long enough for her to really know you. Our culture and expectations are different from yours. Our family is well respected by society here and in Boston. Elizabeth is used to prestige and acceptance. Could you give her any of that?" Mr. Elliott paused, peering at Louis with raised bushy eyebrows. "Love alone will not sustain her. Her loyalties are tied to this city, this family, and this way of life. And where are your loyalties—for the king of France or the king of England?"

Throughout the monologue there was a variety of concerns, but Louis wondered if the last statement and question were the true reasons for the man's objection.

"My loyalty is to neither king, sir. I'm committed to God first, then to Elizabeth, and lastly to the colonies. Elizabeth and I strive to always put God first. We feel our decision has nothing to do with society and outside circumstances." Louis strode toward the large desk and faced the giant. "As for stability and comfort, I have the means to give her all the necessities of life. I've already adopted her language, culture, church, and beliefs. Now all we ask is your permission to marry." He exhaled again. His knuckles whitened as he clenched his fists at his sides.

"I won't say no yet, Louis. But I want you and Elizabeth to take a month to properly court and to rethink your decision. If you feel the same way then, I will reconsider and give you my answer. I'll have the same conversation with Elizabeth and her mother. I can only hope that you take into account your differences and the difficulties the marriage will encounter."

Louis willed his jaw to work. Now was not the time to be speechless or to stutter. "Thank you, Mr. Elliott. I will endeavor to meet your expectations." Louis extended his hand. As they shook hands, Louis saw a glimmer of hope. But he wouldn't read too much into Mr. Elliott's last words. At least he hadn't been rejected outright. All Mr. Elliott required was a month to make sure this was really right for them. Louis didn't even need an hour or even a minute to answer that, but he would bide his time.

Monday afternoon at her home, Elizabeth had a piano lesson with her favorite student, Martha Laurens. The girl was a blessing more than a student taking a lesson.

As Martha played the final notes of Handel's "Rejoice, the Lord is King," Elizabeth felt more than saw Louis' presence in the music room. She turned her head to confirm her suspicions. Since she was at the end of the lesson, it was perfect timing on his part.

After Martha left and the door closed, Elizabeth easily slid into Louis' brief embrace, then grabbed his hands and led him to a sofa. "So unexpected. I'll take this kind of surprise every day. Why are you here?"

She noticed he was not in his usual work clothes. His current cravat and waistcoat wouldn't have withstood the manual labor necessary in the store.

"I had business to attend to, and I made you my final destination," he said, not giving her any information.

She wiggled closer to him. "So, I'm part of your business now?" She laughed as she joined his light demeanor. *What is he hiding?*

"In a way, I could say you are my business. Everything you do is my affair, my concern." His tone and words changed from light flirtation to serious in an instant. "You are my purpose and my life."

"That sounds so possible, so conceivable. If only—" Elizabeth paused.

"What did I tell you about thinking that way? Anyway, that is why I'm here. I received some good news, under the circumstances." He smiled. "I went to see your father today."

She crinkled her forehead with concern and doubt. "Oh, Louis." Did his news stall their dreams or...? It had to be more positive than a firm no, she decided, or Louis would be more agitated.

"Yes, I couldn't wait any longer. I've been robbed of too much sleep already. He received me at his office, and we had a talk. I asked him for your hand in marriage." He took her hands. Her fingers tingled and twitched. "He wasn't surprised or shocked. He actually knew it was a possibility. He did hope you would change your mind or that I would stay in France. But he was ready. Ready to face the truth." He paused, turning her palm upward, and placed a kiss in the center. The tingle reached her toes and invaded her heart, leaving her breathless.

He sighed and spoke slowly, as if checking his words. "I'm sure you'll hear the rest from him about all of my shortcomings and all the woes that a marriage like this would bring. But in the end, he said he wanted us to take a month to rethink everything and then, if we still desire to marry, he would reconsider my proposal."

She jumped up and twirled around before sitting again.

"We are to marry with his blessing?" Elizabeth couldn't stop the tears that flowed and dropped to her flowered skirt. She pulled a handkerchief from her sleeve before Louis could volunteer his.

He brushed a tear from her cheek. "Yes, I think so, but with a month of formal courting. Of course, his answer could be no. I'm sure you'll abide many lectures on your decisions. Do you think you can survive the barrage of comments intended to cancel our plans? It won't be easy."

"Oh, yes, it will, Louis." She leaned her head on his shoulder. "I know my heart, and I know my reason for marrying you. My doubts disappeared when you accepted Christ into your life. I have been sure and free to make this decision since then. So, let them say what they must. In the end, I'm yours."

Hearing a noise at the door, Elizabeth turned to see her mother round the doorway.

She glanced at Elizabeth, eyebrows raised in question. "Louis, I had no idea you were in here. Would you like some tea? I was just going to have some in the sun room." How much had she seen or guessed? "Did you fail to offer him refreshments?"

Would Mother ever have affection for Louis after he took her away? If not affection, then at least respect? Hopefully, Louis would be patient for Elizabeth's sake.

Elizabeth bowed her head to hide her giggle. "I'm sorry. I clearly forgot." Tea, indeed. She had other things on her mind. The teapot would not bode well with her shaking hands.

Responding quickly, Louis managed to cover her *faux pas.* "If you don't mind, I would love a cup of tea, and then I must be on my way."

The sun room, though less ornate, didn't alleviate Elizabeth's tension. She wanted to burst out her news, but Mother had to bring up the subject first. Surely, Father had involved her in his decision. She had many questions, but perhaps instead of demanding answers, she could wait in God's will and timing.

Leading them to the other room, her mother commented, "You are calling at an unusual hour, Louis. You are most welcome any time, of course." Mother seemed to be friendly. Or was Elizabeth's state of happiness coloring everything?

"I finished some business early and had a few minutes. I do need to be checking in with Uncle Henry soon."

"How are your aunt and uncle doing? I don't have any time to speak with them except after church. The mercantile must keep them very occupied." Her mother sipped her tea and placed her cup and saucer on the table. Elizabeth chose to leave her tea on the table. No need to draw attention to her nervous state.

"It is a full-time business. They both enjoy the work." Why didn't his hands shake? Louis seemed calm around her mother.

Elizabeth realized Mother wasn't going to introduce the subject of why Louis was here, not at this setting.

Louis finished his drink and rose to depart. He took Mother's hand and bowed. Before Louis said goodbye to her in the same way, Elizabeth jumped up and walked him to the door. Her hand found its place in his as she waited for his kiss. She could get used to the warm sensation infiltrating her veins.

"Goodbye for now."

"Let me know what your parents say about your 'disappointing' almost-fiancé."

She smacked him lightly on the arm. "You'll see. My parents will become loving toward you."

After Louis left, Elizabeth didn't have to wait long to hear from her father. He wasted no time calling a family meeting. He didn't even wait for dinner to be served. Before she entered the library, Elizabeth said a quick prayer. She was grateful Louis had had the forethought to warn her. Because of her commitment to God, she didn't feel alone now.

There they were—her mother poised in a chair close to the window with her father a few feet away. Elizabeth walked in ready to endure the stares and the words. *Give me strength to overcome this and the ability to see your purpose.* She chose a chair close to her mother.

As usual her father took control of the conversation and the inquisition. That was too harsh an assessment. Perhaps questioning was a better word.

"Elizabeth, I'm sure you know why I've asked to speak with you. You are indeed aware of Louis' intentions in regard to his relationship with you?" he said. She nodded and gave him her full attention. "It seems that your mother and I were the ones not privy to your plans. We tried to sway you from this sort of situation, and we had hoped the time apart would cure you of your fascination with him. Do you have the same feelings for him as he says he does for you?" Her father couldn't be more unapproachable with his arms crossed tightly in front of him.

"Oh, yes, Father, I do. I have, for a long time now. We knew it wouldn't be easy, not in this political climate and economic uncertainty, but—" She caught her mother's hand and tried to see behind her downward gaze. Then she turned to her father. She wanted him to give her a look of devotion and love, not a cool façade. She dropped the search and her mother's hand. "We don't want politics or the economy to deter us from marrying."

"Have you thought about your differences in culture, in language, and even in religion?" Father posed these issues as if on a list to be checked off.

"Father." She found the strength she had prayed for moments before. "Louis has chosen South Carolina as his home with all the positives and negatives of life here. As for the language, his English is as perfect as any Englishman minus a slight accent. And French is a beautiful gift—a language I have always loved. As for religion, he came here not knowing God at all and has since embraced Christ and His teachings. So, I see these three areas as positive influences on our decision," Elizabeth responded with honesty.

Her father didn't move an inch, nor did he release his tight soldier-like posture. "And then there is the issue of loyalty to his country and you to yours. How can you reconcile that? He will always be a foreigner, a citizen of another nation."

Elizabeth knew what her father wanted to hear. That Louis was willing to subject himself to the rule of England and to following King George. Even she could not do that. Suddenly, she realized this was the true key to her father's blessing. It appeared he wanted his household to remain subservient to the past ideals of sovereigns ruling overseas, even at the expense of giving up love.

"Father, I respect you enough not to lie to you. Louis and I have the same convictions about the colonies and the rights of the people. Neither of us feels a strong tie to the Crown. You have known this for a while. As much as Louis tries to please you, he cannot in this area. None of us know yet what will become of the present government." Her steady voice surprised her. "I do know that we both pray for a peaceful resolution without separation or fighting." Elizabeth tilted her head, imploring him to try to understand. "But you must know we can't change how we feel. Our loyalty is to the citizens of these colonies."

Her goal had been to state the truth as clearly as possible without opening the discussion to the chasm of difference of beliefs. Without a word, her mother reached for her hand and held it. Elizabeth smiled at her mother's gesture of support and squeezed her hand. How comforting to realize Mother could relieve her nervous heart. The pounding eased even as her mother released her. Would her father ever give the parental support for which she pleaded? If not, she had made her decision—one with Louis for life.

"You seem to have thought of everything. The terms I gave to Louis are one month of open courtship before I give my final decision. I want you to know of all the hardships this marriage will bring." Not exactly words of encouragement. But when he opened up his arms to her, she collapsed in them.

She would do everything in her power to make him realize she had made the right decision. God had led her to Louis, and God would lead her as she obeyed her father. In the protection of her earthly father's arms, she felt surrounded by her heavenly Father's love.

Two days later Elizabeth encountered the scorn of her brother. It appeared Father had not waited long to share the news. She had anticipated George's disapproval, but hoped he would have the attitude of her parents at least: disapproval, but within the confines of love. George certainly wasn't going to take the news of Louis as a permanent fixture in his family with few words or opinions. He stormed through the parlor door and pulled Elizabeth to her feet by her sleeve. His strength still took her by surprise.

He commenced without any formality or civilized greeting. "I don't see how you fell for his French charm. You usually see through that entire pretense in people. What does he offer that someone like William Burns doesn't? You had a great arrangement with a military officer, and you threw it away last year. Do you know what kind of man Louis is? Compared to Captain Burns, he's a nobody." George let go of her and paced around the tea table and pounded his fist on anything in his way. Elizabeth wasn't afraid. She was used to his outbursts.

"George, I really don't expect you to understand. First of all, William and I parted as friends. There was no love there, and our plans and dreams were so different. Louis and I didn't mean for it to happen or even want it to, but love permeated every area of our lives, bringing us together. Our dreams and plans are one, with God to guide us."

She followed George with her eyes. Back and forth, hands shoved in his pockets. His anger engulfed the area, making everything else seem small and insignificant in contrast. The furnishings and tea set faded to the background. Somehow she had to see more than his image of disdain and scorn.

"God, dreams, love." He shouted. He suddenly stood still, then lowered his voice and shook his finger in her face. "That is so unrealistic. What of power, prestige, loyalty? You act as if you could exist on your feelings. One day you will want a name and a position. No one will cater to a Frenchman and his doting wife."

Elizabeth couldn't help but laugh. Did he not know the position other Frenchmen held in Charles Town? She knew at the base of his opposition was Louis' leaning toward the views of the Sons of Liberty. Her brother held such high Loyalist views. He couldn't see life in any other form.

"George, one day I hope you will fall in love and see that there is more to this existence than only living for yourself. Until then you won't understand our decision."

With one last pound on the doorframe, George left fuming. She wondered where he would find release for his anger. No matter. She would leave this room, still reverberating with George's words. She had good news to share. Anne was at the top of her list. An unannounced visit to her sister's house would surely clear the harsh reprimand of her brother from her day.

She walked quickly over to Anne's, where the house servant let her in. Elizabeth poked her head into the parlor and then the drawing room before finding Anne in the library with the boys. "Excuse me for coming unannounced."

Anne and the boys surrounded Elizabeth with hugs and a barrage of questions. She spoke before she exploded without answering any of them.

"Louis and I are officially courting now with Father's permission, though without his blessing." She grasped Anne's hands. "We have one month, and then Father will give his decision."

Anne lead them to the sofa to sit. "I know you can weather anything Father says," Anne said. "He will let you know, as he did when Robert and I wanted to marry, all the drawbacks of your marriage. Listen to him, but don't overreact. He is being a father, doing his job."

"I know, but Louis has things working against him that Robert never had."

Anne cocked her head. "Like what? Robert is a seafaring captain gone for half of each year. You don't remember, since you were so young, but Father had a lot to say about Robert's career choice."

Elizabeth nodded, understanding the obstacles her sister had in her life and the ones she had overcome. Still, it seemed her personal situation weighed heavy. "Well, Louis has his nationality and his Partisan leanings against him. Father can't get over the division in loyalties. But I can't marry anyone with Father's views. I just can't." How long would she stress over the issue of the inevitable separation from Britain?

Anne pulled Elizabeth to her feet. "Concentrate on Louis and your courtship, not political turmoil. You should be happy to leave your Loyalist home for a fairer, sensible one. So, we're going to cheer you up. First, let's start thinking of some new dresses and china and linens and..."

"Slow down a bit. We don't even have a date. Nothing is official yet." Elizabeth pulled in the reins on her sister's spending spree.

Anne raised her eyebrows in question. "You're right. So, one new dress?"

"All right, just one. I'm going to tell Sarah my news. How about I invite her to go shopping too?"

Anne nodded, looping Elizabeth's fingers around her arm. "Tomorrow afternoon is a good time for me."

"All right. I'll meet you here at one o'clock."

Elizabeth, Anne, and Sarah walked to Jeanette's the next afternoon. The plan centered around finding the perfect material and trimmings for a party dress—one that Louis would love. And what better place than his own mercantile?

Jeannette greeted them. "Good afternoon, ladies. By the smiles on your faces, it seems you have a mission. Elizabeth, Louis isn't in the store at the moment."

Elizabeth kissed Jeannette on her cheeks. "That's fine since I'll see him soon, I'm sure. We have other plans that don't involve our men right now. I need to look at your latest material and patterns."

Jeannette showed the ladies the newest arrival of satins and silks, a selection appropriate for the season.

"Who made the dress in the window?" Sarah asked. Elizabeth saw her gazing at the headless mannequin. The sun reflected on the charming taffeta dress in hues of orange and yellow.

"Mrs. Engle and her daughter," Jeannette commented. "Tom's mother and sister. You know Tom; he works here at the store. The ladies really are very talented, and they need the money. Elizabeth, you might want them to make your dress."

"It would relieve the time factor, giving me more time for teaching and for Louis." Just saying his name made her smile. For now, she still kept his ring pinned within her bodice, a reminder that in a short time, she could wear it in public. "I want all of you to help me pick out fabric for a courting dress."

The four quickly scanned the bolts and found material for four to five dresses.

"Only one for now," Elizabeth reminded them.

Sarah took Elizabeth's mandate to heart and narrowed her search to one —a soft blend of cotton and wool, light enough in weight for the cool fall season. Delicate without being ostentatious, it featured narrow purple, yellow, and green stripes on a white background. Perfect for a white eyelet-lace petticoat and a solid-color bodice and stomacher.

Elizabeth beamed at her success, made all the more special because of her three dearest friends. "I think you've found it, Sarah. I'll take it with all the trimmings—lace, ribbon, buttons. Now, I need to contact Mrs. Engle and set up a fitting." She looked around, hoping she hadn't forgotten anything. "Jeannette, can you join us for tea now? It would be the perfect way to end the afternoon."

"I can if it is close by. Maybe the tea house around the corner on Queen Street," Jeannette responded, catching Henry's attention. He could handle the customers for a few minutes.

Arm in arm, two by two, the ladies exited the store for a cozy table for four, overlooking the busy street. Elizabeth's heart was full. *Blessings all around me. All in the simplicity of friends, family, and future hope.*

CHAPTER 7

*R*elief. Was that what he experienced? His confrontation with Mr. Elliott reminded him of a college exam—the process of dread, facing the unknown, and coming out with hope at the other end.

As he had done several times, he pinched himself to confirm he was indeed in one piece. With the trial behind him, Louis could now concentrate on enjoying his courtship. He planned to guard all areas of his life with a spiritual shield. If that slipped out of place, he feared the crumbling of all other areas.

Louis spelled out his courtship plans to Aunt Jeannette and Uncle Henry. Aunt Jeannette focused on the romance and found ways to help Louis enjoy his courtship. He didn't mind. If she could derive pleasure from advancing their love, he wouldn't deter her. She seemed to have total confidence that, after a month, Louis and Elizabeth would be able to plan their wedding.

Henry approached the subject of romance like a business. Louis had never expected his uncle to advise him on his relationship with Elizabeth. Louis cocked his head when his uncle spoke.

"I've been married almost as long as I've been in business. As long as you keep the customer happy, the business will thrive." He elbowed Louis. "The same applies for courtship and marriage. Remember, she is number one."

Louis could wrap his mind around that concept, although he would never refer to Elizabeth as a business. No, she was his reason for pursuing a successful career.

Uncle Henry and the intricacies of Charles Town prevented Louis from concentrating all of his time and thoughts on Elizabeth. As his uncle reiterated, "This is a crucial time in the history of this town and country. Of course, you know that, Louis. I do wonder if you and I, and even France, are ready."

The discussions surrounding politics had crept up after a routine dinner at the Wilsons' on Tuesday evening. Aunt Jeannette settled in her reading chair in the parlor while the Louis and his uncle occupied the study.

"I have a strong feeling, Uncle, that France is poised for a key role with the colonies. The people I heard from and spoke with actually want a reason to side with us. And a fight for independence gives them a keen sense of purpose." Louis rested his head against the leather high-backed leather chair.

His uncle settled deep into the cushioned sofa. "I hope you're keeping the lines of communication open with your brother and sympathizers in France."

Louis viewed his uncle between half-opened eyes. "I send a letter to André weekly, keeping him personally informed about the state of events here. Do you think we'll hear more details on Thursday?"

"I know the Liberty Boys well enough to suspect they'll have information and plans to relate. I'm anxious to hear."

His uncle's keen interest was from the impact any action from overseas or home would have on his business. But more than profit, Louis surmised, his uncle was convinced that his family and his store were part of a bigger picture. Louis wanted to be as ready as his mentor to play his part whenever, wherever, and in whatever way God led.

❧

On Thursday evening, Louis and Henry made their way to Gabriel Manigault's house. The weather was warm and breezy, so they walked the fifteen minutes to the great mansion. The last time Louis had entered the house was for his first social event in Charles Town a year ago. Tonight, the drive was lit with only a few torches, and the temporary ballrooms were converted back to their original drawing-room status.

Louis noticed immediately that the size of the group had grown in the last five months. The twelve men had multiplied to a full house of close to forty. This time Louis was not a stranger to the townsmen or to the cause. By choice and conviction, he had become one of the Sons of Liberty, also referred to as the Liberty Boys.

Christopher Gadsden, a prominent leader of the Sons of Liberty, could take credit for Louis' conversion to the cause. Christopher's often overzealous conviction for independence and representation had led many to join the league of planters, merchants, and artisans all over the city.

Louis spotted Christopher right away. Without waiting, he entered a circle of men that included Christopher, Gabriel Manigault, James Laurens, and Paul Turquand as well as a new face: Peter Timothy, the editor of the *South Carolina Gazette*.

Christopher greeted Louis with an outstretched hand. "I'm glad you're here, Louis. Could you do us all a favor and tell us a little of your findings in France—just an overview of the situation?" Louis hadn't expected to be put on the spot. So much for wanting to simply listen. "I'll call on you during the meeting, if you don't mind." Christopher patted Louis on the shoulder.

With all eyes on him, Louis had to respond, "Of course." He hesitated when he pictured himself standing in front of these prestigious men. But he wanted to help. Although the opportunity to speak tonight surprised him, the confidence that Christopher had in him was no shock. From early on, the two had trusted each other enough to become business partners. The joint business venture with their ship, the *Rose,* promised many successful voyages in the future.

"All right, gentlemen, let's get started," Gabriel commenced, and the men found their seats around the large room. "Tonight, Christopher is going to lead us in an update of the Tea Act and possible plans. All ideas are welcome."

Louis found a seat to the far side of the room with an overall view of the crowd. He knew Christopher took his role as the spokesman seriously. The Liberty Boys had a good leader in him. Louis admired the gumption of the man. Of all the men. They appeared ready to make a vital difference in Charles Town and the rest of the colonies.

"Good evening," Christopher began. "I assume you know where the Sons of Liberty stand. We stand together as a strong voice for equal representation in our government." The crowd clapped in unison. "For five years now, the South Carolina Assembly has put up with attacks on our rights as citizens. There is still no tax bill that has passed the house that would include our rights and privileges as valuable members of the British Empire. We have demanded that the past British-run government officials leave."

Christopher paused. Louis glanced around to catch heads nodding, recognition of the facts evident in their responses.

"We have also curtailed the power of the Council with our demands—enough to send the royal appointee, Egerton Leigh, on his way. The plea for liberty has been heard, yet the government has not altered its policies regarding a tax bill. Five years without representation."

Louis had only experienced one year and only half of that as a concerned citizen. If he felt so strongly about the cause, the others surely had a multiplied degree of concern.

"Recently the South Carolina Assembly asserted its own will

and issued certification of indebtedness to pay off long-standing public debts. In short, gentlemen, the Assembly is willing to proceed without the crown officials' approval. The Tea Act was the last of many actions that have put us on this road toward independence." Christopher finished his brief rundown of the state of South Carolina's Assembly.

Louis, poised for the revealing of the next step, was perched on the edge of his seat.

"Once again, the power of the Assembly, the ones who represent the colonists, is threatened." Christopher's words were strong and pointed to his sincere belief in the cause. "If we accept the Tea Act, then we're accepting the right of Parliament to tax us without our consent, with absolutely no representation from her subjects." The passion in Christopher's words attacked Louis' inner core. Before the next sentence hit the air, Louis knew he supported the outcome.

"My friends, the first ships with the crates of tea under the new Tea Act are scheduled to leave London in the next week or so. The question is what do we do with it? Many merchants and maybe even some of you have ordered tea. Others have no choice but to accept it and sell it. Mark my words. It will arrive in our harbor as well as in New York, Boston, and Philadelphia. They are having the same kinds of meetings. How should we respond?" He paused. "Any suggestions?"

Louis calculated that most likely Christopher had his own idea, but he had opened the floor for others. Many of these men already had the answer, Louis suspected. But what would they be willing to do?

"Turn the ships away."

"Prevent them from being unloaded."

"Capture the ships."

"Destroy the crates."

Some violence was implied, but not supported. How could the ships be forced to leave? After all, they were possessions of the

Crown. Would the militia be involved? Would the authorities simply step aside?

Christopher cleared his throat and used his fist as a silencing tool. "We must have a plan, for in a few weeks, a ship will appear in our harbor with tea on board. Remember, this is tea consigned to our merchants through the East India Company." Christopher managed to keep the group on task. He sought to let them know of the seriousness of any action. But Louis understood no action was not a solution. It would be a grave mistake just to sit back and do nothing.

"What are the other ports doing?" Mr. Timothy from the *Gazette* asked. Louis hoped the man was here as a friend of the cause, not as a reporter. If Louis guessed right, Mr. Timothy would only print what furthered the cause as well as what Christopher suggested. The editor's words mimicked others in the room, confirming Mr. Timothy as a Son of Liberty through and through.

"The consensus is to turn away the ships and not to let them unload the crates. If they cannot gain entrance and deposit their loads, then we send a message to Parliament once again that we will not participate in another insult to our rights. Of course, the local citizens in the cities must also approve of these actions."

If Louis blinked, he would miss a prominent piece of the puzzle. Christopher had his answers ready to put in place.

"Will there be fighting?" Reverend Turquand asked. "I, like many others, want a peaceful solution or a peaceful demonstration."

If needed, would those in the room fight for the rights of the people? Louis looked around. Only a few were trained in battle tactics. Most were businessmen. He was positive no one in the room wanted a physical fight. After all, the local loyalists were friends, family, and colleagues.

Christopher bowed his head, then took a deep breath. "I would hope all of the negotiations would be verbal and after talks with both parties, the ships would leave peacefully. That's the plan right now."

Louis wondered if King George and Parliament knew of the unrest in the colonies and that the road had been set for independence. The Mother Country's refusal to listen to her subjects would result in a separation—peaceful or violent. The choice was in the hands of the British government. The only way the colonists could be louder or clearer was to take up arms. No one but a few radicals really wanted that option. But Louis knew from his personal role in accumulating weapons and ammunition for later use that people were preparing for the worst-case scenario.

Making eye contact with many in the room, Christopher pulled his shoulders back and let his voice echo clearly around the room. "In conclusion, we have two months to prepare. The only question is when, not if, the tea arrives. Closer to that time, there will be a meeting and a proposal that has to have the support of more than the forty of us here." Then, he gave the floor back to Gabriel.

All the men clapped in response to Christopher's proposal. There was no great dividing line in the room over the rejection of the tea. Louis suspected that other merchants in town would have a different reaction.

Gabriel interrupted the applause and Louis' musing. "Now, let's hear a word from Mr. Lestarjette about the feelings in France regarding our situation."

Louis adjusted his jacket, strode to the front of the room, and looked out at the many faces. He recognized them as friends, not foes, and his nervousness disappeared.

"Christopher asked me to speak about the citizens of France. They are ready to support the colonists in a fight for liberty and justice." His report was short, only the facts he had shared with others on occasion. A sea of hands rose for questions.

"Will they support us with goods?" Gabriel asked.

"Yes. Goods like staple food items and other relevant

commodities." Louis meant arms and ammunition. Nods of understanding circled the room. At least the paper wouldn't read Louis supported the import of weapons.

"What about finances?" James ventured.

Somehow, Louis managed to keep his hands immobile at his sides, although he realized his palms were moist. "Many wealthy French citizens stand ready to transfer funds to support the cause with their own personal backing and corporate loans. They see this call to freedom as one of their own."

Louis remembered the men who were ready to set aside cash for the colonies to use; although this summer he had not felt that the time was right for that step.

"And in the case that we need men to join us on the battlefield, are any willing to serve?" Mr. Raley posed the question others didn't want to voice.

How to answer without condoning an all-out war? History would speak for itself. Louis wiped his brow of imaginary sweat. "In the past, the French have fought against the British for even lesser causes than freedom. So in looking to the past, I believe they would fight."

Gabriel motioned for Louis to be seated. The crowd applauded Louis' efforts. One last remark from Gabriel ended the session. "Enjoy your tea while you can."

The laughter around the room momentarily gave the evening a lighter air, a reprieve from the serious talk of war. The brief conversation after the formal meeting pushed all the statements to a neat, defined area in Louis' mind. The information Louis had been wanting—he expected no less from the Sons of Liberty.

From a merchant's point of view, the rejection of the ships could harm business, whether businesses were Loyalists or Partisans. However, Wilson's Mercantile had been making adjustments for over a year. Any supplies Louis and Henry ordered from Britain in the past had recently been ordered from France or the West Indies. Already their loyalist clients had moved on to other stores to find British products, but their business remained constant. Local merchandise was becoming a valuable, high-quality alternative to being "made in Britain."

Louis left the meeting with Uncle Henry. More than ever he knew his business decisions were correct, but no longer a private matter. "I have a feeling I'll be called on to personally support the rejection of the tea." Louis stopped and turned to Henry.

Henry understood the people and the tough decisions they had already made. They had the same thought process at this time. "Yes, you will. And other businessmen will follow. We are not alone."

What would it take for others to join them? "I do hope when it comes down to profit or progress that others will choose progress for the colonies and the people over personal gain."

Paul Turquand caught up with them. "Going to Church Street? I'll join you."

"*Bien sûr.*" Louis lapsed easily into French. He had profound respect for the Huguenot minister.

Henry patted Louis' back. "I'm going to walk ahead with Mr. Laurens."

Louis nodded and watched him depart. "See you tomorrow."

Paul picked up the pace and conversation in French. "I'm interested in your recent voyage to France. Have you found things much changed in the last year?" Louis recalled that Paul had left France with many Huguenots for a chance in the New World. Louis understood all of this from his family's personal experience.

Louis began to fill in some pertinent news. "For the past ten years or so, the unrest has been growing among the citizens, leading to many nobles discarding their titles and affiliations with the aristocrats. What I noticed this time was a keen interest in what the colonists of America will do next. Personally, I do wonder if they want to mimic our story later."

Paul shook his head. "I hoped they would respect our desire

for freedom without war. As usual the French choose war over peace."

"Unlike the colonists who basically want a peaceful separation or resolution," Louis said. "I don't understand the French wanting a war. Is it their universal hatred of the British, or is it just a worthy cause, one of liberty, that they find appealing? If we want an ally, the French are willing—the people that is, not necessarily the king."

"I prayed things would settle in France," Paul said. "For so long it has been a hot bed of lava just waiting to overflow. I fear for our fellow Christians there," Paul said.

When they arrived at the Turquand house next to the Huguenot church, Louis asked, "Do you have some free time tomorrow? I need to discuss another matter with you." The respect Louis had for Paul bound them in a close friendship, not just layman to minister. They shared the bonds of Frenchmen, Partisans, and Christians. He knew Paul could help him a bit in his decision making.

"Of course. How about eleven o'clock at the church?" Paul answered.

"Fine. I look forward to the conversation. *À demain.*"

Before his appointment on Friday morning, Louis stopped by the Elliotts'. Most likely Elizabeth was already occupied with her morning tasks. She liked to use all her daylight hours for a purpose, not just relaxing in bed or daydreaming over a big breakfast. He felt she would be up tending her garden beneath the clear blue sky.

The only person he saw was the house servant who politely showed him to the back door and the garden. Right where he had imagined her. Today she wore an old cotton day dress that had seen many days in the yard. However, the vision of her wasn't spoiled, but enhanced as he advanced onto the scene. Elizabeth, with trowel in hand, weeds by her side, dirt on her dress, and grass in her hair, looked more beautiful than Louis could imagine.

"Ahem," he cleared his throat to warn her.

"Oh, Louis," she squealed in surprise. Accepting his extended hand, she struggled to rise. "I must look a fright, but I don't care. I have looked worse, I'm sure."

Louis pictured her as a little girl being offered a new kitten or a special gift. She placed a light kiss on his cheek and led him to the bench.

"The reason I have interrupted your morning activity," he stated, as he plucked a piece of grass out of her hair, "is because I wanted to tell you of my intention to talk to Reverend Turquand today—in just a few minutes, actually. I know we won't be married in the Huguenot church, but for some reason I want his blessing and support. I want him included in my life as much as possible. Can you understand that?"

Her clear blue-gray eyes engaged his. "I can, and I do under-stand. He probably fills a need in your life like your aunt does in mine. She was instrumental in my personal search for answers about faith and God. I remember she explained it so simply: 'Each of us has to make a personal commitment to Jesus Christ as Lord and Savior. No one can do it for anyone else.' No one had ever told me that. Maybe it goes back to her Huguenot beginnings. The church's belief in a personal, simple, and straightforward relation-ship drew many French people through its doors."

"Maybe so, yet I had not thought of it that way. That is exactly what Rev. Turquand did for me. The huge concept of religion was brought down to a single personal acceptance of Christ. Yet I had avoided it all my life."

Louis was honored, privileged, and even humbled to share his deep commitment with Elizabeth. Together they were tightly bound to Christ—a three-fold cord not easily broken. A bond for a lifetime, for an eternity.

"I'm glad you are sharing our plans with him. His wife is a very interesting, caring woman who does a lot for the community too. And on a less spiritual level, they are both very involved in the Partisan movement." She dusted her skirt to dislodge stray debris.

"I know. The movement is becoming more personal to me all the time. The amount of prayer I give to the issues. Prayers for peace, for discernment, for direction centering on a possible separation and war. I want to discuss that with him too."

"Well, I hope you find answers. I'm just glad that I'm facing all of this with you now." She placed her hand in his. He responded to her impulsive act by latching on to her grip. "I feel surrounded by love and protected by hope."

"One more thing: after you finish playing in the dirt today, would you like to go out to dinner at the Grand Hotel around seven o'clock?" He teased her once again and kissed her hand, dirt and all.

After rubbing her hands together to loosen the dirt, she grinned. "Of course. I promise there will not be a speck of dirt on me."

"Or weeds in your hair?" He waved a leaf he had rescued from her mass of brown locks. Then he exited through the front gate to the street, thinking about the life he would share with his attractive gardener.

Ten minutes later, Louis stood in Reverend Turquand's office. He admired the dark wood paneling. The large window gave the walls a shiny hue.

"Have a seat, Louis. What may I help you with today? You seemed a little eager last night. I hope I can help."

"You have shared in other decisions in my brief time here. So, I want you to be a part of this very special one." Louis paused to breathe. He still had a hard time voicing a sentiment he had silenced for months. "Elizabeth Elliott and I will be married soon. Hopefully, with the permission and blessing of her father.

Although he has given us the right to court openly, his blessing is pending."

"You're doing the right thing by desiring the blessing of her father. In the long run, you'll be happy that you gave him that respect," Reverend Turquand responded.

"I know that Elizabeth and I are facing a few challenges from Mr. Elliott's viewpoint. But we feel that God approves of our decision. My question is if God has ordained this marriage in our minds, how can there be the remaining challenges with her parents?" Shouldn't God-ordained relationships and situations be easy and worry free?

"Louis, remember that God doesn't promise you an easy life with no problems. You must do what He is telling you to do. I have seen your relationship with Elizabeth grow, but only after I witnessed the change in your life when you accepted Jesus Christ as your Redeemer. Only then did God make a way for your love to become stronger."

All credit was due to God who alone had made the aimless rocky path of Louis' life meaningful and promising despite the challenges still to come. "So, we are to be obedient to Elizabeth's parents and confident that God is in control?"

Paul ran his fingers through his thinning hair. "Correct. It's the best way—although not necessarily easy."

"I just needed to hear it from you. Someone I trust." Louis cleared his throat and peered at his friend. "You know that I want you at the service even though Reverend Smith will officiate."

"I understand. You have my prayers, Louis, and Elizabeth too." Reverend Turquand ended with a prayer from his heart blessing Louis' decision. He promised to be available to listen and support him.

Louis stopped by his house for the noon meal. Mrs. Engle, who was now working at his house a few hours each morning, had placed a meat pie on a warmer in the kitchen. Louis' mouth watered. Quickly, he ate it with a piece of the small loaf of bread and brown-sugared apples. It almost felt like a home. He wanted his house to swell with life. At least someone's presence each day added the semblance of vitality.

"Thank You, Lord, for the hope you give me through Paul and now through the kindness of Mrs. Engle. Please bless this food to the nourishment of my body and my body to your service. Amen." The walls breathed with the fresh words.

Louis relaxed in the sunroom near the pianoforte. A few hours left of work, then an evening with Elizabeth. No more hiding. The Elliotts expected their outings, and this one marked their new relationship.

Louis presented himself in style at the Elliotts'. From the rented, shiny black carriage drawn by a white horse to his flawless black felt hat. Elizabeth wondered if he were trying to impress her parents. All the trappings were moot, since Elizabeth's attention remained on Louis' deep-blue eyes, crinkling at the edges due to his smile. *What is he expecting of me? Would this evening be different?*

She slipped up in front of him on her new tiny blue slippers, which felt like pillows of cotton. Her soft blue dress swished around her, leaving satiny tingles on her legs. Did he want to reach out to her as much as she wanted him to?

In such proximity to her ever-watchful parents, Louis took only her gloved hand in his and bowed his head in a light kiss. Somehow, she managed to refrain from drawing him closer. She knew her parents would be on the lookout for inappropriate action. But they needn't worry. Louis was a model gentleman. It was the major obstacles—his nationality and political views—that remained permanent, unwavering, and non-negotiable.

Her mother and father were cordial in their greeting. "I see you have taken me up on my suggestion to court my daughter properly." Although not exactly cold, Father's words were not full of warmth either. "Remember, my position in this town as you step out with Elizabeth on your arm. Have a pleasant evening." He turned and entered his library.

She was disappointed in her father. He treated Louis like a man right out of boarding school instead of a mature, educated businessman. But she held her tongue, and Louis said to the older man's back, "Yes, sir."

Elizabeth's mother squeezed her hand. "Don't pay attention to him. Have a good time tonight, you two. I'll take care of any unpleasantness here."

Dinner in the elegant hotel restaurant, though not private, allowed enough distance from nearby hearers for Louis and Elizabeth to speak openly and emotionally.

"I'm determined to make the most of our time alone." She removed her gloves.

Louis sighed. She followed his gaze to her left hand. The diamonds and rubies sparkled in the candlelight. "You're wearing your ring. I'm pleased. This is only the second time I have seen it on you. The first was months ago when I placed it on your finger." He brought her fingers close enough for her to feel his warm breath.

"I think it's time to show the world. I've worn it hidden every day, wanting to avoid the explanation and the confrontations with my parents. Now, I'm free. Well, almost free. Free to show my love and to share my joy. Nothing will get in the way of our marriage." Elizabeth declared this barely above a whisper, but with enough intensity as if she were shouting. "I know I can't wear it officially everywhere yet. I will. Soon."

"You make me so happy. You seem to imply that your father will not stand in the way of our wishes," he added. He laid her hand back on the table. His eyes traveled up to her face.

"Why would I think any differently? My optimism can't hurt the outcome. If Father can understand how happy I am, he'll have to consent and grant us our one desire."

The steamy meal of roast lamb, boiled carrots and potatoes, and asparagus in lemon sauce interrupted them. Between bites, the conversation steered to her teaching and his work and on to their joint effort in preparing their house. Louis would be ready to move in soon. He already ate his noon meals there and oversaw the progress.

"We still need to decide about any servants we might need," Louis added. "Mrs. Engle is working out nicely a few hours a day. By the way, she's an excellent cook." He licked his lips.

"Oh, yes, I'm glad. My interview with her was very successful. I see no reason why she wouldn't be the perfect choice to help run the house; she cooks, cleans, and sews. She said that the rooms upstairs would be ample for the two of them. Her daughter, Amy, will help in lots of ways. I do think we should engage their services permanently."

"I'm glad to hear that. I have already asked Tom to help around the house, mainly with the garden and repairs. He would live in the back of the kitchen which has a large room, lots of space for Tom and another hand in the future. I want him to move in soon."

"Do you want me to work out the details with Mrs. Engle? They could join the household in a month or so," Elizabeth suggested.

The whole conversation was dreamlike.

"Of course. Until then, I'll keep Mrs. Engle as a temporary cook and housekeeper."

The days inched away. By the following week, Elizabeth seemed to receive a little extra attention through smiles from mere acquaintances, along with zealous salutations. Perhaps her own smile was contagious. Very few of her thoughts strayed far from Louis.

"Are you oblivious to the stares and whispers?" Sarah asked after class. "Let's watch as the other teachers leave their rooms."

Elizabeth's curiosity was peaked. "What do you mean?"

"Just wait." The two stood side by side in the hallway.

One by one the teachers emerged, stared at Elizabeth with huge knowing grins, then bent their heads in whispers with others nearby. What was so secretive? She held Sarah by the elbow. Her friend wasn't escaping without an explanation.

Sarah cocked her left eyebrow "You should be able to guess, unless you are walking around with your head in the clouds." Elizabeth turned to face her.

"Tell me—now," Elizabeth pleaded. "Please."

"You and Louis have turned quite a few heads. Your names are linked together in the tea houses, business meetings, restaurants, and shops. You know everyone loves a blossoming romance. And you must admit you are a striking couple."

"Are the whispers good or bad?" Elizabeth grimaced. She didn't want negative words spoken about her.

Sarah reached for Elizabeth's hand and squeezed. "The ones I hear are all good. The girls here are so excited. My parents think Louis is the most promising catch in town. And of course, Samuel and Mr. Gadsden only have praise for Louis."

"If only the whispers would make it to Father's ears." Elizabeth shook her head. Would he listen if he had the chance? Would the words make any difference at all?

Whether or not her father heard any of the positive publicity or not, he had to relay his opinion as promised by the end of October, and that was close. She knew Louis would not let the impending date slip by when it was just days away. Elizabeth held out hope even as doubts lurked in the dark. Yet God persisted in his consistency. *Let Me continue to hold you close. Let My love surround you.* Sanity returned with the promise.

On the last Friday evening of the month, Louis joined the Elliotts at their house for dinner. Afterward, on this occasion, the men joined the ladies in the parlor. That was strange. Elizabeth questioned with her tilted head toward her mother. Her mother shrugged. Louis followed his host into the room. He took a seat on the sofa a fair distance from Elizabeth. Mr. Elliott stood.

"Elizabeth and Louis, I must admit that I had my doubts about your relationship and that I was hoping to find a clear, obvious reason to reject your request. Everywhere I turned, I heard good things about you, Louis. I do believe you can provide for Elizabeth." He stepped closer to Elizabeth. "Are you happy?"

She reached for her father and grasped his hand. "Yes, Father. Louis makes me very happy."

Her eyes locked with Louis'. *I couldn't be happy without you. I love you.*

"Well, since that is the case, you have my blessing to marry. Mother and I welcome you to the family." Father extended his hand to Louis.

Elizabeth ignored their handshake and jumped in front of Louis to hug her father. She laced her fingers around his neck. "Thank you, Father."

Louis peeked around Elizabeth and said, "Thank you, sir. I hope I'm never a disappointment to you."

"Don't worry about me. I'm not an easy man to please when it comes to my daughter. You just be sure to take care of her." He smiled, relieving Elizabeth's remaining fear.

"I will, sir. I will."

Elizabeth turned her attention to Louis. Words would come later. It was enough to know that he would endeavor to keep his promise daily with God's help.

CHAPTER 8

*E*lizabeth, Sarah, Mrs. Engle, and her daughter, Amy, sat in a circle in Elizabeth's sun room putting the finishing touches on two beautiful gowns. Mrs. Engle had helped the young ladies turn pieces of satin into light creations of shimmering beauty—masterpieces. The intricate application of lace, tiny buttons, and trim occupied their hands. Otherwise, they were free to enjoy the others' company.

Along with the fall and early November came the time of year when Charles Town woke up from its lethargy, having conquered the annual season of sickness, heat, and abandonment. The streets and shops were full again of eager people relishing the busyness of the town and society. Calendars were overflowing with balls, soirées, and other entertainment.

Mrs. Engle lightly ran her fingers over the newly sewn fabric. "Miss Elliott, this sea-green material with the sheer gauze overlay is perfect for you. You'll be beautiful for Mr. Lestarjette." She was becoming more than an employee to Elizabeth with her motherly ways.

As she finished the sleeve, Elizabeth held it up to her face, batting her eyelashes in fun. "I'm glad. I knew when we picked it out, you could work miracles with it."

Sarah laughed at the sight. "That is well enough, but I think it still needs to be attached to the bodice to have the full effect."

"Oh, all right. You always want perfection." Elizabeth passed the sleeve to Mrs. Engle and took up the other to finish.

Sarah frowned at the material and dangled the button by a thread. "Amy, I need help with this button. You have such a delicate touch, and I seem to be clumsy."

Amy, very talented for a twelve-year-old, gladly took over the project. The satin-covered buttons matched the pale-blue material of Sarah's dress. Sarah could easily wear light colors with her dark hair and complexion.

The young girl looked up from her work. "If you don't mind my asking, Miss Collins, who are you going to the ball with?"

Glancing over at Elizabeth with a semi-pained look, Sarah said, "It appears that this meddlesome miss over here has managed to convince Mr. Evans to escort me. Or did you pay him, Elizabeth?"

"Don't look at me like that. I had nothing to do with it. You must blame Louis this time." Elizabeth eyed her friend's slight smile. "I didn't think you minded. Did you have another suitor in mind?"

"Ha." Sarah blew air through her lips, deflating her cheeks. "You know I don't, but I also know Samuel isn't really interested in me."

Elizabeth winked at Sarah. "We'll see."

"What do you know about the Pinckney ball?" Sarah concentrated on her needle and delicate stitches.

Elizabeth looked at Sarah through her lashes, hoping for forgiveness. "The event will not be as large as the one last year at the Manigaults'. I enjoy the more intimate situations. Still, there will probably be seventy-five people there."

"And I'm sure you'll be occupied the entire time with Louis."

Sarah shrugged. "I'm used to losing your company to the gentlemen on your full dance card."

How could she make her friend understand that others want to be around her too? "Maybe a bit of boldness will give you the confidence to move out from the shadows so that men can actually see you."

"Or maybe Samuel and I will find something to talk about as he spins me around the room." Sarah gently took the gown from Amy's hands, completed to perfection. Twirling around the room holding the dress to her, Sarah danced while humming a tune. Amy covered her mouth, stifling a giggle. But soon all four ladies joined in the merriment, clapping their hands, moving their feet, singing out loud.

Sarah left with her dress wrapped neatly in a cloth. Elizabeth found it a relief to have the gowns completed and hers hanging in the armoire awaiting the ball. She knew Louis was glad they had been invited to this party. Mr. Pinckney was well-respected and active with the Sons of Liberty. Personally, she liked Mrs. Pinckney with her friendly comments, so she didn't think twice about accepting the invitation.

Later in the afternoon, Louis joined Elizabeth in the garden for tea and scones. She soaked up the cool breeze under the magnolia tree. She gently placed Cleo on the soft grass in order to serve the simmering brew.

"My dress is finished for the ball. I hope you're looking forward to the event. It should be entertaining," Elizabeth ventured.

Louis sipped his tea. "Well, I think the guests will be a diverse group, considering Pinckney's past relationship with the government. I'm hopeful that politics will be nominally banned from the ballroom, where I would rather concentrate on you."

She blushed. "Perhaps on the dance floor, but not from the library or study. I doubt if you can control the conversation for the entire evening. Whenever men get together, the subject just pops up unannounced. It's so much a part of all of us. Women just know when to keep quiet." Elizabeth knew that was not true. How did Victoria survive on words of controversy? The thought of her being at the party bothered Elizabeth. Probably she'd accompany George since the Elliotts were invited.

Louis sat back with his tea and changed the subject. "Progress is being made on our home. All the furniture is ordered. Each day a new piece arrives. Still, the house is so empty without you there. Tom is a little company, but he stays mostly with his mother for now."

"They are so excited about moving into the house. I still can't believe we have such a wonderful opportunity to help this family." Elizabeth was a bit nervous being mistress of the house with such a capable woman already in charge. Hopefully, Mrs. Engle would become her teacher in the running of a house.

Leaning forward, Louis returned his cup and saucer to the tray. "I see it that way too. From the way you talk, Mrs. Engle is more than a house servant; she is becoming a friend."

Staring into her teacup, she tried to interpret what he saw. How easily it would be to confide in Mrs. Engle. "It's something Grandmamma taught me this summer. Well, something I knew all along. Getting to know people by name and relationship, no matter what the social status, comes with many blessings. If we let them, they can become like family to us."

Louis grinned. "Knowing you, that's exactly how it will be. It could be that we need them as much as they need us."

"I'm glad you feel that way." What she knew about running a household was not enough to give her complete confidence. Could she share that with Mrs. Engle?

"Before I leave your ideal sanctuary, let's finalize the plans for Friday night. I'll pick you up in the coach at six o'clock. Then we'll collect Samuel, then Sarah. Dinner reservations are for seven o'clock. After that, I plan to dance the night away with only you in my arms." He took her hand, leaving Cleo basking in the sun.

111

"If only that could be. Protocol says no to your delightful suggestion," she teased as she walked him through the house to the front door.

As he retrieved his hat and gloves, he whispered for her ears only, "I love you more each day."

"And I love you too." She reluctantly ushered him out the door.

Friday night arrived, the beginning of parties that would continue week after week through the winter season. Homes opened up in gestures of friendship as the town bonded together again under familiar gaiety and society. Elizabeth in gleaming sea green, and Sarah in delicate light blue on the arms of their men in black tails and top hats, turned quite a few heads at the elegant Grand Hotel restaurant.

"Why are they staring at us?" Sarah whispered to her friend as they advanced to their table by the far window overlooking the garden.

Elizabeth stole a casual glance around the room. "Because we all look so regal, that's why. Don't let it bother you," she encouraged.

Since the beginning of the evening, conversation between the four of them had volleyed back and forth with reasonable ease. Elizabeth wondered at the possibility the night held. At times she wanted to shake Sarah and tell her once again how perfect Samuel was for her. At the moment, though, Elizabeth observed that Sarah's usual shyness had disappeared. She contributed to the table talk like it was second nature. The once demure lady perked up with comments on the social season, the boarding house, and even politics. Samuel made it seem like Sarah's opinion mattered, although he spent most of his time simply looking at her. His occasional comments spurred her on. At times Louis coaxed his friend to join the conversation.

"You were saying, Samuel, that business has picked up a bit lately," Louis interjected. The tablecloth fluttered. Had Louis just kick Samuel under the table to get his attention? Elizabeth covered her giggle with her napkin.

Samuel jerked his head around. "Yes. Of course. Houses, businesses, even plantations. Many people are moving here. It keeps the office very busy. I had to hire more help to handle the land outside of town."

"I think you handled the purchase of property for my uncle in the Orangeburg community," Sarah said as the lamb chops smothered in gravy, cheese potatoes, biscuits, and mixed vegetables disappeared and were replaced by hot gingerbread with a sugar glaze and coffee or tea.

He nodded and stared at Sarah for more than his normal few seconds. "Yes. He bought a nice piece of farmland."

By half past eight, the two couples entered the Pinckney home, a cypress and heart pine house with a stout brick basement. After discarding her coat and being announced, Elizabeth paused a minute to take in the vast ballroom already teaming with guests. Familiar faces and pleasant music surrounded them. With Louis by her side, Elizabeth greeted her parents and friends around the room. Already Sarah and Samuel found others to greet.

Elizabeth watched the couples dancing and pulled on Louis' sleeve. "The orchestra is playing a minuet from Boccherini's Cello Sonata in C Major."

He stood by her side ready to lead her to join the others. "Do you know every piece you hear?"

"No, but I do recognize many of these performed at local balls."

Louis whispered in her ear, sending warm tingling to her toes. "Before your dance card fills up, will you dance the next minuet with me?"

She purposely handed Louis her dance card, allowing him to fill up many of the slots. Her father and Robert had already claimed a few spaces. It was perfectly fine with her if Louis claimed the rest.

Accepting her card, she started tapping her foot. "Here's one I know. Listen. It's by Francois Joseph Gossec, a Frenchman by adoption since he was born in Belgium. It's a new piece, Symphonie no.2." Louis took her hand and led her to the floor for a contra dance with two facing lines. Midway down the line, she spied Sarah and Samuel facing off. They seemed happy, all smiles, eyes glued to each other.

As their brief steps came close together, Louis commented, "I wish we were dancing the waltz. It's a new dance out of Austria that has captivated France." He stepped away to complete a movement, then back again. "The couples dance entirely alone as they float in each other's arms. It can be very lively. Maybe it will catch on here soon."

The thought pleased Elizabeth, as she was continually in and out of his arms.

Before they had a chance to join the next round, Elizabeth saw George's finger tap Louis' shoulder. "My turn now." Louis bowed and exited.

Louis sought some cold punch. When he returned, Victoria Seymour, in a deep-orange gown, trapped him by a column and a chair. No quick escape, he realized. Her stiff stance and unmoving facial features were exactly as he remembered.

"I should've known you would be here with Elizabeth." Her unfeeling voice had not changed either, lacking warmth. "George tells me that you are courting now. What is it that she sees in you?"

"You'll have to ask her that question." Changing the subject, Louis asked, "How do you like this premier event of the season?"

"Rather small, wouldn't you say? You can't make me believe

that balls in Paris are this size. Just look out there at the styles from the hair to the slippers. Plain colonial. But in Philadelphia, the latest style and fashion are observed."

Luckily, he hadn't expected a different answer. Miss Seymour appeared to be made from an unchanging mold. But he wouldn't let her words stick, not while he had the opportunity to uplift his family, his country.

"There is nothing wrong with this group. I enjoy the lack of pretense and prefer the genuine actions and attitudes of most of these citizens. Maybe you should consider returning to Philadelphia, Miss Seymour, if only for a season."

Her lips barely moved even as she threw her response. "Not a bad idea, Mr. Lestarjette. I will leave this pile of commoners to you." She left as he grimaced at her constant curt cuts about the backbone of Charles Town.

"I see you were cornered by the pessimistic Miss Seymour. Clearly, a raving beauty with a poisonous tongue," Samuel voiced.

Louis visibly shuddered. "What is it about her that makes me boil? You would think she would choose to stay away from anything beneath her, like a Charles Town ball." The two men stepped outside onto the porch for fresh air. "How are things with Sarah?"

"Fine. She has a full dance card." Samuel paused. "She has changed from last year with Elizabeth's coaching. Your fiancée has turned a wallflower into a butterfly. It's hard for me to keep up."

Elizabeth's plan of creating this couple was proving to be hard work for all involved. Louis found his coaching skills lacking. What would Elizabeth advise? "Maybe you need to try your wings too and meet in the middle."

His friend sighed heavily. "I am. The prospect of finally landing on common ground is tantalizing. It won't be easy, though."

Gazing at the well-lit lawn, Louis added his own sigh. "Sarah is still the same young lady. She's just not wrapped up so tightly in her shell." He turned and catching Elizabeth's eye, he excused himself and claimed the next dance.

Patting her hand on his arm, Louis concentrated on the most important person in the room, in all of Charles Town. "I thought you would never return. No more turns around the room with anyone else." He didn't expect her to agree, just perhaps nod in agreement to make him feel in control.

He wrinkled his forehead. "Was George that bothersome?"

Squeezing his arm, air whistled in agonizing release from her lips. "Well, yes, he was. His entire dialogue had to do with Victoria and Loyalists. I have a funny feeling about him—like he has a plan up his sleeve. I don't trust him. Yet, I can't tell you why."

"He's young and a bit confused with the present state of things. All we can do is try to steer him in the right direction," he suggested, trying to relieve her fears.

"I'm afraid any advice we would offer is the opposite of what he would do."

Only the lively music from the orchestra lightened the prevalent downcast thoughts. Sparkle returned to Elizabeth as a lively piece played like a cool breeze. "Let's dance. This is one of Abel's concerti for keyboard and strings."

Louis took his vision in radiant green to the ballroom floor and joined other assembled couples for the dance. He didn't care if it was Mozart, Haydn, or Abel; all that mattered was Elizabeth at the moment. She could make any music come alive.

Faces blurred as they spun around. So many friendly guests to brighten their evening, ones that had become dear to them— Gibbes, Rutledge, Motte, Savage, Ravenel. Not just acquaintances anymore, but cohorts, comrades, Partisans. It appeared that all had accepted their formal courtship.

Even the political division halted where love was concerned. Those present of the Loyalist camp overlooked agendas tonight. The social season was open to all parties, all ages. The prominent men of the town put aside differences for certain periods of time. At least that was how it was done in the past. Young men like George had lapses of when to speak and act and when to leave it alone.

The night ended with little concern for opinion or comments as Louis walked Elizabeth to her front door after depositing the other young couple at their homes. Alone for a moment, he took her hands in his and lightly brushed her lips for the briefest kiss. Pulling away slightly, he stepped back, taking her with him out of the lamp light. With his hands on her cheeks, he moved in closer for a deeper kiss. To his surprise she joined him, her arms wrapped around his neck, eyes closed. *Was that a sigh? Mine or hers?*

He pushed against her shoulders lightly, hesitant in breaking the contact but determined to not overstep the boundary lines.

"I really feel there is a bright future for us, Elizabeth. Nothing will get in our way. I love you."

His words were a promise to Elizabeth. A promise he hoped would propel her through the next few weeks.

CHAPTER 9

*L*ouis and Elizabeth set their wedding date for December tenth. He couldn't believe he was getting married in just over a month. They set an appointment with Reverend Smith at St. Philip's Church. For a brief moment, Louis contemplated having the service at the Huguenot Church, but their mutual decision guided them to the church they attended regularly, the church of their families and friends.

He dropped by Reverend Turquand's office to satisfy his guilt. Since Louis found his relationship with the Lord in the spring with the Huguenot minister's guidance, Louis still shared important matters with him.

"Louis, I understand," Reverend Turquand declared. "That has never hindered our friendship. I want to give you a Scripture passage to help you through whatever you face. It's from Isaiah fifty-five. 'For my thoughts are not your thoughts, neither are your ways my ways, saith the LORD. For as the heavens are higher than the earth, so are my ways higher than your ways, and my thoughts than your thoughts.'"

When the issues of the welfare of the country and town overwhelmed or overburdened Louis, he claimed the truth of the passage. It seemed to him that every conversation led to the uncertainties of Parliament and the repercussions of inevitable events. Charles Town was simmering. The people anticipated the boiling point, but no one knew what would trigger it.

And his marriage was right in the middle of it all.

While Louis talked of the rising political heat, nothing seemed to really matter to Elizabeth except the wedding, though her days still consisted of teaching piano and theory. Sarah and Anne guided her through much of the preparation. Her mother and Jeannette gave practical advice. And somehow, with the help of these four women, Elizabeth knew there was hope of a beautiful, successful wedding down the road.

One afternoon at Jeannette's over tea, Elizabeth continued to wonder how her mother would fit into the preparation and, more importantly, the reality of having Louis in the family. A smile, an idea, a word of encouragement—anything would do. Would her mother finally let go of her worries?

Her mother sat across the room from Elizabeth, smiling and talking with the others. "The dress will be altered and ready in two weeks," Mother said. "Now what about food and flowers?"

Elizabeth's jaw dropped. Was Mother taking control? A real interest?

"I'll make a menu for the wedding lunch," Anne said.

Sarah smiled and clapped her hands. "And I'll ask my mother to help me with the flowers."

Jeannette brushed a few crumbs off the tablecloth. "That leaves Louis as my project."

Elizabeth laughed, relieved. "You all make me realize my wedding is really happening. Thank you." Slowly, she ceased to wonder about her mother's role. She needed those around her who were able to force her feet to the ground. Left to her own thoughts and reveries, she would have spent her days dreaming of her future with Louis and nothing more. Usually very practical, it seemed that she was lost in the activities surrounding her love.

With a date set, the list made for the arrangements of the event and divided among the ladies, Elizabeth settled into enjoying her time with Louis.

The first dinner party, hosted by Christopher Gadsden, set the stage for the rest of the month of November. Louis sat next to Elizabeth at the table set for twelve in Christopher's expansive dining room. "How many of these do we have?"

She grinned. "I know how you feel but look at everyone's face. We've given each one something to celebrate. And the answer is five, right now."

He found her hand and held it tightly. "That's five evenings I won't have you to myself."

"You wouldn't have me to yourself anyway, Mr. Lestarjette," she whispered, claiming her hand in order to cut her veal.

Before dessert Christopher offered a toast. Elizabeth glanced quickly around the table. Eyes darted to the host, and each raised a glass. "To Elizabeth, our Charles Town belle, and Louis, one of our most outstanding citizens. May your lives be blessed through your union."

"Huzzah. Huzzah."

With a sideways glance, Elizabeth caught her father's eyes as he gave her a wink and nodded in her direction. He had come a long way. She winked back, lifting her glass toward him, then to Louis.

"To you, *ma chérie*. Forever," Louis said.

"Forever, *mon amour*."

Aside from dinner parties, Elizabeth attended quite a few afternoon teas without Louis. One was given by Sarah and Mrs.

Collins and another by her mother's friends. The girls at the boarding school hosted a special tea. Elizabeth smiled at their youth and innocence, enthralled with the vision of love and weddings. They saw a fairy-tale scenario with Prince Charming and a happily ever after, complete with riding into the sunset on a white stallion. Louis fit their image of a gallant gentleman. She had seen enough marriages to know that the day-to-day married life was not as romantic as the fictitious tales. But why burst the imagination of the young? They would form their own opinions in the next few years. *Anyway, mine* will *be a happily ever after.*

Martha Laurens, who was like a little sister to Elizabeth, composed a piece especially for Elizabeth, complete with the sheet music and words. "Thank you, Martha. I'll play it for Louis often." The young girl blushed. Elizabeth knew Martha felt the same kind of friendship.

Other gifts from the girls included books of poetry, ribbon, plants, posies, cards, dainty handkerchiefs, and many homemade items crafted by girls of all ages. These meant more to her than crystal or china, silver or gold.

Preparations continued. Her mother retrieved her wedding gown from the safe storage in an armoire. She wanted Elizabeth to wear it, if it was her desire. At first sight Elizabeth adored the blue satin gown with its long train and tiny pearl buttons. Anne had worn it ten years ago. To a nine-year-old, her sister had looked like a princess. Her small fingers had carefully touched the miniature buttons and the fancy lace and pearl bodice. Now she was to be the bride, the princess.

Elizabeth didn't have to ponder long over bridesmaids. No one else would do except Anne, Sarah, and Martha—her dear sister, her best friend, and her extraordinary "little sister."

Louis asked Uncle Henry to stand with him at the wedding, as well as Samuel. The only chink in the plan was the third attendant. He dreaded asking George, yet time was passing.

At the Elliots' house one evening, Louis asked the hovering question for Elizabeth's sake and for a future relationship with his brother-in-law. "George, Elizabeth and I would like you to take part in our wedding."

Unfortunately, George did not take the invitation well. "No, I won't be a part of something I don't believe is right for Elizabeth. You are wrong for asking her." With that, he exited the parlor, leaving no room for pleading.

Elizabeth's reaction to her brother's rejection surprised Louis. She accepted it without malice. "The success in our marriage is not dependent on George or on anyone for that matter, except God," Elizabeth promised.

"You're correct. Anyway, I'll ask Robert. He's a close friend and will also be my brother-in-law. He'll be pleased to accept."

She kissed him and smiled. The wedding party was set. And soon, very soon, she would not have to say good-bye.

Elizabeth noticed the changes in Sarah as she was thrown into the presence of Samuel at all of the wedding parties. Late in the summer, her friend had told her that Samuel showed no interest in her after a few outings. Even though her feelings were more than those of an acquaintance, Sarah had shared she was deter-mined to move on and to let go of romantic dreams where Samuel was concerned. Elizabeth had stopped pressing the matter.

So, from where did this new Sarah full of confidence and assertiveness come? Elizabeth still did a double take when she spied Sarah and Samuel with their heads together as if sharing a secret or a pleasant story. Her friend laughed more, smiled often, and joined in conversations with new and old acquaintances. Samuel's rejection had seemingly changed her outlook on the whole social scene.

Elizabeth could never confront Sarah with her observation.

But Anne seemed a good substitute. She tested her theory at a ball at James Laurens' house.

She poked Anne's upper arm. "Watch Sarah. Do you notice how she joins in without hesitation?" Elizabeth guided Anne's search to the center of the room.

Anne followed Elizabeth's directions. "She acts like she is really interested. I think she has realized she has nothing to lose."

"My shy little wallflower is blossoming into a beguiling rose. Ha. I wonder what Samuel thinks now?" Elizabeth found the gentleman mentioned.

"Now he's the wallflower. And look who he's following with his eyes. We'll have to encourage where we can without telling either one of our plans," Anne said.

Elizabeth knew this added challenge would be a pleasure to perform. Since her last endeavor to put the two together, Samuel hadn't made a move on his own.

"That will be very easy, considering they're invited to every one of my parties, and they're always seated at the same table. I'll make sure their place cards are always next to each other, not just across the table." She grabbed her sister's hand and giggled like a child planning a prank; only this one involved hearts and emotions. Would it work?

"If you are going to spend so much time watching her," Louis said to Samuel, "you might as well get a little closer and talk to her."

"Who?" Samuel asked.

"Who? You can't fool me. Sarah, of course."

"Sarah?" Samuel shook his head firmly. "You know we tried that before, last spring, last month. Nothing happened. It was a dead end. We had nothing in common." He turned his palms up and shrugged.

"She seems to have something in common with all these

people now. Maybe you should give her another chance. I've seen you talking to her."

"Always about you and Elizabeth. I think her interest, if there was any, is gone. I was too cautious before," Samuel pined. "Somehow she's different. Instead of her standing alone, apart from the crowd, I am. She could have anybody here."

"Well, you'll never know, my friend, unless you enter the game again." Louis' words contained a challenge.

"The 'game'? I wonder if I would be one of many players this time." His friend stared at his hands.

Louis put his arm around Samuel's shoulder. "Chin up. You'll never know until you try. I know if you can figure out your business deals and court cases, you can muddle your way through love. Look at me. I was the worst candidate for marriage." Louis laughed. He gave his friend a strong pat on the back and a gentle push in the right direction—in Sarah's direction. Louis watched Samuel's feet moving awkwardly, even shyly, toward her. Would he interrupt her conversation with her friends? He had to, or he would stand there dumbstruck until she noticed him. Louis wanted to cheer him on. Instead he moved closer to listen.

"Hmm...Hmm." Samuel cleared his throat. "Excuse me, ladies. Sarah, I would like a word with you, please."

"Of course, Samuel."

He guided her by the elbow to two vacant seats. Now, Louis could only see his friend's mouth move. Then it all ended. The dinner bell rang, and the couple glided to the table.

As Elizabeth sat next to Louis, she winked at Anne. He noticed the exchange between the sisters. What were they plotting? They had watched the same scene between Sarah and Samuel as he had. Perhaps their plan was the same as his.

Louis' head turned to the sound of Samuel's close voice. "I did it. She said yes to a drive and picnic on Saturday."

Another success on the social scene. The dinners and parties were a reprieve from the world's issues brewing around them.

Louis wondered if perhaps the political affairs had come to a halt, if in this season they'd all found a place where the differing opinions could reside in peace. Perhaps it was good for Louis that he couldn't see around the corner. For now, the immediate future looked promising.

CHAPTER 10

*E*arly the next week, Louis escorted Elizabeth home from the boarding school by way of their new house. "You'll be so amazed at the changes a few pieces of furniture have made. It has all been delivered, even the pieces by Mr. Elfe. Everything looks strikingly better than the pictures in the catalogs." Louis tucked her arm in his and stroked her hand as they walked.

She tilted her head and added a crooked smile. "You seem quite pleased. Is it that perfect?"

"No. Not perfect. It's lacking something. Maybe you can figure it out."

"Well, I'm astonished. I would think with the amount of money and time you have spent, you would settle for nothing less than perfection."

"I have an idea how to fix it, but I need to test my theory." He left her clueless as to the problem.

To Louis, the scene awaiting them as they stepped through the front door of their home was a vision of comfort and style. Elizabeth twirled around in all directions.

"Not perfect, Louis?"

He kissed her sweetly and quickly before letting her return to her investigation of every room. "Now it is. I knew with you in the room it would be."

Elizabeth had chosen the different furnishings, most made with mahogany from the Caribbean. A lot of the items were neat and plain, very functional and sturdy, like Louis preferred. A few elegant pieces accented the drawing rooms and parlor: Queen Anne upholstered easy chairs, corner chairs, and camel-back sofas; drop-leaf, tea, and card tables of maple and walnut; candle stands and cupboards. The items that filled the room had turned the house into a home.

Louis had helped her pick out a walnut desk for her use, complete with a writing surface that folded out to rest on two short pulls and plenty of pigeonholes and little drawers. It occupied a corner of the drawing room facing a window overlooking the back garden. Her pianoforte graced one side of the large room.

"This will be my favorite retreat," she said.

Louis leaned against the doorframe and watched her reaction as she took it all in for the first time.

Sticking her bottom lip out in a pout, she said, "I can't believe you got to move in without me. How unfair."

"It won't be long. Now come look at the library. I hope you'll feel cozy in here while I work in the evening. I made sure there is a comfortable chair by the window for you. Perfect to read a book, take a nap, or join me for tea."

The room intended for male occupants was in fact cheery with the drapes and rug that Elizabeth had added. His new desk with the bookcase set on top was much larger than Elizabeth's desk, but it was made of the same beautiful mahogany. The room had two card tables against a side wall ready for use, along with a tea table.

Moving toward him, she laughed. "I can picture me curled up here just watching you work. I don't know how much reading I will accomplish."

He caressed her cheek, gazing into her eyes for the briefest of moments. "I think we better see the rest of the additions and get you home. I don't know that I trust that imagination of yours." *Or mine.*

He allowed her to glance for half a minute into the master bedroom. The elevated bed with its posts reaching eight feet was in place. He heard a sigh before she followed Louis to the double drawing rooms.

She advanced toward the window. "I had no idea that we ordered enough furniture to complete all of the rooms. I think you added a few pieces." The light shone around her, casting shadows on the floor. He envisioned entertaining their friends in this less formal atmosphere. Or better yet, just Elizabeth.

"You're right. I did. This chest of drawers was made by Mr. Elfe. It sat alone with this unique corner cabinet. Since his work is in such high demand, I grabbed them on sight."

"Oh, Louis." She touched every piece of furniture. To him, she christened every item with her approval. "Our house is more than I expected. Just to have you in a little cottage would've been enough."

"I can't promise you that it will always be this way, but while I'm able I want you to live in style. It's not a mansion, but it's a place we can entertain and enjoy living with any family that God gives us." He contemplated their future. Would there be little feet sliding on these floors and fingerprints all over the shiny wood?

"You're right. I'm thankful for the present, knowing God's love surrounds us now and holds our future," she said.

As they left the house, he silently prayed God's blessings on their life together under the roof of their new house.

They rounded the corner onto Queen Street. Approaching them was a man in military attire. "Look, Elizabeth, does that man look like George?" Louis pointed discreetly.

She broke away without answering and stood in the path of the young man.

"George? Is that you?" she asked.

Her brother smiled and chuckled. "Yes, it's none other than your own brother. I expected to see you at home. But I should have known you would be roaming the streets with Louis." He nodded in Louis' direction. "Lucky for you, I guess. I just left the house with Mother crying and Father railing."

"What have you done, George?" Elizabeth asked. The red jacket spoke the worst.

"I proudly wear this uniform. As of today, I am an enlisted member of His Majesty's armed forces."

"But why?" Elizabeth touched the brass buttons on his coat, her voice quivering. "What happened to the law office, a future career there? This is a total surprise. I really don't understand."

He had never mentioned the military in Louis' presence. And Elizabeth seemed shocked too. George's smirk and overzealous confidence left Louis uneasy. If Elizabeth was confused, what about her parents?

"Don't you understand, sister?" George's lopsided grin dripped with sarcasm. Did he want to cause pain? "Ask Louis; he could probably tell you. War is on the horizon because of citizens like you two—if I could call you true citizens. I'm not going to be caught sitting in an office when the British military goes into action."

Louis registered the open discourse between siblings as a window to their past closeness. Before, their honesty would have contained humor and laughter; now there was hostility mingled with criticism. The two had definitely parted ways. A sad state he had just experienced with his brother, although healing had taken place. Louis didn't want this rift for Elizabeth.

"Where did all this hate come from, George? Don't you have a desire for peace, for a compromise? Do you really want blood-shed? That is not how we were brought up. Even Father wants a solution to our differences."

He put his hands on his hips, feet apart, not very military-like.

"And you sound like him. You want me to sit back and let others fight it out. This time there will be no settlement. Your Partisans or Sons of Liberty have asked for too much."

"George, please don't do this. There—" She wasn't given a chance to finish.

"It's too late." George turned to Louis. "I imagine you will be ruined and your dreams destroyed—either on the battlefield or through the harsh constraints of the government."

"I hope you are wrong," Louis said with a calmness he didn't feel. If screaming would do George any good, Louis would shout his sentiments. "Very soon you will be my brother-in-law, and there shouldn't be animosity between us. I'll pray that you have a change of heart." Louis relayed his sincere sentiments as calmly as possible. He squeezed Elizabeth's hand resting on his arm. For his reassurance and hers.

George straightened his shoulders and adjusted his cap. "The change will have to come from the uneducated, misinformed colonists. The king will not change. So for now, goodbye, Elizabeth. I'll be leaving for Philadelphia soon." He continued his journey toward the barracks without looking back, without acknowledging Elizabeth's pleas to stay, to reconsider. No hug, no touch, no words of endearment.

She turned into Louis' arms, grasping him firmly. "Oh, Louis. What has he done? He doesn't even act like my brother anymore."

He knew no words would help; he only had his arms around her for comfort. He guided her home, gently talking, trying to find words to put her heart at rest, but he knew that the step George had taken was a sign of what other men were doing. A peaceful solution seemed farther away. It seemed as the East India Tea Company ships sailed closer to the American shores, the closer the colonies glided toward conflict. Louis couldn't help but feel the stand they took on the Tea Act would be a deciding factor in the resolution.

Louis followed Elizabeth into her home, hoping she could

console her mother. Mrs. Elliott sat on the sofa with her face in her hands crying. "Oh, Mother. I'm so sorry," Elizabeth soothed. "I ran into George."

Mrs. Elliott sat back, her hands crumpling her handkerchief. "He has willingly placed himself in harm's way. Why would he do that to his family without any warning?"

Mr. Elliott acknowledged Louis' presence with a nod. "If this is any indication of things to come, I feel my house and family are going to be divided. I don't support George's hatred and determination to fight, but neither do I believe the colonists have a right to make demands on the government. I seem to be caught right in the middle." His words contained a deep concern for future events. "At heart, I'm a Loyalist and very much an optimist. I want people like you, Louis, to settle down and accept the rule of the empire. The disagreements are tearing us apart as a country." Mr. Elliott paced, stopping in front of Louis before beginning his rounds again.

As with George, Louis' words needed to remain firm and steady, without harshness and volume. "Sir, you have just stated the problem. The colonists no longer feel a part of Britain. More and more, these people in this new land feel like a separate nation. Like you, I want this solved peacefully. Unfortunately, that decision is in the hands of Parliament."

A few minutes later, Elizabeth walked Louis to the front door, out of view of her parents. "All this talk of George makes me upset about his decision. I see his uniform and commitment as a sign of the battle ahead." Then she smiled, albeit sadly. "But I still feel such joy in our wedding and new life." She reached for his face and stroked his cheek.

He bent and kissed her forehead. "If I could, I would take away this pain. All I can offer is my love."

"Thank you. It is the greatest gift."

CHAPTER 11

*T*he fall school music recital was planned for the last week of November. *What would I do if I didn't have this recital? I think I'd lose my mind.* Elizabeth already spent most of her spare time daydreaming about her life as a married lady. What had she done without Louis a year ago? He was her stability when things became tangled and confusing. This path, this life with a shared future, wasn't her original plan or Louis'. She smiled, for she knew only God could devise something this unique out of two lives that had been set on different courses. *Not anymore. Our path is sure.*

She shook her head and slapped her hands on her knees. The recital now, Louis later. Luckily, many of the details of the recital had been placed in someone else's hands. In spite of her youth, Martha Laurens took over the preparations for the recital: the invitations, the room arrangement, and the printing of the program. The details in capable hands freed Elizabeth to concentrate on the music, the students' confidence, and their performance techniques. Elizabeth made sure a few Christmas hymns were scattered throughout the program, a nice way to usher in the Christmas season.

"Martha, you're a blessing and a true friend. Are you sure your aunt doesn't mind the extra time you're spending here?" Elizabeth asked.

"Not as long as it's with you. She knows you need the help since you are preparing for your wedding." The young girl paused and added, "I hope I find someone as handsome and good as Mr. Lestarjette."

His name made her heart flutter. When, if ever, would the simple things involving Louis seem normal? "You will, Martha. But don't worry about it. I promise it will happen when you least expect it. I wasn't looking for love, but God had it all planned. Now what about flowers for the recital? We'll need some for the corner tables, the pianoforte, and the foyer."

Back to business, although Elizabeth knew Martha had the arrangements ordered and ready for delivery. It never hurt to go over the list several times. She didn't want this special event for parents and friends to be spoiled in any way; after all, the recital marked the end of the term and the beginning of the winter break.

One afternoon Elizabeth and her mother settled around the tea table, pausing between assignments. Anne popped in unannounced, sneaking past the butler and the house servants. How did she do that? Elizabeth rattled her cup against the saucer in surprise. "Anne? What are you doing here? Are the boys all right?"

"All is fine." Anne chuckled and leaned to kiss her mother and hug Elizabeth's neck.

Something is afoot here. Elizabeth wanted to give her time. Perhaps her raised eyebrow and tapping foot would spur Anne on. This visit wasn't merely to see them.

"Are you ready for my news?" Anne spread her arms wide and then clapped her hands in front of her.

Elizabeth scooted to the edge of her chair. "Out with it, my sister."

"Well," Anne paused. "I'm expecting another baby, in May or June, as far as I can tell!" Pure joy radiated from her face. Elizabeth could almost seize it in the air.

Jumping out of her seat, Elizabeth reached for Anne's hands. "And you thought all these years that your two boys were the end. What a wonderful surprise!"

Her mother embraced Anne, adding her tears to the mixture. "I'm ready for another baby in the family. It's been a while since John."

"I know. He's already six years old." Anne managed to rest her body in a high-backed chair. Her fingers and feet still jittered to and fro.

Elizabeth hadn't thought about the possibility of another nephew or niece, at least not from Anne. "I'm so happy for you. What does Robert say?"

"He is thrilled, although naturally concerned about me. It's not that I'm too old; I'll only be twenty-nine when the baby comes."

"You will be fine." Her mother covered her mouth and took a deep breath. "Oh, a baby."

The rest of tea time was filled with plans for the baby, possible names, and overwhelming thankfulness. For the afternoon, the wedding took second place.

Laughter, mixed with concern, escaped Elizabeth's throat. "Do you think you can still fit in your dress for the wedding?" It seemed like a selfish thought, but could she?

Anne giggled, as she covered her belly with her hands. "Have no fear. These next few weeks will not cause a change. You planned the wedding date perfectly."

Later, alone in her room, wanting to read, but with her thoughts elsewhere, Elizabeth not for the first time envisioned her life with Louis and children. Would they be blessed like her sister? Sequestered away were the woes of business, politics, and safety. Elizabeth had decided, together with Louis, to depend on God and his wisdom.

Elizabeth stepped back from the semicircle of young ladies and admired them in their white dresses, each a unique style, but all crisp and pristine, perfect for the recital. "Girls, I'm proud of each of you. You've worked hard this term and now you have the opportunity to present your best work to your parents and family."

She poked her head out of the curtain to view the auditorium. A full house. She wouldn't share that information since the girls' nerves were on high alert already.

"When it's your turn, go directly to the pianoforte exactly like we rehearsed. Don't be concerned about the audience. Smile and enjoy the moment."

In order to relieve their anxiety early, the younger ones were first on the program. "The First Nowell" was the cue for the second group to assemble. The last group consisted of four advanced, talented pianists, including Martha Laurens. She opened the section with Handel's "Hallelujah Chorus" from his "Messiah." The crowd was enthralled with the selection and her performance. A few pieces later Martha closed the program with "Joy to the World." What a perfect way to dismiss the girls for the winter break!

At the conclusion, the girls and Elizabeth formed a long line on the stage, joined hands, and bowed to the audience. When the crowd moved to the reception area, Louis and Sarah approached Elizabeth on either side. She quickly linked arms with each of them, her exuberance shining in her eyes and wide smile.

"Success. Congratulations, Elizabeth," he whispered in her ear. "A major feat is behind you."

"Yes. And now I can fully concentrate on the wedding for the next two weeks," she promised. The lingering touch of his hand on her waist momentarily blocked the guests from her mind. Two weeks? Why not today? Right now? She shook her head.

"All is under control in that department," Louis said.

She was dazed. Louis and Sarah stared at her. "What?"

"The wedding, silly. Don't forget you have your mother and Jeannette handling all of the minute details," Sarah stressed. Elizabeth felt a little relief at the reminder.

"Then I will just have to spend my time bothering you both. How do you plan to entertain me for such a long time?" She laughed, not concerned a bit. She definitely wouldn't be bored with them vying for her attention.

"Well, one of us here has to work. The busy Christmas season doesn't stop for a wedding—even our wedding. But I promise to leave a few evenings free," Louis teased as he released Elizabeth.

Hopefully, as she mingled with the parents and students, Louis didn't mind being a spectator in the room as she floated among the occupants of the hall. She kept him in her peripheral view, and her confidence soared with his presence in the room. Soon, she would call him husband and obtain permission to have him near whenever she liked.

CHAPTER 12

*I*t would have been a stressful week for Louis anyway, with business, preparation for Christmas, and excitement for the wedding—all positive endeavors. But another item invaded, leaving negative thoughts: off the shores of Charles Town, an immense confrontation was brewing. The anticipated, but unwanted, arrival of the promised goods of the East India Company was a powder keg waiting to explode.

Why now?

Louis tried to replace conflicting announcements with wedding bells and solemn vows. But on the evening tide of Wednesday, December first, Captain Alexander Curling ran the *London* over the bar and came to anchor in the harbor.

As Louis finished shelving bags of beans and rice, Uncle Henry entered the front part of the store, chuckling as he leaned against the wall.

"What have you heard to make you so cheerful?" Louis asked.

"Just thinking about poor captain Curly. After a seven-week journey, the captain probably expected an easy distribution of his cargo, maybe a little rest on land before he returned with a new shipment of goods from the colonies and the West Indies."

Louis laughed. "Yes. And now he is stranded in the harbor. I bet he didn't sign up for this treatment."

"I believe the rumors circulating for weeks are really facts, at least according to the *Gazette* and the Liberty Boys," Henry said.

That evening Louis saw a predetermined system of communication take on a life of its own. Mr. Timothy of the *Gazette* and Christopher Gadsden of the Sons of Liberty had already encouraged local resistance to the unloading of the tea and the collection of duties. Their call to action spread across town quicker than any piece of gossip.

On the morning of December second, Christopher sent a message to Louis, requesting a brief meeting at his office. Louis appreciated the chance to hear firsthand what the town could expect. So much had happened so quickly that he hadn't discussed the details person to person.

Louis knocked on Christopher's door.

"Come in. Have a seat." Christopher sat behind his desk. "How are the wedding plans?"

"Fine, as far as I know. I don't have to worry about that part of my life. But tell me about all the rumors floating around."

"Our opinion—meaning mine and the Sons of Liberty—is that the acceptance of the tea on the *London* would establish a precedent. It would confirm the power assumed by Parliament to pass whatever law for the colonies that it wants. We can't let that happen. Therefore, the tea will not be accepted. Timothy has helped by having handbills circulated across the town and notices posted along Broad Street. Have you seen them yet?"

"No, but I'm sure Tradd and Church Street will soon be covered."

"Well, here is a handbill." Christopher handed Louis a sheet of paper with the explanation of the stand the citizens of Charles Town were taking with the tea.

"Hopefully, the people are ready to face life without their usual tea." Louis wasn't surprised at any of the information.

Christopher placed another item in Louis' hand. "Here, take the latest newspaper that has all the comments and further arguments from the British and some of Charles Town's finest citizens."

Louis left with a newspaper in one hand and a handbill in the other. It appeared the Liberty Boys wanted the world to know about their stand.

❀

After lunch, Elizabeth set out for a brisk walk. Actually, she wanted to get away from the demanding, sometimes hysterical, pleas of her mother. Demands to try on the dress again, look over the menu, or confirm the choice of flowers. All had been done numerous times before. Sanity lay just around the corner as she turned onto Tradd Street. She adjusted her hat and shawl, hoping to look presentable for Louis.

A young boy stepped right in front of her, causing her to miss a step, and presented her with a handbill. She accepted the paper with curiosity. "What's this?"

"I don't know, Miss. I just do what Mr. Timothy tells me. Good day." The boy moved on, ready to pass along another sheet.

She read it as she walked slowly:

All citizens of Charles Town and surrounding areas, including land-holders, artisans, and merchants, are invited to assemble in the Great Hall over the Exchange at three o'clock on Friday afternoon. The sense of the people will be taken, and plans formulated on what should be done about the recent arrival of the cargo of tea.

Before she could grasp what she was reading, Elizabeth faced Jeannette across the counter at Wilson's Mercantile, her destination. She must have maneuvered herself by instinct.

She placed the paper on the clean, white surface. "Have you seen this, Jeannette?"

Her usual greeting contained a brilliant smile, but not today

"Yes, a few minutes ago one appeared on my desk. Henry had alluded to something like this after the last Sons of Liberty meeting. It seems the hour of action has come." Jeannette didn't bother to hide her disappointment.

"What do you think will happen?" Elizabeth sought any sign of encouragement.

"I say, you don't worry about it, and let the men reach a decision." With no word of encouragement, Jeannette looked away.

A heavy weight of uncertainty entered her domain. "But don't you see? This will decide whether we reach a compromise. Our safety and future are at stake." If she were honest, it was subconsciously there all along. The potential for conflict loomed daily, not just in the handbill.

"Elizabeth." That voice put her smile back in place. "I knew you would come see me today." Louis came up behind her and spun her around. He openly planted a kiss on her cheek and secured both her hands in his.

She twirled her skirt and tilted her head to the side. "Well, my visit wasn't entirely selfish. Mother needs a few things and desires confirmation that her order will be delivered on time. Louis, I had to escape. The house is—"

"—full of love and preparation for the wedding?" He laughed. "Or is it a mad house?"

"I was going to say, 'crazy house.' I think the only sane place is wherever you are." Her mother's dominance over the wedding and the Sons of Liberty's preoccupation with the tea left Louis as the only safe place in her life.

"What's this?" he asked as the paper in her hand interfered with holding her fingers. He didn't wait for her answer. "Oh, the handbill. I saw one earlier. Christopher didn't waste much time getting them out."

Rising on her tiptoes, she searched his face for clues, for excitement, anything. "Are you going, Louis?"

There, in the crinkles by his eyes, if not excitement, then questions. "Of course. Not many of the businessmen in town will miss this meeting. Not only will it affect all of us now, but it will lay the course for any future assemblies."

"What do you think the answer will be?"

"At this store, we no longer order or handle their tea. We've made the switch, but for the others, the loss of the tea will be a shock."

Now, it was her turn to raise her brows in question. "So, you feel the town won't accept the shipment?" she restated.

"Not if the majority of the citizens see matters the way we do. This is our time to take a stand. Maybe this will work even better than the boycotts before. Anyway, don't think about it too much. Think about becoming my wife in eight days. I never thought I would be this happy about sharing my life with someone. You changed that, Elizabeth."

Her smile pushed the boycotts to the background. "Yes, I did. And don't you forget it. Now what about meeting me for tea down the street at four o'clock before all the tea is gone?" She challenged lightly, breaking the sense of doom.

Even though the talk of the town was focused on tea, well-wishers about the wedding managed to cross her path. Since the banns of marriage had been posted for the last two Sundays, parishioners of St. Philip's had offered their genuine words of encouragement and blessing. At least she took it as acceptance and good will. Knowing how some viewed foreigners and Partisans, Elizabeth was aware that some negative gossip existed.

On Friday afternoon, Elizabeth planned to spend her time with Anne, mostly to escape her father and his ranting about the Liberty meeting. She would wait for word from Louis about the proceedings, but she couldn't stand the huffing and puffing seeping through the walls of her house.

Elizabeth hoped to find Anne happily sewing or reading, performing some fretless task. Instead, her sister carried the same concern about the meeting as Elizabeth. At least she had the boys to occupy her time. No one could keep a solemn face for long around them. And here, Elizabeth had someone on her side, unlike at home with her parents.

"I'm so tired of all the meetings and agendas. I keep hoping for a practical, positive solution, and most likely there isn't one. Louis is becoming entrenched in the cause." Elizabeth raised her eyes from the boys to Anne. "I'm sorry to burden you with my concerns."

"Robert is as deeply involved with this as Louis and any other businessman. He relies on the ability to transport items across friendly seas," Anne shared as they watched the boys play on the floor with their building blocks. "I don't see how any of us gets out of this unscathed. But what can we do but support our men?"

The boys made a stable and fortress for their horses and men. Were they soldiers? Elizabeth noted the irony of that since the town was facing such a volatile situation. Boys and their toys. Men and their weapons. And the role of women? Was it to watch their world fall apart, to do nothing? Hardly. She knew the women would do their part to protect their way of life, their children and husbands. Right now, it was a wait-and-see proposition.

On the other end of town, Louis noted it wasn't a tea party or a quiet get-together at which he sat. No nice china, amber tea pouring from silver pots, or tiny sandwiches. No talk of the weather, balls, or family. Strictly politics, money, and loyalties. A newspaper reporter's paradise or a politician's platform. Without realizing the overall ramification of decisions made that Friday, men filled the Great Hall of the Exchange by three o'clock. Louis felt energized and ready to face the decisions to be made. Looking around the room, he saw only four other merchants present. The artisans and planters were out in full force, probably since they believed they had the most to lose.

Louis faced Henry. "It appears that other merchants in town have declared their allegiance to the Crown by their lack of attendance."

"Don't be too surprised. They profit from selling British goods, and the decision today might set them back in profits. Don't forget, we had to make that decision earlier," his uncle emphasized.

With his elbows on his knees, Louis looked at the planks on the floor. "Even so, I think I would want to know firsthand what was being decided for me." He looked around at the anticipation on the faces of many.

A distinguished man who had been elected to preside over the meeting stepped forward. Christopher made the introduction. "Colonel George Gabriel Powell will serve as moderator for us. As you know, he has been an advocate of our rights in the assembly when it was functioning. His experience in the Craven County militia, his ownership of land and dealings with the issue at hand, has moved him to give his time to try to unite all artisans, merchants, and planters on this one issue."

Louis could tell that much work had been done beforehand by a handful of people like Gadsden, Timothy, Laurens, and Manigault, who were outspoken for the colonists' cause. They presented a document drafted for consideration.

Christopher read it aloud: "We, the undersigned, do hereby agree not to import, either directly or indirectly, any teas that will pay the present duty laid by an act of the British Parliament for the purpose of raising revenue in America."

Straightforward enough. Louis and Henry's foresightedness not to place orders with Britain over the last year had relieved them of any repercussions on profit. It would hurt other merchants, though.

A committee was appointed to circulate the letter and secure the signatures of all merchants involved in the import trade with Britain. Then Powell stated in a firm voice, "Those of you present who want to sign the resolution now, we give you that opportunity," Powell stated.

Henry stood up and turned to Louis. "Let's be the first in line and show them how it's done." As they stepped forward, a line of artisans, planters, and the general population present formed behind them.

Standing there at the table, for a fraction of a second, Louis held the quill poised over the document. Then resolve and commitment determined his signature. *I refuse the abuse of Parliament.*

This was the first radical act in which Louis had participated, if one didn't count storing and shipping arms. There was no backing out from here. His signature bound him as his word did also. His future father-in-law was sure to hear about it. Louis wasn't one to stand on a corner and protest or proclaim liberty, although he accepted the cause in his heart. But his name on this important document sealed his promises, no longer by word only.

Commotion from the back doors of the room came at the conclusion of the meeting. "Who could that be?" Louis turned with the crowd to see three men being led by three Sons of Liberty members to the front of the room. The crowd split as if the newcomers were performers entering the audience, allowing important actors a grand entrance. If only the whole situation were a play.

"You know them," Henry whispered. "They're agents of the East India Company, well-known merchants in town."

Louis did recognize them. But why were they here? Christopher introduced them as Roger Smith, Peter Leger, and William Greenwood. They stood and faced the large group. Louis wondered if they had been forewarned about what was expected of them, because they didn't speak, yell, or protest. Possibly the men had been coaxed with harsh words or vague threats before entering the building that they wouldn't receive the tea.

"It appears these men want to join you in signing the document and rejecting the tea," Christopher's voice boomed across the room. Facing the dominating forces and faces of friends and fellow businessmen, the three signed the document. Immediate clapping and roars of approval greeted them. Louis wondered if coercion was the best form of action. Once again he was glad he'd chosen months ago his present side.

"Huzzah, huzzah for liberty."

As Louis walked home with Uncle Henry in the fading light of the late December afternoon, he tried to get a handle on what just transpired. In its basic form, a ship with a cargo of tea was anchored in the harbor, and some of the citizens of Charles Town now protested the unloading of the goods. Simple, in a dramatic way, with formidable potential.

"I don't envy the committee trying to secure the other merchants' signatures. It was wise for them to put Christopher on the team. He is powerful, wealthy, and well-known. The other four are also well-to-do, respected men," Louis paused. "Now what do we tell the women?"

"The truth," Uncle Henry responded. "The truth, for it will affect them as well. I know Jeannette and Elizabeth won't shrink from the implications of the resolution."

CHAPTER 13

"I just don't see a peaceful solution." Louis sat in the Cochrans' parlor immediately after the meeting. "The captain of the *London* would have to leave with his cargo intact and be able to convince the British to compromise. And he really has no say in the politics or the Tea Act." Louis sat forward with his elbows on his knees. After looking at Elizabeth's face full of concern and question, he couldn't have hidden the truth. It appeared Robert felt the same way.

Elizabeth looked back and forth from Louis to Robert. "If that's the case, how long will the ship remain in the harbor?" she inquired.

"For a few weeks at least. We're now most likely to hear from the British Crown. I wish we knew what the other ports are doing. Shipments were to arrive in New York, Boston, and Philadelphia about the same time," Louis said.

"So, we wait," Anne commented as she traced the pattern on the chair with her finger. "I wish all of this would go away. I feel like we've been living under a shadow for a long time. Could anything good come out of this meeting?"

Robert grasped Anne's wayward hand. "In an ideal world, both parties have an opportunity to make compromises and mend fences. But in our present reality, I doubt many concessions will be made."

Louis' eyes connected with the clear gray of Elizabeth's as she smiled and focused on him. "Nothing can be done today. Surely there is something on the horizon to lift our spirits."

"Why don't you two stay for supper with us?" Anne suggested.

With clapping, Elizabeth sealed the invitation. "I have no plans until Grandmamma arrives tomorrow."

Anne rose and informed the cook of the additional guests.

Elizabeth turned to Louis, pulling him to his feet as she focused on her grandmother. "You'll love Grandmamma, Louis, just love her."

"I have no doubt." He would love anyone who held Elizabeth's heartstrings. The reportedly vivacious woman arriving on the ship the next afternoon would indeed bring much joy, if he read Elizabeth correctly.

The next day, Louis found Elizabeth in her parlor. "It's time. The ship is pulling into the harbor right now," Louis said. "Are you ready to go?" He'd promised to call for her the minute he heard. She peered out the window at the carriage. He'd handled every detail down to saving her grandmother a walk from the harbor, as if anyone in the family would have made her leave the ship and arrive to the house on foot.

Excited or anxious? Elizabeth found it hard to keep still. Nothing could stop her from meeting her grandmother on the wharf. "On time, like the messenger told us yesterday. What time is it?"

Louis checked his pocket watch. "Four o'clock."

"The ship is even a little early. Let's go." She put on her blue wool coat, placed her straw hat on her head, and grabbed Louis' sleeve. "I want to be there before she comes ashore."

Louis stopped her before they ran out the door. "Aren't you going to tell your parents?"

"How silly of me. Of course." She left him in the foyer and found her mother in the drawing room.

She almost skidded into the chair, grabbing the back before tumbling into her mother's lap. "Louis and I are off to meet Grandmamma. He has the carriage waiting outside." She felt like a child getting a puppy. "I'm so excited."

"I see that you are." Her mother leaned back peering at Elizabeth. Did Elizabeth look strange or something? She checked her hair with her fingertips. All seemed in place. "You enjoy yourself, and I'll see you when you return. Tell your grandmother I'm waiting for her here."

No one, except maybe Anne, shared her enthusiasm for Grandmamma. Her mother certainly didn't. Whatever their disagreements or past problems, Elizabeth wouldn't let that upset her visit.

At the waterfront, Louis stayed by her side. She wanted him to have a firsthand view of one of her favorite people. In only a few minutes, the petite woman in a gray wool overcoat with a hood pulled closely around her face appeared on the walkway.

"Grandmamma." Elizabeth traded Louis' arm for her grandmother's embrace. "How was your voyage? I have so much to tell you. But first, I want you to meet Louis Lestarjette."

"I would have traveled twice the distance to see you this happy, Elizabeth. Now let me look at you, Louis."

Elizabeth stepped back and watched Louis and Grandmamma exchange kisses on the cheeks. Theirs would be a fine and fast relationship. She wanted to clap her hands, but instead she secured them behind her back. All was working as she'd imagined.

Elizabeth took her grandmother's hand and Louis' arm and moved to the carriage. "Let's get you home out of the cold.

Mother has everything prepared." She couldn't think of any two people she would rather be with.

Half an hour later, after Louis brought them home with the luggage and left for the evening, Grandmamma was safely and securely nestled into one of the Elliotts' most comfortable chairs. She had everyone waiting on her. Elizabeth didn't want to leave her side. "You are the best wedding present ever. Thank you for coming, Grandmamma."

"I couldn't miss this event. I'm not that old, and I'm not an invalid, although your mother treats me that way."

Elizabeth peered up at her from her perch on the floor. She wanted to be close, so sitting at her grandmother's feet gave her a place to talk cozily and hold the woman's hands securely in hers. Mother and Father had disappeared to dress for the evening meal. The time alone with her grandmother seemed like a precious prize.

"I have a gift for you, Elizabeth. Hand me that bag right behind you, dear." A sturdy, heavy canvas bag rested close to her chair. "Elizabeth, this was a wedding gift to me from my mother. It came from Switzerland, her homeland. I want you to have it."

Elizabeth carefully unwrapped a beautiful silver sugar bowl. "But this is the one you use at your home." Elizabeth caressed the piece.

"And now, you are to use it at yours. You are to make your own new memories around it. Picture your family and friends enjoying time with you over tea."

Her grandmother handed her another item and then another until a complete tea set emerged on a silver tray. Elizabeth placed it on the table. "Thank you so much." She kissed her grandmother on both cheeks. "The set will have a special place in our home. Louis will love it as much as I do."

The older woman had a sparkle in her bright eyes as if giving Elizabeth a part of herself. "Now show me to my room and help me find a dress for tonight. We mustn't keep your parents waiting."

❀

The Sunday service was special to Elizabeth—as the third Sunday of the bann, it was the last she and Louis would attend as an unmarried couple. Were there more people than usual? Elizabeth looked around. After seeking a closer assigned section, the Wilsons had moved nearer to the Elliotts' row over the last couple of weeks. And today Louis occupied the seat next to her.

It was hard to concentrate with Louis so near. As she sang, Elizabeth found herself listening to his strong voice. The words of the hymn "Praise the Lord who reigns above" rang true, and soon she worshipped, despite the momentary distraction. She closed her eyes, concentrating on God alone.

I must keep those words of praise in the forefront in the days ahead. I must focus on the power and control of God. He is the answer to any dilemma on the horizon, even a horizon with unwanted ships, with uncertainty on the waves.

As if the words of the hymn weren't enough, the Scripture that Reverend Smith read eradicated any feelings of fear or doubt and once again focused on God's power. Rock. Shelter. Tower. Tabernacle. She planned to make Psalm 61 a part of her daily prayer. *If I can keep God in His proper place as number one, then I can keep fear at bay.*

When Louis greeted Grandmamma after the service, Elizabeth almost felt the embrace, devoid of pretense and formality. The graceful woman's actions implied acceptance, but also expectations. Elizabeth wondered if Louis could see the challenge her grandmother set forth to take care of her granddaughter in every way. She wasn't privy to their words of exchange, however, for her grandmother passed them off in a whisper. Already they were

150

sharing secrets. She smiled at the indication these two would be close.

Elizabeth placed herself in front of them. Would she have to physically separate them? "You two can continue your conversation over dinner, if you would care to join us." She laughed.

"I think we can manage that. Don't you, Louis?" Grandmamma winked at him and set out to join Elizabeth's parents.

Louis crossed his arms and brought a finger to his lips. "How different your grandmother is from your mother. I can see who you take after," Louis reasoned.

"I'm definitely taking that as a compliment." She linked her arm in his for the journey to the Elliotts'. Although skipping was out of the question, Elizabeth saw no harm in bouncing a bit.

Every minute of the next week was full for almost everyone involved in the wedding. Elizabeth popped in with Jeannette at Louis' house on occasion. There Mrs. Engle, Amy, and Tom worked especially hard on various projects, from polishing, placing greenery, pressing sheets and tablecloths. It seemed they were determined to make the Lestarjette house as close to perfect as possible. She tried to tell them that they needn't work so hard for her benefit. Since Louis had occupied the house on Church Street for a few weeks, the rooms appeared lived in and inviting. But not quite home to Elizabeth—not yet, at least.

On Tuesday afternoon, Mrs. Engle helped Elizabeth arrange her clothes in the armoire. It was all rather strange to Elizabeth. For the first time, she really thought about being in charge of her own home. She stopped in the middle of placing a dress on a hanger, dazed and confused.

Mrs. Engle approached her with furrowed brow. "Are you all right, Miss Elliott?"

Elizabeth snapped out of her dead stare and began moving

again, but rather slowly and deliberately. "Yes. I think so." She looked at the older woman. Elizabeth didn't know how much she should share. "You'll think I'm silly, but it just dawned on me, like waking from a dream, that in a few days I'll be mistress of this house and a wife. And honestly, I don't know if I'll be good at either. What if I mess it all up? What if I make lots of mistakes? Am I fooling myself, thinking I can be what Louis needs?"

Mrs. Engle reached out for Elizabeth's hand. "Miss Elliott, do you mind if I say a few words?" Elizabeth nodded and let Mrs. Engle guide her to a big stuffed chair by the window. "I don't think you have anything to fear from Mr. Lestarjette. All he talks about is your living here and filling the house with your presence. I promise you the rest will take care of itself. I'm here to help you."

On impulse, Elizabeth hugged her as if it was something she did every day. Actually, she wished she had that kind of relationship. "Oh, Mrs. Engle, you're such an encouragement. I know I'll depend on you a lot. I do hope we can be good friends. May I call you Ellen?"

"Of course, ma'am." The request put a huge smile on Ellen's face.

In those final days, many of Elizabeth's hours were spent with her family, her grandmother in particular. Most of the time Elizabeth felt like she was simply supposed to show up on time for each event—dinners, visits, parties. She loved having her grandmother around to fill her days of waiting.

"Grandmamma?" Elizabeth searched each room downstairs. "Where are you?"

"In here." Elizabeth followed the familiar voice to the parlor. Sitting in the corner chair with embroidery in hand, Grandmamma stopped her task and looked up. "What do you need, dear?"

Elizabeth plopped down, feet sprawled out, hands upturned. "Nothing, except a quiet place, or not even quiet—just a place to exist without boxes, baskets, and trunks of things. Getting married is exhausting."

"I guess it is, dear," Grandmamma said.

Elizabeth giggled and brushed a curl off her forehead. "Do I want this? So many decisions. It goes on and on. Does anyone ever elope anymore?" She closed her eyes and sighed. "I thought we were going to have to do that. I didn't know how soon Father would relent."

"You went about it all in the right manner, with patience." Elizabeth cherished her grandmother's words. She supposed it was worth it all, just like her grandmother insinuated.

Shrugging, Elizabeth knew those words did not describe her. "I don't know how patient I was. Luckily, Father only put a one-month trial period on us. Would I have waited two, three, or six months for an answer?"

Was her grandmother chuckling as she tried to speak? "Yes, you would have. You're young, and the time would have hurried by. But God saw fit to grant you a quick answer to your prayer, and here you are a few days before your fairy-tale wedding."

Yes, but still, elopement would have had the same results. Elizabeth sighed and kissed Grandmamma on the cheek. She would have understood.

The last chance for Louis and Elizabeth to go out together before the wedding was on Wednesday evening. Elizabeth chose her green taffeta dress with her red wool cape, thick black boots, hat, and gloves—none of it new, but all dependable to fight the chilly night. Louis picked her up in a carriage at seven. Once inside the warm interior of the coach, Louis sat close to her. "I wonder if we could have dinner in here instead," he suggested.

"Hmm, and what would the neighbors think?" she responded, knowing full well that he would stick to his plans. In answer, he knocked on the ceiling, the driver guided the horses into the breezy night.

"One thing different about Charles Town is that distance is not a major factor. In Paris this carriage ride to dinner would take thirty minutes or more. Here ten minutes is a long drive." He pulled her closer still. "Not long enough for me to just sit back and enjoy your company in silence."

"You could have the driver go around in circles," she proposed.

"He's already taking the long way around to add a whole five minutes."

"Oh." She snuggled in to his warm embrace, coerced to stay there by the fact that it would end soon.

Dinner was at the Grand Hotel. An elegant table was set with the finest china and silverware. The meal—consisting of pheasant and venison, legumes and pasta, cheese quiche, biscuits, and soufflé for dessert—tasted delicious to Elizabeth. The candlelight and Louis satisfied her expectations of the evening. Part of her wanted it to last and the other part to hurry so she would be married.

"A toast to you, Elizabeth, for making me the happiest man alive!"

"I think you mean, 'To us.' To a lifetime of happiness and love." As the glasses clicked together with harmony, Elizabeth's heart somersaulted.

"I have a surprise for you at the house—at our house," Louis added.

"Another surprise for me, Louis? It seems I get something every day." She really didn't mind all the attention, but her one wish was to have Louis as her husband.

"This one is my wedding present to you. I won't tell you, so be patient."

She was curious. Excitement exploded with anticipation of a special, meaningful gift. She still hadn't given Louis his wedding gift. Soon she would.

After the carriage ride to their house, Louis escorted her through the entrance hall to the formal parlor with her eyes closed. She trusted him as he guided her across the room around the furniture to the fireplace on the far wall.

"Now, open your eyes," he whispered as his hands touched her shoulders.

Dominating her view, shining and sparkling with the light from nearby candles, stood two solid silver candlesticks unlike any she had seen before. "Oh, Louis, they are marvelous, beautiful. Where in the world did you get them?" Words tumbled from her as she reached for one and held it in her hands. Holding it close to her heart, she took one step toward Louis and kissed him.

"Was that a thank you?" he teased as he returned her kiss. The candlestick between them urged him to step back. "These came from Paris, especially made and crafted for you. If you notice the base, you'll see tiny flowers tapering into the stand reminding me of you." She studied the one in her hand and traced the delicate pattern. "The pair will represent our marriage and the light that will come from it." He paused and breathed the words, "I love you, Elizabeth."

"And I love you. Thank you." As she placed the candlestick back on the mantel, a tiny tear landed on its base. A tear of joy and love. Life with Louis was full of surprises. But even if she never received another gift, their shared life would be enough.

CHAPTER 14

The politics of the town had not ceased simply because of his wedding. Louis found it hard to separate one subject from the other. "I know politics doesn't recognize the events of death, birth, and marriage—only of power, money, law, war, and sometimes peace. But I do wish for one month when we wouldn't be bombarded by the news of Parliament and committees." Louis looked at Henry.

"Have you heard anything from the Signature Committee?" Uncle Henry asked. His uncle certainly didn't have the power to stop the political drama. Did anyone?

Louis paused after placing a sack of flour by a front row of shelves. He leaned on the edge of the top row and wiped his hands on his apron. "According to Christopher, the committee is still trying to secure the signatures of more members. It appears the pressures of the wealthy and powerful leaders did not influence all of them. A group of merchants have refused to join."

Henry replaced a canister of nails on the shelf. "I know why they're taking a stand: for profit."

Louis nodded. "Exactly. They have ordered tea from the East

India Company. It's their business, their livelihood. They see personal benefit by accepting the tea."

"I hear there's a meeting this afternoon at Mrs. Swallow's Tavern on Broad Street." Henry adjusted a row of preserves and spices. "They plan to form the Charles Town Chamber of Commerce in opposition to the Sons of Liberty's signature proposal."

"So, the debate is on, and the lines are drawn," Louis stated. "And the tea, all 250 or so chests of it, is still rocking on the ship in the harbor—to land or not to land?" *And our lives are expected to continue in some kind of normal fashion, including my wedding?* Louis drew in a deep breath with no way to solve this issue, not today.

In the middle of organizing wedding gifts in the parlor, Elizabeth spied Louis leaning against the doorpost. "How did you sneak in unannounced?" She raced to him and draped her arms around his neck. He drew her closer and kissed her.

He smiled and pushed Elizabeth gently out by her shoulders, looking over her shoulder for any prying eyes. "I brought items from the store for your mother."

"What an excuse, Louis. I know Tom could have delivered them." She pulled him into the parlor. From a table beside the door, she hoisted a wrapped gift in her hands. "But since you're here...this is your wedding gift. I thought this was appropriate since our love is based on God's love."

Louis removed the paper and exposed a new Bible with black leather binding. He ran his fingers over the smooth surface. "It's cherished already, Elizabeth. And it will always be the center of our lives together. The Lestarjette family Bible." He turned to the page near the front reserved for recording the family information. "Here, we'll write our names and our children. All the births, weddings, baptisms, and deaths."

Elizabeth leaned in and followed his finger down the page with her own. He trapped her hand under his and brought it to his lips.

Her voice had a wispy cadence as a prayer. "Our family, Louis. All those written in here will be part of us."

Our family. Words she wanted to hear every day to carry her through the years, especially the near future with all the newness awaiting her.

The bridal party and family gathered at the formal celebration of the wedding the next day. Sheer joy replaced Elizabeth's nerves and fears of a few days before. Not even the absence of her brother marred the occasion. All of these people gathered because in some way each had a connection of love for her, for Louis. Elizabeth brought her hand to her heart as she focused on each one. *Thank you, Lord.*

The little boys delighted in the food and the attention from the adults. Tonight, her nephews were not sent off to separate rooms. Elizabeth was thrilled to have them active around everyone, playing with their wooden soldiers and horses. The eldest of the guests, Elizabeth's grandmother, sat in regal fashion on a sofa, offering lively conversation to any who stopped by her. Robert stayed close to Anne, placing an arm lightly behind her back, obviously proud to be an expectant father again.

Her mother scurried around as she kept the refreshments flowing and plates full. Delightful sandwiches appeared, garnished with shrimp relish and muscadine jelly. Dainty, flaky pastries filled with lemon and peach preserves disappeared quickly. While Mother bustled around in her element as hostess, her father entertained the guests, a task he did easily, always able to find a topic of interest. Elizabeth had requested politics be banned tonight.

Her gaze settled on Louis. Louis, the one who caused her heart to expand with love she hadn't known existed. Because of him, this celebration brought them all together.

Louis stood beside his aunt and uncle, his only family in this vast country. Before long Elizabeth realized Jeannette and Henry were very comfortable with the others, especially Reverend Smith and his wife, Louise.

Martha Laurens, a little young for a grown-up party, stayed close to the Smiths. Elizabeth made her way through the group to her side. Martha whispered, "I feel so proud to be a bridesmaid. My aunt has made sure I have new dresses for my role in the parties."

Elizabeth mingled with everyone, ending up with Sarah and Samuel—the only two without partners. Elizabeth looked closer. They did seem remarkably comfortable together. She wondered if she was interrupting something. Never had she felt like an intruder with them, usually the opposite, always the one to keep Sarah on her feet. She raised her eyebrows at the questionable difference tonight. Though the two included her in their conversation, they definitely had the situation under control. Finally, after months of placing them together, it appeared they were finding each other's company enjoyable and even desirable.

When Louis distracted Samuel with a question, Sarah linked arms with Elizabeth as they walked across the room. "Elizabeth, you don't seem nervous at all. I think I'd be in a state of shock, unable to function properly. But you're all smiles, and there's not a jittery thing about you."

Elizabeth hoped her smile was contagious, causing all in the room, even her fretful mother, to rejoice. She hoped all could forget the outside world for a few hours.

She patted her friend's hand linked in her arm. "You'll understand one day, Sarah. When it is right, there is peace and serenity."

Glancing across the room, Elizabeth found Louis still engaged in a conversation with Henry and Samuel. But not so involved he didn't search out Elizabeth every few moments. Their eyes met, confirming Elizabeth's words—peace, serenity, and love.

The sounding of the dinner bell gathered the party at the large, elegant mahogany table with six legs surrounded by mahogany Queen Anne chairs. The table extended to seat the fourteen guests. The men seated the ladies before taking their places. Her father offered a toast. Elizabeth knew, despite his twinge of misgiving, he trusted God, Elizabeth, and even Louis. If he didn't, how could he give his daughter away?

"To Elizabeth and Louis. May you find life together to be full of blessings and many years of happiness."

"Huzzah! Huzzah!" Congratulations came from everyone, including the little boys. Elizabeth noticed their tendencies to mimic the actions of the adults.

Grandmamma pushed her chair back and stood in front of it. "Excuse me, I have a few words to add." She looked directly at Elizabeth and held her glass at elbow level. "I couldn't be happier for Elizabeth and Louis. I don't imagine their way will be easy, but I do predict years of wonderful memories. You have my support and blessing." She raised her glass and winked at Elizabeth and then at Louis.

Elizabeth covered a giggle with her closed-mouth smile. She didn't doubt her grandmother's sincerity. But she also knew Grandmamma's bias. She'd probably love anyone Elizabeth loved.

The meal was more like a feast to feed royalty. Mrs. Engle from Louis' household and Anne's cook partnered with the Elliott household to prepare the succulent fare—pork, venison, soup, hominy, lentils, lima beans, meat pies, breads, plum pudding, ratafia drops, coconut puffs, and jumbles.

"My favorite—venison topped with tomatoes and steaming brown rice," Louis commented as he took a generous serving.

Elizabeth noted the smile on her mother's face as all of the guests savored the vast amount of food. "Mother, why did you let out the secret about the ice cream? Look at the time Robert is having with his sons." Elizabeth laughed.

It was hard to contain the boys' enthusiasm for the desserts, but Robert was firm. "Pork before ice cream," Robert said. They settled down and made a dent in their food.

Not a glitch or a pause took place in conversation throughout the evening. Elizabeth stole quite a few glances of Louis, brushing hands under the table with him, whispering between discussions. Stolen seconds promised to be numerous and unhidden tomorrow. These precious moments bore witness to the immense love binding them together.

Louis took her hands and slipped with her into the tiny space under the stairs in the foyer. "Elizabeth, tomorrow we'll take the most important walk of our lives, down the aisle to make our vows before God and all our family." He placed her face between his hands and drew her lips to his. "A promise of many days of kisses whenever we want. And a promise of my unending devotion."

She followed his example and held his face in her hands. "I promise to love you forever and make your life exciting and a bit unpredictable."

"That I can believe." One last kiss before they faced their guests again.

Even after the departure of guests full of ice cream and delicate cakes, Elizabeth found it hard to sleep, knowing tomorrow her life would change forever. Forever to be the wife of Louis Lestarjette. Only by praying and thanking God for all her joy could she calmly close her eyes in a restful, deep sleep. She'd need the energy for the event of a lifetime.

CHAPTER 15

"I can't believe this day is here." Elizabeth twirled around in her wedding gown in the antechamber, awaiting her cue to enter the sanctuary. Although her hands remained steady, her heart beat a little faster. How was Louis? Did he have any qualms about their marriage? She prayed, and knew deep down, that his love and resolve was rock solid as hers. *God has joined us and is right here with us.* Fortunately, her physical appearance did not show her nervous anticipation rumbling in her inner core.

Anne fixed Elizabeth's veil one more time. "It is, and you are beautiful, my sister."

Elizabeth walked to the stained-glass window, closed her eyes, and soaked up the rays of sun shining through. It enveloped her. "It doesn't seem like December." The mild weather seemed appropriate to Elizabeth. Why shouldn't this day be beautiful?

Elizabeth paced the small room. "Has it really only been a few months since I fell in love with Louis? At times it feels like years and that this day would never get here." Anne was the only attendant remaining in the room. Sarah and Martha waited outside the door. Elizabeth was envious because they saw all the activity and even Louis. *If only I could see him for a moment. To tell him, what?*

That I love him. He knows that. Just to see that promise in his eyes. She'd see him soon enough.

"Love doesn't understand time," Anne said. "It can happen quickly or over a period of time. Yours needed little nurturing."

"Well, right now I want to run, not walk, down the aisle." *Straight into his arms.*

Anne covered her mouth and lowered her hand, hiding a giggle. "Elizabeth, you can't skip everything but the 'I do.'"

After Anne straightened Elizabeth's long, flowing, ivory silk train, she held Elizabeth at arm's length. Elizabeth focused on her, hoping to see wisdom and strength there. But she knew Anne could not go through this for her or even with her. This process, and whatever her life would hold, would be for Louis and her to figure out.

"You're so beautiful, my little sister. I know it seems like forever until you're finally married. But take hold of each moment. Enjoy each stage, each step, each part of your marriage. Soon you'll be like us, looking back over ten years. Make them memorable. But for now, breathe."

Elizabeth mimicked Anne's gentle breaths, in and out.

"I'm so happy you found your love." Anne hugged Elizabeth tightly.

"I couldn't have a better sister and friend. Thank you for giving me encouragement."

Elizabeth's eyes gleamed with hope and great anticipation. Her fears of being a good wife dissipated with the kind, wise words from Ellen earlier and now from Anne. What remained was a true desire to be the person God wanted her to be in her marriage. She didn't fear losing her identity, being swallowed up as merely a wife. Instead, she claimed the promise that she would be a help-mate, a partner in the journey.

Elizabeth grasped the bouquet of red camellias draped with greenery, received one last kiss from her sister, and took a deep, cleansing breathe. "All right, I'm ready. I think I hear the music."

She glided out of the chamber into the arms of Sarah and Martha and then to a sanctuary glowing with brilliant sunlight from the stained-glass windows, streaming colors across the pews and walls. She remained veiled until her father gently lifted the lace in order to kiss her cheek and place her hand in Louis'.

A single tear glistened as she searched Louis' face and found the reassurance and promise in his blue eyes. She would trust those eyes every day of her life. A blush spread across her cheeks as his gaze pierced deeply into her soul.

After she saw Louis, Elizabeth didn't notice the beautiful flower arrangements around the altar or the numerous candles glowing down the aisle any more. She noticed her husband-to-be in his cream-colored suit, complete with a long jacket with tails. It would not have mattered to Elizabeth what he wore, as long as he would say the words she longed to hear.

"I, Louis, take thee, Elizabeth, to be my wedded wife. To have and to hold from this day forward, for better, for worse, for richer, for poorer, in sickness or in health, to love and to cherish, till death do us part, according to God's holy ordinance. Thereto I plight thee my troth."

Elizabeth watched his lips move and felt each word in an intensity of shivers all the way to her toes. She wanted to touch his lips as he spoke, but vaguely remembered where she was and that her hands were grasped in his. She had to follow the order of the service.

Somehow her voice, a few levels above a whisper, pronounced each word clearly. "I, Elizabeth, take thee, Louis, to be my lawful husband."

She wanted to bounce up and down. Instead, her feet remained in place, and her vows promised Louis love to last the tests of time.

With a solid gold band on her finger and a kiss for the world to see, she heard the words she had longed to hear, for perhaps a lifetime, come from Rev. Smith's mouth.

"I now present to you, Mr. and Mrs. Louis Lestarjette."

After staring at her new husband for what seemed like hours, Elizabeth turned to Anne, Sarah, and Martha to receive their silent adulations. Even her mother and father beamed, despite the tears in her mother's eyes. Her grandmother gave her a knowing nod, confirming her confidence in Elizabeth and her right decision. Jeannette extended her hand to Elizabeth, and Henry smiled at them. So many people—and all Elizabeth wanted was one. She squeezed his arm as they walked into the foyer of the church.

"Let's run away straight to the house," Louis whispered. Elizabeth felt he was ready to bolt and pull her behind him.

"And miss the meal?" she teased. "What would the town say? What would Mr. Timothy place in the paper? 'Husband and wife unaccounted for moments after their vows.'" She giggled, realizing the suggestion was in jest. A good one, but highly inappropriate.

The meal at Anne's house gave guests the opportunity to mingle with Elizabeth and Louis. Elizabeth understood the necessity of the event and wouldn't deny the friends and family members the opportunity to celebrate.

Father sat beside Elizabeth for a few minutes. He placed a kiss on her forehead. "I'm happy for you, Elizabeth. Remember you and Louis are welcome at our home at any time. We haven't lost a daughter, only gained a son."

Elizabeth kissed his cheek, and he disappeared. All summer she had prayed for his respect and blessing. Now she had so much more than she asked for—she still had her Father's love.

"Grandmamma," Elizabeth called. "Come sit by me, please." Her grandmother's petite form brushed next to Elizabeth's gown as she claimed her seat. Their hands clasped in Elizabeth's lap, and their heads leaned together. "I'll take any advice you have to give."

All Elizabeth really needed was the smile that had not left her grandmother's face. "You don't need my wisdom. You have your heart to guide you. You've married for love, so you are ahead of a lot of couples, including me. I married at the request of my parents. Your grandfather and I had to find love later. Your way is easier and right."

Placing her forehead against her grandmother's, Elizabeth studied their hands laced together. "Thanks, Grandmamma. I'll do my best to keep the love in the forefront."

Others had congratulatory words to pass on, but for some reason, her father's and grandmother's words outweighed all of the others.

After a while, Elizabeth knew the time she'd chosen today to spend with the people she loved most somehow made sense. They sent her out with blessings she needed to hear. Besides, she had the rest of her life to share in her home with Louis. Yet, she was ready to have him to herself.

Amid the talk of Christmas plans, Anne's baby, Robert's next trip, business, and school, Louis heard the results of the meeting that had taken place the previous night. He felt a bit guilty even thinking about other events while he celebrated his wedding. He watched Elizabeth across the room with her family members and friends. This time was for them to express blessings and wishes. But Louis just wanted to whisk Elizabeth away for himself.

And yet, while he looked forward to his marriage and life with Elizabeth, the town approached a major battle line—even on his wedding day. Would the merchants come around in support of the boycott, or would Louis and Henry and a hand full of store owners stand alone? Was the tide turning in their favor and carrying the dilemma away to sea? Or would the controversial cargo be bought ashore? The last scenario seemed very unlikely. A mass of citizens wouldn't allow it.

Samuel punched Louis' upper arm. "I think your plan to exit is in order. Go, collect your bride, and leave this talk for another day." He didn't have to use much persuasion to divert Louis' attention from politics to the greater, sweeter purpose of the day. Not just the day, but the year, his life. Nothing would distract him from caring for Elizabeth—not business, not war, not society.

After they had embraced their guests and said goodbye, Louis and Elizabeth—Mr. and Mrs. Lestarjette—boarded the shiny black carriage, enclosed from the world's view. A secluded paradise for the few minutes it took to arrive at their destination.

"You are more beautiful and precious then I could ever imagine," Louis stated, trying to translate his love into words. "I promise to fulfill all my vows to you and even more."

"I know, Louis. You have already given me more than I thought possible. I have no fear about the future with you. Whatever comes our way, we'll be in it together," she promised as she leaned into his embrace.

Whatever comes our way encompasses a lot of unforeseen territory. He kissed his bride with freedom, not holding back his passion. Holding her a little tighter, the kiss lingered, offering suggestions for the rest of the day and the night to come.

CHAPTER 16

"*M*rs. Elizabeth?" Ellen found her in the parlor. "Miss Collins is here. Should I show her in?"

"Of course." Elizabeth put down the garland and raced to the foyer to find Sarah discarding her coat and gloves. "Sarah, I'm so glad you're here. Come join us as we decorate the house."

Elizabeth embraced her friend she hadn't seen since the wedding five days ago. Sarah leaned back to stare at Elizabeth. "You don't seem any different. You're still the same Elizabeth, right?"

"You're so silly. I'm just a better me. I love being married and mistress of my home." Elizabeth spread her arms wide and pivoted in a circle. "What do you think of the house?"

"It's beautiful. I'm surprised the Christmas decorations aren't up yet. You always are the first to deck the halls."

"I've been a little busy." Elizabeth giggled and turned away from her friend. She didn't need to share the ways she'd been occupied.

"So, when is your honeymoon? Have you finalized the date yet?"

"You sure are full of questions." With a lowered head, Elizabeth looked at her friend from beneath a fan of eyelashes. "Well, the actual honeymoon will be in March with the prospect of better traveling weather—a journey to Boston and maybe Philadelphia. Louis hasn't seen or experienced those places yet." The thought of showing him her Boston thrilled her. She'd go with him now if it were possible.

"I'm so jealous. I've never been either. Maybe one day I'll be able to travel some." Sarah examined the glass donkey on the table. "Is this new?"

"Yes. It's from Grandmamma. Another one of her surprises. Look, it's a complete nativity." Elizabeth took out Mary, Joseph, the shepherds, the wise men, an angel, a cow, sheep, and of course, baby Jesus. "There. The complete set."

With the help of Ellen, Amy, and Sarah, Elizabeth's home turned into a picture of Christmas, complete with greenery, wreaths inside and out, candles, and bows. Tom showed up with more cedar boughs and a box of decorations. "Where do you want this box?" he asked.

"On the table in the corner, please." Elizabeth clapped her hands, glanced at the additional greenery, and smiled. As Sarah helped her retrieve each ornament, Ellen and Amy added their oohs and aahs and praises as they helped Elizabeth place them on tables and in the greenery.

"Where did you get such beautiful ornaments, Mrs. Elizabeth?" Amy held a crystal teardrop up to the light.

"My mother and grandmother collected them over the years for me, just waiting for this occasion when I had my own house." Elizabeth peered into the box and searched for a very special ornament. "This one is from Grandmamma. She says it's from Switzerland. If you look at it closely, you can see the mountains etched in its surface. See?" Amy responded with wide, expressive eyes. Elizabeth placed it carefully on a wreath in the window for all to view.

An hour later, Elizabeth pulled Sarah to the other side of the room with Ellen and Amy following. "The room is perfect. Thank you for helping. Do you think Louis will like it?"

The chorus of yeses from the three more than convinced Elizabeth of success. The colorful glass and silver balls, stars, and bows caught the afternoon light and told their own story of beauty and peace.

❀

Impressed with the transformation of the home, Louis requested Elizabeth play the piano after dinner.

"Of course, I'll play all my favorite carols—if you promise to sing with me."

"Are you sure?"

"Of course, I love your voice. Anyway, it's just for me."

Louis was still amazed they had both settled into married life so easily. He shouldn't have been surprised at Elizabeth's adjustment, but his was nothing less than a miracle. Who would have thought it possible for him to commit, for life, to anything, much less a person? His brother had warned him that love would change him. It had. Evenings like this were proof that God had taken a selfish man and turned him into someone with purpose and design. Here in their home, Louis was able to sense that plan completely.

"Are you happy?" Louis placed his hands on her shoulders as Elizabeth faced the keyboard.

She turned around to look up at him. "Oh, yes."

"I believe you are."

The music was forgotten for the remainder of the evening. Louis desired to make their own song as he fulfilled his husbandly role with love and respect for Elizabeth. It was by far his easiest challenge.

❀

A week after the wedding, Louis ran headfirst into the tea fiasco.

Samuel confronted Louis at the mercantile Friday morning, December seventeenth. "Come on, Louis. The world hasn't stopped because of your marriage. I'm here to take you to the meeting at the Exchange."

"Slow down." Louis laughed as he hung his apron on the hook in the back room. "Henry already informed me. I'm five minutes from being ready. I wouldn't miss this, married or not."

Louis, Henry, and Samuel joined many other artisans, merchants, planters, and citizens at the Exchange. "Standing room only it seems." Henry led the men through the crowd to an open space across the room.

"From what I'm hearing, this is about the fate of the *London* still rocking in the harbor." Louis pieced words together, surmising others were speculating just like him. It didn't appear he missed much as he hibernated with Elizabeth the past week.

Henry pointed to the five men sitting at the table on the platform. "Those were the ones appointed in early December who are to decide the fate of the tea."

"Remind me again of the men sitting on the opposite end of Christopher, beside Mr. Charles Pinckney and Daniel Cannon." Louis crossed his arms and nodded in the direction of the platform.

Henry whispered, for the hall had silenced. "On the far end is Thomas Ferguson and next to him is Charles Cotesworth Pinckney."

Christopher stood and called the meeting to order. "The Committee proposes a resolution, which prohibits the landing or vending of tea from the East India Company until the tea tax is repealed."

"Huzzah, huzzah!" Louis resounded with the majority of the crowd. The chant wrapped around the building. Finally, an answer to the blight on the horizon.

"The members of the General Committee have already

endorsed the bill. All two hundred and fifty-seven chests of tea will be sent back to England."

The prompt handling of business impressed Louis. Less than half an hour later, he and Henry were headed back to work. Christopher met them on the walkway outside the Exchange.

Henry turned to him. "Well, Christopher, it looks like a victory."

"But at what cost? I know these men, and they won't let it just go away. I'm afraid some of our men want to put action to the resolution. Some of the more radical spirits—anonymously, of course—have threatened to burn the tea ship. I hope it's peaceful and that doesn't happen."

Henry grunted and shrugged his shoulders. Louis knew that sound from his uncle. Henry didn't expect peace from the British.

"I hope the tea ship is spared and somehow drifts out of sight. We have other things to think about besides tea," Louis said.

"True." Christopher turned toward the harbor and his office. "Merry Christmas."

With thoughts of the holiday, Louis hoped the subject of tea would fade into the New Year.

Elizabeth closed her eyes at the Elliotts' table. "Christmas Eve. It's almost tangible. I feel it, smell it, and see it." Light danced around her inner eyelids, and aromas of food and greenery accosted the air.

Anne laughed at Elizabeth's description. "I guess you would cut it up and put it in a box to bring out every day if you could."

"And what would be wrong with that? I could have this perfect shepherd's pie, these sandwiches, and soup ready at my fingertips all the time." *And all my family too.* "Louis, let's walk to the church. I don't want to be enclosed in the carriage. You don't mind, do you, Mother?"

"Not at all. We'll take the boys with us and leave more room for Anne and Robert in the second carriage."

Anne huffed. "Do you think I need all the extra room already?"

Robert responded quickly. "She didn't mean that at all, did you Mrs. Elliott? Anne, with your coat, you don't appear with child," he consoled.

Anne pouted. "Right. With my coat."

Elizabeth and Louis left fifteen minutes before the others. St. Philip's steeple shone in the distance. She tucked her arm in Louis' and stuffed her gloved hands into her muff.

"I love the season of Advent, but now the waiting is over. The celebration of the birth of Jesus begins." Elizabeth breathed in the cool air as if inhaling a promise. The same hope the baby Jesus brought every year and every day. Hope of peace on earth and good will to men.

Louis patted her hand and guided her to the church doors.

To Elizabeth, the service this night in 1773 was extra-special, since Louis was now a permanent part of her life. The Christ child was firmly placed in his heart and life, as well as hers, making Him the center of their joined existence.

Elizabeth kept her hand in Louis' as the traditional verses of Isaiah 9:6-7 were proclaimed:

For unto us a child is born, unto us a son is given: and the government shall be upon his shoulder: and his name shall be called Wonderful, Counselor, The mighty God, The everlasting Father, The Prince of Peace. Of the increase of his government and peace there shall be no end, upon the throne of David, and upon his kingdom.

On the walk home, Elizabeth imagined Jesus born on a cold and clear night just like this, with a million stars as a canopy in the midnight sky. Tonight, she could say she was at peace, content. She was quick to acknowledge her protection and safety within God's love, surrounding her as a canopy like the stars above. Yes, tonight she could rest in His love.

173

The house was quiet Christmas morning as Elizabeth prepared the tea and scones. Louis would rise soon and join her. The fire drew her to a comfortable chair, and she pulled her legs up under her. Her view encompassed the many candlesticks on the mantle and then the crèche on the table. She lit the candles and let the light reflect through the crystal objects.

The crèche told an amazing story—one never to grow old. Besides bringing Jesus to mind, Elizabeth's grandmother's image radiated from the peaceful holy scene on the silk cloth on top of the marble table.

As she contemplated the crèche, letting her thoughts mesmerize her, Louis entered the serene scene and placed his arms around her. "Why am I not surprised to find you here in perfect peace? *Joyeux Noël, ma chérie.*"

She uncurled her feet from beneath her and placed them back in her warm slippers. After patting the seat for Louis to join her, she poured him a cup of rich tea. "And Happy Christmas to you. Since we are having such a big meal today, I asked Ellen to leave a few scones to hold us over."

"Perfect," he agreed.

And it was, breakfast or no breakfast, as long as Louis was there.

"Would you like your gifts now?" he asked.

She bounced on her seat and clasped her hands under her chin in enthusiasm. "Oh, yes. Of course. You know I've been staring at these for days now. And since I promised not to peek, I've been very obedient."

"All right. I see it would do no good to ask you to wait any longer. Let's see—how about this one first?" He presented her with a flat, square velvet box tied with a red satin ribbon.

Elizabeth quickly dispensed with the ribbon and lid. A sparkling pair of ruby drop earrings and a gold chain with a cluster of rubies forming an elegant *V* presented an image of rare beauty and sophistication.

"Louis, they're beautiful. How did you know I wanted rubies?"

"I know because I listen, and I watch. I've noticed how you place your ruby ring next to your pearls or your other pendants. These are an ideal match for your engagement ring." Louis gently took the necklace from the case and secured it around her neck.

"I'm sure it goes astonishingly well with my dressing gown." She laughed and caressed the jewels against her skin.

"I didn't even notice."

"Now, you must open a gift. This one." She handed him a long, oddly shaped package.

He loosened the wrapping and held up a walking cane of dark mahogany wood with intricate etchings of birds and wildlife and topped with a silver handle. "Now, I'll really walk around in style. A true Carolinian gentleman."

"A great addition to your robe too." Weren't they a fine pair, prancing around in their finery and bed clothes?

Elizabeth received two additional gifts of extraordinary value, at least in her mind. A leather-bound book of Voltaire's writings in French and the work of Louis-Claude Daquin, a French composer.

"How did you come across these? Certainly not in Charles Town."

"I have my connections. Remember you married a Frenchman with close ties to the latest Parisian artists." He made it sound auspicious but confessed. "It was André, per my instructions."

Elizabeth was glad when they set aside the gifts. They stood in the morning light pouring through the windows. Louis filled his hands with Elizabeth's face and brought her lips to his. She melted at his touch. For the next few minutes, she had no idea why she desired any presents. She had everything she wanted.

At the Elliott home, the big festive Christmas meal started in the early afternoon and carried on for two hours. The Elliotts, Cochrans, and Lestarjettes feasted on fare prepared the day before. Since all the house servants celebrated with their own families, the capable wives took over the menial chores for the day. Elizabeth thought it a welcome change to freely move around and wait on herself and her family.

Anne's boys maintained this was "the best Christmas ever." Robert received a boy-sized rifle with the promise from his father "to shoot a nice-size turkey very soon." Although acting a bit envious, John contented himself with a coonskin hat and a wooden sword, as close to authentic as he would get at age six.

The women organized the leftovers in the kitchen. "This would have been the perfect Christmas if George had been here. He's the only one missing." Mother sat down and let the tears flow.

"Ah, Mother, lamenting won't bring him home." Elizabeth ached for her at the pain George caused, but she wanted her mother to see the many loved ones about her.

"I just don't understand." Her mother wiped her tears on her handkerchief. "Why would he choose to alienate himself from his family, all the way in Philadelphia in the bleakest part of winter? He should be here with us on Christmas." What could Elizabeth say to console her mother when she was also wondering the same thing?

There was more to the situation than an absent son and brother. Underlying it all was the fact that this man had joined the militia. His sisters were firm Daughters of Liberty; the men, except for his father, were staunch Sons of Liberty. Her mother was somewhere in between. And George? He flaunted the bright-red uniform of a loyalist, the symbol of continued British rule. Elizabeth shook her head; a family dilemma, for sure.

As Elizabeth thought, Anne saw the George issue as she did. "Mother, there's nothing we can do. George is now a man of eighteen years. He has made a choice that he has a right to make. And we can't plead with him or beg him to change. Only God can direct him."

"So, as a mother, I just sit back and let him ruin his life, possibly be killed, and do nothing?" Mother let her tears dampen the towel as she dried a plate.

Elizabeth hated seeing the tears but didn't know how to change the outcome or the reality. "No, I don't think Anne is saying that, Mother. You can still tell him how you feel and pray for him. Write to him often. And when he does come home, welcome him back like a prodigal son. I feel a mother's prayer and love can go farther than any others. Just don't give up on him! Never despair totally." Elizabeth meant these words, but practically, she didn't see how they could help in the present situation.

December ended quietly, or so Elizabeth thought. Was the calm just a disguise for some troublesome instances or clandestine activities? She watched January 1774 bring the end of the holiday season. Time to turn to new beginnings, new directions, and new decisions.

She extended her left hand in front of her and turned her wedding ring until it set perfectly centered. *I have the whole of 1774 in front of me with a new husband. I'm constantly surrounded by God's love and new possibilities. Now, if only the political climate will cooperate.*

CHAPTER 17

*E*lizabeth entered Wilson's Mercantile in the middle of a cold, early January morning. She glanced around the room, searching for Jeannette, and found her friend engrossed in the newspaper, not even acknowledging the sound of the bell on the door.

"Jeannette. Jeannette?" Elizabeth had no luck attracting her attention until she was at the counter.

"I'm sorry, Elizabeth. Have you heard the news?" Even as she asked, Jeannette unfolded the paper to show her friend.

"What news?" Curious, now that the paper was in her hands, she turned her eyes to where Jeannette pointed.

"Right there. Mr. Timothy describes the event so well. Read it."

The news of yet another incident in Boston captivated Elizabeth. Apparently, on December sixteenth, a group of patriots disguised as Indians boarded the East India Company ships in Boston and dumped about nine-thousand British monetary pounds' worth of tea into the harbor—the equivalent of three hundred forty-two chests of tea.

Elizabeth tapped the paper, releasing the crease. "Listen to the words of John Adams of Boston: 'The die is cast: The people have passed the river and cut away the bridge: last night three cargoes of tea were emptied into the harbor. This is the grandest event, which has ever yet happened since the controversy with Britain opened. The sublimity of it charms me! This is the most magnificent movement of all. Their destruction of the tea is so bold, so daring, so firm, intrepid and inflexible.'"

Elizabeth looked up from the paper. "By his words, I can surely tell which side Mr. Adams is on. The report also states that New York and Philadelphia turned away the tea. Isn't that what we did?"

"Yes, but read on," Jeannette coaxed, as she leaned on the counter.

Elizabeth found her place in the article and continued aloud. "Since no one in Charles Town appeared to receive and pay the duty on the tea aboard the *London* within twenty-one days after its arrival, Crown officials seized the tea on December twenty-second. That is the law. It is being stored in the cellar of the Exchange." Elizabeth glanced at the second column. "So, the tea is here in Charles Town. No wonder Mr. Timothy made this editorial remark: 'Charles Town is the only colony that allowed the tea to land. That is an embarrassment and a shame.'" Elizabeth folded the paper and set it on the counter in front of Jeannette.

After putting the paper behind her on a shelf, Jeannette sighed. "I don't know if Henry and Louis have seen this yet. It will awaken the town to questions about what to do next. Imagine a sea full of tea. A waste for sure, but maybe it served a purpose."

Shaking her wandering thoughts into submission, Elizabeth remembered why she had come to the store. "By the way, is Louis here? I wanted to remind him about dinner tonight at the Laurens'."

"Check in the back. He'll love your surprise visit." Jeannette smiled. Elizabeth loved being considered as the daughter Jeannette never had. "Don't forget lunch with us tomorrow. I promised to cook Louis a French meal."

"Ellen and I need to try a few of your recipes. Turning Ellen into a French cook—that's an idea." Elizabeth laughed, as she made her way to the storage area. Louis would surely be surprised if his cook became a chef *française*.

Henry and Louis, deep in conversation, didn't even notice her knock on the door facing. She hoped she wasn't intruding on anything.

"The 'Boston Tea Party' is what they are calling it. Can you imagine the look on the faces of the officials? A sea of tea," Henry said. They both laughed, probably at the vision in their heads of so-called Indians and chests of tea.

She approached the men with her hands clasped in front of her and cleared her throat. "Excuse me, gentlemen."

Startled heads turned to her voice. "Elizabeth, how long have you been there?" Louis asked, wiping his hands on his apron.

She smiled at the dusty men who still had the sparkle of mischief in their eyes. "Only long enough to be entertained by your laughter. I would have thought the destruction of the tea would be a more serious matter. But seeing it as you described it does make me laugh too."

"Sometimes, you have to laugh at the harsh situations," Henry explained. "We were just counting how many bricks of tea we have left. We expect some more in the next shipment from the islands, but we won't depend on it. We don't even know if customers will continue to buy tea from any source."

Louis cleared the top of a crate for her "Have a seat, Elizabeth. You can watch us work." She kept her gloves and coat on in the cool room. "I don't suppose you have a newfound love for coffee, do you?" He raised his eyebrows to emphasize his playful concern.

"Not yet. But if it comes to that, I won't think all is lost without my daily dose of tea." She sighed as she took mental note of the shelves surrounding her. Tea, sugar, coffee, flour. They had plenty for now.

Oblivious to the occupants of the storage room, Tom Engle

stumbled through the door, humming a catchy tune while perusing the words on a sheet of paper.

Henry stepped closer to the young man. "Stumbling and mumbling, Tom? What has your undivided attention?"

"Oh, I'm sorry, Mr. Wilson. Someone handed me this on the street. It's a song called 'Tea Rally.' And a group sang it on the corner. It's sort of a lively tune," the youth explained.

"Let's see." Louis held out his hand to take the newest pamphlet on the fiasco in Boston, read it and chuckled. "I'll not sing it, but here are the words:

And tell King George we'll pay no taxes on his foreign tea,
His threats are vain, and vain to think,
To force our girls and wives to drink his vile Bohea!"

Louis folded the tract and placed it in Tom's pocket. "We can laugh now at the image of a tea party. Yet, a time will come when the king will take this as a serious act." He thumped a nearby chest. "Back to work for us."

As his uncle led Tom to crates that needed unpacking, Louis extended his hand to Elizabeth. "Now, what may I do for you?" He brushed her cheeks with his fingertips.

"Just a reminder about dinner at the Laurens' tonight. Martha would be very disappointed if we forgot."

"I have every intention of escorting you there. I wouldn't want to disappoint Mary and James Laurens either."

"So, I'll see you at home later." She ran her fingers down his arm. "By the way, I gave Ellen and Amy the afternoon and evening off to visit friends."

Capturing her hand, he kissed her fingers. "You won't be lonely?"

"Not me. I have Cleo under my feet, lessons to prepare for the school opening, and books to read. I will patiently anticipate your arrival." She planted a kiss gently on his lips and departed swiftly.

January brought the arrival of the girls at the boarding school, ready to commence their education. Music was a gift Elizabeth wasn't willing to relinquish. Although Louis didn't mind the hours she spent teaching, he didn't want it to overburden her.

"How could a few hours tire me? Ellen handles the house, and all I have to worry about is you. I thought I was doing a fair job of that."

"No complaints here. Have you worked out the details of your absence in March?"

Surely, he knew he was most important, and to him, their voyage was a top priority. *Have no fear, my dear.* "Except for a few details. Sarah will help Mrs. Singleton with the theory classes, and Martha will teach the younger students individual piano lessons. That just leaves my advanced students without a teacher," Elizabeth explained.

Nothing would deter her from their delayed honeymoon to Boston in March. Louis was anxious to get away and see another part of the country. What better place than her former hometown? After all she had lived there for sixteen years and still had a fondness for the people and vistas. She rubbed her hands together in anticipation as ideas churned in her head. It would be perfect.

Louis' favorite part of a normal day was dinner for two in their drawing room on a small oval Queen Anne table placed next to a window. The thick drapes, closed in the winter, gave the room a cozy, homey feeling. The crackle and warmth of the fire lent an air of comfort and relaxation, a needed commodity after a day's work. For those few minutes, the world was left outside. Dinner conversation was never heavy or controversial. Their routine offered a time to reconnect and share.

Tonight, Ellen served a hearty clam-and-potato chowder followed by a flaky crusted quiche. Dessert was always served later while reposing on the sofas next to the fireplace and piano. Some evenings Elizabeth played for Louis to soothe him and to give him rest. Tonight, though, he had something on his mind.

Although talk of politics was not prohibited, Louis preferred to avoid it when he could. Not now. Elizabeth asked him to promise to include her. "It's time for another meeting of the Sons of Liberty. It will be at Christopher's house. He also suggested that the ladies meet. It seems there is information that will interest all of you as well." He paused and glanced at her. He didn't know what answer he expected. "Would you be able to have them come here?"

"Here?" She smiled. "Of course. But I never thought my first party in our house would have a political venue. Our house will get a proper Patriot christening."

Louis relaxed, taking his chocolate croissant from his plate. "Somehow, I knew you would jump at the opportunity. I'm sure you ladies will turn it into a social event as well."

She pulled her shoulders back as in defense. "There's nothing wrong with mixing business with pleasure, Louis." Of course, she had nothing to fear from him. He'd rather not be parted and preferred a mixed meeting if ever offered.

One more surprise. "Did I mention it would be next week? Next Thursday night?"

"No, you failed to share that piece of information. One week. I can do it with Ellen, Amy, and Anne's help," she proclaimed. "Louis, I think I'm going to ask Mother to come. I don't know if Father will let her, but I can't help thinking she needs to know what is happening before it happens." Her brow furrowed as she considered the consequences of the invitation.

Louis reached for her hand. "She can always say no. Do what you feel you should," he encouraged. "Mary Laurens will moderate the meeting. All you need to do is provide the place and a few refreshments."

"I know. I'm excited about the opportunity. Is that strange, to be looking forward to a politically charged gathering?" Political or not, he could tell from her expressions that plans began formulating in her mind as she envisioned the prospect of her first role as hostess.

The next morning, Louis turned his attention to his import ventures. As far as Louis could tell, it was business as usual with regard to his shipping endeavor. News from his brother in France relayed words of encouragement that French ports were open to his ship. More so because it was not owned and operated by the British government. His latest letter stated:

Keep the goods coming. All is on schedule for the shipment of French goods to arrive in March. The Tea Act has helped to stabilize and to benefit French items being shipped to America. The Frenchmen want to support an independent citizen of the New World over the British tyrant.

Louis could feel André's strong political sentiments across the miles. His brother had made the shipping venture with Louis into a political agenda. Anything to thwart the progress of England. Well, André didn't have to live the day-to-day life of a semi rebellious colonist. It might be smooth sailing now, but Louis felt André's constant optimism was going to be tested. Soon, if what he heard was correct, the King and Parliament would speak out against the bold colonies.

He left his letters at the house and joined Christopher at a public house for lunch.

"So, I assume that the meeting will focus on the retaliation of King George." Louis would have preferred to stick to business, but their business was connected to the political climate. Christopher never seemed to mind the subject. In fact, Louis wondered how he kept his family life intact.

Christopher sat back with his coffee, a commodity seen more and more since the tea chests were locked away in the Exchange in Charles Town. "Yes. Mr. Timothy is receiving news daily about the reaction to the defiance of the Crown. He'll do a lot of the talking at the meeting. The information is too much to print in the paper. Besides he can't simply print what we want. He does have the other half of Charles Town to please. The information he has collected about the response could fill a book. How he'll break it down for us will be a feat to witness."

"Do you predict it will hurt our future shipments?" Louis sought the truth from his partner.

"Not today, but later, yes. If the ports are closed, if shipments are searched and confiscated, if the government even remembers Charles Town so far to the south. The circumstances and 'if' factors will play a role. We do have contracts with France and the islands, a plus for our side. Our cargo doesn't depend on Britain. But access to our ports and the open waters could become a big issue."

A big issue? What about a huge issue? Their livelihood. His uncle's mercantile. The citizens of Charles Town. Louis leaned forward. "This could ruin us, couldn't it? Be honest with me, Christopher. We could be ruined."

Christopher ran his finger around the rim of his cup, giving Louis the hint that his friend didn't want to answer. "Honestly, we could, if our ship cannot move freely in and out of port. I don't see action coming to a halt. There will be a way to divert the government. We could even load and unload further south. But today, Louis, we need to concentrate on what we can see and control. I haven't seen this defeated look on you before. Why all the doubt?"

Yes, why? Only one thing had changed in his life. But that one thing rearranged all the others. God remained on His throne as number one in Louis' life. But marriage, commitment, and love for Elizabeth pushed his own welfare and that of business down a few notches. No longer was he haphazardly running his life for himself; he had Elizabeth to consider. He had promised to care for

185

her, to cherish her—even in a world that would be turned inside out. So, yes, a business that had the potential to collapse was an issue.

"I must provide for Elizabeth. I know you understand that, Christopher. You have a family. You need this business too."

"I do. But I know that if needed, I can live frugally. I can survive on less." Christopher adjusted his coat in order to place his elbows on the table. "I can turn my knowledge and business into something else. And I feel God has a complete plan with or without monthly shipments. You need to grab on to that deep faith of yours, Louis. Don't let doubts and fears lead you. Use hope and promise instead."

Louis realized his friend was not pointing a finger only at him but at himself too. "You're right. For a moment there, I was lost in a world of what-ifs. Aunt Jeannette always says, 'Don't borrow trouble from tomorrow.'" More and more, Louis found he needed to live that way and enjoy more of the everyday moments.

He didn't shy away from sharing his feelings with Elizabeth. At dinner he repeated the conversation he had with Christopher.

Louis held his breath when Elizabeth responded, "We shouldn't fear the future, so I won't. I'm glad you're thinking of us, but so is God." Why had he been concerned? She was wiser than he was at times. "Psalm 46 says 'God is our refuge and strength, a very present help in trouble. Therefore, we will not fear, though the earth be removed, and though the mountains be carried into the midst of the sea.'"

Later, over a game of chess, Elizabeth held her pawn above the board. "Do you think Mr. Timothy will share his information with the ladies?" Then, she calmly captured his knight.

"I'm sure someone is passing on all of the pertinent information. You won't miss much except some loud, robust-sounding men."

"Checkmate."

How had he let that happen? Even though Elizabeth beat him

half of the time, it still surprised him. "You like to do that, don't you? More often it seems. Either I can't concentrate around you or you are taking lessons on the side." He smiled as he gazed at her smug grin.

"Neither. Why can't I just be getting better? I'm able to anticipate your moves. You're going to have to use different strategies to outmaneuver me over the next fifty years."

"Fifty years. That sounds like a challenge. Half a century of chess in front of a warm fire." The game was over, but not the evening. They had hours yet to experience a portion of their remaining years. He vowed to not lose his concentration for the rest of the night.

CHAPTER 18

$\mathcal{B}$y Thursday evening, Elizabeth's excitement had grown concerning the simultaneous meetings. She imagined spouses all over Charles Town had made plans to part for their different destinations. To Elizabeth's surprise and extreme pleasure, her mother accepted the invitation. For some, like her mother, this would be their first encounter with the Sons of Liberty or Daughters of Liberty in action.

"What did you tell Father?" Elizabeth pried as her mother helped her with last-minute preparation and presentation of the hors d'oeuvres.

"The truth: that I wanted to be with my daughters. That I needed to see firsthand where their commitments lay. And that is the truth, Elizabeth. I don't really know what you girls believe."

"Then you have come to the right place. Please, Mother, keep an open mind."

"I will. An open mind at the back of the room out of the way." Most likely her mother had taken her biggest step in a long while. Elizabeth wouldn't push for more involvement. Part of her prayers had been answered. What more could she need for one night?

Elizabeth gave her a quick hug of encouragement. They turned back to the business on hand, making sure Ellen and Amy had filled an oblong table with mouth-watering appetizers—small lemon tarts, cheese puffs, scones with jam, candied fruit, ginger snaps, apple crisps, and a cranberry fruit punch.

When he came downstairs, Louis sampled the overflow of goods in the back hallway and planted a kiss on Elizabeth's cheek. "Do I need to remind you to relax and enjoy yourself?"

"No. But you do the same, Louis." She straightened his coat lapels. "And try not to come home with the weight of the world on your shoulders. Leave that at the meeting or, better yet, in God's hands."

As Louis stepped out of the house to attend his meeting, Anne stepped inside. Her coat could not hide her expanding waistline. Elizabeth felt she would have no desire to disguise her condition from the world if she were with child, yet Anne admitted being a little self-conscious of the way her clothes fit her these days.

Mother rushed to Anne's side to relieve her of her coat and coax her to have a seat.

Anne rolled her eyes in Elizabeth's direction. "I'm not an invalid. This isn't my first time at this." Then she simply defied her mother and offered to lend a hand instead of taking a seat. But with Mother in charge, the only thing left to do was to await the arrival of the guests.

Ellen acted as greeter and usher, announcing each guest as she arrived. The group as a whole was prompt. Quickly, the ample parlor filled with chattering friends and acquaintances.

"Please sample the light fare in the dining room," Mother encouraged. It satisfied Elizabeth when her mother found a place of confidence, even though the whole organization was new to her. It appeared any social event functioned on the same social etiquette.

Every available chair and sofa had been placed in the front room. The scene thrilled Elizabeth as she perused the multiple

189

groups of ladies. Even with their less-formal attire, the women were a stylish bunch. Bodices and skirts of blues and greens, reds and oranges, browns, and her own of deep golden yellow animated the room and filled it with warmth and purpose. She was too excited. She couldn't just sit and eat, so she roamed the perimeters making sure all were content.

There were a few new faces, at least new to the cause. In particular she noted Mrs. Reynolds from the boarding school; Sarah, a new, bolder version of herself this year; and Mrs. Turner, a friend of Jeannette's. Elizabeth stood to the side and counted the attendees—twenty-eight ladies. That could be a record. For a political gathering of women, this was a strong statement. The concerns and need of information were apparent. These women came to accept their place in the fate of the country.

In her role as hostess, Elizabeth welcomed the guests and prepared to introduce the speaker. Her nerves subsided once she began. Filled with confidence, she smiled and proceeded. "Mrs. James Laurens has graciously agreed to be the speaker tonight. I know we are all—"

Elizabeth was interrupted by a commotion in the hallway behind her. The late arriving guest had escaped Ellen's side and made her loud entrance herself.

"I'm so sorry, ladies, to be late. Please don't mind me," the young woman stated, waltzing into the middle of the room in her elegant, showy furs.

Elizabeth's mouth dropped, and she gasped. The latecomer was none other than Miss Victoria Seymour. George's Miss Seymour. *What is she doing here? She's certainly not a reformed Loyalist.* Elizabeth didn't have time to carefully formulate her opinion. Somehow, she had to continue her introduction. "You're welcome to join us, Miss Seymour. As I was saying, Mrs. Laurens is prepared to share some of the latest news that will affect us all. Mrs. Laurens."

Taking her place in the front row, Elizabeth fidgeted, knowing

Miss Seymour was behind her. With determination, she promised herself she wouldn't allow the presence of one woman to mar the evening. After all, the meeting was open to anyone who desired to come.

Mary Laurens chose to stand behind a table that held her notes, instead of sitting in the overstuffed chair facing the audience. "As most of you know, the month of December was a lively one for the ports in the colonies, including our own. Our experience was just one of many. As a summary, I am going to give a few facts about the recent results of the Tea Act in Boston, Philadelphia, New York, and Charles Town." Mary stated the facts clearly, sometimes pulling from her notes, at other times from newspaper writings. "All ports had thwarted the deliveries of tea. So, you see the colonies as a whole, though, acting individually, have taken a stand. A stand for our rights against an unfair act of Parliament. As you can guess, repercussions most likely will be rendered by the king."

Whispers around the room confirmed the concern of the ladies. Elizabeth noticed the only one unaffected was Miss Seymour, grinning like a tiger just waiting.

Mary continued, "Of course, it is too early for the British government to put action to their threats of punishment. But I do have a few quotes from the Crown." She procured a sheet from the stack. "It states: 'Even though the Charles Town tea party was not equal in criminality to the proceedings in other Colonies, I consider it a most unwarrantable insult to the authority of the Kingdom.'"

A heavy chuckle echoed around the room. Elizabeth saw Miss Seymour's gloved hand covering the escaped, wordless comment.

It didn't faze Mrs. Laurens. She leaned forward and seemed to make eye contact with each person present, even Miss Seymour. "And that, ladies, is what has been debated these last few months, especially since the Tea Act. What exactly is the 'authority of the Kingdom'? Across these colonies people—men and women—are meeting, just like we are here, debating the role of Parliament, thousands of miles away, in our lives. This colony took a stand by not accepting the tea, although it was unloaded and stored. Mr. Timothy said that 'it is Charles Town's shame'—the only port where the chests of tea were landed. I wonder what will happen next time?"

"Will there be a next time? Will England send another ship with tea?" Mrs. Singleton asked, opening the discussion.

"Knowing some of the merchants here in town, I believe the East India Company will not give up so easily. We should expect more," Jeannette voiced as others nodded or verbalized in agreement. Miss Seymour sighed and clicked her tongue, the only one failing to believe Mary's words. Yet, Elizabeth's mother could have the same opinions, though, perhaps a bit more open to a second opinion.

"It appears this will be a wait-and-see matter," Sarah added shyly, a step out of her shell.

"Yes. You just wait and see." Miss Seymour's response was volatile. The woman stood now, pointing at those gathered in the room. "Just wait and see what the king will do to you. None of this should concern you. You are just a few wives, listening to your weak husbands. You don't have a chance with your tea parties. Just wait until the guns and soldiers arrive to determine who is right. It won't be the Sons or Daughters of Foolishness." With that acerbic attack, the tyrannical spokeswoman departed taking her fumes and flames with her. She bumped a few chairs while weaving her way to the door.

At once everyone in the room let out a collective sigh of relief. Mrs. Laurens returned to her stand by the table. Elizabeth was sure if she had a gavel she would use it. "Well, I'm glad that is over. Obviously, she has her own opinions." She managed to turn the tide of the conversation back to the issue at hand. The conclusion was that the women would have to be prepared to support the efforts of the Partisans as they sought a repeal of the Tea Act.

With the business concluded, as Elizabeth expected, the ladies returned to socializing. Food and punch flowed, plenty for the second round of conversations. Overall, she was pleased about a successful evening with only one hazard who seemed to enjoy whirling in and out of Elizabeth's life.

Sixty men gathered at Christopher's house in his parlor and over-flowed into the library and drawing room, all within the hearing of the speaker, Mr. Timothy. Louis knew the man needed no introduction. His name had been linked with the Sons of Liberty since the first meeting under the Liberty tree. He knew firsthand about persecution and the consequences of taking a stand.

Louis studied the crowd and noted the attendance was what Christopher had expected. Recent events involving the Tea Act and the people of Charles Town had presented a need to consoli-date their numbers and come to mutual agreements and under-standings. Merchants, planters, artisans, doctors, lawyers, businessmen, and educators were scattered across the rooms. It was obvious to Louis that they all had their lives and livelihoods at stake or at risk of being altered. He realized this group did not expect a solution without sacrifice. No one was naïve enough to imagine the Crown gracefully withdrawing its power.

"You by now have read the reports of the response of the king. We are to beware of repercussions for our rebellious acts. If only we had been as brave as the Patriots in Boston," Timothy stated in the form of a criticism.

"If there is a next time, I feel the citizens will take direct action," Mr. Raley, a gentleman known for speaking out, predicted. "I, for one, will not be disgraced again."

The popularity of his statement received a round of applause before Mr. Timothy gained control of the crowd again.

"Don't be deceived into thinking Boston will simply receive a warning. Give Parliament a few months to devise a plan of retribution, not only for Boston but for all of us. Listen to what John Adams, a prominent statesman and lawyer in Boston, wrote the day after the dumping of the tea. 'Last night three cargoes of tea were emptied into the harbor. This is the grandest event.'"

"Mr. Adams is perhaps right," Reverend Smith commented. "This is the grandest event so far. Are we ready for the results? We have prayed for a peaceful solution. That is what I would want foremost. But honestly, do any of us see that happening? With God on our side and a united front, tyranny can be replaced with freedom. Ultimately, we are seeking equality and fairness. What price is each of us willing to pay?"

Louis was surprised to see—and much more, hear—the reverend of the local Church of England taking a stand for establishing their rights. Wasn't he bound to the Crown? Wasn't he an important British citizen? Of course, as were all the men in these rooms, except for Louis. Men bound, but willing to break these ties for a higher cause: freedom.

Mr. Timothy continued, "John Adams has the same questions as you do. 'What measures will the ministry take in consequence of this defiance? Will they dare to rescind the act? Will they punish us? How? By quartering troops upon us? By annulling our charter? By laying on more duties? By restraining our trade?' You see, gentlemen, most believe something more than the Tea Act is coming." Mr. Timothy concluded his talk, stacked his many papers, and put them away in his case.

Christopher took the lead. "Gentlemen, you are welcome to remain for more questions or discussion or just to mingle. Thank you for joining us here. And thank you, Mr. Timothy, for sharing your conscientious insight."

After the applause, the men formed loose groups of four to five men and remained for another hour discussing the options of the Parliament and the colonies. Louis joined a group consisting of Henry, Samuel, and Reverend Turquand.

"I hope our ships from France can continue to make it through the harbor." Henry placed his hand on Louis' shoulder.

"Perhaps my brother has a plan to avoid conflict with the British in the French ports and on the open water. It will be tricky." Louis crossed his arms. Really, no one had any answers. The limbo they had experienced in waiting for the British to act seemed to bring another prolonged period of unanswered questions. How long would they await answers? No one expected good news, which made the waiting more difficult.

As the groups dispersed, Louis thought about Elizabeth and her meeting. Did her mother comment? Did they receive enough information? It was after nine o'clock, so Louis assumed the ladies were safely home. He easily made his exit. Nothing more to do tonight. As he walked home alone, he considered the implications of the meeting. No mention of war or violence, but he knew that, under the surface, it was possible. The issue required diplomacy and two willing parties desiring to communicate and compromise. Of course, a perfect solution would be for Britain not to use force or troops and to give America her desired representation.

What was God's perspective? *How do I act in obedience to God's will?*

No answers satisfied Louis before he entered his quiet home. Elizabeth embraced him with a calmness he didn't share, not at the moment.

He relaxed beside her on the couch. "So, it was a success I presume by looking at your contented expression?" His disturbing thoughts remained, but a streak of hope seeped in just because Elizabeth sat by him.

"Yes, a very positive, successful endeavor. But the meeting held a few surprises," she said as she placed his jacket on a chair. "Do you want a few of the appetizers before I tell you about the intruder?"

"Food and an intruder? I'm intrigued." His mind couldn't grasp what could have happened.

She set a plate of tempting pastries and a cup of punch on the small table before trying to sit next to him. That didn't last long, for she couldn't be still. She was animated by the story she had to tell.

"I'm listening, so you can spill the mystery." As he faced her, he turned his shoulders, anticipating an interesting scenario.

"As I was introducing Mrs. Laurens, the last person on earth that I ever expected appeared. Can you guess who?" Louis shook his head and continued to grin at Elizabeth's excitement.

"None other than Victoria Seymour. I would have said she had the wrong meeting, but her entrance and words were well rehearsed. Her exit was more dramatic than her introduction. For a second, I was even embarrassed for her behavior." Her sympathy obviously had not lasted long then or now as she shared the details with Louis.

"Do you think George put her up to it?" Louis questioned as he tried to decipher what purpose her attendance served.

"We haven't seen George for over a month. I guess he could have somehow convinced her to gather information. I thought maybe Mother invited her. But the look on Mother's face proved that notion incorrect. I don't think we'll ever know."

Louis settled Elizabeth next to him on the sofa now that the retelling was complete. "So, intrigue at the Lestarjette house. Not bad for your first entertainment. Well, any chance to talk to your mother?"

"No. She was quiet and left with Anne soon after the meeting. Either her questions were answered, or more were added. I'm sure I'll hear later." Elizabeth sank further into the comfort of Louis' arms, releasing a yawn with a sigh.

CHAPTER 19

The end of January ushered in an influenza epidemic. Elizabeth credited the cold weather and winter conditions for the severity. One of the areas with the most cases was the boarding house. Within literally hours, the dormitory was turned into an infirmary. Many of the girls couldn't go home due to the roads and weather. Dr. Ramsey did his best to confine the ill girls to one floor of the house. Fifteen girls were quarantined away from the other twelve.

Elizabeth remained with the well girls in the boarding house, while other adults played nursemaids to the sick ones. She didn't think it was fair for her friends to be alone in the middle of the danger, for she was just as strong and healthy. Louis wanted her to be helpful but careful. She understood her husband's concern, and she tried to convince Sarah to stay away. But Sarah attached herself to the side of Dr. Ramsey and Mrs. Reynolds, doing all she could to help.

"Please don't work too hard, Sarah. Your body can't take being around illness all the time. Why don't you go home for a few days?" Elizabeth encouraged Sarah out the door after four straight days of caring for the most severe cases.

Sarah drank some tea in a few gulps and headed back upstairs. "No. I feel fine, and the doctor needs my help. Don't you worry so much." Quickly, she disappeared, not heeding Elizabeth's advice.

The local girls were sent to their homes until the doctor gave his approval for their safe return. The hours were long for Elizabeth as she took over menial jobs like cooking and cleaning to allow some to attend to their own families and to help upstairs. The laundry and dishes were endless. The girls who were well needed to attend their studies in order to stay occupied and out of the way.

On Friday, five days into the crisis, Mrs. Collins pounded on the front door.

"Come in, ma'am." Elizabeth stepped aside as Sarah's mother bustled into the foyer.

Mrs. Collins grasped Elizabeth's hand in hers and squeezed it. "I need to see Sarah. Is she well? Is she eating and resting?"

"She is well, and I do know that she eats." But she couldn't vouch for the rest. "I'll go tell her you are here."

Elizabeth left the woman pacing in the parlor. Standing at the foot of the landing to the second floor, Elizabeth called, "Sarah, your mother is here to see you."

The nurse nodded from a doorway. Soon Sarah appeared, washed her hands in a basin, and discarded her apron. "Why is she here?" Sarah inquired as she tucked her hair behind her ears.

"She is very worried about you, as I am." What more could she say? Sarah would hear it all in a minute. Elizabeth stood by her friend, facing Mrs. Collins.

"I had to see for myself. You looked tired." Mrs. Collins felt Sarah's forehead with the back of her hand. "And now I see that you must come home with me this instant before you get sick."

Her chin went up as high as the walls in the room. "But, Mother, I am the doctor's assistant. He needs me. The girls need me."

"I agree with your mother now, Sarah. You must go home to rest or you will be sick." Elizabeth pleaded, but deep down she knew she fought a losing battle.

Sarah brushed her hair aside. "I'm fine. The doctor makes me rest every few hours, and Mrs. Reynolds feeds me soup and tea very often."

"I don't feel you would tell us if you weren't doing fine." Mrs. Collins twirled a wisp of Sarah's hair, then patted her cheek. "Your father won't be happy with this decision. You know we'll be waiting when you change your mind." Mrs. Collins kissed Sarah's cheek and hugged her to her bosom.

Elizabeth and Sarah worked for four more days along with the skeleton crew. Surely, the end was in sight. All the girls had fought the fever and won; they were weak and pale—but out of danger.

All except Sarah.

A week and a half after the outbreak, Sarah was the last one to become ill. Weak from lack of rest, she collapsed as she made her rounds.

"Sarah. Sarah." Elizabeth held Sarah's head in her lap in the library where she had found her minutes before on the floor. "Doctor!" she called frantically. "Help me. Someone help me."

Dr. Ramsey entered the dark room. He lifted Sarah's eyelids. "She's unconscious with a raging fever."

Mrs. Collins arrived, and with the doctor's permission, she moved Sarah home to convalesce.

Dr. Ramsey saw them to the carriage and continued his rounds. "She's a strong girl, Mrs. Collins. I'll be by to see her in a few hours."

Elizabeth's concern transferred to Sarah, her best friend, who was now fighting for her life. Even Louis couldn't keep her away. "I'll be careful, Louis. I want to help her. She gave so much to those girls. They are all recovering because of her. At least I can be there for her."

Palms turned upward, he acquiesced. "All right. Perhaps part of the day wouldn't hurt you."

They reached a compromise: Elizabeth spent the afternoons by Sarah's bedside. She read to her, wiped her brow, gave her water, and prayed.

"Sarah will survive," Dr. Ramsey encouraged on a visit several days after Sarah had fallen ill.

His words were meant to comfort Elizabeth, but the tiny form under the covers didn't show strength or health. Was he just placating her? If he was, she didn't want to know the truth. She had to believe her friend would recover. "She has to, Doctor. I know others have died in the city. I won't let her be one of them."

"There have been only eight confirmed deaths from the influenza," he confirmed. "I feel the worst has passed. We fared better than past times. Keep doing what you're doing."

As Dr. Ramsey left, Samuel Evans entered with his hat in his hand. He had been a daily visitor at the boarding house and here, asking about Sarah. Elizabeth noticed the lines of concern on his brow. His soft words were spoken as if he was scared he might disturb the patient. "How is she?" he whispered.

"Come in, Samuel, and talk to her. I think she hears you." Elizabeth stared at Sarah's pale still hand and then placed it gently in hers. "I talk to her all the time."

After returning Sarah's hand to rest on the covers, Elizabeth directed Samuel to a straight-backed chair beside the bed. At first, he didn't say a word, didn't even look up from his hands, turning his hat round and round. Finally, he gazed at Sarah as she slept with sweat forming on her forehead. Elizabeth felt like an intruder and decided to stand by the window, letting her eyes wander occasionally to the couple.

Samuel reached for Sarah's hand and took it in his, caressing her fingers. "Sarah, this is Samuel. I'm so sorry you're ill. The doctor says you're getting better every day. I don't want to bother you, but I had to see for myself."

He gently pulled out a pressed flower, an early crocus, from his pocket and laid it on her pillow. "Well, I'll check on you tomorrow." He stood and turned to Elizabeth. "She'll be all right, won't she?"

She nodded. "Of course, Samuel. Yes, she will." Elizabeth lightly touched his sleeve and squeezed, wanting affirmation to sink in to relieve his creased brow.

What had she seen in his eyes and in his touch as he leaned over Sarah? Could it be love? Could the confirmed bachelor have found the love he'd been missing? He would never admit to searching for it. At thirty, he vowed over and over that he was content in his bachelorhood. But recently, Elizabeth felt she had witnessed a different side of Samuel. She couldn't wait to tell Louis their matchmaking might be paying off.

Elizabeth spent another few minutes rearranging the many cards, posies, and delicacies—like candies and pastries—on Sarah's dressing table. Between Mrs. Collins and Elizabeth, most of the well-wishers were sent on their way with a heartfelt "thank you," and "She is getting better." And she was.

A few days later Sarah was warmly dressed and comfortably wrapped in blankets in front of the fire in the back drawing room.

"You gave us a scare, Sarah. But now I strongly believe you're on your way to a hundred percent recovery." Elizabeth tucked the blanket in tighter around Sarah's legs. The February morning was bright but cool. No reason to take any chances.

"Thanks to you and Mother. I'm really not used to all of the attention. Now sit down and stop waiting on me. Tell me any news, please." Sarah smiled, one of the first such times in a week.

"News. Let's see. The school is back open in full swing—missing you, of course. The museum celebrated its first anniversary last week. And there's a ball at John Fullerton's house in a week. I do hope you're able to join us. Samuel will—" Elizabeth stopped to check the response at the mention of his name. Sarah's alert eyes and tilt of her head were proof enough for Elizabeth.

"Samuel will be joining us as I hope you will. He has come by almost every day to check on you."

"Really, I had no idea." Sarah giggled. "Well, that's not entirely true. I was awake the last few times. And I do have his card here, though, stating his plans to come by this afternoon."

At least, Sarah recognized his concern for her. "I think he really cares for you, Sarah."

"It's only because I was ill. Nothing more." When it came to men, even this man, Sarah seemed to give up hope, never really believing someone would be interested in her. Although her confidence had risen a bit, she still held back. Elizabeth didn't want to annoy her, but why was Sarah attempting to close off a part of herself?

Elizabeth shook her head in frustration. "If you and Samuel would ever shed your fear of—I don't even know what to call it. Fear of sharing your true feelings, I guess. Then maybe you could truly appreciate the other person. He cares for you. Somehow you'll just have to accept that." Since she couldn't shake sense into her friend, Elizabeth prayed she'd ponder the situation.

Soon Elizabeth exited, for she had fifteen eager girls awaiting their music class—an energetic group of fully recovered girls. They would delight in the news that Sarah would join them again next week.

Elizabeth stopped by her mother's on the way home. With the recent epidemic, there had been no time in the two weeks to follow up after the Daughters of Liberty meeting. She deposited her gloves on a tea table, empty except for a vase of camellias. "I know I've been neglectful of visiting you recently, Mother. How are you?"

"As you can see, I'm fine," she answered, not adding any details.

"Yes, you look it." Elizabeth stalled, putting her nose close to the enticing flowers. The promise of spring. "Tell me what you thought of the meeting at my house. Do you have any questions?"

Her mother didn't avoid Elizabeth's stare or question. Maybe she had thought through the information she had received and heard.

"I was very impressed by Mrs. Laurens and her wealth of knowledge and presentation. I do, finally, see the purpose of the group." Mother set her needlework aside, studied her hands a second, and lifted her eyes again. "You're supporting a cause that you believe will be better for the colony, Charles Town, and all citizens. I understand now. I no longer feel ignorant. But you do see my dilemma? What do I do about your father? I must be supportive of him too."

Elizabeth reached beyond the problems. Her mother held a belief in a good cause. Finally, Elizabeth saw an intelligent woman who was searching for knowledge. "I know. Has it caused problems yet? Does he know your beliefs now?"

"Yes. I couldn't deny them. He deserved to know the truth. After all, I have to live here with him. I couldn't hide that every day."

"Well, what did he say?" Elizabeth sat forward with her elbows on her knees.

"He was calm and unsurprised. He doesn't agree with me, and we don't discuss the matter. We are at a mutual standstill about the subject," her mother concluded, not in defeat, but with perhaps hope. That was more than Elizabeth thought possible.

She clasped her mother's hands in hers. Even though by a single fiber of thread, her mother's budding quest tied the two together. It could only grow stronger. *Who knows? Perhaps Father would join the women in his life on this matter.*

"Let me know what I can do to help. We'll have more meetings, and I hope you'll come. Anne and I feel so strongly about this cause for which our husbands are willing to sacrifice wealth and possibly even their lives."

It wouldn't come to that—not in Charles Town, not to Louis. Elizabeth shivered.

Hugging her mother, who was always straight-backed and

proper, Elizabeth felt her mother bend a little to the embrace. If she could let loose and show some maternal affection, another fiber in the thread of their relationship would strengthen.

Later the same week on Friday afternoon after a filling afternoon tea, Elizabeth strolled with Louis through the streets of Charles Town, basking in the cool breeze from the ocean.

"Peaceful, after a long tiring week at work," Louis said, as he absently patted her hand, resting in the crook of his arm. "You make it all worthwhile, Elizabeth."

She pulled him to a halt. "You exaggerate, Louis. You love your work. Admit it."

"True, but I love this more. Listen. Birds, the ocean, children. Peace." The serenity did indeed surround them for a few moments. They headed to Mazyck's Pasture near Alexander and Charlotte Streets, where the peacefulness dissipated.

"What is the shouting about? Let's find the voice." Louis guided Elizabeth to the muffled voices. "It could be interesting."

Under a giant live oak tree, appropriately called the Liberty Tree, stood Christopher Gadsden and a crowd of men, women, and even children. Elizabeth knew meetings under the tree had happened over the past few years, but she had never joined one in progress.

"I should have recognized the voice." Louis leaned his head on a nearby tree and pulled Elizabeth to him. They settled for a side-view position of the speaker and the crowd.

Christopher's voice boomed across the green area, resounding against the trees. The tall statesman was surrounded by other devout Liberty Boys—or Charles Town Whigs, as they were being called. "So far Britain has not repealed the Tea Act. If the statements from Parliament are correct and presented to us in their true form, King George has no plan whatsoever to repeal the act. That, my fellow citizens, is a blatant disregard for our rights."

Someone in the crowd—a familiar, but unexpected voice—volleyed back to Gadsden's proclamation. "You'll have more than the Tea Act to contend with soon. More acts than you can handle."

Elizabeth searched for the owner of the remarks. Other heads in the crowd also turned.

"There, Elizabeth. Off to the right side. The man in the red coat, military, of course." Louis pointed to a spot Elizabeth had overlooked.

"Yes. And if I'm not mistaken, that's George." She shuddered, thinking he was a figment of her imagination.

Louis turned his head to the voice and then to Elizabeth. "Our George? I thought he was in Philadelphia. Look. He's backing away from the group now. Let's talk to him." Louis pulled Elizabeth gently in George's direction.

He didn't need to encourage Elizabeth more. She loved her estranged brother, even though he chose to disassociate himself from her life.

"George. George, wait!" she called and ran after him still holding Louis' hand. When she had three feet to go, she let go of Louis and attached herself to George's arm with a strong grip. She briefly looked into his eyes, hoping to see the old George. None of that was apparent. It hadn't been for over a year.

"Good evening, Elizabeth. Louis. What a pleasant surprise. I should have expected to see you here following your distinguished leader." His words, laced with sarcasm, pricked Elizabeth's heart, not because of the words themselves, but because of the venom dripping from them. The sneer added a dimension of unpleasantness.

She had so many questions about his life, his plans, and his happiness. "How are you, George? What are you doing here? Are you home for a while?" Did she speak like a stranger? She tried not to react to his coolness, but George didn't give her much of a chance to shower sisterly love on him. She dropped her arm and straightened her jacket, attaching herself once again to Louis. Perhaps his strength could help her remain strong and upright.

"Only a short leave. I came to see Miss Seymour and happened upon this interesting sideshow." He grimaced while stretching out his hand to encompass the speaker and his audience.

Elizabeth didn't take the bait. She could feel Louis' upper arm muscles tense as he held back words for his brother-in-law. The hurt he had caused Elizabeth was inexcusable in Louis' mind. She knew her husband would be seething inside.

"Miss Seymour? Are you still courting her?" Just her name sent shivers up and down Elizabeth's spine. She wanted to tell him again to flee from her crafty clutch. "I thought maybe the distance would deter you."

"Not at all, sweet sister." *Sweet sister, indeed. I'm not fooled.* His words hurt her. "Letters do a world of good, keeping the fires burning. I wanted to surprise her."

"Where are you staying?"

His hands clutched the edges of his red jacket. "At the barracks. I'm used to the cot by now."

"You should at least go see Mother and Father. Please, George." She grabbed his coat sleeve and pleaded, knowing it wouldn't procure a desired result.

"Perhaps, for a few minutes. By the way, it looks like marriage is good for you. I hope this Frenchman is taking excellent care of you." George turned to Louis.

She transferred her hand to Louis' arm, feeling the warmth instantly. "That's one thing you don't have to worry about. Louis continues to make me very happy."

George nodded in his direction. "Great. Now I'll be on my way. Romance is waiting." He turned quickly so no more words could be said.

"Goodbye," Elizabeth whispered to the silent air. A part of her wanted to run after him, turn back time, beg him to be her brother again. She wiped a single tear from the corner of her eye.

❀

Elizabeth had put aside her disillusioned picture of George and concentrated instead on the Fullerton Ball. On Sunday afternoon, just six days before the ball, Sarah found her in the sun room having tea.

Sarah joined her. After setting her tea cup on the tea table, her friend cleared her throat. "Samuel convinced me to go to the Fullertons with him. I couldn't say no to his invitation. He came to see me every day until I was completely recovered. I still feel he was only concerned for a friend. So, my acceptance is a natural gesture of appreciation, nothing more."

Elizabeth laughed for her friend could not see what she saw. "I'll be watching for that 'nothing more.' You go on fooling yourself." She continued to sip her tea as if the problem had already fixed itself.

❀

Sarah dressed at Elizabeth's house on Saturday night almost like they were young girls again getting ready for their first ball. Of course, Elizabeth didn't feel the jitteriness her friend felt. Although she still wanted to please Louis with the clothes she wore and to coif her hair perfectly, she knew he belonged to her no matter the state of her appearance.

"I'm so glad you chose the pink dress, Sarah. It makes your dark hair and brown eyes shine. You're beautiful." The questions, the words—Elizabeth meant for them to soothe Sarah. Hopefully, they didn't just sound like noise. "Do you like the way Amy fixed your hair? She has improved so much."

Sarah toyed with the tight ringlets around her face. Her

modest bodice was trimmed with a row of sheer lace bordering the neckline. The ivory-colored wrap draped across her shoulders finished off the captivating image. "Yes, it's amazing. Thank you, Amy," Sarah said. The girl dipped her head in acceptance.

Elizabeth took the compliments personally since she had been a part of Amy's rescue. It had been a joy watching Amy Engle mature and grow these few months. More like a sister than a housemaid.

"Samuel will be very attentive with the prettiest girl at the ball on his arm." Elizabeth took Sarah's seat in front of the oval glass. "Now it's my turn." Amy put the last touches on Elizabeth's hair, adding a sprig of Queen Anne's lace behind her ear. She was pleased with the creation Ellen and Amy had designed from the material she had brought home from Wilson's. Any shade of blue accentuated her eyes and hair. Ready.

Descending the stairs, Elizabeth glanced at Louis waiting for them in the foyer. She wondered why he was pacing. It's not an important date for him. Was he nervous about Samuel?

He reached out his hand. "I see the extra time you took was worth it, ladies. Come now. I know another gentleman who is bound to be more impatient than myself." He placed a lady's hand on each of his arms, led them to the carriage, and made sure they settled in comfortably. The seat next to Sarah was left vacant for Samuel's long, imposing form.

Once they picked up Samuel, Elizabeth made it her role to keep the conversation flowing. But she soon realized there was no need. Samuel and Sarah took over rather quickly, leaving Elizabeth and Louis to become quiet spectators.

She knew the Fullerton house well. The single house, which she liked, was situated on Legare Street. As she peered at the three-story frame, she noted its light and airy feel. She and Louis ascended the staircase first, followed by Sarah and Samuel. The rooms, normally divided by folding doors, had been transformed into a large ballroom. The ingenious concept created an elegant space large enough for a well-attended party. Their house could almost fit in this one area.

Unfortunately, Mr. Fullerton didn't ban the discussion of politics from his home. In fact, it appeared to be part of the entertainment. Louis and Samuel quickly found the men gathered in various circles. She had no choice but to release him.

The women enjoyed appetizers and punch and their own topics of conversation about fashion, weddings, and courtships. Elizabeth usually slipped away when the gossip started, but tonight she was drawn in as her brother and Miss Seymour were discussed. The women tried to hush it up, but Elizabeth had heard too much.

"Please, continue. What did you hear about George?" she inquired as she entered the tight circle. She prepared for the worst with shoulders back, lips tight, and head slightly cocked.

"I was just repeating what I heard about the military ball," Mrs. Raley continued. "It appears that Miss Seymour was the guest of Captain William Burns. You remember him—don't you?"

Of course, she did. The woman was baiting her for an emotional response, but she gave none.

The woman continued unperturbed by the awkward conversation. "Well, neither knew that your brother was in town. When George saw Miss Seymour on the arm of the captain sharing an intimate *tête à tête*, he stormed across the room and demanded an explanation."

Elizabeth could imagine the scene with her brother's temper, never mind the purposeful exaggeration of Mrs. Raley. The lady knew Elizabeth and William Burns had courted. What did she want Elizabeth to say?

"Anyway, Miss Seymour was pulled away by George, only to be rescued by Captain Burns. Her tears and screams resulted in her exit with the captain behind her. George was asked to leave Charles Town immediately."

Not only booted out of the ball, but the whole town. All over

Miss Seymour? Elizabeth would never understand the attraction. She was still in shock when Louis claimed her for the first dance. She spilled out the story with as little expression as possible, not wanting to bring attention to herself.

"What was he thinking, Louis? What was she doing with William?" she whispered, enclosed tightly in his embrace.

"We don't know the whole story or the true story. Unfortunately, it sounds like the way George would handle the situation," Louis concluded and spun her out and back into his arms.

"What kind of game is Victoria playing? I wouldn't put it past her to have orchestrated the whole thing, string one along to make the other jealous." Her honest musings always spilled out with Louis.

"Now, clear your mind of any thoughts of them. Right at this moment, we have Mozart in the air and a dance floor to twirl around. Relax and enjoy." She noticed the sparkle in his eyes. Around and around the floor they went, all other dancers blurred in her vision. No Sarah. No Samuel. No circles of ladies gossiping. No men discussing politics. Just Louis for a few moments.

The news of George left a small gray cloud over Elizabeth's otherwise pleasant evening. She didn't expect any answers and wasn't surprised when she heard from her mother that he had returned to Philadelphia, leaving Miss Seymour to her own devices.

But that one bit of gloom didn't overshadow all the other rays of sunshine filling her days. One was the anticipation of their voyage to Boston—six weeks with Louis to herself away from the mercantile and his business deals. She wasn't naïve enough to believe everything would always be perfect with their time and life together, but this trip would be a memorable event.

Another bright spot in her life was the upcoming arrival of

Anne's baby. Daily the baby seemed to punctuate with his kicks that he was eventually going to enter this world.

"Oh, Anne, you look wonderful." Elizabeth entered her sister's house and found the expectant mother with her feet up on a stool in the sitting room. "I just know this baby will be such a joy and comfort."

"Well, we sure didn't think we'd have another one. So, any way we look at this, it's a miracle and a blessing. One day, Elizabeth, you'll know exactly how special," Anne whispered, as she captured her sister's hand.

Yes, one day. Elizabeth cherished the thought.

Amid the packing of their traveling trunks and telling friends and family goodbye, Elizabeth carved out time to talk to Louis, even in the upheaval. "I don't know what to do anymore about Sarah and Samuel. I want to advance the romance and help it along." She folded another petticoat.

Louis added a few items to his pile of stuff, a few books and papers. "You can't do anything about it. Samuel is very set in his ways. But I do see a slight break in his armor. Maybe with us gone for a month, he'll step out and—"

"And what? Court her without our arranging it? Actually talk to her parents? Can you see him doing that?" She placed another dress on top of the others in the trunk. Elizabeth paused and watched Louis place his hand on his writing desk and reach for his Bible.

"He's not a totally lost cause. He did come to church Sunday. He's asking me questions. I gave him some verses to read, the ones that helped me when I was searching. And you know he cares for Sarah. He was at her house every day while she recovered."

He stored his Bible and writing material in a trunk and secured Elizabeth in his embrace, preventing her from more packing. "That can wait. While I have you securely in my arms, let's talk about Boston and our time away."

Yes, packing could wait. She couldn't resist his playful, then serious attention. He kicked the bedroom door shut, barring other noises and images from entering their domain.

CHAPTER 20

*S*ince Louis had traveled all over Europe with his mother and endured various setbacks, he tried to anticipate all of the events wrapped up in a voyage with Elizabeth. He chose a ship taking a direct route to Boston. The ship was a medium-sized vessel, and the trip would take six to seven days, weather permitting. Although small, their cabin at least had a bed, a desk, chairs, and a place for their luggage. Louis was thankful to be within view of land for most of the journey. "It won't compare to the monotony of the wide-open ocean," Louis informed Samuel. "Anyway, I have Elizabeth to occupy my time."

"I don't envy the sea voyage. Keep me on land any day." His friend shrugged his shoulders and gritted his teeth.

"And that is why you will never get much farther than the next town. The King's Highway overland from Charles Town to Boston is thirteen hundred miles of good and bad roads, much improved over the past years though. At twenty-five miles per day, the journey still would be arduous." Louis laughed, knowing Samuel had no desire to leave the area. "Are you sure you don't mind checking in with Christopher every week on any business needs?" he asked.

"Not at all. It's my job." The lawyer side of Samuel convinced Louis that a few weeks away would cause no damage. "I can't believe you're leaving before your next shipment arrives."

"It's now or never. Elizabeth's sister is expecting her child in May. And frankly, I don't know how feasible travel will be with turmoil on the horizon with British ships appearing daily. I still get a strange, eerie feeling about possible repercussions from Parliament." Louis stared out the office window at ordinary people doing mundane routine chores like shopping and delivering.

"There's nothing you can do about that, my friend. Just go and have an enjoyable time," Samuel said.

"'God is our refuge and strength,'" Louis added, as he replaced his hat and took up his gloves and cane from the chair in front of Samuel's desk. "I must believe He is in control. It makes things a lot easier. You should try it, Samuel."

"I'll leave God to you."

For now, Louis would let Samuel's spiritual condition stand, but not forever. "Until April. Don't forget to check on Sarah for Elizabeth." Louis exited, leaving Samuel with legal instructions and, hopefully, hints about seeing Sarah.

Louis had said his goodbyes to his aunt, his uncle, and Christopher. He saw the trunks delivered to the ship. All was in order—at least all that he had control of personally. The weather, the government, and the rumors were out of his control and unpredictable.

Elizabeth spent time with her mother and father at morning tea and promised to see Grandmamma as much as possible when in Boston.

"You know she'll have many activities arranged for you. Be kind even if she's too presumptuous," Mother said.

"I can take care of Grandmamma, I promise. We understand each other, and she knows Louis is my number one concern." Elizabeth rose and kissed her mother's cheek. "I'm off to see Anne now."

A light midday meal with Anne reminded Elizabeth how much she would miss her sister. "Be sure to wait until I return to have your baby."

"The birth will still be a month away when you return. So, you are the one who needs to hurry back safely, please."

"I will. I'm so excited to show everything to Louis. It's not Paris, but I think he can enjoy Boston and what it has to offer." Elizabeth bit her lower lip. She hoped he would relax in a new place, leave his worries behind in Charles Town.

Elizabeth next popped into Wilson's Mercantile to kiss Jeannette and Henry good-bye. "I'm going to miss you. Thanks for watching things at the house for us. Ellen will enjoy your visits."

"My pleasure. You just go have a good time." Jeannette grabbed a bag from under the counter and stuck her hand in the big sweets jar. Elizabeth licked her lips, imagining sugar crystals lingering there. Lemon and peppermint were her favorites. "Here's a handful of treats for you and Louis as you wile away the hours on the ship." Jeannette deposited a nice-sized parcel filled with candies of all sorts into Elizabeth's hand.

"Louis will love these. But if you make me fat, Jeannette, I'll not forget it." Laughter and hugs followed before Elizabeth sought out Henry in the storeroom.

One more stop. It was perhaps the most difficult. Although Sarah had recovered from her illness and had become bolder through the year, she still seemed to depend on Elizabeth. Perhaps this time apart would cause her friend to branch out and be more independent. Maybe even welcome Samuel in her life. *Big steps for my petite friend.*

"Be sure to let Mrs. Reynolds know if you and Martha have any problems with the girls at school," she told her friend. "I'm sure you'll be fine. Martha will look to you for guidance since she's so young. I hope that I haven't put too much pressure on her."

"Elizabeth, we've been over and over this. We'll be fine, as long as I only have to handle theory classes and Martha has all the actual piano lessons."

"If you need anything, just ask Anne or Samuel. They have orders to look after you as needed."

"I wish you wouldn't act like my mother. I'm not a child."

"Speaking of your mother, she'll keep you company too." Elizabeth giggled as they embraced.

All farewells accomplished allowed a calm evening at home and an early start in the morning. Off to see Boston, but more importantly, to have time alone with Louis. No business and no family, except Grandmamma.

The early March weather was perfect. As they stood on the deck of the ship, their home for the next week, Elizabeth stared at the big beautiful homes with their wide balconies and porches and huge oak trees gracing the lawns. Home would be there when they returned, but now was the time for a little adventure.

Passengers waved and shouted to loved ones on the shore. The sails rustled in the wind, sending the air spiraling down, blowing her hair away from her face. The cool breeze from the ocean forced them to wear their cloaks over their travel clothes. Louis had a camel-toned wool overcoat that hung to below his knees, with a collar at the neck and a cape over the shoulders. Elizabeth's full-length, green wool cape fastened under her chin and down the front to keep the nippy wind at bay. She held it tight as the ship pulled away.

The houses, the piers, and then the harbor disappeared from view as they made their way into the Atlantic channel. "*Au revoir,*

Charles Town," Louis whispered as he settled his arm around Elizabeth's shoulders.

They settled into a shipboard routine for the next six days. Activity abounded all over the ship as they approached the active Boston harbor. Excited to be almost safely deposited on land, Elizabeth experienced an added urgency to show Louis her birthplace.

Standing at the rail, Elizabeth pointed to the activity on land. "It all seems so familiar, yet busier than I remember. Look at all the people and activity. Has it changed so much in the past nine months?"

The usual port activities permeated their view—loading and unloading of goods, passengers coming and going, ships from many different origins, men discussing business, ladies strolling with their parasols to the shops, and always the predominant red coats of the militia.

"That's the difference," she proclaimed with a frown.

"What is?"

The uniforms, the guns, Loyalists. "More military, and they appear to be stationed in larger groups all over the port." They walked down the crowded walkway to the busy square. "Could the military be so dominant because of the recent tea party?" Had Boston as a whole made its choice?

"No doubt. Rumors abound about new acts on the way to curtail future disobedience. Where's Griffin's Wharf where the tea was dumped?" Louis asked.

"I don't know for sure." She looked around and speculated that the crowd gathering to their right, surrounded by soldiers, would give a clue. Without discussion she followed Louis to the back fringe of the crowd.

Beneath a structure resembling a tree, a man waved a pamphlet in the air and screamed out "Read all about the abuses of Parliament and King George."

Leaning close to Louis, Elizabeth whispered, "This is a lot like what Christopher, James, and Mr. Timothy do in Charles Town, but this isn't a real tree." The item posing as a tree was a little dramatic, although the symbolism was appropriate for the Sons of Liberty. Their speeches had begun years ago in Charles Town under a live billowing tree.

"Let's go, Louis. We've heard it all before. Remember, this is our wedding trip. No politics if we can help it."

"You're so right." He followed her lead away from the tree. "But I sense the tension here is more prominent. Perhaps the concerts, plays, shopping, and parties will keep us occupied. Now for the luggage and our awaiting carriage." His gait quickened as if to escape the images of tyranny.

In their brief absence, the trunks had been loaded in the carriage, and the driver stood patiently waiting for the mean-dering couple to return. Louis had chosen an elegant hotel away from the harbor complete with the appropriate amenities for an extended stay—a sophisticated, upper-class establishment. Once in the entrance hall, she knew his contacts had pointed her husband to the perfect accommodation—lofty ceilings with sparkling chandeliers suspended above their heads, exquisite tile flooring, shiny dark-wood paneling ending at a chair rail, colorful fabric covering the wall to the ceiling. The elaborate sitting area provided comfort and ample room to congregate, relax, read the paper, or assemble before meals. She peeked into the dining hall with Chippendale tables of all sizes, from massive ones seating up to twelve guests to cozy oval ones for two to four.

The noontime activities and the carriage ride to the hotel left Elizabeth in need of exercise. She wasn't used to sitting around all day. A tour of part of the old town filled her restlessness. She opted for a light straw hat with a red ribbon, complementing her red-checkered skirt. Her white bodice and underskirt hinted at the fresh, spring season. They left their coats at the hotel and set out on foot.

In the Boston Common, she enjoyed the sunshine of the

cloudless day. The public park was a favorite gathering place for young and old, especially on a day like this one. She felt free of any agenda or obligation. For a few days she didn't have a house to run, lessons to teach, or charity work to administer. For a brief period, she'd set out to relax in the sole company of Louis. Through the guidance of her grandmother, Elizabeth committed to four of the Boston events. That would still give them time for concerts, lectures, and individual invitations.

She took Louis' hand and pulled him to her side. "What do you want to see first?"

"Surprise me. The afternoon is yours to govern. I don't want to have to make any decisions today."

She understood. A holiday from ordinary day-to-day life begged to be experienced and celebrated, even more so since it was a honeymoon.

"Then off we go to King's Chapel." Ready to show off her birthplace, she pulled Louis to his feet. "I always stop inside for a time of prayer. It is a peaceful place. If only the statues and pews and windows could tell of the first members. The burying ground shares some of the stories—some tragic, some commonplace." She almost skipped but progressed in an even gait instead.

Louis tipped his hat to quite a few friendly ladies and gentlemen. "Not knowing a soul gives me time to take in all of my surroundings. It still amazes me that buildings and monuments and even burial grounds could not be much more than a hundred years old. Such a young world compared to Europe. History is still being birthed here, the beginnings of something great and flourishing."

Elizabeth turned to him, pulling on his sleeve to have him face her. "You sure do put a unique spin on things. How old is the cemetery where your ancestors are buried?"

He shrugged, stuffing his hands in his pockets. "I can't say for sure, but at least seven hundred years. Some tombstones have eroded through time and taken their dates with them. You must have relatives buried someplace in Europe."

"Yes, my grandmother speaks of churches and cemeteries in Switzerland. But I never asked her about the dates. There must be sites in England too. I expect one day our great-great-grandchildren will be touring the grounds of South Carolina for our tombstones."

"Today is too pretty and fresh to talk of our demise."

She smiled at the thought of her future with Louis—not concerned with a hundred years in the future. "Tell me more of your old world."

Louis patted her hand and focused on a distant object. "Europe, and more personally France, has already experienced many reshaping, reconstructing, and reforming eras." He described the ancient stones, some crumbling, some firm with reverence but in a dreamy, vague veil. "And I'm fearful she is in for a big change as she's watching what the colonies do. America is just beginning the process of making history."

Elizabeth moved her hand from his arm to clasp his hand. His past, one she was not a part of, was emotional for him. *Does he miss it? Or does he miss the ghosts of it—something that no longer remains?* All Elizabeth had to compare his world to were history books and now Louis' own account. Instead of Boston's being an old, stable city, her Boston was a youth. She now saw it through Louis' eyes.

"Maybe this New World won't have to participate in the growing pains like other nations." He paused. "Or does all growth involve pain and heartache? I remember my Huguenot upbringing and the persecution, the loss of land and title and the disdain of aristocracy and privilege. I wonder if America could avoid these lessons."

"Freedom of worship is a big issue." Elizabeth picked up the thread of conversation. "Charles Town handled it outwardly just fine with several different houses of worship scattered throughout the city. But will England continue to let the many beliefs stand alongside the Church of England?"

Louis shrugged. "So far, at least in Charles Town, that doesn't seem to be a problem."

As they approached the façade of King's Chapel, she remembered how it had dominated the street. She caught Louis' inquisitive, leaning head, and she laughed. "I know it appears to be incomplete because the steeple is missing, and the colonnade is under construction."

"Perhaps that is what's puzzling me." Louis straightened his stance.

"All of this stone structure was built over the original 1688 wooden church. Before completion about twenty years ago, the old church was thrown out of the windows," she explained while laughing as she visualized a group of people pitching wood and furniture to the outside.

They stepped inside and found a quiet pew in the middle of the church. Elizabeth wondered if Louis could be impressed with something so new compared with the older churches in France. The light hitting the windows was comforting and cheery. Surely it could console anyone. She glanced at Louis with the light dancing on his cheeks. His upturned face and grin confirmed her suspicions about the inspiring atmosphere.

They knelt for a time of prayer in the serenity of the moment, the past and future set aside. She thanked God for Louis and this time away from the ordinary.

Finally, she touched his arm, and they walked silently out the side door. Immediately, she skipped a step or two forward. "Let's wander through this graveyard." They were here, so surely, he wouldn't refuse.

"I don't understand you and cemeteries," Louis commented. "What do you see here that draws you to relinquish your time?" He stood with his arms crossed as Elizabeth crouched next to an old stone.

"Is it that strange? Aren't you just a little curious about who this lady was and how many children she had? How did she die? Each marker has a story. It causes me to want to make sure my story is complete exactly the way God wants it for me."

"So, you aren't sad for these people?" He gestured with both arms, circling the tombstones in view.

"Not at all. You do realize that they aren't here? Surely most of them are in heaven. The rest, well, they aren't here either. But they made their decision by not accepting Christ while they had time. Anyway, all this inspires me to live my life fully."

She wondered if Louis might view the next graveyard in a different light.

"Next stop, Faneuil Hall. You might know it from a forum where the first Partisans protested the Sugar and Stamp Acts and more recently some meetings of the Sons of Liberty before the dumping of the tea. But before all that, it was designed as a center of commerce. On the first floor are wonderful, busy market stalls. That is my destination."

"Of course, it is. Shopping." He laughed. "So where were the meetings?"

"Right above it on the second floor. You might want to peek while I browse the goods."

Out of curiosity, he took a few minutes to see where famous speeches had been made—the most powerful one involving the doctrine of "no taxation without representation." Louis recalled that Samuel Adams had held a funeral for the victims of the Boston Massacre here. The story circulated that later Mr. Adams offered his personal family burial site in the Granary Burying Ground to the massacre victims. What a predominant, confident man. He wondered if Mr. Adams was in town now.

His thoughts strayed to the political scene for a fraction of a minute before he remembered the purpose of this trip and his conscience brought his thoughts to a halt. This was his honeymoon, and he had a beautiful wife to attend. When dwelling on her attributes and living, breathing body, the thought of politics scurried away.

The days and evenings passed pleasantly. He was good to his word and stuck to his vow to focus on Elizabeth with vigor. The couple attended a harpsichord concert at Concert Hall performed by Mr. Selby one afternoon and another evening concert including the orchestra's rendition of Hayden's Keyboard Concerto No 10 in C and Mozart's Kyrie in D and Church Sonata in B flat. The names and pieces meant nothing to him outside of the radiant smile and warmth of her by his side. He spent more time watching her and listening to her sigh and breathe than to the concert.

She included walking tours every day until he had seen all the important sites. While she explained what they meant to her growing up here, Louis attached them to political events, though not always aloud. They viewed the Townhouse, presently the seat of the British government in Boston. Within the walls, great debates between Samuel Adams and the government had taken place. As the center of Boston's civic, commercial, and political life, he could almost hear the taxation issues resounding inside.

Elizabeth's knowledge continued to enlighten him. "On the top is the cupola with the lion and unicorn on it, symbolizing royal authority. And right outside the building is the site of the Boston Massacre." He didn't want to visualize that gruesome scene. Would Charles Town ever be a repeat of death in the streets? He prayed not.

Each Sunday they joined Grandmamma for the morning worship service at Christ Church. He looked around the fifty-year-old building that boasted of being the oldest standing church in town. For sure, no one could miss the hundred-and-ninety-foot steeple from any vantage point.

Although the ceremony was the same from the Book of Common Prayer, Louis missed Reverend Smith and his own church family. He believed worship could take place anywhere, though, so he opened his spirit to hear God's Word.

"The Gospel of Matthew states in Chapter 5 verses 43 and 44, 'Ye have heard that it hath been said, Thou shalt love thy neighbor, and hate thine enemy. But I say unto you, Love your enemies, bless them that curse you, do good to them that hate you, and pray for them which despitefully use you and persecute you.' Who are your enemies? Your neighbors? Your countrymen? Or do you treat everyone as a brother or friend? In the coming days, remember Jesus's words about unconditional love." The minister's voice boomed from his pulpit.

I have brothers and even friends to whom I have a tough time giving my good thoughts and prayers. How can I love my enemy when I don't even know from day to day who that person is? Today he might be a neighbor and tomorrow a British spy. The minister surely doesn't know what I know.

Later, after a satisfying meal of stewed lamb and fresh vegetables in a cream sauce, Elizabeth said, "Every sermon I hear lately is focusing on loving our enemies. It's as if the church is trying to prepare or warn us about things to come. I don't feel that I have enemies. But I do disagree with certain views and want different outcomes."

Louis sat back in his chair. "I know. Those that disagree are all around us." Rifts in their own community confronted him every day. As a husband, he wanted to protect Elizabeth, but it seemed she was more aware of the rifts than he was.

"I worry about George and his hatred of any belief that is not his." She sighed and rose to pace the room. "If this is hard for me, I know it must be hard for a clergyman to support a Partisan cause, especially if it goes against the king, but that is what appears to be happening. The minister today admitted it to a certain degree."

"I agree. Even Reverend Smith has attended our Liberty meetings at home. I think he risks a lot by taking a stand. Maybe by subtly preparing us for the plight, these ministers are taking a stand for what is right for their parishioners."

"Yet, their positions in the church are securely tied to the British rule," she responded.

He didn't claim to understand it either. "I hate to keep saying this, but we need to be prepared. Boston is a pivotal player in this game much more so than Charles Town. Whatever this city does, ours is sure to follow."

Already it was Tuesday night and the soirée at Mr. and Mrs. Randolph Cookston's. "I promise to introduce you to some interesting people," Grandmamma said once again. "Since your marriage, you are now old enough and mature enough to attend all these high-society events. Remember how you dreamed of them as a little girl?"

"And now I could just as easily stay at home with a book and my handsome husband." Elizabeth turned as Louis entered the drawing room. "Are you still sure about going tonight?" She knew he was interested, although not thrilled, to be thrown into society. In Charles Town, he was now well known. But here he probably felt he was once again a stranger.

"I've done it before; I can do it again." He convinced her he was comfortable with the parties.

She twirled in her new ball gown created by a local seamstress. The satin material was light to the touch, perfect for the warm weather. She'd chosen a new color—chartreuse—with a faint flower pattern. The bodice fastened in the front with a wide ecru lace neckline and satin ribbons with two jeweled buttons. She turned around, enjoying the feel of the satin underskirt showing its off-white hue down her front.

Louis delighted her with his tan breeches, white ruffled shirt under an ecru silk waistcoat, cravat, and a royal-blue coat. She admired his ability to present himself wigless, not even bothering to keep one on hand. She knew he preferred his thick brown hair to be naturally tied with a casual bow. She did too.

"I don't know if I want everyone staring at you tonight. You're beautiful." Louis drew her into his embrace.

"Then be sure to stay close. I don't want too many strange men to claim me on the dance floor."

"Only if your grandmother approves of them will I let you accept."

"So, they have to be her age or older?" she teased.

"We'll see." He kissed the tip of her nose before leading her out the front door to the carriage.

The Cookstons' small palace was the perfect place to host a party for the hundred-plus guests. It was easy to flow from room to room, always enticed by flowers, food, and drink. Her grandmother kept the couple close as she introduced them to many neighbors and friends. The list could have read like a prestigious roll call of old Boston families.

"Mr. and Mrs. Cookston, I present my granddaughter, Elizabeth, and her husband, Louis Lestarjette."

The couple in their mid-fifties, obviously at home with the crowd of sophisticated citizens, shook their hands and nodded. "Welcome to our home."

Grandmamma led them further inside. Soon they greeted other guests; the names drifted in and out of Elizabeth's head, few really sticking. Until—

"I would like you to meet Mr. and Mrs. John Adams, Mr. Samuel Adams, Mr. Paul Revere, and Mr. Silas Deane."

How did Grandmamma know Samuel Adams? Over the last weeks the Adams name had shown up everywhere. Louis spoke of them often on their tours around town. She struggled to force her jaw to remain in place with her smile. If she was in awe, what about him?

"Please join us for a while, Mr. and Mrs. Lestarjette," Samuel Adams said, coaxing them with his pleasant smile.

"Yes, please." Mrs. Adams commented, standing beside John. "I dislike being the only woman in the group, but if I leave my husband, I will never see him again."

Grandmamma squeezed her hand and wandered off, leaving Elizabeth to fend for herself. Well, not totally alone. Louis would carry much of the conversation, she supposed.

"What brings you to Boston, Mr. Lestarjette?" Samuel Adams asked.

"A belated wedding trip," Louis answered. "Elizabeth wanted to show me her hometown."

She grinned, surprised he didn't overflow with questions. Was he awestruck? She gave him a sideways glance. *Come, Louis, here is your chance to meet some political rebels.*

"Are you from France, sir?" Mr. Deane questioned. "I noted a slight Parisian accent. I hope to have the opportunity to travel there one day."

"Yes, from Paris. Now I'm a merchant in Charles Town, as well as a ship owner and businessman."

"What do you think of our outspoken city? I'm sure you've gotten wind of our messy events." Mr. John Adams got straight to the point. Was he testing Louis? He knew enough about Samuel Adams and John Adams to know he spoke with true Patriots.

"I have read as much as I can on the issues. I attend local Sons of Liberty meetings, and I support unashamedly the actions and beliefs of my fellow Partisans," Louis said.

"Well said, young man." John patted him on the shoulder. "We could use a man like you. I think knowing French will be valuable over the next few years. I'm sure your friends have told you that."

"Yes, sir. Already I've made a trip to France to set up contacts, but I still hope we don't have to use any force," Louis stressed.

"Keep listening, Mr. Lestarjette. Any day now we'll hear from Parliament, and it won't be to our liking." Samuel nodded to the group. "I hope to speak with you again soon." He left the room, taking Deane and Revere with him.

"My cousin seems to thrive on this debate. As a lawyer, I want it all to be settled legally." John paused as his wife pinched his arm. "Well, I made a promise to my Abigail not to talk politics. I've already broken that pledge tonight. How about joining me for a lecture at Harvard University on Thursday?" John asked.

Louis glanced at Elizabeth, who slightly lowered her head. She wouldn't let him pass up a chance to congregate with John Adams.

"And I'll take Mrs. Lestarjette for tea or coffee and shopping. An afternoon away from the children would be a great incentive for me. Would you like to join me?" Mrs. Adams had no airs, even with her outspoken husband attended by numerous men vying for his attention. Her plain attire—not of silk or satin, like much of the crowd—emphasized her matronly role. Her rosy cheeks and friendly smile provided Elizabeth the hope of a friendship with the older woman.

Elizabeth didn't need to contemplate her response. "Yes, Mrs. Adams, I would."

She patted Elizabeth's sleeve. "Just call me Abigail."

"Elizabeth." She reciprocated at the request.

After plans were finalized for Thursday, she enjoyed the rest of the evening with no renewed talk of politics, of acts, of the king. When she danced with Louis, the other Bostonians faded in and out of view. He was her center—not the prestigious Patriots. But outside the circle of his love, she found the Adams impressed her as no others that evening. The married couple held on to each other as if newlyweds. Their love beamed even after five children and a life of upheaval.

On the ride home in the carriage, Elizabeth caressed her

grandmother's gloved hand. "How do I thank you for introducing us to a very lively and interesting Boston tonight? You could have warned us."

Grandmamma grinned. "And spoil seeing your expressions? I take it Samuel Adams and John and Abigail Adams met with your approval."

Elizabeth nodded and kissed her grandmother's cheek. "More than you know."

"And that goes for me, too, Grandmamma." Louis faced Elizabeth and Grandmamma and leaned forward to embrace their locked hands.

CHAPTER 21

*E*lizabeth straightened Louis' cravat. "Our first afternoon apart since we arrived. I still don't know if I approve of Mr. Adams taking you away from me."

"I could hardly say no when a well-known man privy to many other prominent Bostonians extends an invitation. How could I refuse?" He raised his hands in surrender.

Hands on hips, she agreed. In fact, she didn't mind associating with Abigail. After all, they couldn't entirely avoid the things dominating their world. Boston wasn't an island. It was the bed of free-thinking men at the center of civilization.

"You don't have to give me an excuse, Louis. I'm glad you're included. Now go and have a nice time with the academics at Harvard. I'll scour the town with Abigail spending your money." With that playful note, Elizabeth sashayed out of their suite to meet the carriage sent by her new friend.

Shopping was one of Elizabeth's favorite outings in Boston. It wasn't a new experience by any means, but she now viewed shops and purchases from a different perspective. No longer a young girl envying other customers and their packages, shopping had become a social event, more of a conversational opportunity than a spending frenzy. The time with Abigail would also be an educational one, Elizabeth had no doubt.

"I've left five children at home," Abigail commented as Elizabeth joined her in the carriage. "This is truly a treat."

This talkative woman, about ten years older than Elizabeth, had accomplished so much, at least along the lines of family. *Maybe that will be me one day.* She admired Abigail's simple attire— a clean, crisp blue dress with a tiny lace trim. A few ringlets of her shiny brown hair escaped her perfectly positioned bonnet. Perhaps Elizabeth should have changed her dress of olive green with dainty yellow flowers for a plain day dress. Anyway, this was her honeymoon, and she had her new dresses for the occasion. Perhaps when she had five children, her attire would take second place. That was years away, however, and she planned to keep Louis gazing at her for a few more years.

"Please tell me about them. They seem to be the center of your life," Elizabeth returned, truly interested in the woman's full life.

"I never have a moment's peace. Lessons, meals, squabbles." Abigail laughed. "Enjoy your days with a quiet house."

It took about five minutes for Abigail to transmit the pride she had for her active, large brood. Even the negatives of sickness and mischief sounded like a positive situation to Elizabeth.

Elizabeth let the words trickle to each nerve. *This is what I want, to be so much a part of Louis' life and the center of my children's. Abigail is doing it, so can I.* "You make it seem like a joyous experience, even though you emphasize the noise and constant activity. Motherhood must be the greatest accomplishment a woman could have."

"One of them. I know many women who aren't mothers and have fulfilling lives as wives. Even a few of my friends who have remained unmarried and tend to excel in their freedom and make an impact. So, I guess what I'm saying is being a mother is right for me, but maybe not for everyone."

Why couldn't Elizabeth's mother have passed on the same wisdom?

"I do hope that is what God wants for me. But I've never really thought about life without children." For some reason Elizabeth didn't find it as negative a prospect as before—not as long as she had Louis.

"Now, let's not dwell on my brood this afternoon. I want to know all about you and Charles Town and your handsome Louis."

They had a lot in common, which surprised Elizabeth. But why should it? She was also a woman in the public arena who was active in church, took part in charitable projects, met the needs of the poor, as well as loved music.

"Use your time without children to polish and practice your music. I can't imagine sitting at a pianoforte for an hour with five ruffians running around," Abigail laughed.

After a round in the shops, Abigail guided them to a corner café. "Let's rest over a cup of tea."

"Good, because I still have unanswered questions," Elizabeth said. They ordered their refreshments and settled in for a time. "Tell me about your role in the Daughters of Liberty. I wonder if your group is more active than ours." Elizabeth wanted to learn so much from her friend and felt like a girl in school sitting on the edge of her seat.

"Well, we meet regularly. Over the past few months, our group has expanded, especially since the incident in the harbor. The men are concerned about the consequences that will be sent as punishment. I feel I need to be ready to support John and protect our children."

"How are you preparing for that?" Elizabeth asked.

"We're willing to make sacrifices in the area of boycotts and rationing. If it comes to it, we'll store up supplies and food for any kind of siege or threat from Britain." Abigail gestured for Elizabeth to lean in closer. "We've even sown extra pockets in our petticoats as a place to hide documents, jewels, money, or weapons. If you think about it, lots could be stored under a big, billowing skirt." The woman's huge grin shed a comical light on the discussion.

"You almost sound excited, like you are a spy or a pirate." Elizabeth gasped as a tiny chuckle escaped. "We could employ the same preparations in Charles Town. In fact, I'm going to propose it at our next meeting."

"Well, our prayer is that it won't come to any of that. But the things I hear John say don't support a peaceful ending."

Elizabeth nodded, still contemplating the deep pockets. "Will you show me a petticoat with pockets?"

"Of course."

"And I'll give the Boston ladies all the credit." She giggled, trying to imagine having to actually conceal secrets in her petticoat.

Louis wondered about the ladies. *They're probably nibbling on pastries in a comfortable tea room.* He sat next to Samuel on a hard bench at Harvard, listening to debates on the past acts of Parliament and the historical penalties and outcomes of disputing Parliament. His mind wandered in and out of the meeting, finally homing in on John's speech.

"My point, gentlemen, as I've said before, is that our provincial legislatives should be fully sovereign over our own internal affairs and that the colonies are connected to Great Britain only through the king, not Parliament."

"Huzzah! Huzzah!" Louis noticed the crowd predominately supported the cause for equal representation. Obviously, the gatherers had not invited their Loyalist counterparts.

John concluded with a bold statement. "If a workable line cannot be drawn between parliamentary sovereignty and the total independence of the colonies, then the colonies will have no other choice but to choose independence."

Louis realized that this lawyer had fought this battle before. The man didn't want a war or a battle, but it appeared that Parliament did.

The spokesman continued. "Parliament and the king are separate. These colonies should have their own voice to the king. The fight is against Parliament, laws and regulations—not against the sovereign king. If only King George would listen to us personally."

John returned to his seat in between Samuel and Louis. Louis looked around and listened as John pointed out the local characters from the Sons of Liberty attending the political debate, which in fact was one-sided. It had turned into a rally for support and ideas. Groups formed around the hall to casually discuss the past events. No one seemed to know what the future held for anyone.

Mr. Deane spoke briefly to Louis. Both came from regions outside of Boston, and Louis was drawn to him—possibly because of their lack of local roots.

"How did you find connection with Mr. Adams?" Louis asked.

"I'm involved in legal matters in Connecticut." Mr. Deane's answer should have been obvious to Louis. "I have a great admiration for Mr. Adams and the Sons of Liberty. So, I spend as much time as I can with men like him, the finest lawyers of our day. I feel we'll soon all join as one body, and these colony borders and distinctions will come under one banner."

Another soul reminding Louis of Christopher. "One banner, as in one nation?"

"Yes, exactly." His new acquaintance stared at Louis, not allowing him to retreat.

Did Louis want to hear the commitments of yet more citizens? One nation? "Therefore, you are telling me that independence from Britain is the outcome according to many of these men present?" Louis waved his hand toward the crowd.

He nodded once. "It completely depends on what Parliament

sends our way. Mr. Lestarjette, you, and possibly France, might be involved in some radical actions soon. I'm not an alarmist. But give the British a few more weeks."

Mr. Deane's keen interest in France sparked concern and curiosity. Louis knew it wouldn't take much to involve his countrymen. "What's your involvement with foreign support?"

"I won't say much now. My prediction is that the colonies will need an active presence in places like France to gain financial and material support. I'd be willing to serve if duty called. The only drawback for me is that I speak very little French. People like you could become a great asset to the colonies, if the need arises."

Secrets. In other words, this new nation would seek the support of France to build protection against Britain. At present, Louis had no concerns about shipments from his brother, even with the questionable cargo. But would his opinion change during a war? Putting his ship and crew in harm's way posed a different set of problems. Were all these men willing to make that firm, unyielding stand, placing their lives in the hands of a new nation? Was he?

A few more weeks. Would there be a peaceful resolution or a promised revolution? Louis began to recognize the strengths of the colonists. Strength in numbers. Solidarity in mission. A winning combination. But at what cost?

After sharing their experiences later over dinner, Louis suggested a stroll in the Common. He linked her arm in his and moved toward their destination. "Let's get lost in the crowd of Boston and pretend we don't know anyone." Perhaps Louis could concentrate so profoundly on Elizabeth that, in fact, the rest would disappear.

"You seem distracted, Louis." She obviously had picked up on his disheveled ponderings. "Tonight, you can discard politics and look around you at the beauty—the stars, the green grass, the flowers—and breathe the air of spring."

"And gaze at you, by far the most beautiful in God's creation. You're right. I need to leave my visions of unrest in the lecture hall." Louis adjusted his thoughts to include the calmness surrounding him now. Love from Elizabeth and God could permeate him and surround him even in the turmoil boiling in their homeland.

CHAPTER 22

"I can't believe our time here is almost over." Elizabeth peered into an empty trunk, waiting to be filled.

Louis reached around Elizabeth from the back and pulled her close. "We shouldn't be sad. Look at the new friends we have made. Our wedding trip doesn't have to end once we get home. I hope that it is a little calmer, with not so many parties and gatherings."

As he rocked her back and forth, pressing his cheek against hers, he felt a special warmth for Elizabeth's Boston. Her grandmother and the townspeople had made Louis feel welcome and not so much a foreigner. He was glad once again that he had given this new land a chance.

Louis spun Elizabeth around and kissed her deeply. "Thank you."

"For what?" She ran her fingers through his hair.

"For giving me a reason to stay in Charles Town, for marrying me, for showing me Boston, for loving me," he said.

"All of that?"

"And more." Much more. A knock on their door broke up their embrace. "Yes, enter." The butler presented a single letter on a

silver tray. "Thank you. If I have a reply, I'll leave it in the foyer."
He opened the missive. "It's from John Adams. He's invited us to
an important meeting at Faneuil Hall this afternoon."

Elizabeth raced to the wardrobe, rummaging through her
dresses. "With no other warning? How could a meeting be called
so quickly?"

"All I can think is something political has happened." Louis
raised his eyebrow and looked through his lashes at Elizabeth.
"I'm surprised he has invited you to a place known for controversial assemblies."

"But I am invited by name, and you will let me go, right?" Elizabeth crossed the room and stood with arms crossed in front
of Louis.

Looking into her determined eyes, Louis grinned and realized
he had no intention of leaving her behind. "You will not depart
my side, my dear." Elizabeth clapped like he had given her a gift.

He kissed her before they turned their attention to finding the
appropriate attire, choosing comfortable everyday clothes for the
brisk walk to the market building. Wall-to-wall people packed the
second floor of the space. Louis marveled at how word had
permeated the city in only a few hours. He chose a place at the
back close to an exit. This many people in one place caused Louis
a bit of concern. It was a mixed group of merchants, farmers,
lawyers, and townspeople. Loyalists and Liberty Boys.

He kept Elizabeth's hand looped on his arm. Feeling her close
gave him the sense that he protected her from the crowd. She
didn't seem worried, but he could feel her rise and fall on her
tiptoes as she tried to see more clearly.

Samuel Adams spoke from the lectern on the stage. Louis
could see his new friend's animated face and hoped he could hear
the words from such a distance.

"Prime Minister Lord North has sent the latest act of the
government. In response to Boston's dumping of the tea, the
English government resolves 'to pursue such measures as shall be

effectual for securing the Dependence of the colonies upon the Kingdom.' The first of these measures, my fellow citizens, is called the Boston Port Act."

A roar of whispers arose as those assembled voiced their suspense. Elizabeth squeezed Louis' arm. "I can't imagine that it is good for Boston," she whispered.

As Adams raised his voice to continue, a hush hovered over the crowd. "This is the first of several acts. The port of Boston shall be closed to commerce until the East India Company has been repaid for the destroyed tea and until the king is satisfied that order has been restored."

Objections rose from the floor.

"Not fair!"

"The punishment settled on Boston—not New York, Philadelphia, or Charles Town?"

"Boston is the target to teach all a lesson in obedience."

Louis remained quiet but perplexed. One of the objections spiraled loudly over the crowd: Samuel continued, "The Port Act is punishing all of Boston rather than just the individuals who had destroyed the tea. We're all being punished without having been given an opportunity to testify in our defense." He paused, scanning the audience which had ceased chattering. "They are in hot pursuit of revenge. Today is March 31, 1774, three months after the ports turned away, dumped, or stored the East India tea. It's penalty time. Beware that other acts will surely follow," Samuel concluded.

Louis didn't want to stay for the debate to follow. Crowds and worried or irate citizens didn't mix well. "Let's make our quiet departure before the real debates begin." Louis eased Elizabeth through the door. "I know enough, and there's always tomorrow's paper. I wonder what the reaction will be in Charles Town."

A shadow accompanied him on the walk home, one not visible before. Not noticeable at times but ever-present. The shadow of conflict, of change.

Elizabeth clung to Louis' arm, her fingers gripping his tense muscle. "Louis, will we still be able to leave on our ship next week?

"Yes," he said, hoping he was right. "Minus any cargo, it seems they can't stop passengers. But we won't tarry any longer. It's time to get back home."

Elizabeth stopped and pulled on Louis' sleeve. "Will Grandmamma be safe?"

"For now. She can always come stay with us if she feels threatened." *Surely common citizens are not in harm's way. Not yet, at least. God, I pray I'm right.*

The Sunday service at Christ Church should have given Louis a respite from gloom and doom. He willed himself to concentrate on worship. His faith remained in God—not in man. So surely, he could praise Him.

Even though Louis refrained from an alarmist role, the pieces all lined up and pointed to a tremendous time of change. The sermon from Psalm 46 depicted a trembling nation surrounded by enemies, calling on God. And His answer rang out, "Depend on Me. I will sustain you." Louis claimed the promise now for his family, town, and new homeland.

On the morrow Louis and Elizabeth would head home, leaving a place full of memories, but ones they could recall anytime they needed. Louis said a quiet prayer before leaving the sanctuary. *Guide us through whatever circumstances await us in Charles Town. You are in control of our lives, and our hope is in You.*

The carriage ride to the home of Elizabeth's grandmother was somber, considering the sermon, the recent political news, and their departure so soon. All afternoon, as they spent precious hours with Grandmamma and then returned to their room to make their final preparations, Louis noted Elizabeth's watery eyes. He knew leaving not only her grandmother but also the city of her birth was hard. His past goodbyes echoed in his mind, reminding him of how difficult the day must be for her.

On Monday morning, after watching the trunks load, Louis took Elizabeth to her grandmother's house for the last time. She ran into the older woman's arms and embraced her through tears.

Tears meandered down Grandmamma's cheeks. She pushed Elizabeth a few inches away in order to look into her eyes. "Now, child, go with Louis and continue your life in Charles Town. And I'll be here praying for you and writing you soon."

"Yes, Grandmamma. I know I must, but I always miss you."

Louis entered the circle and received his goodbye kiss. "I'll take care of her, Grandmamma."

"I know you will." She patted his cheek. "Now you must leave, or you'll miss your boat."

Minutes later with Elizabeth tucked under his arm, Louis stood once again looking at the harbor with new eyes. His visit to Boston had cemented his loyalty. Stationed with more of a purpose on this day in April, the militia appeared on duty and on guard for any ships with cargo. They enforced the act by a shield of redcoats.

A different picture from a month before. Louis saw Elizabeth's childhood Boston as a mature, slightly battered city. No scars on the outside, but ones on the inside, on the hearts of her people.

By the time they arrived home a week later, Charles Town was abuzz with the latest news. Although Louis had attended the meeting in Boston, he wanted to be a part of the ones here, too.

At King's Tavern the night after Louis returned, Christopher,

Samuel, and Henry met with Louis to fill him in on all the events. In March, Christopher, before knowing about the Port Act, had called the Sons of Liberty together in secret to rededicate themselves to resistance. "We resolved that our present conduct depends on whether we shall in the future be taxed by any other than representatives of our choice. Our province shall preserve its reputation or sink into disgrace and contempt," Christopher shared.

"And when did you hold the group meeting?" Louis asked.

"March sixteenth," Christopher said. "Our group led the movement to establish a standing General Committee. It will act as a temporary executive branch and will rally the people against any further efforts at tea importation."

"Do you think our port will be closed?" Louis asked all the questions he'd wondered about in Boston but that no one could answer.

"Not yet. It seems all of the acts are aimed at Boston and the Massachusetts colony."

"Acts? I only know of one, but there were rumors of others." Louis wondered how one week on a ship sheltered him from so much news.

"Here's the paper listing them." Christopher handed him a folded copy of a local newspaper from his jacket. The front page covered the Coercive Acts. "We call them the Intolerable Acts. See what you think, Louis."

He skimmed the article until he found the list. Added to the Port Act, the Massachusetts Government Act stated all positions in the colonial government had to be approved by the governor and the king. Town meetings were limited to one a year.

Louis looked up to find Christopher waiting. "Will they administer the same penalties and restrictions to the government of South Carolina?"

Christopher drummed his fingers on the table. "That's the fear. That our fate will be the same as theirs. Read on."

"'The Administration of Justice Act allows the governor to move trials of accused royal officials to another colony or even to Great Britain.' So," Louis said, "a Loyalist could get away with any crime and be shipped home to escape a true trial." All men nodded.

The fourth one was the Quartering Act, which applied to all the colonies, allowing a governor to house soldiers in unoccupied buildings if suitable quarters were not provided.

"Do you see what's happening here? It's not only Boston being violated. These acts are a threat to the rights of all the colonies. I predict the hatred against Britain will grow," Christopher stated.

"Once again then, it's wait and see." They had all been playing that game for a while—to see what Britain would do. Louis had seen it in Boston and now here. And he could do no more than what he had done for a year and a half: store away supplies in the mercantile for possible future use. He refused to live in fright and dread. Maybe some good news was in store for them soon.

Elizabeth's first contact once home came in a note from her mother. "I need to see you right away." Elizabeth wondered about the meaning. Was someone sick? Had word arrived from George? Whatever the news, she made it her priority. She didn't even send word ahead of her visit. As she barged into her mother's sitting room, Elizabeth sighed, thankful to see her mother in good health.

"Welcome home, Elizabeth. You didn't send word that you were back." Mother rose and approached Elizabeth with open arms. Elizabeth lasted about a second in the embrace, stepped back, and tried to decipher the urgency in the letter.

"I came in response to your note. What's the matter? Who is sick?"

"Slow down, child. It's Anne. Don't fret. She's well. I just haven't known what to do with her since you've been gone. Sit down, please, and stop pacing," her mother coaxed.

"Mother, tell me."

Her mother placed her hands in her lap one on top of the other, a picture of calmness. So why the urgent note? "She's fretting over this baby more than with the boys. She's convinced something will happen to her or the baby."

Elizabeth collapsed on the sofa in relief. "Oh, how silly. Anne's in perfect health. Why now?"

"I don't know. Robert just got back from France. Maybe it is the fear of his leaving again or a war or boycott. I don't know. Do you think you could talk to her?"

Elizabeth bounced up off her seat. "Of course. Right away."

"No, please stay for tea first." Her mother's hands motioned for her to remain. "I want to hear about your trip and your grandmother."

An hour passed as Elizabeth shared the highlights of the trip and of her friendship with Abigail Adams.

"And you and Louis?" Her mother's eyebrows rose in question.

"Oh, Mother." When would they truly accept that her choice was the right one? "You don't have to worry about us. He's perfect for me. I know you and Father were concerned, but you didn't need to be at all."

"Well, fine then. How about coming for dinner on Friday night? I'll ask Anne and her family as well. That might take her mind off her condition."

"We'd love to be here." Elizabeth stood and bent to kiss her mother's cheek. "I'm going right now to see her, unannounced. I'll get to the bottom of her concerns."

And Elizabeth didn't let her older sister hold anything back. Through tears and sniffles, Anne laid out her woes. "I'm older now. I feel different than with the boys. Robert is gone so much. I never expected another child. I feel something bad will happen. What if I die? What if the baby dies? What will I do if something happens to Robert? What about war and money and—?"

Elizabeth stopped her with her outstretched hand. "Now that's enough. This is so unlike you, who is so full of faith and encouragement to others. You weren't this way with the boys. And Robert was gone a lot then too. You're just ready for it to be over. Just a few more weeks, then you'll be holding her in your arms."

"Her?" Anne jerked her head toward her sister and grinned.

"Or him. But I feel like the baby is a girl, and she needs a happy, healthy mother. For the rest of the afternoon, I want your feet up, a book in your hands, and I need you to give me control over the children, the house, and you."

Anne smiled and stared at Elizabeth. "I might be able to do that for a few hours."

"Perfect. Find your perch and your book, and I'll prepare tea." Elizabeth disappeared, giving strict orders that no one was to bother Anne for the next four hours.

After tea, reading, and a nap, Anne returned to a cheerier disposition. Elizabeth prayed for her sister as she left. *Heavenly Father, give her the rest she needs and the assurance that you are in control.*

Elizabeth looked out of the sunroom window and viewed the flowers and shrubs in full bloom; azaleas abounded, as did the lilies and late daffodils. "Ellen, you even kept the garden free of weeds and bugs. Everything is blooming and welcoming us home, thanks to you."

"Believe me, I had help from Tom and Amy," Ellen said.

The vegetables had sprouted and fruit trees had budded. She smiled and leaned her head against the pane. Another household member had also missed her. Cleo curled up wherever she went, the yard, her lap, her bed, her chair. As she walked, Cleo did, almost causing her to stumble a few times.

With Anne happy and the household humming right along, Elizabeth went to the boarding school the next morning to see Sarah and check on her classes. She would finish the last month of school, relieving Sarah and Martha of the added workload. She waited patiently for Sarah to finish the theory class, hoping to surprise her in the hall. They hugged and bounced around in circles.

"You're back. How was it? Not tired of Louis yet?"

"Not at all. The only reason I came back was to see you." Elizabeth teased as she noted Sarah's glowing complexion, new hair style, and trim frilly dress. "You look different. It wouldn't have anything to do with a gentleman friend?"

Sarah's curls bounced around her flushed cheeks. "There has been one certain man in my company."

"Samuel, of course." Surely, it couldn't be anyone else.

"Louis didn't pay him to take care of me, did he?"

"Of course not. You're silly. I just knew it had to be him. So, what did you two do while we were gone?"

"I can't tell you here." Sarah's hand covered her mouth. "The girls might hear, and then I would never get their attention back. Let's just say that I saw all the plays and concerts that were offered in Charles Town."

Although Elizabeth wouldn't personally apply matchmaking to anyone else, she was thrilled it had worked with Sarah. But seeing the look in her eyes, Sarah shook a finger at her. "Don't go and have me engaged and married. Samuel is too cautious for that."

"We'll see. I think I hear wedding bells," Elizabeth said as she cupped her hand to her ear.

"That is the bell for the next class."

"All right. I'll see you later, then." Elizabeth went upstairs to a small room with a pianoforte placed close to the window, receiving an abundance of light. Martha Laurens soon joined her.

Elizabeth reached for the girl's hands. "Martha, you have grown up since I saw you six weeks ago. Did you manage all right with the students?"

Martha giggled. "Yes, after they realized they would be accountable to you if they slacked off too much."

Elizabeth arranged the music on the piano. "I hear your father is coming home soon. I know you have missed him and your brothers."

"I have. But my aunt and uncle have been very generous and loving. It seems my brothers are staying in England to finish their education."

"Your father will be proud of your progress. I have a few minutes. Would you like to play something for me?"

Her student sat on the bench with her back straight. "I've practiced this one, but it has a few rough spots." Martha chose one of Handel's cantatas. The "few rough spots" were slight and unnoticed by an average listener.

After clapping her hands, Elizabeth laid a hand on Martha's shoulder. "I'll be back at my position next week, so you can rest easy about your duties to the other girls."

"I'm glad, although I haven't minded at all." Martha hugged Elizabeth good-bye.

Elizabeth took the long route home, enjoying the slight breeze from the bay. Upon entering her home, she exchanged the smell of the sea for the aroma of a delicious dinner: tangy spices mixed with lemon and onion. After a dinner of poached fish in a thick cream sauce and red potatoes with onions, Elizabeth moved her chair closer to Louis and crossed her arms on the table. She loved these quiet times with just the two of them.

"Guess who I talked to today."

Louis leaned forward and placed his goblet on the table. "It would be easier to guess who you didn't talk to. So, tell me."

"You're right. Anyway, my talk with Sarah gave me some interesting enlightenment. I think there is a blossoming courtship in the air." Would he be happy about her secret?

"I talked to Samuel too. It appears he saw a whole lot of Sarah."

"Yes. I think that is wonderful." Elizabeth bounced in her seat. "Didn't we do a fine job of it? But now we can let them do the rest by themselves."

"Good. I was beginning to believe it would never work."

With her matchmaking skills shelved for the time, Elizabeth danced through the house, hoping she wouldn't have to work that hard again on bringing two people together.

CHAPTER 23

*a*fter a morning weeding and planting, Elizabeth sought out the nearest chair in the kitchen, discarding her hat and gloves on the table. "It's warm out there. Good for the plants, but for some reason I feel overly taxed."

"Are you well, Mrs. Elizabeth? Here's some water," Ellen said, offering Elizabeth what looked like a piece of heaven. She sipped it as she looked out the kitchen window. Her garden flourished, as did her desire to make Louis happy in his home. Ellen helped by making it her goal to maintain order and meet all Elizabeth's expectations.

"Thank you. I'm fine, really. This will help. Maybe I haven't rested enough from our trip. I just seem tired, not sick." Sitting with her eyes closed, Elizabeth rested for a few minutes, oblivious to the activity around her. She found it hard to keep her eyes open. The fresh air and inactivity lulled her to sleep...

Had it been seconds or minutes? "I must have dozed off. I'm sorry, Ellen. I wanted to help you with the vegetables," Elizabeth said as she stretched her sleepy frame.

"I think I can handle a few vegetables." Ellen wiped her hands on her apron. "Why don't you go relax, and I'll bring you some tea."

Elizabeth took her suggestion, although reluctantly. *What is wrong with me? Can't I even work an hour in the garden without feeling droopy?* Since she had already had a nap, she wasn't about to lie around the house all morning. Deciding to practice several pieces from French composers, including Leclair and Daquin, she found her missing energy as the notes rang across the house. Ellen arrived, set the tea tray on the table beside the piano, and turned to leave.

"Won't you join me, Ellen? This will be just what I need."

This wasn't the first time the two women had shared a half hour together just chatting as friends. Amy was at her lessons—lessons that Elizabeth had insisted she start. In Elizabeth's mind, every young girl needed to be able to read, write, and decipher—no matter her station in life. Ellen's daughter was no exception.

"Mrs. Elizabeth, if you don't mind, I have a question to pose. A personal one." Ellen's voice quivered a bit.

It would be a change if Elizabeth could help Ellen. "Of course. You may ask me anything at all." But what advice could she give the older woman?

"I was wondering—hmm—I've observed that—" Ellen paused. "Well, are you expecting a baby?"

Shocked and wide eyed, Elizabeth exclaimed, "What made you think that? Could I be?" Shock turned to surprise and surprise to laughter.

"The past week you have seemed unusually tired, though healthy, and you've eaten more than normal, although you could stand to gain a few pounds."

"Yes. I guess I could be." Elizabeth's hands held her cheeks, feeling their warmth. A baby! "I just thought with the excitement of the voyage and a disrupted routine was the reason for these symptoms. Oh, Ellen, wouldn't that be wonderful?"

Perfect was more the word to describe the possibility of a baby. After counting up the months, she realized it would probably be due in December. Her favorite month. Christmas, her anniversary, and a baby.

"You just take care. You'll know for sure soon enough," Ellen encouraged.

After changing from her dusty garden clothes, Elizabeth felt she needed to tell someone, especially Louis. But how and when? Elizabeth couldn't wait until he got home. She had to share with someone. Anne, being nine months along with her own baby, was her perfect choice.

The exercise to her sister's house left her flushed and exuberant. "Anne. Anne." Elizabeth shouted as she bounced through the front door. Her sister was sprawled out on a daybed in the sunroom, watching the boys play in the back garden.

"You're going to bounce every item off the shelves with your actions, Elizabeth. I couldn't even take one of your lively steps. Sit down and tell me your news." Anne rolled herself into a sitting position and placed her hands on her belly as if reassuring her child of his security.

"Oh, it's the most wonderful news. I think I'm going to have a baby. Anne, I'm going to be a mother." Elizabeth wasted no time with guessing games, as she grabbed her sister's hands.

"I'm so happy for you. Look what you get to look forward to, little sister: becoming a big, fat elephant."

But instead, Elizabeth gazed out the window at the boys playing instead. "No. I'm looking at what I get to enjoy. A child of my own to watch grow and play. That far exceeds the temporary inconvenience of being a huge whale," she commented, turning her attention back to Anne.

"A whale now? You just wait until I call you names," Anne teased.

Elizabeth turned serious, thinking about the newness of this baby. "I need your advice. How do I tell Louis?" Surely, if anyone knows, it would be Anne after three times.

"No advice there. You just tell him. Any moment will be right."

What? No help from the one she came to first? "Do you think he suspects anything?"

"Robert never did. Each time he was very surprised and exceedingly happy."

"All right. I'll do it as soon as Louis comes home." She dreaded wiling away the hours alone. "You and the boys will have to put up with me the next couple of hours." Elizabeth helped with the boys' refreshments and hemmed a blanket for Anne's baby before she escaped out the door.

She knew she couldn't hold off the announcement. The minute Louis settled into his comfortable stuffed chair, Elizabeth crawled into his lap and offered him no way to escape. She took his face in her hands, making sure she had his undivided attention.

"Louis, I have the most wonderful, exciting, special news. I just hope you're happy too."

"If it has made you this animated, then I can assure you I'll be happy." His brows rose in anticipation as he searched for understanding. His hands caressed her arms, sending shivers to the tips of her toes.

"Ready? I think you are going to be a father!"

Silence for half a second. "A father? Me? You're going to have a baby?" He stood with her in his arms and twirled her around. He appeared to be totally enthused about a little Lestarjette.

"Yes, I have all the signs, although I haven't seen the doctor yet. We're going to have a baby—possibly in December." Tears escaped and landed on Louis' shirt. "Then our home will be complete."

"Oh, sweet Elizabeth, you made my life complete months ago."

She understood a baby didn't make or break their strong bond of love, but what a different dimension it would give to their life. Elizabeth settled onto Louis' lap for his congratulatory kiss, affection she returned freely.

Louis read to Elizabeth over a late breakfast after her announcement last night. Words from Prime Minister North to the House of Commons reached the *Gazette*.

"Listen to this."

The Americans have tarred and feathered your subjects, plundered your merchants, burnt your ships, denied all obedience to your laws and authority, yet so element and so long forbearing has our conduct been that it is incumbent on us now to take a different course. Whatever may be the consequences, we must risk something; if we do not, all is over.

Louis let his coffee cool and laid the paper down. He stared ahead, not at Elizabeth or the garden but at a point in the distance, blurred like the future. He lifted the paper again.

"The Coercive Acts are the 'something,' and that something is having the opposite effect." Louis deciphered, throwing in his opinion. "Christopher's comments in the paper state that 'Great Britain hopes that the Coercive Acts will isolate radicals in Massachusetts and cause us all to concede to parliamentary authority. It was a risk, and my fellow citizens, it has backfired. More than ever, the colonies stand together backing the colony of Massachusetts.'"

"Do you think most citizens think like Christopher?" Elizabeth asked. Louis looked over the top of the paper. He had hoped Elizabeth was listening and smiled at her comment, despite the gravity of the situation. If only they could talk of their baby or the next picnic instead.

"The Sons of Liberty do, and more join daily—in every city. With South Carolina supporting the other colonies like Massachusetts, the numbers are increasing against the British." Louis shook the paper. "And this is proof." Proof of the shaking and jostling of life as they knew it. Louis would have to seek stability in all parts of his life if he wanted to remain standing on the other side. *Somehow my growing family and my love for my home must survive.*

April passed, and May ushered in blankets of green grass and delicate flowers, blossoming fruit trees, and flowering vegetables. Elizabeth compared her life to the vibrant nature around her. To keep things positive and fresh, she let the stories of Parliament float in and out of her mind.

The one thing Elizabeth allowed to take priority was the birth of Anne's little girl, Charlotte Elizabeth Cochran. The Elliotts, the Cochrans, and the Lestarjettes ecstatically welcomed the newest member to their family.

Elizabeth hadn't wanted to leave the baby's presence. "Anne, she's beautiful. I told you that you would have a girl this time. You aren't disappointed, are you?"

A tired whisper issued her response. "Not at all. I'll cherish doing the things one does with a daughter, like pretty dresses, parties, sewing. Don't you remember the fun times we had with Grandmamma? We'll do that with our girls."

Elizabeth stared at little Charlotte, hoping she would have a daughter. "Now are you making a prediction?"

"I predict that you'll have three girls and three boys."

"Oh, my. I certainly will be busy." Elizabeth laughed, then kissed Anne goodbye for the day.

Elizabeth became very protective of her own unborn child, especially since confirmed by the doctor. A December birth had been her prediction and she was right. She understood a bit of Anne's fear, however unwarranted. Somehow the expected baby weaved himself into every part of Elizabeth's being. She felt great, with enough energy to take her through the end of the school term complete with an afternoon recital. Martha shone brighter than any of the girls, displaying her superior talent with her Missa in C by Mozart. Sarah, Samuel, and Louis attended and applauded as much as anyone.

"Let's celebrate. How about dinner at the Grand Hotel tonight?" Louis suggested after the finale.

"Dinner it is. About seven o'clock?" Sarah said.

"Perfect." Elizabeth needed the opportunity to release her pent-up nerves over the recital.

Later, around a corner table at the Grand, Elizabeth raised her glass with the others. "What are we celebrating?"

"The end of a very full season and month," Louis offered.

"Here, here," Sarah and Samuel commented.

Elizabeth concentrated on her plate of fish and fresh steamed vegetables. Her appetite surprised her. She had to slow down to match the others' pace or she would be finished with the fruit and cheese before anyone else. She set her fork down for a moment and giggled.

Louis was in the middle of speaking when she turned her attention back to the group. "This month marked the anniversary of the Tea Act and a year since my departure for France. And speaking of France, King Louis XV died recently, leaving the nineteen-year-old King Louis XVI as ruler. A lot has happened this month to be recorded in history."

"You don't miss France, do you, Louis?" Samuel asked.

"No, I have Elizabeth, a baby, a family, and friends." He reached for her hand.

Elizabeth remained speechless as she realized she also had all she needed surrounding her. But would her baby have the freedom to travel to France to visit grandparents and relatives? She didn't expect to visit France, but that didn't mean her child had to stay in Charles Town forever. Things had to change. Wasn't that what Louis implied? Yet would the outcome be something she wanted for her child?

CHAPTER 24

The exhausting heat and the long summer days didn't interfere with the search for answers to the offensive Acts of Parliament. Almost daily Louis ran into a new figure or another who had joined the Sons of Liberty. He watched as the force of disheartened citizens gained momentum. All he tried to do was his part to lessen the adverse effects of any port closure or boycott.

Henry approached Louis in the storeroom at the Mercantile. "Thanks to you, Louis, the mercantile now operates on a hundred percent local, French, and West Indies products. We haven't had to order any supplies from Britain in over six months."

His compliments reinforced Louis' confidence, but would their choices hold them up for the long haul? "You're the one who helped me see the need to focus elsewhere," Louis said. "Of course, I would like the French merchandise. But I've been greatly impressed by the materials and craftsmanship made right here in the colonies. You made a believer out of me, Uncle. In fact, Elizabeth only wants furniture made in Charles Town now. We have converts all over the place." Louis laughed, covering the fact that it was anything but funny.

Why did we even have to take this action? Will it hold out? What happened to the peaceful solution? All the talk and the debates didn't seem to influence the answer in any positive way. A peaceful solution seemed to have diminished about four Acts ago, out with the tea in the harbor in December. Was peace not even an option now?

Elizabeth wasn't ignorant of the murmurings and activities around her. At the moment though, she chose to occupy herself with more pleasant possibilities. Unlike ever before, she was drawn to baby Charlotte. Her maternal instincts led her to give her full attention to the new little bundle of joy. In truth, she considered any new life a hope for the future. As politics raged, she concerned herself with making life better for everyone, especially the children.

Elizabeth visited her sister as often as she could. "Anne, doesn't it scare you just a bit with this talk of fighting around us? Has anyone considered what it will do for this little one? Part of me wants it all to just go away without a whisper. And then the other side wants a government for the people and for the colonies that are made of up of colonists like us," Elizabeth rambled as she played with the baby's toes.

"What do we do as women? Make our homes and husbands comfortable and happy for now," Anne said.

Elizabeth believed she could continue to please Louis by surrounding him with love and appreciation for a lifetime. But could she avoid an active role and pretend the conflict didn't exist? Images of large, secret petticoat pockets spurred her imagination. Could she be as supportive as Abigail Adams?

The social scene was almost nonexistent in the summer. People left the city for the country life or stayed inside to avoid the insects and heat. Except for forays to Anne's, her mother's and church, Elizabeth stayed inside like the other remaining citizens.

Elizabeth fanned herself on the sofa in the sitting room in the back of the house. "It's so hot and dull today." She had her feet resting on a floral stool.

Louis handed her lemon water. "Here, enjoy this." He chose a wicker chair close to an open window. "Would you like to go to the country for a week or so, just to get away?"

She glanced over the rim of her glass. Something was behind his question as if he wanted her to say yes before he revealed the details behind why he'd asked. She smiled, proud that she knew him so well. "What's the big event?"

Draping his arm over the arm of his chair, Louis looked casual, which contrasted to his serious tone. "Well, it seems a very prominent figure, William Henry Drayton, recently a devout Loyalist attached to the king and his government, has drastically altered his sympathies. He's joined ranks with the Sons of Liberty. The Coercive Acts have outraged him and aroused his influence in our cause."

Another casualty of the oppressive acts. She wasn't surprised, not with all the news in the paper. "I've heard of him. Wasn't he friends with Christopher and the Laurens in the past?" Elizabeth inquired.

He nodded. "Christopher expects his zeal to be as strong for equal representation as it was for the king. We'll see," he added.

"What does this have to do with a week in the country?" She leaned forward awaiting the reason for the offer.

"Drayton is opening his home for a social gathering of sorts." He smiled, and Elizabeth understood why. He had wanted to visit the Drayton estate that he had viewed from the river. "I expect many of our friends will attend." He scooted forward in his seat, resting his elbows on his knees. "So, what do you think?"

Even politics was a good reason to leave the city for a while.

And how could she let Louis have this experience without her? "Let's go. I could do with a change of scenery."

They decided to spend a few weeks at the country home of Elizabeth's cousin Lucy, and from there make visits to Drayton Hall and Middleton Place when organized dinners and events occurred. As long as Elizabeth had a little rest in the afternoons when she tired, she found she had surplus energy—enough to attend teas, gatherings, and late walks with Louis.

An added incentive was that Middleton Plantation was only two miles from her cousin's house. Elizabeth had fond memories of the March weekend retreat there last year, a time when she and Louis had advanced their relationship. Negative references flitted in her mind, ones of George's return and the introduction of Miss Seymour. Much had changed since then. Could she disassociate her disappointment in her brother from the place? She'd try for Louis' sake. George was someone she could not understand. *Who knows? If Mr. Drayton can change, perhaps there is hope for George?*

During an afternoon tea with Marianne Middleton, a new friend from last year, Elizabeth enjoyed the beautiful view of the gardens and pathways, which were cool because of the shade trees. "Have you visited Drayton Hall, Marianne?"

"Yes, often. Many times in the past before the—well, before the rift. It's an impressive structure. You must see its uniqueness, unlike anything around here." Her hostess poured some more tea for Elizabeth. "John Drayton borrowed a book from my husband's father and found an architectural design he liked. The structure resembles classical Roman architecture by Palladio."

For now, Elizabeth was glad her hostess changed the subject from the person to the mansion. Placing her cup and saucer on the marble table, Elizabeth perked up as Marianne explained the details of the mansion. The stair hall served as the stairway and entry to welcome guests arriving from the river. The great hall opened onto four large corner rooms on the first floor and upstairs. It sounded like a huge structure, surpassing any in Charles Town. But of course, it could because of the vast expanse of property.

Elizabeth sipped her tea and hung on every word. "I can't wait to see it. Will you be at the ball Friday night?" She truly wanted her friend's company.

"Yes. I wouldn't miss it."

Marianne's details escalated Elizabeth's excitement. She felt more comfortable this year as Louis' wife than as the unmarried daughter of Mr. Elliott. With marriage came some self-confidence. What a relief not to have to worry about dance partners and dinner companions. In her opinion, marriage came with many advantages.

The next day, Louis and Elizabeth walked toward the huge structure of Drayton Hall. Even arriving in a carriage left a long walk to the entrance. Louis explained as they approached the house that Mr. Drayton was as dynamic as Christopher Gadsden and called by some "our converted countryman."

As Elizabeth entered, she could feel the atmosphere tingle with fiery statements and debates. Impressed with the great open spaces and extremely high ceilings, she breathed in the warm breeze from the river. The open porches and huge windows allowed the air to circulate and cool the guests.

Her elbow rested in Louis' fingers. She was thankful to have someone to lead her through the crush. Louis took them on a snakelike trail. "Let's weave our way over to the window where I see Christopher and Samuel," he explained.

As they went, Elizabeth looked around, hoping to catch a

glimpse of Sarah. Had she decided to come with Samuel? Her last answer had been no. But perhaps?

Her eyes locked on the petite lady in a light-green dress.

"I'll be right back, Louis." Elizabeth slowly meandered to Sarah's side. "Sarah, I'm so glad you're here. But surprised too."

"I know. I wasn't going to come, but Mother insisted I get out of the house. So, I came along with them," her friend explained.

"Then you're not with Samuel?" Elizabeth knew her pout wouldn't help the outcome. Sarah had her own reasons.

"No, I'm not. He prefers the company of Mr. Gadsden, it seems. Anyway, I'm going on to my grandmother's estate with my parents after this."

Elizabeth managed to pull Sarah aside for a more personal interrogation. "Are you and Samuel not getting along? I thought you and he were—"

"Were what?" Had Sarah just stomped her foot? Her clenched teeth and false smile didn't disguise her anger very well. "I've told you before he has no interest in me, the church, or my family. He's just so predictable."

Elizabeth stifled a laugh. For one who protested her involvement with Samuel, Sarah was inordinately upset at his lack of attention.

Louis stood next to Samuel, wanting to shake him. "Did you ask her to come with you?" Louis asked, shocked at his friend's nonchalant attitude toward Sarah.

Samuel shrugged and looked at the floor. "Not exactly, because she was leaving town with her parents. So, what was the use?"

"The use? To show her you care. You get in more trouble because you keep your mouth shut and assume the worst. Well now that she's here, what are you going to do?" *Why do I still try? This relationship is floundering, even as we speak.*

"You mean besides making a fool of myself? I could probably ask her to dance and to walk in the gardens," Samuel suggested.

"Or both. She's with Elizabeth over there. Sweep her off her feet with your charm." Louis pointed him in the right direction.

As Sarah and Samuel headed to the gardens, Louis stood shaking his head. Elizabeth joined him, linking her arm in his. "Both of them are so awkward at this. Why can we see it, and they can't?"

"Because, my dear Elizabeth, we're in love and want them to have what we have. The rest has to be their doing, not ours. How about the next dance?"

During the evening, Christopher announced a meeting of the South Carolina General Committee for June thirteenth at Dillon's Tavern in Charles Town. In every direction and room, Louis heard cries for desperate measures to combat the oppression of Parliament.

Louis took Elizabeth out on the balcony away from the flare-ups for a while. "The debate isn't subsiding but intensifying. Even the walls of this elegant house can't diffuse the treasonous talk."

Elizabeth leaned on the railing and faced the river. "The women, including myself, have a hard time diverting the conversations. For some reason, art, clothes, and local gossip can't compete with tea and Parliament. So, I've given up the fight and opened my ears instead."

"Do you want to join the parade of meandering couples? Once we return to Charles Town, the evenings will soon become stifling."

"Maybe we'll find Sarah and Samuel in a deep tête-a-tête." She giggled, making her way through the crowd.

"I'll not be a part of spying on them. When I said I wanted to walk with you, it was for your attention only. I don't plan on sharing you."

"Oh? I can handle that too."

Once outside, her pace slowed, and Louis had her undivided attention.

The Drayton party came at the end of their brief time away from Charles Town. Back in the city, Louis focused on settling into the summer routine in their pleasant house on Church Street, watching the townspeople drift briefly in and out of their abodes. Before the extreme heat descended, he and Elizabeth took advantage of a few more mornings and evenings of warm, but not overly hot, weather.

Louis attended the Sons of Liberty meeting the next week along with a few hundred other citizens from all over South Carolina. A question loomed in his mind: *Will Charles Town ban all commerce with Great Britain until the Boston port reopens?*

Even as these thoughts formed in his mind and the minds of other merchants, Louis stood among the participants as Gadsden said, "Cessation of commerce would depend on what New York and Philadelphia do. The Committee voted for the motion to be postponed. A general meeting of representatives from every part of South Carolina is scheduled at the Exchange Building on July sixth. Then we'll decide what to do."

Louis knew Christopher well enough to understand his friend wanted to do something now to help fight against wrongs done to the colonies. But on the other hand, Louis admired him for sticking with the Committee.

Two days later, Christopher called Louis to his office. The usually calm, determined man paced in front of his desk, obviously angry. "I'm going to write to Samuel Adams today to tell him that nothing will deter me from prodding South Carolina to aid Massachusetts. Nothing will undermine this colony's cause for liberty," Christopher promised.

"What can we do?" Louis asked as his eyes followed his friend's constant motion.

"First, we're going to ask for and accept donations for the relief of the distressed people of Boston. Therefore, any rice shipped to my wharf for that purpose will be landed, stored, and shipped at no cost."

"I've no doubt that you'll succeed. Count me in on spreading the word and giving you any assistance."

Honestly, when Christopher grabbed hold of an idea, he didn't let go. His determination was etched into his very brow, making permanent furrows. For his part, Louis sprinkled his life with bits of sanity, mostly found in Elizabeth's presence. He didn't want his facial features to permanently resemble the leaders of the colony, with worry lines and pre-mature aging. They carried the weight of the world, and it showed.

On Thursday evening, Louis joined Elizabeth, Aunt Jeannette, and Uncle Henry at the Wilsons' home. Louis needed the break from a busy schedule. And as long as Elizabeth felt well and wanted to socialize, he would be at her side.

"I'm hearing about rice all over town. Is it really as bad as it sounds for Boston?" Elizabeth inquired as she savored a rare cup of tea after the meal. The tea bricks had dwindled from storage. Although Louis didn't mind coffee, so far Elizabeth had not acquired a taste for it.

Louis glanced briefly at Henry, sharing one of those moments of clarity that they were all in this together. "I'm afraid so. But South Carolina as a group is sending rice very soon. Actually, today Uncle Henry and I convinced a few local planters to donate part of their crop to help. If we put ourselves in their position, how could we not send aid? Who knows, it might be Charles Town one day."

After making sure everyone had been served, Jeannette placed her feet on a stool and seemed to relax. "Who would have thought a port the size of Boston would be closed?" she commented.

"The first shipment should leave early next week." Louis stared at his cup full of amber liquid, the same concoction that had floated in the Boston harbor. "I've never been as proud of a group of people as I am of this colony. Better still, of these colonies."

"Why, Louis?" Jeannette asked.

Choosing his words wisely, Louis continued, "We—I will proudly put myself in the formula—have the opportunity to take a stand for right, for fairness, for a better form of government. And we're taking that chance together, not knowing what the outcome will be. Our hopes and dreams are placed in God's care. And if these men honestly pray for his guidance, the outcome will be more sustainable and reliable than we could ever expect. As daunting as the situation seems, the challenge is not too much for God."

The Louis of the past wouldn't have been able to wrap his mind around a God who cares about the everyday lives of each person. But he'd changed and grasped a little more every day of what it meant to live in God's plan.

At Christopher's office on Friday, Christopher showed Louis a portion of a letter to be sent to Samuel Adams and the Boston Committee of Correspondence.

We're sending a ship with a hundred and ninety-four whole and twenty-one half barrels of rice to Boston to be followed by more—ultimately around one thousand barrels of rice...

We are thoroughly alarmed here and will be ready to do everything in our power.

Louis realized, as he read the letter, this was obviously the sentiment of the colony as a whole, what with the overwhelming donations they had received.

The shipment preceded the next big event: the meeting for the entire colony. Handbills plastered the trees and store windows, as well as stacks on countertops at businesses all over town. Louis saw men on street corners passing along the information about the upcoming general meeting. Taverns and tearooms, dress shops, and mercantiles—no place remained immune to the July sixth scheduled meeting. Excitement from the Sons of Liberty reigned the sparks of anger from the Loyalists.

Sparks that could fuel a fire. Louis prayed for the wind to subside.

☙❧

"Mary, where are you? I have about had it with—" Father entered, waving a handbill and stopped when he saw Elizabeth sitting with her mother in the parlor.

"Elizabeth, it's good to see you." Her father bent down to kiss her cheek, then chose a chair next to Mother.

Elizabeth knew full well how irate her father could become, but she wanted to hear him out anyway. "You were saying, Father?"

Her mother waved her hand in the air. "Don't involve yourself with his ongoing angst against the General Committee," her mother advised.

Her father eyed Elizabeth, who sat up straighter under his suspicious gaze. "I'll speak for myself. Elizabeth knows how I feel. To think I can't even walk in my front door without finding this propaganda on the doorstep. Louis wouldn't have anything to do with this, would he, Elizabeth?" *He is suspicious of us both now.*

"Of course, he knows about it. And he'll be there, I'm sure. Are you going, Father?" She knew the answer.

"I won't have to. It'll be verbatim in the paper if Mr. Timothy has anything to do with it. What do they hope to accomplish?"

A lack of response from her mother or Elizabeth led to a lull in the conversation. Quietly the topic of their newest grandchild, Charlotte, cleared the murky waters. "She smiled at me today. I think she is the smartest little thing," her mother commented. "Artemus, you must drop by one day soon and see her. And just think, by Christmas, we'll have another grandchild."

267

"Well, good." Her father, never comfortable with talk of babies, removed himself to the library. Elizabeth imagined him huffing and puffing about the downhill slide of humanity, while surrounded by his papers and correspondences.

"He's not handling the changes in Charles Town very well," Elizabeth commented to her mother. "What will he do, Mother, when real decisions have to be made?"

"I don't know, dear. I do try to talk to him about it. Now that I see the real issues and understand my true dedication to change, it puts a strain on any deep conversation."

"He's surrounded by family on the opposite side of the issues, except for George, who doesn't even talk to us. Most of his colleagues at the college are members of the Liberty Boys as well as at church and at his clubs. His number of Loyalist friends are declining quickly."

"I know. I pray for him every day. I want peace in our household, and I try to keep it balanced. But I can't be quiet about everything anymore." Her mother showed real concern as she reached for Elizabeth's hand.

"I'll pray for you too, Mother."

CHAPTER 25

*E*lizabeth admired her husband as he dressed for the meeting. "I wish I could go with you. Please promise to tell me everything, good and bad. I want to know who is there, who speaks, what they say." She sat on the edge of the bed, rubbing her hand back and forth on her small, round stomach.

"Slow down. This meeting could go on for days. How about just the highlights?" he said.

"All right. But don't leave out the interesting bits. You know, any arguments or debates."

"If I didn't know better, I'd say you wanted to hear the gossip and the rumors."

"You're right, of course." She smoothed her dress out around her. "Anyway, I'll be occupied with Anne, baby Charlotte, and the boys here today. And tomorrow, I'll rope Sarah into doing something entertaining, and after that I have no idea. Surely, this won't last more than two days." Elizabeth crinkled her forehead and tensed her cheeks.

"It could. Christopher and the General Committee have a lengthy agenda." Louis stared at her concerned features and grinned. "I suppose there's no reason to ask you not to concern yourself with this issue. You are as deeply entrenched as I am. More so with the tension in your family. How could you not be concerned?" He planted a light kiss on her brow.

"And you wouldn't have me any other way. Right?"

"My little rebel. A rebel before I was. Have a good time with Anne and the children. I'm off to change the world or at least to bandage the wounds. The whole time I'll be thinking about you and our baby—my top priority. I don't know if I'd be involved at all without you in my life."

As he left, Elizabeth removed herself from the politics of the day to reflect on the relative calmness in her life, at least compared to two hundred men or more meeting in the Exchange Building. She preferred her organized chaos to the unpredictable a few blocks away.

Knowing the meeting was open to all the inhabitants of South Carolina—merchants, planters, mechanics, and back country settlers alike—Louis didn't quite know what to expect. He knew he needed to ally himself with someone he felt would think like him and help him make sense of the options, preferably Samuel.

John Rutledge had Samuel cornered. "I hope you understand, Mr. Evans. We can't become too radical and move too quickly on decisions. We must have a reasonable plan and see what other colonies do."

It appeared Louis showed up in the middle of a speech. Apparently, Mr. Rutledge was trying to convince Samuel to join a particular faction of the Partisan group.

When Mr. Rutledge moved on to another circle of men, Louis leaned in with a whisper. "If I'm hearing correctly, there is already division within the ranks of the general meeting. A campaign of sorts."

"Yes. I'm afraid so," Samuel said. "Gadsden, the mechanics,

some planters, and the back settlers are being called *radicals*. The merchants and lawyers like us are labeled *moderates*."

"And I was thinking we were all on the same side." Of course, with such a vast range of occupations, special interest groups would emerge. Louis shook his head. Perhaps now he was better prepared for the meeting.

Samuel motioned for Louis to follow him to two vacant seats. "From what I gather, we're just at different response levels. I don't like being labeled before I know what I'm supporting."

George Powell was chosen by the hundred and four legal delegates. The debate began to answer four questions. The voters, at times more than four hundred, crowded the hall. Anyone present, including Louis, could vote on the issues. Hours passed of tedious questions and debates until finally all the votes were tallied.

Later that evening, at home with Elizabeth, he tried to make sense of his position. "The first question posed was should Charles Town join Boston in a boycott of British goods?" Louis paced in front of the windows in the parlor.

"If I only had to think of myself, I would vote yes," Louis explained after Elizabeth coaxed him to relax on the couch. "Especially since we have relieved ourselves of our British goods. But I'm one merchant in a hundred."

Elizabeth ran her fingers along the back of the sofa and landed on Louis' shoulder. "But you didn't live through a boycott. In the past, it hurt the planters, the merchants, and the citizens."

"I know. The moderates proposed a compromise to postpone the decision until the meeting of all the colonies in Philadelphia."

"So that is how you'll vote?"

The moderates won the victory the next day. Both factions agreed on the second question of how many delegates to send to the congress: five. Louis joined Samuel, Henry, and Robert as the debate boiled over which five to send.

"I can understand the undisputed selection of Henry Middleton and John Rutledge—the first a wealthy planter and the other a planter and a lawyer. But this next vote will be a bit sticky," Henry commented.

Powell announced the three radical delegates on a ticket of Christopher Gadsden, Thomas Lynch, and Edward Rutledge. The moderates, on the other hand, suggested Rawlins Lourdes, Charles Pinckney, and Miles Brewton. The voters rallied for the radicals, and Louis added his vote for them too.

"That went smoothly," Louis observed. "Basically, the lines within the group aren't that defined. I'm glad that Christopher is going. South Carolina will be well represented."

"Only one other issue today: what authority to give to the five delegates? I know if it were up to Christopher, South Carolina would be swept into a battle for independence. So, I imagine this will be interesting," Samuel said.

Louis knew the deep-running vein of equal representation ran through the thoughts of men like Christopher. But was it the right time to flaunt independence and separation?

Not according to the voting body. The delegates had unlimited power to make right any legal matters, such as the repeal of objectionable actions by Parliament. But the line stopped before independence or a new boycott. They resolved to fix their differences with the British government.

Louis returned for one piece of business on the third day—the establishment of the Committee of ninety-nine, which would handle the executive matters for future general meetings. In other words, the temporary government of South Carolina consisted of fifteen merchants, fifteen artisans, and sixty-nine planters. The new task force, armed with verbal ammunition, perched ready to act. Christopher would leave this week for Philadelphia. Part of Louis wished he could go with him, but he corresponded with Silas Deane and Samuel Adams enough to make sure he'd receive some information.

Also, Robert would leave again soon distributing goods to France. How difficult must that be to leave a baby? Would Charlotte even recognize him when he returned?

Louis was left in the city with many others, but for what purpose? He'd rely on God to show him what to do as he worked along others as the delegates worked for them all.

CHAPTER 26

*J*uly and the lazy sunny days exited, and politics entered in with gusto. From all the pulpits across the city, Louis heard hints of support or condemnation expressed over the sending of the delegates to Philadelphia. Yet, he didn't waver in his views. He knew Christopher represented him well, whether a hundred percent of the citizens thought so or not.

While Reverend Smith of St. Philip's sent Christopher Gadsden and Thomas Lynch off with a prayer of safety and wisdom, the Reverend John Bullman of St. Michael's condemned them as traitors along with the other three. Every day, Louis ran into people of the opposing side, but the traitor label, what did that mean?

"Traitors? That's a bit out of line, I think." Louis stood with Elizabeth on the dock on the hot afternoon of August fourteenth. The Sunday offered a cloudless day for a departure. The other three delegates had left earlier in the week. Louis listened to a few words of derision from one group of citizens on the wharf when Gadsden and Lynch walked by. Others offered their family's prayers and respectful words. The lines were drawn, more permanent every day. How long until people could not change sides? What about Mr. Elliott? Or George? Was there yet any hope?

Christopher turned to Louis before boarding the *Sea Nymph*. "I'm thankful for your support and friendship. There's no stopping this country now from accomplishing great things. Traitors to some, heroes to others. We've made our choices."

Christopher with his seventeen-year-old son and Lynch with his wife and daughter sailed away. Canon fire saluted them on their journey.

Walking home under the shade trees, Elizabeth said, "What will the Congress decide?"

"I don't know." Louis didn't want the stroll to end. He felt in tune with her steps, her thoughts, her concerns. At least, he knew she wouldn't suddenly cross to the other side. "They'll represent the people in all things. I feel South Carolina will follow the collective decisions of the other colonies. While these men determine the fate of the colonies, you and I will continue to figure out ours."

She placed herself in front of him, walking backwards a few steps before he pulled her to the side of the walkway. "My place in all of this seems so small. Organize a household, teach piano, garden, and help the poor." Was she actually belittling her role? Did she want to shoulder a rifle too? Or speak in front of the Congress?

Hands on each of her shoulders, forcing her to look only at him, he said the only thing that mattered, "Carry my child and love me."

Instinctively, as of late, her hand went to her stomach as in an embrace. "Of course. And above all do what God wants me to do," she added.

"And we can't forget to be content in our calling. Remember Reverend Smith's sermon from Philippians. 'For I have learned, in whatsoever state I am, therewith to be content.'"

"I can do that." She looked at her hand caressing her belly. "I have you and the baby and my family."

Louis believed in a higher purpose. But he wanted it all: Elizabeth, the baby, and prosperity. But with Elizabeth beside him, any situation that they could find themselves in together, he would be content.

Elizabeth was still surprised when Louis showed such faith. Such a mature grasp for a new Christian. His growth challenged her often stagnant acceptance.

How can I regain that calm, deep faith? The faith I had as a child?

She had a lot to learn from Louis. She would take that step now, at this moment of reflection. "How do you do it, Louis?"

"Do what?" He appeared genuinely perplexed.

"Contentment. Acceptance. Calmness. In the middle of impending boycotts and war, imposing taxes and regulations, an unstable economy and trade. You carry such a heavy weight, yet you are content." Although she didn't mean for them to, her words sounded almost like an accusation.

"Elizabeth, it's not that difficult anymore. Last year I made the most difficult decision of my life, and the best one. By turning my life over to Christ, I relinquished the outcome to his promises. Ultimately, He is in control. My job is to do what He wants even if it is hard or uncomfortable. This is one of those times of trust. As long as I am doing what I feel God wants me to do, I'm resting in His love, and I'm content." He let out a pent-up breath.

How far was he willing to take this? "Even if your business fails?"

He rocked back and forth on his heels. "Yes, even then."

More? "Even if—you have to go to war?" Would she find any contentment then? Would she be willing to give him to the war?

"Yes, dear girl, even in that worst-case scenario."

She debated whether she should voice the next scenario. It would be the hardest. "Even if something happens to me or our baby?"

His pause lasted only for a brief second. "That would break my heart, but even then, my faith rests in Christ." She believed him even with the slight quiver in his voice.

"Thank you, Louis. God knew what He was doing when He sent you to me," she admitted humbly through sparkling tears.

He wiped a stray tear from her cheek. "I'm the one who profited. Remember, I was the one needing salvation, not you."

"True." She smiled at the truth. "But I needed to be a part of the miracle He worked in you."

August ended with a brief word from Christopher:

I've found lodging with a widow in town. It's very comfortable, and one of the other guests is Silas Deane, a very interesting, promising young man, just like you said. Due to the lack of passage by sea, the delegates from Boston have not yet arrived. They're due to arrive by coach at the end of August.

While Christopher geared up for Congress, Charles Town showed signs of deliberate changes. Louis saw British items boycotted by the majority, leaving the demand for local goods at a record high. Supply and demand raised the prices of many items.

Louis and the Wilsons survived with their present stock and costs due to major decisions last year. They always had contracts with local planters and artisans to fill their shelves.

Whereas Louis wasn't adversely affected, his friend Samuel didn't fare so well. Louis spent a few hours with him in his law office. It appeared land was not a commodity that exchanged hands during unsettling times. Although Louis had bought a house in the past year, he hadn't thought about increasing his own property.

"The boycott and uncertainty of the future has caused land sales to slow. Not only that, some of my Loyalist clients found new lawyers with Loyalist sympathies. By openly siding with the Sons of Liberty, my practice has diminished," Samuel admitted. But he didn't hang his head or wring his hands. He was very matter of fact. Louis realized a sack of flour or a bolt of material never wandered to the side of a slow commodity. Need verses want.

At least Samuel had a plan. "I'll have to do a lot more of the research and documentation myself since I can't afford the extra help. If I don't lose too many more clients, I can keep my house, office, and present standard of living," Samuel shared, putting his pen in its stand. "But I don't know what to do about Sarah."

Sarah? "What does Sarah have to do with this?" Louis asked, choosing not to reveal his suspicions.

Samuel stood and shuffled his feet, eying Louis. "In short, I want to ask her to marry me."

Jumping to his feet, Louis caught Samuel in a bear hug. "It's about time, my friend. What's the real reason for the hold up? Is it just your business?" Did the man not know that everyone had the same questions?

"I told you, my business is hurting. How could I bring her in to that situation, with an uncertain future?"

Louis stepped back, crossed his arms, and leaned against Samuel's desk. "Do you love her? Does she love you?"

Samuel's arms hung limp by his sides, but his eyes were sharp and focused. "Yes. Yes to both questions."

"Then she will do fine." He pointed to the busy world outside the window. "Look around you. Every man is facing challenges. Maybe at different levels or extents, but challenges still. And they are married, have children, servants, dogs, and cats. You name it. Life goes on. Look at me, directly in front of you. A wife, a house, a business, and a baby on the way. Would I discard any of that during these challenging times? Not at all. Why not share it with Sarah?"

"I guess you are right." Samuel seemed serious. "Don't tell Elizabeth." Almost in panic.

"Not tell her best friend? You must be kidding."

"Well, at least don't have her mention anything to Sarah before I do. This takes more courage than speculating in land. What do I know about marriage?" They exited and continued their conversation along the wharves.

"Speaking from a little experience," Louis sighed, "one cannot know much about marriage until he experiences it. And believe me—I'm still learning. I had to settle the question of who was going to be in charge of my life. Last year I was doing such a poor job of it. Once I settled that issue, the rest started making sense, including marrying Elizabeth."

Samuel shook his head, staring out to sea. "I've seen you, Louis, actually living out your faith. I don't think I can do that, not like you, Elizabeth, and even Sarah. You all have something I don't. And maybe I can't ever have that." Samuel appeared resolved, as if God didn't need or want his life, not when God already had the exemplary lives of his friends.

Louis understood the words of rejection embedded in his friend's heart, for he had been there a year in the past. How could he be the person to explain any of the Almighty's plan, like Reverend Turquand did for him? "It all starts with a simple faith. Accepting Christ as your Savior. The rest will come later, possibly slowly. Changes in your thoughts and actions will happen when you place your trust in someone other than yourself," Louis explained.

"Is that what you did?" Samuel asked. Louis saw the signs of a questioning and searching man.

"Exactly. I had had enough of a pointless, purposeless life. And the only way for it to have meaning was with God in control."

Samuel gave his full attention to Louis. "Well, I do believe in

God. But I want it to be more personal, like what you are talking about."

Louis' hand rested on Samuel's shoulder with the pressure of a believer desiring for his brother to share in what he had. "It comes down to knowing and accepting Jesus as Your Savior and Lord."

The next words that came from Louis' mouth flowed with faith to what God wanted. He recognized the opportunity to share Christ with his closest friend. *If only I was more prepared.*

He felt if not heard the response. *You are my child. You are prepared.*

The words tumbled out of his mouth as if he had no choice. "You can take that personal step right now. Right here."

"Right here in the open air with people passing by." Samuel took his eyes off the water and peered inland. Louis saw it to—people conversing, children playing, all in their own little worlds.

"Why not? I'll help you," Louis encouraged. Although his acceptance of Christ had been in the Huguenot Church with a minister, Louis saw no reason to delay this God-given encounter. "I'll pray, and you repeat my words."

Both men removed their hats and lowered their heads as Louis led his friend down the marvelous road of forgiveness and redemption. To the entire world, it appeared like two men gazing out at the Atlantic Ocean. But to one man, the moment would change his life forever.

At home on Church Street, Elizabeth spent an hour with Amy in the kitchen, a place she ventured often. Baking and cooking, pleasant pastimes—plus teaching Amy, who was now thirteen—added a joyful addition to her days. She saw her own childhood in this ambitious girl. Although her own mother never stayed long in the kitchen, Elizabeth had spent hours with their cook, trying to learn the family recipes sent down from her grandmother.

"This one is a favorite of mine." Elizabeth pointed to a worn piece of paper on the counter. "We call it Cottage Cheese Delight Bread. I think you will like it. All the ingredients are here, I think. We start off like normal bread with the yeast and water. Then we add honey, cottage cheese, and molasses, followed by the oil and flour. We'll let it rise while we make the Crumb Custard, one of Louis' favorites." She hummed the tune of "This is the Day the Lord Has Made" as she mixed the eggs, bread crumbs, milk, sugar, butter, nutmeg, and vanilla. Soon the two added the words to the song as they worked.

After finishing the lesson in the kitchen, she found Louis ensconced in his library huddled over the daily paper. He brushed it aside when she entered all cleaned up. In the library he had added a comfortable settee just for the times when she joined him.

"Come, sit for a while. I have so much to tell you." He patted the cushion next to him.

"Really? Is that why you are home early?" She sat with her back against the arm in order to gauge his expressions.

"It is. Some exciting news I can only share it with you, and you can share with no one."

"No one?" The thought of a secret shared only with Louis held potential.

"You have to promise. You won't have to keep the secret for long though," he interjected.

"Tell me. I promise to keep quiet." Her hand casually rested on her extended belly as she remained poised and ready to receive the secret.

"I'm not very good at telling stories, so straight to the point: Samuel intends to ask Sarah to marry him. And—" He prevented Elizabeth from speaking by placing his fingers on her lips. "And today Samuel gave his life to Christ."

Both pieces of information were so extraordinary, given Samuel's character. Elizabeth didn't know how to comment. Two miracles had transpired. Miracles related to prayers she had prayed, but that had remained unanswered. Until now.

"And Sarah doesn't know about either, I assume." She realized why Louis had made her promise.

"Right. Samuel came to me full of doubts but left full of faith and hope. Who knows what action he will take and how soon he will truly grasp what commitments he has made all in one day." Louis studied her face. Did he see her wheels turning? "And you can't help. He has an appointment with Reverend Smith tomorrow. We'll wait until Samuel makes the move."

She had many reasons that she should tell Sarah, but her promise to Louis remained firm. And he was right, Samuel needed to work this out in his own time and way. "Sarah will be so happy. She knew she couldn't have him while he ran from God, but now they'll have a complete union."

"And that's the best way. There was no hope for us either until I found that out."

Elizabeth had a clear memory of the days when Louis blatantly turned from everything, except making money. Now money was at the bottom of his list. A complete reversal from his old self. Today, God, Elizabeth, family and then somewhere further was patriotism, pleasure, and profit. If Louis could change, so could Samuel.

Against all her feelings of wanting to burst with her information, Elizabeth did as she was told. Sarah seemed normal, knowing nothing of Samuel's intentions. The young women saw each other often at the boarding school. In her less strenuous role as a piano teacher to Martha and one other girl, Elizabeth served in a minor role, assisting the housemother in errands and chores. She was able to rest when she felt tired or to leave when she had appointments. Being an extra pair of hands proved a different role for her, but she intended to keep her word to Louis and for their baby.

On an afternoon in late September, Elizabeth and Sarah walked home by way of the market, taking in the fresh air and smells of the earthy produce. Sarah was unusually fidgety. She stopped Elizabeth, placing her gloved hand on her friend's arm. "I need to talk to you."

Elizabeth sensed panic, not jubilation. "Why you are shaking. What's wrong?" It must not be good news.

"It's Samuel. He asked me to dinner this Saturday night. Just the two of us at the Grand Hotel. He's acting strange, different somehow."

"Different good or different bad?" Elizabeth couldn't tell by her friend's confusing expressions.

Sarah tilted her head and pinched the pleats in her skirt. Finally, she looked Elizabeth in the eyes. "I don't know. Good, I guess. He comes around the school often. And then he calls at the house. He talks a lot to my father, mainly about the banking business, and he sits and listens to my mother. But there are always people around. It's as if he plans it that way. Maybe he doesn't like being alone with me."

Elizabeth screamed inside, wanting desperately to tell Sarah the truth. *Silly girl, he loves you.* But she had promised. Maybe Sarah's suffering would end this weekend. Calmly without releasing any information, Elizabeth smoothed her delicate friend's concerns. "If I were you, I'd think of what good he might have planned for you."

Heavy sighs accented her fatalistic response. "Easy for you to say. You have Louis and don't ever have to doubt him."

"True enough, but Saturday will be here soon." She smiled, covering her secret.

The political buzz brewed as Mr. Timothy sent pages of congressional information back to the *Gazette*. Since he was a fellow printing comrade of Benjamin Franklin, he had joined the group in Philadelphia to report firsthand. As the *Gazette* flowed with news, so did the pen of Christopher Gadsden to Louis. By the end of September, Louis had received two letters since the September fifth convening of the First Continental Congress. The first detailed his dealings with the other delegates. In all, fifty-six delegates arrived from twelve colonies. Not really surprised, he commented that Georgia did not send anyone. "The colony is far away, relatively young and tightly controlled by the Crown."

Christopher went on to describe others who had chosen to represent the colony:

The Virginia delegation appeared on the scene last. Although I hadn't gotten to know them very well, they are a distinguishable group consisting of Benjamin Harrison, Patrick Henry and George Washington, to name a few. I think you would get along well with this group. Mr. Deane and the Adams cousins speak often of you and send their regards.

The most recent letter Louis brought home to share with Elizabeth. The firsthand messages and descriptions brought the validity of the event closer to them. Not that they didn't believe or trust Mr. Timothy, but with Christopher, they felt personally involved.

Over a cup of tea, Louis read to Elizabeth, who, as much as she could in her present condition, was curled up in an overstuffed chair.

The delegates from the north, including Connecticut and Delaware, were surprised that our southern colonies were so ready to be united with the other. Mr. Deane even described us as men of firmness, sensibility, spirit, and thorough in our knowledge of the interests of America. That's high praise for South Carolina.

He looked up from the letters to make sure Elizabeth was still awake. "I knew Christopher would gravitate to Mr. Deane, as he did to Samuel and John Adams. He says here that even after disagreements and arguments, no one has been sent to Philadelphia to start a revolution."

Elizabeth perked up, chin raised. "That is great news! Maybe there is still hope. I want our baby to be born in a time of peace —not war."

"That is why these men are meeting. To find a reasonable solution to our plight. For you, for me, and for our baby."

Elizabeth took the letter from Louis and studied it. "You are holding out hope for a compromise from Britain then?"

"Hope, yes. I still want a peaceful conclusion. But we can't be naïve. We have to stay close in our commitment to prayer and God's guidance." Christopher's letter was forgotten as he comforted Elizabeth. *If only I could relieve this burden from her life.*

As the bells of St. Philip's competed with the bells of other churches after the services, Sarah caught Elizabeth in an exuberant embrace whispering, "Samuel proposed."

"How wonderful. I assume you are accepting his proposal." Elizabeth hoped, and prayed that Sarah could see the good in this man and accept that he really did love her.

"Yes, silly. My parents approve too. I had no hesitation after he told me about his new commitment to Christ. We can weather anything with that strong bond."

"Just imagine. Mrs. Samuel Evans does sound nice." Elizabeth wanted Sarah to have a fulfilling marriage like hers. At least their first nine months displayed a good start to years to come. But right now, this was about Sarah, not her own almost perfect marriage. What did she really know anyway?

Samuel and Louis joined the excited pair of ladies who acted like giddy school girls. "I guess the secret is out now," Samuel stated, as he tipped his hat to them.

Sarah naturally linked her arm with her tall, handsome fiancé as if she had always done that. "Samuel, you will have to get over people talking about you. For a few weeks, we'll be the talk of the town within our circle."

"When is the wedding date?" The practical side of Elizabeth chimed in, hoping she wouldn't be in confinement at that time.

"In November for sure. You must be there. So, for you, the sooner the better," Sarah said, eying her friend's obvious condition. Elizabeth's pale-blue skirt no longer had a waistline. The faux stomacher lacked ornamentation to draw the eye away from her stomach. The cooler weather required a light jacket, which concealed a bit of her extended figure.

"As an honorary bridesmaid, perhaps, because I can't stand in front of the church like this," Elizabeth giggled.

"I know. But as long as you are there, I can feel like my day will be complete."

There wasn't much Elizabeth wouldn't do for her closest friend. She would definitely be present.

CHAPTER 27

The wedding was the subject of many conversations between Elizabeth and Sarah. A little over a month to plan the event. A short engagement, but the couple didn't want to linger as the political scene heightened in uncertainty.

Amid the planning in early October, Elizabeth visited her mother with her sister Anne and the children. "It's good to get out of the house," Elizabeth shared. The boys occupied the floor with a basket of toys while the adults were served tea and biscuits.

"I wish you'd bring the children by more often, Anne. Why did you leave Charlotte?" Her mother raised her arms as if wanting to cuddle the baby. "I guess I'm going to have to visit you more often." Mother laughed.

Unannounced, George stood in the doorway of the sunroom almost filling the area with his tall, broad frame. The red uniform with shiny buttons reminded Elizabeth in an instant of his chosen profession. "Well, well, well. What a pretty scene."

The boys attacked his legs immediately. Elizabeth grinned, wondering if his remark stung with sarcasm or with truth. Everyone smiled whether in surprise or just the joy of seeing him among them. Too young to attach misgivings to his uniform and his absence and harsh words of the past, his nephews delighted in their uncle's presence.

Their mother accepted his kisses on her cheeks with a smile. "George, we had no idea you were coming for a visit." She really seemed joyous about his surprise visit. Elizabeth covered her stomach, noting that a maternal love could forgive many disappointments. Would she have to do that for her children? Had her parents done that for her? Yes. And through it all their love for her remained firm, exactly like that for George.

"Only a short one," he replied, accepting the hugs and kisses from Elizabeth and Anne.

Mother patted the cushion next to her. "Have a seat. I'll order you some tea and sandwiches."

He stood straighter, drawing all their eyes upward. "Mother, that can wait. I have some news. Important news."

Surely, he couldn't shock them anymore. With all of his rash decisions in the past, what was left to say or share? Elizabeth wanted to go to her mother's side. Would anyone be able to help or change any of his news?

"Go ahead, then," Mother said in a stern voice as she straightened her shoulders as if preparing for a blow of bad news, as if trying to reach his height.

"Well, I have a surprise for all of you." Turning his head, George's hand followed as he motioned to each of them. "You see —well, I am married."

"Married?" Elizabeth's word joined the other two women's startled words, all overlapping sounding like a hoarse, breathless whisper.

Crossing his arms, he seemed to be enjoying the reaction. "Yes, just recently in Philadelphia, to Victoria Seymour."

All of the air felt like it was sucked out of the room, making it difficult for Elizabeth to breathe. Of all his choices, he chose her! "Victoria Seymour? I thought she was with—" She couldn't believe she voiced her thoughts out loud. Was it her place to react first? "But wasn't she courting William Burns just months ago?"

"She was, but now she has chosen me." He turned briefly and put out his hand. With her nose in the air and body stiff, Victoria walked into the room, wearing a pink dress dripping with feathers and lace.

Victoria, as haughty as ever, married to her brother. A surprise and a shock. Her nemesis was now a member of her family—in the role of a sister.

Anne was the first to offer a word of congratulations, bringing everyone back to the present. "Welcome to the family, Victoria."

Elizabeth must have said something, following Anne's example, although she couldn't remember what. She could tell there was more George wasn't saying. "How long will you be staying?" she asked.

"I only have a few days." He shuffled his feet and turned his head to look at his wife. Elizabeth wanted to laugh at the red and pink portrait they painted, yet the scene was all too serious. "But, Victoria needs to stay longer."

Their mother lifted her chin and asked, "Needs to? Why is that, son?" Could her mother see through the wall her son had built? Elizabeth felt this was no casual visit. She glanced back at her mother. When the woman wanted to show authority, she could pose as regally as a queen. *Why doesn't she say more?*

"To tell the truth, Victoria has been sent away from her home by her parents since she married me. They will not keep her while I am on duty. She needs a place to stay for a while." No other details. Except, "Here is my wife, take care of her." It sounded too rehearsed, perhaps hiding a plan. But a plan to what?

Elizabeth noticed fear on Victoria's face in the form of heavy eyelids hiding her large, expressive eyes. As much as she disliked Victoria, Elizabeth didn't want her to be homeless for whatever reason—even a reason they were not honestly revealing. What was it about George's controlled speech and emotion?

Mother barely moved, only her mouth appeared to be alive. "Of course, son, she can stay here while you find a house in Philadelphia."

"Thank you, Mother." Turning to his wife, he said, "You see? Nothing to fear."

The forced smile on Victoria's pretty face revealed a not-so-complacent attitude. From all appearances, even with her guarded expression, the woman did not share her husband's decision that this was the best of situations.

"Thank you, Mrs. Elliott. I will try not to be a burden." With emphasis on the last word and a clipped look at George, Victoria obviously was not a happy participant.

Elizabeth viewed the players before her with speculation. No one had a positive outlook on the new predicament. Mother had unexpectedly gained a daughter-in-law and an additional houseguest for an indefinite period. Anne and Elizabeth had obtained a sister-in-law, someone who would be present in everyday gatherings. A fixture in the house.

"You may have Elizabeth's old room, Victoria. I think you will be very comfortable. Will you show her where she can store her trunk and belongings, George?"

In an instant George was leading his wife up the stairs to the second floor. Footmen followed with not one, but five trunks. It seemed like a whole household of goods.

The three women were speechless. Numb? Perplexed? Elizabeth almost burst with the silence pressing in around her. "Mother, what just happened here? George married that—that—"

Luckily, her mother calmly interrupted her before Elizabeth found an appropriate word for the new member of the family. "Girls, it really doesn't matter what you thought of her in the past. She is family as George is family. And as Christians, we will accept her with charity. I don't expect instant friendship or even trust, but kind words and actions must prevail." What controlled speech, calling upon the one thing her daughters could not refute: charity.

"There has to be more to this than George is saying," Anne commented, still staring at the staircase as the last trunk disappeared.

As quickly as that brief encounter, Victoria became a permanent member of the clan.

Louis deciphered the latest from Congress from the paper while in the storeroom with Henry. "The delegates voted to condemn the Coercive Acts. They have adopted a Continental Association that pledges Americans to boycott most British goods. They also sent a formal list of grievances to the British government. If redress is not forthcoming, they would meet again in May 1775. That is very straightforward. I can't imagine that the Continental Association was adopted without controversy," Louis commented as he glanced over the rest of the article. "Here it is. The divisions or concerns. 'Earlier some delegates argued that a boycott would not work because Virginia would not agree to ban the exportation of tobacco.' I could have seen that coming."

"What did South Carolina—or, in particular, Gadsden—have to say? No way would he remain quiet," Henry said.

"Mr. Timothy reports that 'Gadsden supported a boycott without Virginia: Boston and New England cannot hold out—the country will be deluged with blood, if we don't act with spirit. Don't let America look at this mountain, and let it bring forth a mouse.' He surely did take a strong position. I would have loved to see Christopher's fiery stand. According to this report, it worked. Congress, including Virginia, resolved to prohibit all trade with Great Britain effective December first this year."

Propped against the table, Henry balled his fists resting beside him. "Things will really change for the planters with export options decreased." His uncle always saw the big picture, who would be hurt and who would have to sacrifice. The boycott would affect all the colonies and colonists eventually. A few doors of trade were still open—France and the Indies—but Americans would have to learn to be self-sufficient.

Louis set the paper aside. "I have a feeling we haven't heard the end of news from Congress. It almost seems too easy. Mark my word, Christopher has more to say."

Louis finished his work early. He found Elizabeth dozing on the daybed with her right hand reposing protectively on her belly. Even his quiet entrance, though, brought her out of her peaceful reverie. Looking at her in that moment, she appeared as one without a care in the world. But only briefly.

"Oh, Louis! I'm glad you're home." She accepted his hand as she adjusted to a sitting position, not the easiest feat of late. Her emphasis on his name, made him wonder how her day had progressed.

"Good news or bad news?" he teased, not expecting the latter.

"Horrible news. Just unbelievable." She shook her head and sighed, her breath coming in short puffs.

It couldn't be that bad. No tears. No blood. No black mourning clothes.

"George has married none other than Victoria Seymour. He brought her home to Mother's today. No warning. No big wedding. He broke the news abruptly and established Victoria in Mother's house." Finally, she stopped. Her flailing arms again rested calmly beside her.

He chuckled at her passion. "George and Victoria. Well, I thought he had better sense and would leave her to William Burns. She changed course quickly."

"Why do you grin so? Don't you see? She's here to stay. George is leaving her with Mother. It's awful. She's in my old bedroom." Frustration dripped as she spoke. He wouldn't have been surprised if she stomped her foot next.

"I see what you mean. I thought her family moved back to Philadelphia." Something wasn't adding up as truth.

"They did, but they don't want her. How could a mother not want her own daughter? Even one like Victoria?"

"You don't need to worry about that. It will work out." Victoria was one of those situations he'd never figure out, at least in the immediate future. No need to dwell on her. "Now tell me what you decided about the party for Sarah."

She sighed but followed his lead. "The party will be here in two weeks on a Thursday evening. She wants to keep it small— church friends and family. So far the list comprises twenty-five names."

"That's small?" Not to him. "Are you well enough to do it?"

"You know I have Ellen and Amy. And I promise to keep it simple, stress free for me and not a huge burden on them. Anne and Mother will bring food items from their kitchens too."

"If there's anything that Tom and I can do, let me know." He enjoyed seeing her animated, with a project to keep her mind busy. "Promise not to overdo your activity, Elizabeth. Remember your fragile condition."

"I don't know about fragile. But it is certainly a condition I can't forget."

The week before the party, Sarah and Elizabeth took the buggy to the political meeting at the home of Mrs. Savage on Church Street. Louis said he didn't want Elizabeth walking the streets even for a short distance. He tried to prohibit her from going to the meeting, but she was determined and won the argument, promising to stay with Sarah at all times.

The Daughters of Liberty group had grown, especially since the Continental Congress was meeting. It seemed few wanted to miss the news from the halls of Philadelphia. Elizabeth glanced through the large drawing room and two parlors. Plenty of space for the women present so far. Sarah grabbed her arm and pulled her to a comfortable chair.

"Why are you rushing? No one else is seated yet." Elizabeth looked around at the milling groups.

"You need the best seat in the house," Sarah said. "Anyway, Louis insisted on this part of the bargain."

"How will he know where I sit?" Elizabeth didn't understand all the fuss; she wasn't an invalid. By the looks of the older matrons, however, she might as well have been on her deathbed. "Obviously, these women haven't seen a woman in my condition in a while. Maybe I should lock myself in my room."

While they waited for the official meeting to start, Elizabeth shared a plan with the few women around her. "Just think what we could hide under layers of petticoats within the folds of material. Mrs. Adams showed me how to make pockets that can be used for almost anything—letters, food, money, medicine, even weapons. We could be the 'petticoat brigade,' able to walk past any soldier with our secret stash."

"What an ingenious idea. You should share it with the rest of the group," Sarah urged.

She wasn't quite ready to admit the possibility of even needing the petticoat scenario. "I will, but on another occasion. Not tonight. I'm sure we have a full agenda."

The spokesperson was Mrs. John Rutledge, the wife of one of the South Carolina delegates. She was only a few years older than Anne.

"The last news we heard was about the boycott of all British trade by December first." The woman had a crisp, clear, articulate voice. "Things have changed a little from then. According to my husband, four of the South Carolina delegates, including him, walked out of Congress in protest of the Continental Association." She unfolded a sheet of paper and held it closer to the lamp. "Here is what he wrote."

We flatly refused to cooperate unless the exportation of rice and indigo was exempted. The

Congress compromised and agreed to exempt rice, but not indigo. With that revision, we

signed the Association. The resolution states that Congress resolves not to import any

goods, slaves, or duty-laden tea from Great Britain from December 1, 1774, through

September 20, 1775. If by that latter date Great Britain has not repealed all objectionable

laws, then all exportation, except rice, to her and her possessions would cease.

Elizabeth knew that was only one side of the story, but, unwilling to enter the discussion with a counter statement, she sat back and listened as Mrs. Rutledge continued. "'The vast majority of the delegates, including the five from South Carolina, hoped England would make the concessions needed to end the crisis.' And that is all. It gives us something to think about."

Mrs. Savage distributed copies of the local paper. Elizabeth read a quote from Christopher on the front page of the day's news. "Our seaport towns are composed of brick and wood. If they are destroyed, we have clay and lumber enough to rebuild them. But if the liberties of our country are destroyed, where shall we find the materials to replace them?"

Elizabeth hadn't understood why her husband and others were collecting and storing arms. Yet more and more, it became clear that America was willing to do battle. What would happen to her life of music, family, teaching, and gardening? Strife and discord seemed to knock more and more often on her door.

Elizabeth remembered the feeling—the one she saw glowing on Sarah's face. This time last year she had been the bride.

"I never thought this day would come. I'm really getting married." Sarah bounced on her tiptoes, twirling in her light-green party dress.

"Of course, you are. And Samuel is the luckiest groom in town." She followed Sarah to the table piled with gifts. "Look. Everyone on your list replied."

"We appreciate all the gifts," Sarah said to her guests. "Samuel and I are blessed to call you friends. I really don't know where I'll put everything." Elizabeth recognized all the essentials displayed, the china, crystal, silver serving pieces, all similar to her table of gifts last year. Honestly, Elizabeth could not have predicted her best friend's wedding.

"Well, Sarah, the banns are posted. Your dress finished and the date around the corner. No turning back now," Mrs. Collins said.

Elizabeth knew Sarah had no intention of letting Samuel go after it took so long to turn him around.

Louis went to the Elliott house for the duration of the wedding event. He found himself cloistered with Mr. Elliott in the library discussing politics, a subject that Louis fervently avoided with his father-in-law. But tonight was different. Gone was the defensive, stubborn stance of Mr. Elliott. In its place was a truly concerned, contemplative, almost fearful man with shoulders drooped and fists clenching and unclenching at his sides. What had caused this strong, stoic man to resemble defeat?

Mr. Elliott paced and placed his hand on his chin. "I hope I'm not too late."

"Too late, sir?" Louis looked for a letter or a bearer of unwelcome news and found none. "Too late for what? What has sparked your concern?"

Mr. Elliott sighed and stared at the ceiling. "All the events of the Continental Congress and the decisions made. For the first time, I see the futility of siding with Britain. I see it as a lost cause." He stopped pacing and looked at Louis. "Britain won't change. I finally realize Parliament cannot rule this country. And as of today, I'm going to stand as a Partisan for the cause of liberty." He stopped and dropped his hands again by his side and shrugged, leaving the impression of defeat or resignation. Or could it be the final shedding of unwanted conflict that he'd battled for too long?

Louis stepped closer to Mr. Elliott, a bit scared he might suddenly disappear as an apparition. Could Louis trust his ears? "I don't know what to say, except I didn't see this coming." For over a year, a thick wall had existed between them. Louis almost felt it physically crumbling.

"Well, let's say it was your prayers." Mr. Elliott wasn't going anywhere, and if his smile was any indication of his happiness, the man's decision was here to stay too. "God convinced me I was being selfish in my stand. I was only seeing the benefits to me, while an entire group of people was suffering and willing to possibly die for a chance at freedom and liberty."

On its own volition, Louis' head turned back and forth, wondering at the result of this confession. "Have you told your wife yet?"

Shaking his head, Mr. Elliott frowned slightly before he put his smile in place. "No. You're the first. I've really just now come to this conclusion. I'll have to take small steps until I grasp the whole picture. Would your uncle mind if I visit with him?"

Henry had prayed for Mr. Elliott's mind to search for the right answer. Of course, to the Sons of Liberty, the fight for freedom was the sensible way to live. Henry would probably not be as shocked as Louis. "Not at all. You don't mind if I share this with Elizabeth, do you? She's been so concerned."

Mr. Elliott clapped his once fisted hands together, announcing it was time to celebrate this feat and not look back. "No, you're free to say whatever you want. I'm tired of fighting. I'm content with my decision. I'm sure Anne will be pleased to tell Robert when he returns."

"There's only one, now two, who will be furious with you," Louis suggested.

"You mean George and Victoria." Louis nodded. "They'll not understand as I did not understand all of you before now. Each man must make up his own mind."

Louis extended his hand. Mr. Elliott grasped it and pulled Louis to him for a quick embrace and a pat on the back. As Louis accepted his father-in-law's commitment with respect and awe, he realized George would now see his flesh and blood, his own father, as an enemy, as he saw his sisters.

Louis' determined, energetic gait guided him home. He practically raced with the news. The Engles were putting away the last of the stray party items, and Tom had already rearranged the furniture. Louis had spent longer with Mr. Elliott than he had intended. Yet the transformation he had witnessed was worth the time. He shook his head in disbelief.

He found Elizabeth already resting in bed, her beautiful hair flowing over her shoulders. He loved this time of night when she had her book propped on her belly, using it as an easel. "Such an inspiring picture. I wish I could capture you forever like this," he commented, as he leaned over her for a brief kiss.

"You say the sweetest things. If you can love me like this, I don't have to worry about your love at other times."

He placed his hand on their baby who gently kicked him back. "How long now? Six weeks?"

"There about. Our little anniversary gift." She giggled, causing her book to rise and fall.

He gently stood up, not wanting to disturb her comfort, surrounded by perfectly fluffed pillows, by rocking the bed. "I have some news, but don't try to jump out of bed when you hear it." He removed his jacket and cravat, followed by his waistcoat.

She placed her book face down beside her and waited. Her mouth turned up, then down, obviously confused about the subject of his news. Should he prolong the suspense? Maybe not in her condition.

"I had a nice long visit with your father tonight." He took her hand and kissed it. "Our prayers have been answered. He's finally accepted the views of the Partisans. The walls came down in front of my eyes. I could see God's hand as He performed this miracle." The story unfolded as Elizabeth's smile grew more permanent.

"Oh, Louis." In her excitement, her book tumbled to the floor. Luckily, she remained stable. "Now my entire family is on the same side, no longer split in two. I feel like I've my dear father back, like I'm no longer a rebellious child going against his will."

Louis realized in her enthusiasm that she had forgotten an important detail. "Not your entire family. Don't forget George and Victoria."

Her smile diminished a bit. "Oh. For a minute I did forget. Prayer worked for Father; now I'll continue until all is fine with George and his wife."

Louis didn't see that conversion happening, but he hadn't seen her father's either. "I've invited your father to the next meeting. I know he'll feel a little awkward just like I did at first, but everyone will welcome a new member of your father's position."

"Go easy on him. Remember his pride is a big part of him. He'll not budge very easily."

"Thanks for the warning. I'm glad that family quality passed over you." He whispered, as if not to let the baby hear. "Hopefully, this little one won't have to deal with a pride issue."

"She'll be full of goodness and grace—not pride and mischief," Elizabeth stressed.

"She?" Louis chuckled.

He had battled with pride all his life. From stories, he knew that mischief was Elizabeth's childhood trait. Their baby, son or daughter, would enter a world where love and commitment were better choices.

🍥

The Sons of Liberty met soon to discuss plans for a debriefing once the delegates arrived. Louis offered Mr. Elliott a ride in the carriage to the home of Mr. Singleton. Introductions didn't need to be made for a man like Louis' father-in-law. Attached to the college and the church, he was known to many, especially the educated, wealthier citizens.

"Welcome, Mr. Elliott," James Laurens said. "I didn't expect to see you here. I won't beat around with pleasantries. What are you intending to gain from being here?"

Louis crossed his arms and listened. James's straightforward manner didn't seem to dent Mr. Elliott's confidence. "To be honest, I have questions, and this is the place I can get them answered."

"Let's start, then. Join the group in the parlor, and I'll tell Mr. Singleton we're ready." James motioned to the almost full room. Louis found two seats in the middle, avoiding the ones vacant in the front. No reason to draw extra attention to his father-in-law.

An overview of the political scene took only minutes. The role of Charles Town required the bulk of the hour. Louis tried to listen with the ears of a new Partisan to better understand Mr. Elliott's position. For his part, his father-in-law nodded and clapped with the others. At times, however, he shifted his feet and clenched his fists. What was his concern? Was he having second thoughts?

"Any questions, gentlemen?" Mr. Singleton glanced around the room.

Mr. Elliott stood. "I understand where the line is drawn, and I've shifted to the side of the rights of the people. But if this is not solved peacefully, how will the citizens of our town defend themselves?"

Of course, Mr. Elliott didn't know. While he was pandering to the Loyalists the last few years, he'd missed the storing of arms around the city. Louis didn't know how much the men trusted Mr. Elliott at this early point.

"Without revealing any secret plans at an open meeting, I promise you strategic actions have taken place to enhance the safety and security of the citizens," Mr. Singleton said.

Mr. Elliott looked in every direction, even turning to include the audience behind him. With his arm, he drew a circle in the air to encircle everyone. "And this group is willing to defend and protect at any expense."

"Huzzah, huzzah." Those present voiced their support.

Mr. Elliott received his answer and sat down. Leaning toward Louis, he said, "I'm convinced this group has the means and ability to make a stand."

Louis felt confident that having Mr. Elliott as an ally would be a plus for the overall cause of freedom. Slowly, he would come to understand the cause and accept the price of freedom, just as Louis had. Struggles loomed in the future for all, no matter what side one chose. Louis was glad Mr. Elliott had finally aligned himself with the Partisans.

CHAPTER 28

*H*aving adjourned on October twenty-sixth, the delegates from the Convention and their families made their way back to Charles Town. Louis heard the brigantine was to arrive on Sunday, November sixth. After church, many citizens greeted the delegation, though he chose to bide his time until later.

That evening the delegates presented papers and extracts from the Congress to the General Convention and others present at the Exchange. Louis' curiosity propelled him to attend.

Elizabeth laughed. "I'm not surprised. If there wasn't a meeting, I don't know how I'd keep you from Christopher's house." She kissed him and pushed him out the door with her blessing.

Even though he had kept abreast of the progress through letters from Christopher and the paper, the firsthand report assured Louis the five men were together in their beliefs. Louis found Christopher before the reporting began. "I saw your name in the paper so often I was beginning to think you were on your own. But now I see the respect all of you have for each other. Welcome back." He patted his friend on the back.

"Thanks. I appreciate the support. Not everyone can go home and find that the majority of the town welcomes him."

"Let's get together soon, away from politics." Louis settled in a seat, appreciating the work of these citizens.

The Committee planned an elegant celebration in the delegates' honor at Ramage's Tavern on Wednesday. Christopher extended a personal invitation to Louis, Henry, and Samuel. "I'm anxious to hear more about Lieutenant Governor Bull," Christopher said, gaining Louis' attention.

"You must have heard the rumors," Louis said. "Supposedly he was scared that all the pomp and celebrations after the Continental Congress met would erupt into violent defiance of British authority. Word leaked out that he had promised Britain he would do all in his power to arrest, detain, and secure any gunpowder, arms, or ammunition that might be imported into the colony."

Christopher's shoulders rocked as he laughed. "He was probably wise to be scared into leaving. But it sure does make the British seem weak—or at least their puppets representing them." Louis imagined a bit of smugness lurking at the corners of Christopher's smile.

Louis leaned in closer. "This news concerns me because Robert's shipment contains more secret crates of just such items. Hopefully, he will arrive soon, bringing the cargo safely to harbor."

At the festive occasion, Louis stood with Henry in the back, preferring the fringes away from the layers of participants. The room suddenly seemed very small.

Christopher read from the address to the people of Canada and the petition to the king. Then Lynch explained the non-exportable agreement. Christopher stood and interjected, "I want to go on record as I did in Congress that I don't think South

Carolina should have special rights to export rice to Britain. All colonies should be treated the same. But my opinion didn't pass." He sat down.

There was the man Louis read about and knew. The rebel among rebels, not scared to make a stand and stick to it even on the losing side. Whispers resounded throughout the hall. Others could perceive the bold statement out of place at the celebration, but Louis knew his friend would use any situation to declare his stand.

Louis received word from a messenger: The *Rose* had pulled into the harbor and had docked early this morning. He wasted no time walking to the wharf. Robert's safe passage boded well on many levels. For Anne, Louis was thankful the family would be reunited, and for business, a successful voyage completed. He didn't know that it would always be the same in the future. He prayed so.

He walked the distance up the ramp to meet Robert. "Welcome back. Thank you once again for a fruitful voyage. I admit I was concerned this time more than others."

"It's good to be home—or almost home. I have much to tell you, but I think it can wait," Robert said, looking past him to the wharf, where stood the boys and baby Charlotte in her mother's arms.

The plan worked, almost to perfection this time. All weapons, ammunition, and items to be stored for possible future use went undetected. Louis thought God must have put a shield over the ship. In his practical mind, he knew since their ship didn't go to England, the General Committee didn't question the contents. Charles Town wasn't Boston, thankfully.

After the delivery to the store, Louis searched the crates. Special items—gifts for Elizabeth and the baby from his mother—spurred his inspection.

There in the third crate, with various bolts of material, patterns, and books, was the item he awaited. He gently ran his hand over the old wooden cradle. The cradle, which was over a hundred years old, had been passed down through his family. Would Elizabeth cherish it like his family had?

There was also another box wrapped in paper with a note. "Louis, open with Elizabeth. *Amour, Maman.*" He didn't have a clue. Anxious to return to Elizabeth, especially with the gifts, Louis instructed Tom to deliver the cradle later. Grabbing his coat and the mysterious box, Louis walked briskly to his home.

Arranging flowers in the parlor, Elizabeth turned at the click of the front door. Louis had arrived before she had expected. She clapped with delight as he dangled a box in front of her. Since it was from his mother, a woman she might never meet, the moment was dear.

"Do we open it now? Or wait?" Louis shrugged, but before he could answer, she continued. "No reason to wait. Sit down next to me. Do you know what it is?"

"I have no idea. You do the honors and open it."

Her fingers slipped through the paper packaging to find three beautiful items: a silver beaded porringer, a silver baby cup, and a silver baby spoon.

"Louis, the note says that these were your baby items. That means so much to me." She pulled each item to her heart, her tears mingling with laughter and joy. "Our baby is already so blessed and so loved. I'll write her a letter right now."

"Wait a few minutes before you do that. I'm expecting another surprise any minute now."

Louis made her sit and relax. She tried but staying still was not high on her list. "Here, put your feet up and let me tell you about Robert." Louis helped swing her legs around to rest on the sofa and added a pillow behind her back.

"I suppose Anne and the children made it on time." Nothing could have kept her sister away.

About ten minutes later, Tom entered the front door, making loud grunting noises. Elizabeth was surprised when Louis acted quickly and placed himself in front of Tom. "Close your eyes, Elizabeth, and don't peek." She obeyed with a giggle. "Tom, put it right here. Gently now. Thank you."

Elizabeth sat as commanded, tilting her head from side to side as she followed the sound of the placement of the item. Louis had already given her one surprise gift. What more could he have for me?

"Now, open them."

Her hands covered her mouth for a moment as her eyes connected with the beautiful cradle. "Oh, Louis. It's beautiful. So perfect." As she touched the cradle, she could feel his past written into the wood grain. And she could see their baby sleeping there as she rocked it back and forth.

"It's over a hundred years old. A bit of Lestarjette history, including some teeth marks and scratches." He rubbed his fingers over some tiny indentures.

"Hopefully, we'll add a lot more. Now can we write that letter?"

"Of course."

She chose a flowery print stationery. Would Louis' mother be able to comprehend the love Elizabeth felt for her? A love for someone she might never meet.

She combined her proper, but limited, French with her stylish handwriting and with Louis' help produced something she hoped conveyed her affection and appreciation for all his mother had done. That complete, she placed her hand on her stomach and prayed for their baby. One month and she'd hold her baby girl or boy. The cradle would bind the family across the miles as her arms surrounded her baby right now.

The wedding was beautiful as was the bride. Elizabeth missed standing up front with her best friend. But at least on the front pew, she felt confident in her new hunter-green dress with cream lace and a tan jacket.

Sarah and Samuel Evans—another marriage with God in the center. Elizabeth placed her hand in Louis' as the minister spoke the vows. She repeated them in her heart and received a loving look from her husband.

Afterward, in the foyer of the church, Louis pulled her aside and kissed her.

"What was that for?" she asked.

"For marrying me a year ago." And another. "For having my baby." Another... "Because I love you."

Elizabeth wrapped her arms around Louis' neck, stared longingly into his eyes, and pledged through tears, "I'll love you forever."

CHAPTER 29

"*E*lizabeth, I won't be home for the noon meal today. Christopher sent a note about an event taking place on the wharves today," Louis said. "It appears that the recently arrived *Britannia* carried seven chests of tea that were consigned to merchants in town. Today the General Committee is going to force the consignees to board the ship and get rid of the tea. He wants me to be on hand to support the cause."

"Please be careful. Don't be involved in anything dangerous," she pleaded grabbing his sleeve.

He patted her hand. "I'm sure with a few convincing words the Committee will turn the merchants around. This tea was ordered months ago, not yesterday." One more kiss goodbye didn't really convince her.

As Louis walked to Christopher's office, he noticed about two dozen men gathered near the *Britannia*. Louis joined Christopher, Mr. Timothy, and Mr. Lynch.

"I sure do hope the men know what to do," Christopher said uneasily.

Louis watched as about ten men boarded the ship and proceeded to the chests of tea. With hammers and axes, the men smashed the chests and emptied the contents into the Cooper River. Where was the militia? Not that Louis wanted someone like George to appear. The waters bubbled with the tea bars as they dissolved into amber foam. With a repeat of other tea parties around the country, the hope of reconciliation swirled to the bottom of the river like the forbidden tea.

The crowd had grown, including representatives from the government, but no one interfered or came too close. Louis felt the heartbeat of the men around him, although he had not lifted a finger. How could the British government watch and not defend the cargo? Fear? Orders from above? The men and the General Committee had free rein to perform this act. The calmness and acceptance of the dumping of the tea surprised Louis. Would he calmly allow someone to come in and rid the store of valuables from France and the Indies? He didn't quite understand the lack of retaliation, but he was suspicious of the Loyalists and their lack of action. No harsh words. No violence. Nothing except their watchful eyes, which could in the future work against this act of destruction. Who truly had the upper hand in this game of power?

A few days later, noise from the street brought Louis and Elizabeth out onto the steps of their house. "What's happening?" Elizabeth grasped Louis' arm and rose on tiptoes to see.

"I don't know, but it looks like the whole town is parading down Church Street." Several hundred citizens, if Louis guessed correctly. He stood in amazement, watching the mass marching to the city limits.

"I'm going to follow them. You stay here where it's safe." He squeezed her fingers as he removed her hand from his coat sleeve. He knew she wouldn't want to follow, not in her condition. Any other time and he would not be able to stop her.

She stepped back closer to the door as he peered into the crowd. "Does that mean you won't be safe?"

Safe? With the number of arms tucked in basements and cabinets and he assumed in jacket pockets, he wasn't sure. Elizabeth didn't need to know that he had thought of carrying a weapon at times. "They aren't armed, so I'm assuming it is a peaceful demonstration. But I want to find out. I'll stay on the outskirts of the group."

He kissed her and stepped into the organized mayhem—if there was such a thing. Like a sly fox, he stayed close enough to the action without being part of it. The group ended up in an open area where they burned effigies of agents of the king and tax collectors. Then, as if enough tea hadn't been destroyed already, a large quantity of tea fed the flames. Things had surely changed in favor of the Sons of Liberty and the General Committee. Still, he wondered at what price.

When he spied Robert, Louis stood with him away from the bulk of the crowd. "Who do you think organized this?"

"I don't know. But I heard it was a local effort. Basically, the townspeople wanted to show support for the Congress and Sons of Liberty," Robert said. "The people even supplied the tea."

"I should have realized it would only take a little time." With arms crossed, Louis stared at the black pillars of smoke rising above the trees. "The same thing started in France, which led to animosity toward the aristocracy. Here I see ordinary people, not only the wealthy and educated, willing to take a part in government. This group confirms Charles Town might be ready to be self-governed."

Robert nodded. "I think you explained it well." He turned from the fire toward Louis. "Do you have a few minutes to talk? I need to share some information from your brother. Could you come by the house now? I want to give you the letters personally."

"Of course," Louis agreed. "I was going to drop by today anyway."

By maneuvering away from the crowd with their backs to the intense fire, they managed to avoid the crowds. The streets appeared almost empty since hundreds remained in the park. Robert talked of the mood of the French public. Louis found he was a little envious of Robert's opportunities to do business with the French in person. At times, Robert appeared more in tune than Louis. But, if Louis spent all his time crossing the ocean, how could he conduct his business in the colonies?

As they choose short cuts through the city, Robert continued, "Wealthy investors have a desire to support the colonists in any skirmish against the British. It's as if they want a war. But I think they want a cause. Some are willing to give their service, as well as their money, in a military endeavor. André said his contacts are still willing to aid in any items that we might need."

Louis once again found himself debating whether he wanted a military confrontation. Of course, he would hold out for peace, but everywhere he turned in his world, all prepared for a physical battle. At some point there would be no turning back. "If I'm hearing you correctly, they are even more committed than last year."

"You're right. They see this foray as entertainment, a chance to get back at the British. We need someone in France trying to keep the rumors down and give facts, if there are any facts to give. I feel we are still waiting on Britain's next move." Robert never hinted what that next move would be. No one knew. Or if someone did, it had not leaked out to the colonies.

Robert passed on the letters from André. His brother's news congratulated Louis on becoming an uncle to a healthy boy in July named Charles André: "It's hard to believe we'll have children the same age. I always thought they would grow up together, although I do understand your decision to make your home in South Carolina." Did his brother really understand that for Louis there was no returning to his way of life in France, for family or patriotic devotion?

No regrets, only memories. His thoughts often turned to his own child. From one man all by himself one a year ago, to a family of three. God had been good to him.

Victoria dropped in unannounced in late November. Elizabeth welcomed any visit from the outside—even a challenging one from her sister-in-law—especially since she was confined to her house for the next few weeks. *When did I become so needy? Surely, a book is better for my baby than this?*

Elizabeth pasted on a smile. "Would you please stay for refreshments?" She didn't often see the woman. Today she noticed something different. As she studied her, she had a feeling she was about to learn the answer to a question she'd had from the beginning: why was Victoria in Charles Town? If she could have leaned her body forward, Elizabeth would have placed her elbows on her knees in total anticipation like a child listening to a ghost story.

"I'd love to join you," Victoria answered. She chose a high-backed chair and spread her royal blue skirt from arm to arm, finally resting her hands rigidly in her lap as if clasped too tightly. At least she had a lap, Elizabeth mused.

After Elizabeth asked Amy for tea, she watched Victoria fidgeting with her gloves, searching the room for a place to focus her attention. *I'm ready. Tell me now and stop stalling.* "Why don't you tell me why you're here?"

"Why? Do I need a reason?" As Elizabeth had expected, the statuesque woman put up a wall of defense in no time at all.

"I am glad you stopped by, but I think you have a reason to visit. You can tell me whatever you need to say." Elizabeth pushed back into the fluffy comfort of goose down pillows, ready for drama to unfold. Would the story answer all her doubts? Or simply add more? Could this be better than a novel? Elizabeth knew she shouldn't want any drama for this woman was part of her family.

"I do need to tell someone. George and I haven't been quite honest with you and your family." Victoria paused. Elizabeth held her tongue just in case her eagerness deterred Victoria. Patience would win out in the end. "You see, I'm expecting a child in April." She didn't meet Elizabeth's eyes. "When my mother found out we were married in October, she refused to have her daughter ruin the family reputation." No tears. No remorse. Just facts.

Oh, why did Elizabeth desire the drama? She'd take back all her thoughts for the chance that this wasn't true. Elizabeth understood it all now. The quick wedding. The surprise visit. The housing of Victoria—all for the sake of Victoria's reputation. Why hadn't she picked up on it earlier? She knew there had to be another reason, and this was a very good one.

Seeing the situation in this new light, all barriers were lifted for a moment. George and Victoria were to have a baby. Elizabeth would be an aunt again. Her maternal heart couldn't reject an innocent baby—especially one that shared her blood. For better or worse, this child deserved to be loved and accepted, as did Victoria.

Elizabeth hoped her jaw was back in place and her smile didn't look lopsided or fake. "I'm truly happy for you. You are so very healthy looking. I would never have guessed." Instinct urged her to embrace the mother-to-be. She stood to make her way to Victoria.

But Victoria jumped up instead, almost pushing Elizabeth aside. "Well, if George could see me now, he wouldn't be too complimentary. He prefers me to wear the most stylish and flattering clothes. And this figure is already so unbecoming." Victoria frowned as she glanced down at her royal-blue skirt. Elizabeth didn't notice a difference. "If I grow as large as you, he'll surely never come back to claim me. This is not what he wanted."

Sorrow filled the woman's face as if she wanted to escape her future, exactly the opposite of Elizabeth, who continuously rejoiced in her own prospects of a child. *Can a woman really not want her child?* The thought was inconceivable to Elizabeth as she placed her hands over her own precious unborn child. *Large indeed. I don't think I'll ever complain again about my girth.*

"Victoria, George will love this child. He's so good with his nephews and niece. Children are not a nuisance to him. Yours will be a welcome addition. You must believe that," Elizabeth stammered and rambled, almost pleading for a "yes" in response.

"Love?" Victoria shouted, letting her reserved persona disappear with her harsh tone. "Love a baby that has taken me away from my family, from my freedom, from society, and placed me in seclusion away from all I want? Love is a very strong, misplaced word for what I feel—and definitely from what George feels."

Sorrow filled Elizabeth's heart. All she could think to do was pray for the future of this child. God loved the unborn baby, and undoubtedly her family would too.

As Victoria stomped her way to the door, not waiting for anyone to see her out, Elizabeth bowed her head, and as tears flowed freely, she prayed. *Please, God, help Victoria and George have a change of heart and direction as the child develops and grows. When he is delivered, let them welcome him to a happy, whole family centered on You and on love. Amen.*

Later, when Elizabeth shared the news with Louis, he reacted as she had expected. Although he voiced pain at Victoria's rejection, he transferred his love back to Elizabeth and their child, giving her assurance that he loved them with his whole being.

He held her close. "You need to concentrate on our precious one. Now please don't worry about Victoria too much. There's time for that later. Maybe through our love and example, they'll see how much a baby should be cherished."

As December commenced, Elizabeth had to hear the news of the town from Louis, her family, and the newspaper. She wasn't to venture out of the house before her delivery. As long as there was news, the walls of the house didn't feel so confining. She paced the rooms at times, trying to mentally solve Charles Town's problems, as though anyone, much less a whole city, would listen to her.

Reading anything about William Drayton, the recently converted Loyalist, made Elizabeth laugh. He complained of having to participate in government with men who knew only how "to cut up a beast in the market or to cobble an old shoe." What did he think of Louis' occupation?

Louis hadn't dwelled on Drayton's opinion. "He's not the only one. Many educated gentlemen have a hard time mixing with merchants, planters, and artisans. They're not used to the common South Carolinian serving beside him," Louis added. "Your father is one, although not to the same degree. After all his son-in-law is a merchant."

Elizabeth's response dripped with sarcasm. "Poor Mr. Drayton, to be saddled with people like us. Wonder what he thinks of you?"

"I'm not worried. My education might not be from Oxford, but it is from its rival in Paris. Anyway, listen to what the *Gazette* says today." Louis unfolded the paper. "'George III told North that blows must decide whether they are to be subject to the Country or Independent.' That was his response to the meeting of Congress."

"In other words, fighting?" Elizabeth interpreted.

"Yes. A battle to some degree. We can only hope and pray that he comes to his senses and doesn't really mean a fight." He set aside the paper and spoke of other more soothing things. "Are you getting enough rest?"

"Of course. Ellen and Mother won't allow anything else. I have to beg to get out of bed for even a few hours. Luckily, I have visitors like Anne and Sarah. Any distraction is good for me."

"Do you think we all want to be called distractions?" he laughed.

"I mean it in the most loving way. Somehow you all know what to do. Jeannette has supplied me with the most interesting books, including *Sinners in the Hands of an Angry God* by Jonathan Edwards. I've almost finished it. You might enjoy reading it." He nodded, but Elizabeth knew that meant if he had time.

"Ellen said Mrs. Turquand came by today."

She would take a visit like that any day. The woman always shared positive, uplifting information or scenarios, which was not always easy in Charles Town. "She did. It was a lovely surprise. I'll never forget the role her husband played in your decision of faith. I'm so glad the Huguenot Church was here for you when you needed it."

"And of course, I'll never be able to thank him enough. God used the Reverend and my past church affiliation to work a miracle. The Turquands have been inspiring friends."

Elizabeth leaned back against her pillows after Louis adjusted and fluffed them again. "Are you comfortable for the night?"

"As comfortable as an elephant can be on his back," she sighed. A few more weeks, or maybe days. The doctor said any day would be fine. It was fine with her also.

The atmosphere around Charles Town was a bit tense as the Royalist government held to the right to arrest and detain anyone participating in resistance by importing arms. Louis wasn't naïve in thinking the British weren't worried and suspicious. But Louis heard that the General Committee of South Carolina resolved "no person engaged in transacting public business, or going to, or returning from a meeting to elect delegates to a provincial congress could be arrested, imprisoned, summoned, or otherwise molested by any Civil Process."

Late one afternoon, Louis unfolded the paper, reclined in his study, and tried to seclude his concerns away from Elizabeth. Citizens still assembled, and so far, the British presence in Charles Town had not acted on any of the government's threats of arrest.

Perhaps they didn't know who was storing arms. He chuckled. If they did know, all of his friends and himself would be behind bars instead of working and sometimes scheming at different homes. Even an election was scheduled to be held on December nineteenth to choose delegates to a General Provisional Committee meeting in January. What did Britain think of that? Perhaps the present lack of detainment would last until the election. If not, he pictured it taking place anyway—from prison.

His coffee cooled as he paced back and forth in front of the window, clasping his hands behind his back. The coolness of the afternoon outside, compared to the warmth of the fire inside, fogged the windows and distorted Louis' view of the street. He pulled in the heavy smell of the wood-burning fire and let it settle his restless meanderings.

He stayed close to the heartbeat of the cause. He knew that they were facing a crisis of belief as war was rumored. No matter what he or others wanted, he hoped the decisions were in obedience to God, wrapped in faith.

If Louis was to embrace a possible revolution for freedom, he had to be sure of his motive. Weekly, Reverend Smith's words emphasized a need to look at issues from God's perspective, not man's. "When a man's ways please the LORD, he maketh even his enemies to be at peace with him." Even King Solomon as written in Proverbs 16:7 had felt the tug of his enemies, just like Louis did now.

He still felt the break from an established government could be a peaceful one. God could be giving America the opportunity to form an entirely new government. Would 1775 be the year to determine their destiny?

He struggled with what he could do to protect his family. He'd watch for signs of his role in obedience to God's calling. Surely, God wanted Louis to provide a safe place for Elizabeth and their baby. Was that to be Charles Town?

On Wednesday afternoon, Elizabeth learned from Martha about the return of her student's father to Charles Town. It should have been exciting news. But Henry Laurens announced that he was sending his daughter to England to keep her away from trouble in South Carolina. For a few hours, Elizabeth brooded over Martha's plight. *I don't understand men sometimes.* She crawled up in bed and beat her hands by her side in frustration. Would Louis do the same thing one day? Send her away?

She shared her confusion with Louis later in the parlor. "How could a father send his child away after he's been gone for the past year? She has no mother and basically no father." She rubbed her own baby as she tried to imagine leaving her child or sending her child away.

Louis shook his head. "Henry Laurens returned home most likely because of love for his country. He's another leader of the Sons of Liberty leaning toward the prospect of war."

"So, it's more serious to some men then to us."

"I can't help but think that these men know more than I do about the whys and whens of politics. It's as if they are seeing a future that I can't yet envision." He leaned in to capture Elizabeth's chin with his fingers. "But I'm not going to send you away. It would take a lot more than the present situation to leave your side."

She pushed her bottom lip out with a pout. "You say that now, but there could be a time when all of us have to make tough decisions." If he did have to make that choice, how could she blame him wanting to protect them?

"And then your protection and safety will still be my top priority." He kissed her and turned his talk to the baby. Not really the rallying speech she needed to hear, but she gained some comfort from Louis' promise to protect her. Losing Martha to relatives across the ocean brought the impending trials closer to home than Elizabeth wanted.

❀

As Christmas decorations appeared under Elizabeth's supervision, the atmosphere smelled and looked festive. Ellen always had something simmering or baking, filling the air with the pungent aroma of spices—cinnamon, nutmeg, and ginger. Each day she tempted Elizabeth with a new concoction.

At night, activities centered on placing the finishing touches on gifts, and secrets smuggled in and out of hiding. Elizabeth giggled as each person disappeared after supper to private rooms. Daily, gifts would appear in the parlor on the table draped with a red silk cloth and greenery.

Tom brought in a cedar wreath one afternoon and placed it in a prominent position for all to see. Elizabeth knew passersby would gaze at the decoration on the door with its oranges and pomegranates, ribbons, and lace. Extra globes with candles were placed on the path leading to the front door, beckoning Christmas guests to enter.

But the only visitors she had were family and close friends. No one arrived unannounced, not with an expectant mother in the house.

Elizabeth protested one Thursday afternoon when her mother dropped by. "But Mother, I want the visitors. I want to go places and soak up the Christmas festivities." Her whining was getting her nowhere. "This is taking forever. Did you ever feel the time would never arrive?" She stared at her mother, not really expecting her to answer with any detail.

"That is natural. And yes, I remember pacing and complaining, but it got me no closer to delivery. Relax and savor the attention. The baby will come in God's time."

Elizabeth and Louis' first anniversary came without fanfare.

They had no choice but to celebrate at the house. She felt Louis' and Ellen's eyes on her every move.

"Happy anniversary, Elizabeth. You've made this first year very memorable indeed." He sat across from her under the glistening candlelight. She watched as he stretched his tightly closed hand toward her. Mesmerized, she saw his fingers flutter open, revealing a palm-sized gold pin in the shape of a butterfly, jeweled with tiny rubies and emeralds.

"Oh, Louis, it's beautiful." She took it and held it to the light. "Will you put it on me, please?"

He slid out of his chair, knelt beside her, and pinned the butterfly to her bodice. She watched it glimmer.

"Thank you." She cupped her hands around his cheeks and kissed him. In truth, she wanted to crawl up into his lap and hug him properly. But somehow, she didn't think she and the baby would fit. "I don't have a gift for you."

"Oh, yes, you do." Louis placed his hand on her stomach. "Right here."

Time crawled like a child's waiting for Christmas. Would Elizabeth's gift arrive soon? All she wanted was the safe delivery of her child. On Thursday, December fifteenth, Elizabeth paced the parlor and the morning room, fidgeting with every item in reach.

"Elizabeth, are you feeling all right?" Ellen entered the morning room and clucked her tongue. "Should you be up walking around so much?" She removed the lid of the tea pot and peered inside. "And look, you've not had any tea or eaten your breakfast."

"I'm fine. I just can't stay still. My back is aching, and I don't have an appetite," Elizabeth explained.

"Anything else unusual?" Ellen asked, her hand tried to cover a big grin. Elizabeth didn't know what was so amusing.

"The baby is causing me to catch my breath as my stomach does flips." If this was normal, she wanted it to stop. What she wouldn't give for a peaceful nap or a cozy read in her big chair.

"I think you're in labor." Elizabeth's eyes popped open. Did she hear her correctly? Was it time? Where was Louis? "Now, you remember what the doctor said. You need to time those feelings and rest. Let's get you to bed, and I'll send Amy for Mr. Louis." Elizabeth let the older woman's experience rule her actions. "After Amy goes to the mercantile, I'll send her to your mother's."

Ellen disappeared and most likely had everything under control. Elizabeth rested as best she could in her bed. In what seemed like barely five minutes, Louis was at her side, wiping her brow with a wet cloth.

"Sweet, Elizabeth. Do you want me to do anything?" His hand rested on her shoulder as his fingers gently massaged her tense muscles. The obvious wrinkles in his forehead told Elizabeth of his concern.

Lord, let Louis feel You here. Don't let him worry overly much.

"Pray. Everyone says I'll be just fine. This happens every day, right?" She couldn't take away her inevitable pain or answer any disturbing questions. What did she know of childbirth? All she knew were that any struggles would be worth the pain. *Please, let me be strong.* Another pain caused her to grab the crisp sheets in a tight grip. Breathe. It wasn't unbearable, not yet.

"I've been praying for days." He held her hand, after she let go of the sheet, and brought it to his lips. She melted in his gaze for several minutes, until a pain took her breath away and left her panting.

"Oh, that one was the worst one so far." Tears that she promised she'd shield from Louis escaped anyway. He held her hand, all that she suspected he knew to do.

A knock on the doorframe preceded her mother and Ellen. "Louis, you'd better wait downstairs. Mrs. Engle and I can take it from here."

Louis kissed Elizabeth's forehead and whispered, "I think I'd better obey your mother. I love you."

"I love you too." She gritted her teeth as another pain overtook her. Louis departed, leaving her in experienced hands. How long until she'd be in his arms again, until their baby would be with them?

Without having Louis beside her, Elizabeth had no idea who to turn to in her pain. But of course, both her mother and Ellen had experienced childbirth. She couldn't be in more capable hands. She sighed and released a tiny giggle as she realized it was better to be in their care than Louis'. What did he know of childbirth?

"Anne is on her way. She had to make sure the children were properly placed. Now what can I do for you?" Her mother fluffed the pillows, patted Elizabeth's hands, and checked out the water and sheet supply.

Was it strange to put Louis foremost in her mind? Well, normal or not, his image remained. "Just be here for Louis. He seems nervous. Make sure he's occupied," Elizabeth responded.

Her mother wiped a cool cloth across Elizabeth's brow. "Louis will be fine. You're the one who is important now."

Three hours later Dr. Ramsey and the midwife Mrs. Smyth arrived, taking charge of the entire situation. Elizabeth's mother, sister, and Jeannette joined Louis, who had been pacing in the foyer at the foot of the stairs.

"She'll be fine, Louis," Anne assured her brother-in-law as she touched his arm briefly.

"But what if—what if something goes wrong? I don't want to lose her or the baby." He knew his concerns were not misplaced. Lives were lost in childbirth every day.

Please God, I know You have a plan and a purpose for Elizabeth and this child. Protect them at this hour. I am placing them in Your arms. His prayer was one of many over the next two hours.

A cry pierced the almost stagnant air, tiny but strong. His child. Louis' heart skipped a beat. He grabbed the rail of the staircase, not knowing what his next action should be. He seemed paralyzed to the spot. His gaze climbed the stairs, but his body didn't.

"Louis," Dr. Ramsey said from the top of the stairs. "You are greatly needed up here to welcome your child into the world." The doctor smiled as Louis willed his body to take the stairs two at a time. All was well.

Thank You, God.

He peeked his head through the doorway. Elizabeth, propped up in bed, held a small bundle in her arms. How beautiful Elizabeth looked—even after the exhaustion from her labor. Hers were the eyes he sought. There, she lifted her head from the baby, and gave him the look of love he never wanted to live without.

"A daughter, Louis. Our precious little girl." Elizabeth held out her wonderful gift to Louis, so tiny in his arms.

He sat on the edge of the bed and beheld the most extravagant gift. His daughter. "A beautiful angel, just like her mother. Thank you, Elizabeth." Louis gently kissed his wife and then his daughter. With this gift came the most important responsibility in his life so far. These two deserved his all—all his love, his future, his attention, his protection. *I can't do it without You, God.*

"We need to thank God. He gave her to us." Elizabeth's voice, weak but ever so clear, turned him to the present, one day at a time. The future seemed endless.

"Yes. Do you mind if I do that right now, out loud?" In the circle of three, Louis offered up their thanksgiving for a safe delivery and for the new life God had placed in their care.

Louis stared at the wrinkled bundle of love. "Hello, Harriet

Jeannette Lestarjette. You have a strong beautiful name for such a dark-haired, red-faced beauty." He lifted his gaze to Elizabeth. "Are you ready for the rest of the family to meet her?"

"Yes, of course." She paused and caressed his hand. "Louis, I love you," Elizabeth added before the others arrived.

"And I love you more every minute."

Their moments alone were interrupted by the murmurings of the women in the hall, waiting impatiently. "Come in. All is fine." Louis ushered Mrs. Elliott, Anne, and Jeannette into the bedroom. He felt a pride about his daughter he had never had for anyone or anything before.

I promise, God, to try my hardest to be the best father I can.

A brief quarter of an hour later, all were ushered out, so Elizabeth could rest.

Louis rejoiced that God had brought him into this close-knit family at just the right time to capture the heart of Elizabeth. And now, with the birth of Harriet, he felt more firmly and permanently planted in the lives of this community, its people, and its causes. The newest citizen of Charles Town was a sign of hope and peace.

CHAPTER 30

"I'm ready for a taste of reality, Louis. I haven't heard one word from you about any political news." Elizabeth thought about having Anne sneak a paper in for her to read. Did having a baby mean she couldn't participate in the happenings in the city? She'd appease Louis on this issue for just so long. "I feel wrapped in a cocoon—a comfortable one, but a bit too snug." Baby, feeding, and sleep. Then, repeat.

Louis played with Harriet's toes that somehow had escaped from the warm blanket. "Surely, I have the right to protect the mother of my child as long as possible."

Elizabeth rolled her eyes. "Since when do I stay away from a little trouble?"

"A little?" He raised his eyebrows. Perhaps, she hadn't guessed at the possible turn of events. "I guess I have sheltered you too much. I'll help you downstairs. But I'm warning you, what you hear or read is not my fault." He laughed although weak as if he wanted to cover something serious with a little humor.

He was such a doting man. Tingles crept to her fingertips. Louis had easily wrapped himself up in his family as little Harriet wrapped herself around his heart. Perhaps Elizabeth didn't want

325

to burst her realm of utopia. For a second, perhaps, but her inactivity and lack of intellectual, though controversial, conversation made her fidgety and anxious. Good or bad, she craved to be a part of the real world.

With Harriet in her bassinet and Elizabeth surrounded by blankets in a comfortable chair with her feet propped up on the ottoman, she longed to hear some familiar hymns. She wasn't ready to sit at the pianoforte, so humming "The First Nowell" had to suffice. No political paper or pamphlet graced her lap yet. At least the scenery had changed.

As Elizabeth's thoughts motioned her lips to form a tune, Sarah unceremoniously entered the room. "I'm glad to see you out of bed." Sarah pulled a chair closer to Harriet. "What are you humming?"

"Christmas carols. I long to play the piano, but I'm not yet allowed that luxury." The instrument loomed as a forbidden friend.

"Well, I can pick out the notes if you have the sheets of music," Sarah suggested.

"They're right there on the piano where I left them. Would you mind, truly?"

"Not at all. Although you know I'm not a Mozart or even a Martha Laurens. Bear with me."

Elizabeth sang along as her friend plucked out the notes to favorites like "The First Nowell" and "Joy to the World."

After attending worship service on Christmas Day, Elizabeth welcomed her family in the afternoon to a lively frenzy of gift opening, mainly with her nephews ripping off paper and squealing with delight at their toys, including additional pieces for their township collection—horses and miniature people.

In the evening after all family had disappeared, Louis

presented Elizabeth with two extraordinary gifts. "Open this one first. It's been hard to keep it a secret."

Carefully, she removed a leather box from a silk purse. Inside was a beautiful emerald bracelet; the dainty jewels complemented her tiny wrist.

"Louis, it's perfect. Where did you find this unique piece?" She held out her hand, watching the emeralds sparkle in the candlelight.

"Boston, at a jeweler recommended by your grandmother."

"That makes me wonder about something." She pressed two fingers against her lips, stifling a giggle. "Open your gift now, so I can still my curiosity."

Louis retrieved a neatly wrapped box from the table. Another leather box. "This looks familiar. Could it be the same proprietor?" He popped open the lid to reveal a gold watch with a chain. His initials were on the back and the sentiment "Love, Elizabeth" had been engraved inside.

"Thank you. I will cherish it." He placed in in his pocket and patted it in place. He handed her a rectangular shaped item wrapped in a pretty red piece of velvet. "Open the other one now."

She discarded the packaging that held an elaborately illustrated copy of *Gulliver's Travels,* one of her favorite novels. The gift, perfect in all ways, instigated a stream of giggles then a cascade of laughter from her.

"What is so funny about *Gulliver's Travels?*"

"Nothing. But I bought you the same kind of gift." She handed him another present wrapped in paper.

Once he opened it, he, too, burst into a deep round of laughter. "*The Way to Wealth* by Benjamin Franklin." He ran his thumb over the leather cover. "You know the greatest gifts are you and Harriet on Christ's birthday. Happy Christmas, Elizabeth."

He pulled her into the circle of his arms, hugged her, and settled onto the sofa. No sooner had Elizabeth's head hit his shoulder then Harriet awoke. Louis picked her up and placed her in the crook of his arm.

"It's hard to believe 1774 is almost over. Here we are with our little family. It seems like the unrest in the colony is concealed by the happiness and joy in our house."

Elizabeth stared into Harriet's big blue eyes, and her heart swelled with love. *Lord, protect our family in the New Year.* She leaned her head on Louis' shoulder and wondered about the changes to come. While the ocean roiled and the ground shook, Elizabeth rested surrounded by love.

On New Year's Eve, Ellen knocked on the library door. Louis took the letter from her and turned back to his desk. Before releasing the wax seal, he studied the unfamiliar handwriting on the nondescript paper, then turned to make sure the door was closed. Christopher had told him that he would receive a letter and had asked him to read it and destroy it. He hinted about the possibility of needing his services—although what services Louis had no idea.

Meet at the Exchange at eleven o'clock this evening. Make sure you are alone and not followed. Your attention to this will further the good work. If you choose not to participate, we understand.

No name. *What did he or they want?*

Louis hung his head, knowing his answer would affect his family and his country—no matter which way he chose. He would leave the party at the Elliotts' and Elizabeth's side tonight to assume whatever role assigned to him. If South Carolina could take drastic steps toward a new government, he could at least obtain the information in order to figure out his place. He sighed. A new year with undetermined obstacles.

He heard Harriet crying in her cradle and Elizabeth's soft, comforting voice. They were the reasons surrounding his commitments. He put the letter above the flame, and then dropped the burning missive in a bowl.

Following the sound of cooing and singing, Louis focused on his loved ones for a few more hours. The year 1775 would consume him soon enough.

QUESTIONS AND INSIGHTS

After walking through the streets of Charleston, South Carolina years ago, a profound observation hit me and wouldn't leave me alone. The people of Charles Town 1770-1782 lived their daily lives in a pre-revolution and revolution state of alert. My imagination wondered about how that would have been. My ancestors were some of the ones who survived that time in that city. I asked specific questions which turned into a massive research and writing opportunity, which is ongoing today. Here are some of the questions:

1. As a mother or father, what did they tell their children about the state of their town and their country? What would you tell your children if a war was about to engulf your city and way of life?
2. How did they go about their daily routine? With fear? With hope? With blinders?
3. What did they think about marrying during this time? Would you consider a marriage if war was raging in your streets?
4. Why would they consider bringing children into such a

    volatile situation? Would you have children during
    these scenarios or wait?

5. And a big dilemma, how did they decide to stay and
    fight? Or did they flee? Would you fight for your way of
    life and your town, state, country, if the enemy
    swarmed your streets?

I decided to try to answer these questions in these novels. Elizabeth and Louis and thousands of others continued in their daily lives with mundane chores of eating, cooking, shopping, and working with added events like birthdays, wedding, births, and deaths. Life did not stop with a war. Survival kicked in with the hope of an end of strife.

ABOUT THE AUTHOR

Marguerite Martin Gray is the author of *Hold Me Close, Surround Me,* and *Bring Me Near-- Revolutionary Faith Books One, Two and Three.* She enjoys studying history and writing fiction. An avid traveler and reader, she teaches high school Spanish and has degrees in French, Spanish, and Journalism from Trinity University in San Antonio, Texas, and a MA in English from Hardin-Simmons University in Abilene, Texas. Marguerite is a member of American Christian Fiction Writers, Abilene Writers Guild, Daughters of the American Revolution, South Carolina Historical Society, and Preservation Society of Charleston. She currently lives in North Louisiana with her husband.

ALSO BY MARGUERITE MARTIN GRAY

Hold Me Close (Revolutionary Faith Book 1)
Bring Me Near (Revolutionary Faith Book 3) ~ Coming Soon